THE LAST RETREAT

Marina Palmer is the pseudonym of best-selling British author Imogen Robertson used for her contemporary solo thriller writing.

Imogen was born and brought up in Darlington and read Russian and German at Cambridge. Before becoming a full-time writer, she directed for TV, film, and radio. She is the author of several novels, including the Crowther and Westerman series and *The Paris Winter*, and has co-written novels with former Labour Deputy Leader Tom Watson (*The House*), screenwriter Darby Kealey (*Liberation* as Imogen Kealey) and the legendary Wilbur Smith (*King of Kings*). Imogen has been shortlisted for the CWA Historical Dagger three times and for the CWA Dagger in the Library Award once. She has also written for Hampton Court Palace, chaired the Historical Writers' Association and been mentioned in *Private Eye* twice.

Palmer is Imogen's husband's surname – she is married to the cheesemonger and author Ned Palmer – and she chose Marina as tribute to Russian Silver Age Poet Marina Tsvetaeva. She almost went for Anna, after Anna Akhmatova, but as her mother-in-law's name is Ann, that started getting a bit confusing. She, her husband, and her multiple identities live in south London.

Also by Marina Palmer

The Russian Doll

MARINA PALMER

THE LAST RETREAT

HODDER &
STOUGHTON

First published in Great Britain in 2026 by Hodder & Stoughton Limited
An Hachette UK company

The authorised representative in the EEA is Hachette Ireland, 8
Castlecourt Centre, Dublin 15, D15 XTP3, Ireland (email: info@hbgi.ie)

1

A CIP catalogue record for this title is available from the British Library

Paperback ISBN 9781399709781
ebook ISBN 9781399709767

Typeset in Plantin Light by Hewer Text UK Ltd, Edinburgh
Printed and bound in Great Britain by Clays Ltd, Elcograf S.p.A.

Hodder & Stoughton policy is to use papers that are natural, renewable and recyclable products and made from wood grown in sustainable forests. The logging and manufacturing processes are expected to conform to the environmental regulations of the country of origin.

Hodder & Stoughton Limited
Carmelite House
50 Victoria Embankment
London EC4Y 0DZ

www.hodder.co.uk

To Dad

PROLOGUE

West of Kharkiv, Ukraine, November 2024

They should have got out of here when the French left.

The soldier shoved Tash hard, with enough force to make her stagger then he kicked out, knocking her legs from under her. Tash went down heavily, her right hand protecting her camera, her weight falling on her left as she tried to break her fall. Her palm stung and slid sideways across a patch of dirty ice; her chin hit the ground, rattling her skull, and a metal shell fragment embedded among the rotting leaf mulch and broken branches scattered over the track sliced through her cheek, neat and effortless as a butcher's blade. Tash gasped with the pain, the surprise of it, then coughed as she inhaled the spores of frozen black earth. The soldier who had knocked her down laughed, then kicked her once in the stomach, sending a sudden spiral of pain radiating out from the spot where his boot connected.

She breathed through her nose, trying to lift herself above the pain, biting her lip so she wouldn't whimper. *Stay calm. It's OK.*

Monty would get them out of this. He'd talked them through a dozen dicey encounters in the last six months. He was fast, and clever and everyone liked him. She just had to stay still, not get in the way and hope to hell that kick hadn't done too much damage.

Come on, Monty. Do your thing and in ten minutes I'll be smiling at the fucker who just kicked me and taking his photo.

Monty was talking fast, Karin, their fixer, rushing to keep up with the translation.

'Press! Journalist! Come on, let's just have a drink and a chat. International friendship!'

The soldiers laughed.

Christ, had he actually just said that?

The bastard who kicked her had broken a rib at least, and now the blood from the slice on her face had reached the corner of her mouth. It tasted slightly sweet.

Someone rested a boot on her back, pressing her down into the soil. The image of a game hunter, one foot resting on the back of his kill flitted through her mind.

She stayed very still.

Why hadn't they left with the French? Every photographer, every correspondent, every TV crew knew that when the French leave town, you do too. Crazy bastards the lot of them, teasing the Americans at the bar, dancing on the tables to their Bluetooth speakers in the middle of bombardments. It was a rule. When the French got into their cars and stamped on the accelerator it meant one thing – the shit was about to hit the fan. But Monty had been determined to follow up this tip and that had meant going in the other direction, towards the frontline, which flexed and undulated like a snake through the woods. Why hadn't she said no?

Because he'd said it was important. Because he'd said, 'Tash, you can handle this, can't you?'

And that had been enough. She'd ignored that ripple of caution in her gut and said, 'Of course I can.'

Bloody hell, Tash! You're twenty-seven not twelve. When are you going to grow up?

Possibly never. Not now.

The rapid streams of Russian going back and forth over her head ended in one man's voice issuing a sharp, barked order. Discussion over. Tash turned her face very slightly to try and see the others.

Shit. Monty was on his knees, hands above his head, still talking fast. The contents of his pockets were scattered on the ground around him. Notebook, phone.

One of the Russians was talking on a radio. Another, a heavy-set guy with a face like a shaved pug, had his pistol out, held close to Monty's temple. Karin was flat on the floor like Tash, still trying to keep up with Monty's stream of chat. He was telling them about his family, his flat in London. Trying to establish a connection. He sounded like he was making friendly conversation in a bar. Panic surged through Tash's system. The light stung her eyes, she couldn't breathe, her eyes were gritty and sore and she couldn't move to rub them. *It's OK. Come on, Monty.*

'Journalist,' Karin shouted, abandoning the translation for a second. 'Journalist!'

Like they didn't know that.

'*Spion*,' the pug dog said, staring at Monty as he talked on, smiling up at them, telling them some story about the last time he was in America.

The soldier pulled the trigger.

No.

Time sliced in two by the instance of a bullet.

On one side of the bullet was Monty, talking fast, everyone's friend. His mouth open, halfway through a sentence, halfway through a word, alive. Then came the kick of the recoil, the dull snap of the shot, like a branch breaking, and on the other side of the bullet Monty was dead. He collapsed sideways, and Tash felt the impact through her own body as he hit the ground, then her view of anything else was blocked by the bulk of his back.

No. Not possible.

Not Monty.

This was a joke, a mistake, a stupid dream. Monty could not be dead. That half-smile on his face when he looked through her shots; his hands, his writing, sharp and clear, his impatience with bullshit, his energy. That couldn't be done. That couldn't be over.

There is nothing, nothing in the world, so still as a dead man.

Tash must have made a sound, a grunt of protest. Someone grabbed her wrist, jerking her arm up and back, making her gasp in pain. Was he trying to force her up on to her knees too? No, the foot was still on the small of her back, holding her down. *Just get it over with, you fuckers*, she thought. She gritted her teeth, letting her anger and shock and disgust and the horror of it all lift her up and away from the cold earth. She felt an ugly scraping at her wrist. The bastard was taking her bracelet. It was nothing, just a touristy thing of plaited leather with a silver clasp, but it was hers and he could fuck off.

She knew she would fight then. She tensed her muscles, waiting for him to move a little, so she could take her best shot as his fingers scrabbled over the inside of her wrist, trying to undo the clasp. She'd turn over, kick up and catch this bastard in the balls. She'd bite and stamp and scream, she'd scratch his eyes out. She would go out yelling obscenities at this arsehole.

A rattle, like gravel thrown hard against a window. Gunfire coming from further down the road. The weight of the boot on her back disappeared and her arm flopped to her side. The Russians swore, a flurry of fleeing oaths.

Come back here, you son of a bitch.

She lifted her head an inch above the dirt in time to see the man who had killed Monty stumbling away up the track, holstering his pistol, awkward with panic.

The one who had been trying to steal her bracelet was running too, sprinting up the track trying to get to cover before returning fire. Tash turned her head, looking back into the fractured landscape. The pain in her side blossomed and pulsed. There was movement between the bare trees. Ukrainians? Had the frontline shifted again?

A tree trunk, blown off its roots by mortar fire, partially blocked the track some fifteen feet ahead. Tash lifted herself slightly on to her elbows, and crawled forward, pain spreading through her as she dragged herself over the dirt towards it, past Monty's body, till she was level with Karin. Karin was still prone, hands in fists, her eyes squeezed shut, sobbing and flinching at the short bursts of semi-automatic fire exchanged over their heads.

Tash reached out, hit Karin on the shoulder. Karin squeezed her eyes tighter, and a little plume of grit spattered down on the back of her sky-blue padded jacket. Tash punched her arm again, as hard as she could, till Karin forced her eyes open. Tash pointed towards the tree trunk.

Karin lifted her head, her eyes blank and wide, her skin so pale it was almost the same blue as her coat. Tash pointed again, emphatic, and Karin blinked, nodded, then started scrambling forward.

The tree trunk was miles away. The retreating Russians could shoot them out of spite. The Ukrainians could shoot them by accident.

Just get to cover. Don't think.

She hauled herself another six inches forward, her elbow slipped and her chin hit the earth, a fresh wave of pain radiating through her skull, competing with the throbbing ache in her side.

Monty.

Perhaps this wasn't real. Perhaps she'd wake up back in the hotel room, and this time she'd tell him no, there was no way—

'*Idi!* Come!' Karin hissed at her, reaching back, tugging at her upper arm.

Don't think.

'Fine. I'm bloody coming.'

'Fucking *shift* it, Tash.'

Her brain blinked at the incongruity, that full English swearing with a Ukrainian accent. It gave her something real, something to wrap her fingers around.

Another rattle of semi-automatic fire – she couldn't tell which side it was coming from – and someone screamed, close by, further up the track.

'*Nazad!*'

She understood that. 'Back!'

Karin had reached the fallen trunk. She slid over it, then reached back, hauling Tash after her.

'Who is that?' Karin gasped. 'Who is shooting at them?'

'No idea. You hit?'

'No.'

Tash turned over, her back against the trunk and her hands went automatically to her camera, brushing off the leaf rot and mud.

She lifted it to her eye.

Get up, Monty. Get up and run over here.

'Take the pictures,' Karin hissed. 'Take them now, Tash.'

Don't think.

Karin's face, the terror making her skin taut, her eyes huge in the frame. Then she lay back down on the ground, inched round the end of the trunk, until she could see his body. Monty's body.

Don't think.

The back of his head was undamaged and the breeze ruffled his hair. She could see the pale nape of his neck. It looked like he was sleeping off too much beer till your eye registered the blood spattered across the dirty patches of ice and snow. Figures were moving up the track behind him. She framed up, including the shell fragment which had sliced open her face. Its edge pearled with droplets of her blood. A little colour among all that black and white. Took the shot. Her hands and fingers moved, made her decisions for her. An engine, a truck heading towards them up the track, gears grinding.

She pulled back behind the trunk, shrank into her bones.

Fuck, fuck, fuck.

The engine stopped and boots thumped on to the earth.

The speaker raised his voice. 'Natasha Bell. You here? Call out!'

What the hell?

It was a British accent. She half-turned, her hand on the rough bark of the fallen tree, confused, and wary. South London at a guess.

Karin glanced at her, then called out. 'We're here! She's here with me.' She stood up slowly, holding her hands above her head.

'Get up, Tash!' she hissed.

Tash blinked. The pain in her side was getting worse.

Don't worry about that now. Just stand up.

Knees on the ground, hand on the trunk to support her weight, she moved into a crouch then straightened her legs, lifted her head and struggled to understand what she was seeing. The logging track through pine trees leading back towards the place they'd left the car. Monty's body lying across it. Two men, wearing grey and brown camouflage, crouching down next to him. One was taking Monty's picture with his phone, the other had picked up his notebook and phone and was tucking them into the side pocket of his trousers. A truck, small, but with wheels like a tractor, was behind them.

A soldier, also in camouflage, stood between her and Monty, his semi-automatic rifle held across his chest. She looked at his shoulder. No insignia. No blue and yellow flag, no Russian patch. No marking of rank either, though he was obviously in charge.

'You Natasha Bell?' he asked.

'Yeah.'

'ID?'

She reached for her press pass, but her fingers were strangely clumsy, like trying to use your phone in a dream, and she couldn't undo the button over the pocket. He came closer till he was on the other side of the trunk, then reached forward, undid it for her, and took out the card. He studied it for a second then tucked it back into her jacket. He nodded at Karin.

'This your translator?'

'Yes.'

'We're taking you back to Kharkiv.' He turned round and addressed the men behind him. 'You two up front. TJ and Smith, you're in the back with our guests.'

'Who are you?' Tash said. 'You're British?'

'I'm your fairy fucking godmother. Get in the truck, both of you.' He looked at Monty's body. 'I'm sorry we weren't quicker.'

Her strength had gone. She sat on the log, swung her legs over it. Couldn't stand.

. . . Mother of God.

He glanced at her. 'Injured?'

'Maybe.'

He nodded to Karin. 'Help her. And get a shift on. TJ, check her out.'

Then he returned to scanning the trees, the road ahead.

Karin half-carried, half-dragged Tash towards the back of the truck, and the two men who had been examining Monty pulled her in.

'What about Monty?' Tash asked.

Maybe he's OK. Maybe none of this is happening. Pray God, let none of this be happening.

'He'll be retrieved,' the Londoner who seemed to be in charge said, coming round the back of the vehicle and jumping in. He slapped the back of the cab with his hand. The truck coughed and pulled away. One of the others swung his way across the bouncing truck and sat on the bench next to Tash.

Retrieved.

'Right, love. What's going on with you?'

Scottish accent.

He opened a medical kit and snapped on a pair of latex gloves, then leaned in close to examine the cut on her face.

'It'll scar,' he said. 'Was that casualty a friend of yours?'

Tash nodded. 'A reporter. Monty Young.'

Who were these men? Special Forces? She lifted her camera, but the man in front of her shook his head, slowly. She lowered it again.

The bouncing of the truck made her flinch. The man tending to her wound frowned and then, with a nod of permission from her, lifted her shirt out of her waistband and placed a hand against the skin. Slight pressure. Tash hissed between her teeth.

'Got some internal bleeding here,' he said.

Her tongue was feeling thick and the words wouldn't come.

'Best step on it.'

The leader nodded. He had Karin's ID in his hand. 'Civilian ambulance waiting two clicks away.' He turned his attention to Karin. 'Your mate got shot, then the Russian patrol got scattered by incoming mortar fire and you ran for it. Helped get Miss Bell to the ambulance. You're a fucking hero. That's the story. Don't care who asks. Say any different and I'll come find you. Got it?'

He handed back her ID.

'Got it,' Karin said quietly.

The man in the back with them who hadn't spoken yet glowered at Tash. His nose was too small for his face and his lashes were absurdly long.

'So what makes her so bloody special?' he growled. Tash's vision was getting cloudy, so she couldn't see the look the leader threw at him, but it was enough to make him hunch his shoulders and turn away.

She felt her grandmother's hands around her own and the clouds overtook her.

PART I

The Abbey

I

Belford Abbey, nr Alnwick, Northumberland, 29 June 2025

Light poured in from the floor-to-ceiling windows. Tash crouched low against the back wall of the room, watching it saturate the purples and pinks of unrolled yoga mats, tease halos out of the long hair of the women, and catch highlights in the eyes of the men. One man in his early thirties with a short black beard, had his knee up, arms loosely hanging round it. He seemed absorbed, enchanted. One of the women was lying on her front, her elbows on the floor and chin in her hands. There were about thirty of them in all, lounging on their mats on the polished parquet, all barefoot but expensively pedicured, dressed in soft cotton casuals. Each of them had a water bottle in peach or pink within reach.

The focus of their attention was a woman in her forties with long red hair worn in a half-up style, who sat on a raised platform between the central windows. Jemima Carter. One of the original Instagram wellness influencers; purveyor of body lotions, bubble bath and scented candles to the select, and the best-selling author of self-help books for the masses. St Jemima of the dirty laugh, down-to-earth advice and elegant packaging, offering enlightened self-care in an unsettled age. Everyone's safe space. No judgement, no agenda, no pressure to be perfect, just better. And now she was the owner of Belford Abbey, this luxurious estate in Northumberland where the burned-out super-rich came to be renewed.

Sometimes charisma is a visible thing. It seemed to shiver off Jemima in crenulating waves, trailing from the tips of her fingers as she waved them in the air, conducting her audience. The pomp and grandeur of the space should have diminished her, but instead the attention of the watchers acted like a spotlight. Jemima wasn't wearing yoga clothes but an emerald-green dress with a wide skirt, a red leather belt cinching her tiny waist and the collar turned up. She looked like a Hitchcock heroine.

Tash didn't listen to what she was saying, just watched how audience and speaker mirrored each other. When Jemima leaned forward, so did they; when she smiled crookedly, her palms lifted, they shook their heads and laughed back. All friends together.

Tash moved, finding the shot first with her eye before lifting her camera, letting the colour and light fill the foreground in an impressionistic blur, but with Jemima, small in the middle left third of the frame, in sharp focus – the centre and source of all the energy in the room. Tash released the shutter, then, knowing she wouldn't take a better picture that day, let her Nikon rest in her lap and looked round.

A real stately home. These walls must have been hung with old masters once. Tash had visited enough National Trust properties with her grandparents as a kid to imagine Italianate landscapes and Gainsborough portraits hanging against red damask wallpapers. Now the walls were all white, and hung with huge abstract oil paintings. Good ones.

Tash felt someone's gaze on her, like a fly settling on her skin, and looked around. Bethan, Jemima's PA, had come in through the high narrow door behind her with a large buff envelope under her arm. She crouched down.

Impressive. The crowd watching Jemima might be in yoga pants and baggy T-shirts, but Bethan wore a close-fitting cream dress and four-inch heels.

'Jemima won't be free for another hour or so,' Bethan whispered, her mouth close to Tash's ear, her breath smelling of cinnamon candies. 'Can I take you to your room, Tasha? Get you settled in?'

Tash nodded and got to her feet, but before she left she looked over her shoulder and Jemima caught her eye and smiled. The focus of the room shifted and the heads of the listeners turned in a ripple towards Tash, friendly and curious as small children.

Tash nodded in return and as she stepped through the door Jemima said something which provoked a warm wave of settling laughter in the room.

'You've never visited Belford Abbey before, have you?' Bethan said, speaking at a normal volume now and walking quickly through another drawing room, this one full of sofas and armchairs, then another lined with books. All the furniture was in pastel shades with gold or accents and looked too over stuffed to sit on. Fresh flowers, branches of lilac in tall grey and white ceramic vases stood on every side table.

'No. It's not lilac season, is it?'

'Lilac is Jemima's signature flower,' Bethan replied with a note of reproach, as if Jemima's preferences could alter the passage of time. Perhaps they could. Tash tried to guess Bethan's age. Could be mid-thirties, but she was so groomed she could have been ten years older. *Wellness Barbie*, Tash thought, then breathed in and out, trying to control the feeling of sulky bitchiness this place seemed to provoke in her.

'We're very excited to have you on staff.'

'It's just temporary,' Tash said.

Bethan pushed open another door and paused, halfway on to a stone landing. 'Oh, I hope you'll never want to leave,' she continued warmly. 'No one ever wants to leave. Why would you want to go back to the world, with all its troubles and mess, when you could be here?'

'It's trouble and mess which means you and Jemima have jobs, isn't it?' Tash said, her voice tight. 'If everything was peachy no one would need her help.'

Bethan stopped and turned towards her. She did not look offended, merely thoughtful.

'Yes, that is probably true.' The quick smile returned.

Tash looked around, adjusted her backpack on her shoulder. 'I left my suitcase in the main hall downstairs.'

Bethan waved her hand. 'Oh, one of the staff will have taken that up to your room already.'

OK.

'In that case, can I see my studio?'

'Oh yes! I'm rather pleased with it.' Bethan smiled. Her teeth were very white, and her lips a glossy pale pink. Almost everything in this house was pale. Then she pointed upwards, as if to heaven. 'But as we're here, this is the family wing. I've given you one of the suites on the top floor. Charles Porter, our art master, and Ingrid Moyle, who teaches embroidery, have suites there too. Jemima leads her sessions in the main drawing room, as you've seen, and the creative classes are held out in the garden studios.'

She started down the staircase, her hand trailing gently along the polished banister and Tash followed. 'The gym, sauna and treatment rooms are in the basement, and of course the pool is off the chapel wing in the old greenhouse. FYI, Charles and Ingrid are a couple, and they tend to keep to themselves. He's English, she's French. Charles is a softy, and Ingrid can be a dragon, but she's a fantastic artist.'

'The French photographers are always the crazy ones,' Tash said.

Bethan snorted slightly. 'Ingrid can be very firm, which comes as a shock to our American guests. But her work is amazing. There's a display on the first floor of the pele tower. Have a look. Your photographs are there too, and Charles's paintings.'

'The pele tower is a gallery? I thought it was a ruin,' Tash said.

She'd noticed the pele tower as they arrived, but then it was impossible not to; the whole landscape of the park seemed designed to lead towards it, a great edifice of stone rearing above the ruins of the old Abbey which gave this place its name, now picturesquely flanking the grand 18th-century mansion.

'It's a ruin *and* a gallery. We didn't want to change how it appeared in the landscape, but we wanted to make use of it too. The architects did a brilliant job.'

The staircase was cool and quiet; somewhere below them a door opened and closed, an old latch rattling into place as it did. Tash's step faltered slightly.

'Have you worked with Jemima long?' she asked.

'Five years. So tomorrow you and the other teachers will do the taster sessions in the afternoon,' Bethan went on, 'then once the guests have chosen which creative path they want to follow you'll have two hours of classes each day, Tuesday to Friday. The guests leave Saturday morning, and the new lot arrive Sunday afternoon. Thank you for sending your materials. So helpful if students have questions.'

Tash had found a certain sort of peace, satisfaction, pulling together the workshop plans and slides, whittling down what she knew about film photography into bite-sized chunks with Megan Thee Stallion playing on her headphones. In the evenings she'd taken her own film camera into the streets and shot reflections, the glitter and rain. The people.

Monty's ghost found it harder to slip into her mind when she was absorbed. When it did though, a face in a crowd of revellers, a distortion in the air between her and the world, her heart plunged fast and hard. Like those nightmares where the elevator snaps and you plummet through floors of steel, glass and light.

Tash's fingers touched the wooden banister lightly. It was a deep gold in the filtered sunlight, washing down from a skylight high above her.

The stairs ended in a small lobby, the floor a mosaic of dark-green and gold tiles, the walls another variation of beige and abstract prints. Almost like that of an ordinary house, as opposed to the double-height marble hall lined with statues of graces and gods behind the main, porticoed entrance to the Abbey. Bethan pushed open the door and Tash was blinded by a blast of sunshine as she followed her out on to a broad stone-flagged terrace, then down shallow butter-coloured sandstone steps to a formal walled garden of gravel pathways, low box hedges and flower beds. They were thick with lavender and rosemary, cornflowers and verbena.

'This way,' Bethan said, and Tash had the strange sensation of following her into a dream.

2

Sixty feet from the terrace, Bethan took a sharp right along one of the paths, which led through a brick arch framed by wisteria into another walled section of garden. More paths, scattered benches, more lavender, but in this garden also stood a horseshoe of buildings, converted greenhouses by the looks of them, arranged round a small fountain. A bouquet of outlandish-looking fish fluted water into the air below a bearded and togaed sea-god brandishing a gold trident.

'Here we are!' Bethan announced. She took a key card from her pocket and held it to the lock of the building on the furthest wall. The door had a sign on it:

Natasha Bell, Photography

Bethan tapped the QR code on the sign with the corner of her key card. 'That links to your biography on our website. Our guests like to do their research.' Then she pushed open the door and stood aside to let Tash enter. 'I hope you like it.'

Tash walked into a large classroom with a long table under a whiteboard at the front, and four high benches for the students. It looked like the old science lab in Tash's secondary school. One side of the room was glass, looking out over the fountain, and the sloping ceiling was glass too. The back wall was lined with shelves and cupboards, split between what looked like a library of photography reference and art books and, each in their own individual cubbyholes, an array of cameras.

Tash dropped her bag, crossed the room and picked one up. A Leica MP. Fully manual. There were twelve of them. She'd been shooting for the moon when she'd asked for these, almost teasing by asking for cameras worth five grand a piece. They were worth every penny, but still.

'Perfect,' Tash said, running her thumb over the rough back. 'I never thought you'd be able to get this many in the time.'

For the first time Bethan's smile looked entirely natural, and she wrinkled her nose.

'It was a bit of a push, but I'm so glad you're pleased.' She joined Tash and lifted another of the cameras down from its place, turning it in her hands and admiring it in a way that made Tash suddenly like her. 'My dad had one a bit like this when I was a child,' she said. 'It's great they are becoming popular again. And film still has a certain quality, doesn't it?'

'Yes, all very analogue. Like vinyl records and homemade clothes.'

She nodded. 'You use digital though, don't you, for your work, Tasha?'

'On news assignments using anything else would be daft. But I started with film, when I was a kid. My first teacher was a bit of a traditionalist.'

'Who was that?'

Tash smiled, remembering the feel of the latch on the back gate, the way it rattled when you pushed it open, crossing the little stone-flagged yard with its patch of lawn and reaching up to knock on the kitchen window. The old man looking up from his washing up.

'Mr Race. He ran the corner shop down the road from my gran's house till he retired, but taking photos is his passion. He still has his own darkroom. He taught me a lot.'

Some of the best memories of her childhood were of him, his cheeks, patterned with broken capillaries, tainted purple by the dark light, bent over the developing tank, his long nose and beetling brows.

'I am so glad you are here, Tasha. Belford Abbey is a very special place,' Bethan said as Tash opened the back of the camera, enjoying the click and snap. 'It's remarkable what actually creating things with their hands can do for our clients. Very healing.'

'Yeah.'

'I hope this can be a healing place for you too,' Bethan added, more cautiously.

Tash didn't reply and Bethan sighed, then pushed the buff envelope she'd been carrying across the counter-top to Tasha. 'Your welcome pack. This has your key card, and all the information on the house and spa rooms. We have a nutritionist and personal trainers available too.'

'I can feed and walk myself, thanks.'

Tash bit her lip, she'd found these flashes of irritation harder to hold back since the day in the woods, but Bethan didn't react. 'Mobile signal is patchy at best here, but WhatsApp works and all the staff carry radios, so you'll be able to track us down if you need us.'

Tash took a breath. 'Thank you. Is there a map of the house?'

'Oh, yes! All the communal areas are open twenty-four hours a day. The Abbey Villa, just behind the ruins, is invitation only.'

Tash glanced at her. 'What, there's a whole other house there? Is that where Jemima lives?'

'No, Jemima has a suite on the ground floor of the chapel wing. The Abbey Villa is for guests who need more privacy.'

Tash put the camera to her eye, making the world manageable, watching the responsive twitch of the light meter at the edge of the frame as she pointed the lens out into the garden, then back into the pale shadows of the room and Bethan's symmetrical face.

'We've just confirmed there will be guests in the villa at the end of July,' Bethan said into the camera, 'and no other guests in the Abbey that week. You'll still need to be available to teach classes, but it's much more ad hoc. More a conference set-up than the usual retreat. That OK with you?'

'Sure, as long as the pay is the same. Who's coming to stay then?'

'I'll let Jemima explain.'

Tash nodded. 'And the film pick-up?'

'The courier will come at five-thirty Monday to Thursday to collect the film for overnight processing in Newcastle. The prints will be here by nine the following morning, Tuesday to Friday. We'll see they come straight to the studio.' She was all business now. 'By the way, there's a non-disclosure agreement in your pack. If you could sign that and get it back to me.' She hesitated. 'Obviously it's wonderful to have an artist of your calibre here . . . But your aesthetic is so very different from ours, isn't it? I mean, you will be kind to our clients, won't you?' She gave herself a little shake. 'Sorry, that was a stupid thing to say. If you need anything else, just WhatsApp.' *So Wellness Barbie had views on her aesthetic, did she?*

'It's fine. I promise I'll behave. You've seen the materials; I cropped the body parts out of the conflict shots.'

'Bless you for that,' Bethan replied, a sudden snap of steel in her voice.

Fair enough. Bethan was being decent, and Tash knew she was being . . . what had the agency manager, Najit, said about her recently? Oh, yeah: 'brittle'. She was being brittle again. Like untreated steel in cold weather. Prone to sudden fractures.

'Hang on, I'll sign the NDA now,' Tash said, putting the camera down and riffling through the pack until she found it. There were two copies. She scanned it quickly, then ferreted a ratty ballpoint out of her backpack and signed.

Bethan took her copy with another toothpaste-ad smile, then turned and left, her heels tapping across the polished wooden floor then crunching onto the gravel outside. Tash set the camera gently back on its shelf.

Tash wasn't sure if she had an aesthetic. Her one book, published just before Easter, was a mixture of snatched moments of violence and portraits of individuals: soldiers, mothers, wives. All Ukraine. The book had caused a slight stir. Enough to get her on TV a couple of times, a few podcasts and some newspaper interviews. She'd been asked a lot of questions about being a woman in a conflict zone – Tash had pointed at the images of Ukrainian women in her book. Lots of women in conflict already. Then they always turned to the day Monty died. Sometimes she told them about it.

Sometimes not. Once she'd tried to punch a podcast host who kept pressing for more detail. 'But how did it *feel* when they shot him?' The clip had got her a certain amount of attention and a concerned call from Najit.

When Tash told him about the job offer from Jemima Carter to teach short courses at Belford Abbey, he told her to stop being an idiot and take the gig. Not like she was doing anything else.

She looked through the welcome pack, took the plastic key card out of its holder and tucked it into her wallet, flipped to the page with the Wi-Fi code and added it to her phone.

It buzzed immediately.

A message from her publisher asking her to go to a shop in Alnwick to sign copies of her book.

Yup, happy to.

She had spoken to Monty's family before including the picture she had taken of his body in the woods, of course she had. And they had said yes, they would be glad if she published it. The book was dedicated to him too. Him and the people of Ukraine. It felt wrong and mawkish to do that, she doubted Monty or the people of Ukraine would give a shit, but she hadn't known what else to do. And Monty had had a vain streak. Still, the whole thing – the book, the publicity – made her feel sick. She looked at her motives and they seemed good, but she had still felt, sitting on that talk-show sofa, like a war profiteer. That was probably why she tried to punch the podcast host.

Tash returned to the folder. Among the timetables and dietary preference sheets was a booklet about the history of the house, and one about Jemima. She had read the online versions. Her fingertips left little sweaty marks on the cover.

'Get a grip,' she muttered to herself.

'Tasha!'

She turned round.

Jemima was standing in the doorway, her arms spread out. 'I have to go back for my individual welcome sessions, but I couldn't wait to say hello properly.'

The sunlight behind her fringed Jemima's body with a golden glow. She looked unearthly, standing there, with the gardens and house, the fountain, the lavender visible through the windows either side of the door. Some goddess of healing, arriving on the threshold via Hollywood.

Tash looked at her, taking her in, feeling that beam of her attention, blessed, in spite of herself by a one-on-one moment, the only object of that million-dollar smile.

'Hi, Mum.'

3

Jemima walked into the classroom and hugged her. Tash caught a scent of lilac and foundation, then Jemima took a step back, her hands on Tash's shoulders, and looked up at her. Her mother was still wearing the emerald-green dress.

'You can't do yoga in that, can you, Jemima?'

Jemima snort laughed. 'No. I have a ball gown for that.'

She looked Tash up and down, and Tash felt small under her gaze. Maybe when Bethan talked about her aesthetic, she'd meant the clothes. Combat trousers, loose shirts, no make-up beyond heavy eyeliner, and a ripple of studs in each ear, a cuff of tattoos round each forearm, the leather braid round her wrist rather than a diamond tennis bracelet.

'You're looking well, Tasha.'

'Well, or better than you expected?'

'Both,' Jemima replied. 'I saw you on TV. You come across very well on camera. Ironic, given your profession is to be behind it.' She lifted her hand and brushed her neatly manicured fingertips over the scar which ran across Tash's cheekbone under her left eye. The scar tingled. 'You look almost piratical.'

'Thank you for covering the medical bills.'

'Of course. You know I wish you'd let me do more. How are your grandparents?'

'They're fine.'

Tash's grandparents, Nancy and David Bell, were living the dream in a house Jemima bought for them six years ago, around the time Jemima had made the jump from doing well to doing exceptionally well. Three bedrooms. Period features. Closer to the church for Gran, big garden for Grandad, though he'd kept the allotment on too. Old friends from Shields Road were still coming round even now to admire it, Gran polishing everything with tears of pride in her eyes. She seemed convinced it was God who had given it to her though, as a reward for her devotion and sacrifice, not Jemima.

'How are . . .' Tash didn't know how to say it. 'How are *your* parents?'

'Still arseholes,' Jemima replied brightly. 'Look, I have to get back to my students. I'm so glad to have you here. Has Bethan given you everything you need?' She put her hand on the door.

Tash had a sudden urge to keep her in the room. 'Bethan isn't sure how my aesthetic will fit in with yours.'

Jemima shook her head. 'Perfection is out. I do hope you'll take pictures here – not just as part of the classes – and I'm interested to see my home through your eyes, or at least I think I am.' She studied the ground, the threshold under her feet. 'I just hope your next book isn't all slashed pictures of me and the house.'

Tash squirmed under the vivid, sudden memory.

'I was fourteen then! And it was one birthday card.'

'Maybe, Tasha, but having the card I sent returned, ripped up in an envelope with "cunt" written on it kind of stuck in my mind.'

The fountain chirruped on in the silence that followed. The bleat of some distant sheep the only other sound.

'Sorry,' Tash said eventually, and Jemima suddenly laughed.

'You said that at the time. I guess Nancy was breathing down your neck.'

Tash had never seen her grandmother that angry; she could still see the bright red flush on her powdered cheek and feel her own insides shrivelling in shame.

'She almost throttled me.'

The warm afternoon air stirred, bringing the scent of lavender and mint into the room.

'I shouldn't have snitched,' Jemima said eventually. 'What did she do to you?'

'The apology, and I was grounded. All my birthday money was given to the church roof fund and I had to say Hail Marys in the front room in front of Dad's picture for an hour. Every day for a week.'

Tash was back there in the old house, in Shields Road. The old front living room no one lived in, too warm, and smelling of Pledge; the cream and red striped wallpaper overwhelming in the cramped space. Marshmallow sofas. The photo of Tash's dad on the mantlepiece – a snapshot of him with Tash on his lap. Grinning. Candles standing either side of it. Always lit.

'Sorry,' Jemima said, looking up from under her eyelashes.

'I deserved it.' Tash shrugged. 'It was a crappy thing to do. And if I'd really meant it, I wouldn't have tried to keep the twenty quid, would I?'

'Lucky old church roof. Yes, I noticed that. And I was a starving PhD student then, I could have done with getting it back.'

It seemed impossible that there was a road from the sort of poverty when twenty quid made a difference to here, yet Jemima had, over the last thirteen years, found it and walked it.

'It's on your bio on the website, that you're my daughter,' Jemima said. 'At the bottom. Is that all right?'

'Yes. Sure. What do I say, if people ask. About us?'

Jemima studied the polished wooden floor of the classroom. 'I've always said I had you very young, and you were raised by your father, while I finished my A levels and went to university, and then by his parents after he died. That you are your own person.'

Tash's skin prickled. 'But what do *I* say? I don't want to damage your brand.'

Jemima rolled her eyes. 'What a relief! My "brand", Tasha, is that life is complicated. Say whatever you want.'

'Jesus, OK. Just checking.'

Silence. But Jemima didn't leave.

'The house is very beautiful,' Tash said at last, holding out a tattered olive branch.

'Thank you,' Jemima replied. 'I love it. It took a lot of work. And a shit ton of luck too.' She glanced at her watch, a thin silver band round her wrist. 'I have to go. Look, come and have a drink with me before supper. My room, six o'clock. Till then . . .' She waved her hand. 'Have a wander, get to know the place. Bye for now.'

Then she was gone, and the room became a little darker.

4

Kharkiv, May 2024

Tash shifted on her chair, trying to get comfortable. She could have taken the laptop up to her room and used the desk, but she needed to be around people today, even if she didn't want to talk to anyone. She was adding metadata to three batches of photographs before sending them to the agency. Date, location, names if known. Time of day. Most of the images she sent just as she had taken them. Others she cropped to hide gorier details. No one needed to see that.

'Mind if I sit here?'

She looked up. A tall lanky-looking man in his thirties was standing over her, English judging by the accent. He had dark, wavy hair and a slightly horse-like face which should have been ugly, but wasn't.

Tash looked round. The bar was huge, sprawling, full of booths, tables, little islands of seating like the one she was at with inconveniently low tables and large leather armchairs. Some of the windows had been replaced with chipboard. There were plenty of empty tables. When she'd first come to Ukraine in the March of '22, places like this had been full every night. Two years later, the thirst for news from the country had been slaked to the point of sickening. Tell me when it's over. The remaining correspondents and photographers had shared all of their best stories long ago. This guy, with the boy-band hair and the sideways smile, was new at least.

'Knock yourself out.'

He sat, perching on the edge of one of the wide low armchairs, while she wrote an email to Najit, pointing him towards what she thought were the best shots, then she shut her computer.

'Want a drink?' he asked, seeing she was done, and put out his hand. 'I'm Monty Young, by the way. I know, stupid posh name, but mum had a crush on the gardener from the telly. She didn't even know it was supposed to be short for Montague.'

'Natasha Bell,' she said, shaking it. 'Tash. My mum liked Russian novels.'

He smiled. 'Yeah, I know your work. So, drink?'

'Monkey Shoulder if they've got it in.'

He left his own drink on the table, and returned with a double for her. 'I guessed no ice.'

Tash had sprawled in one of the deep armchairs in his absence, one leg folded under her, her laptop in her bag. She put out her hand for the glass.

'You guessed right.'

He smiled and handed it to her.

'I haven't seen you before,' she said.

'No, I'm fresh meat,' he replied, picking up his own drink again. A pint of one of the local beers. 'I'm writing for the *Independent*. Was on the tech and national security beat for *The Times* before that.'

'What happened to Jonathan? He was stringing for the Indy, wasn't he?'

He nodded. 'Yup. Gone to America to cover the elections for them. It was a bit last minute, me coming here, so I have to find my feet pretty quick.'

'No point talking to me,' Tash said, sipping the whisky, 'I just take pictures. You have to work out what it all means.'

'Yeah, I think I'll be going with "The fucking fuckers have fucking fucked it." Just get that into three hundred words for the website and the rest of the day is my own.'

'Pithy.'

He had a good smile. Tash grinned herself and glanced down at his hand. No ring. Not that that meant anything – war played havoc with everyone's moral codes. Still, always good to know what you were getting into.

'Your mother is Jemima Carter, isn't she?'

He became immediately less attractive.

Tash looked round to see if anyone else was in earshot. As far as she was aware none of the other correspondents knew who her mother was. It wasn't that she was ashamed of Jemima, but it was hard enough as a young woman to be taken seriously for her work. If she had to take all the wits of the international press corps asking her for wellness tips and discounts on scented candles . . .

'I shan't tell anyone,' he said quickly, and Tash was irritated he'd guessed what she was thinking. 'I saw an interview where she said her daughter was taking pictures in Ukraine – then I did a bit of light googling – but unless this lot read *HELLO!* magazine, your secret identity as the heir to a wellness fortune is secure.'

She downed half her whisky. 'It's not a secret. I got four pages in the autobiography, so I'm told. If you're looking for an interview with her, just call her PR firm. They're on her website.'

She finished her drink and stood up. He did the same, stepping slightly in front of her. She looked at him, raising an eyebrow, and he lifted his hands and backed off a little.

'Look, I didn't want you to fall for my boyish charms and then find out I knew who your mum was afterwards.'

'No danger of that.'

She moved passed him, and he groaned, turning after her.

'Don't go, Tash. You haven't given me the opportunity to recover from the posh name yet.'

Tash paused.

'How about this?' he went on. 'I'll tell you three things that will make you like me. Then stay or go. What do you say?'

She said nothing, which was close enough for Monty apparently.

'Last month I was in the DRC and almost got shot by poachers. I talked my way out of it by pretending to be a biologist. Just pointing at plants and saying things I hoped sounded like Latin.' He frowned. 'And . . . I wrote really bad poetry while I was studying French and German at university and I'm terrified it will appear on the internet some day and my editor will sack me on the spot. And . . . and it's good you are doing conflict photography because it's making your style looser. The street art series you did was good, but too mannered.'

Tash was too baffled to reply for a second. 'Hang on, the last one wasn't even about you. And why would any of those things make me *like* you?'

He hunched his shoulders and grinned.

'Yeah, sorry, I panicked a bit. I'm told the pizza place round the corner is decent. Fancy splitting a pepperoni?'

He had something, a sort of restless energy to him. 'No questions about Jemima?'

'Yeah. Not over pizza anyway. And I read the autobiography. Those four pages were the best bit.'

Tash looked around the room. Still no one else here she particularly wanted to spend time with and she was, she realised, really hungry.

'Fine. OK. But you're buying.'

5

Belford Abbey, 29 June 2025

The pele tower was a rugged, asymmetrical construction which made the Palladian elegance of the main house seem vain and a little silly. A mass of ancient stonework, it rose over Tash in the late afternoon light, a remnant of, and a monument to, violent times on the Scottish–English border. A neat information board which stood near the entrance among the flower beds laid out the history of the building in brief. It even had an artist's rendering of how the tower would have looked when it was in use. Around its massive base, very clean-looking peasants clustered with their animals, ready to climb the short flight of stone steps and take shelter from marauders within its walls. A refuge in uncertain times.

She ducked into the tower through an open arch and the air became cool at once. From the clean floor of beaten earth, a modern wooden staircase led up to the second storey, where the exhibition was situated. She climbed it, and was surprised to find herself in a large, much lighter room occupying the whole footprint of the tower. Part of the southern wall had fallen away, then been shored up again. Rather than replacing the lost stone, the architect had taken the opportunity to introduce a single huge window. Beyond it was the gentle undulating park, dipping down to the woodlands which lined the river Aln. Above her, a skylight of thick glass bricks allowed more light into the space, casting subtle shadows over the rough walls. Tall white panels hung with artworks stood around the room, and in the far corner, an unlit stone arch gave way to another internal staircase, built into the wall itself. The arch was discreetly roped off, with a sign standing beside it:

NO UNAUTHORISED ENTRY

Her photographs fitted in surprisingly well with the work of the embroiderer and the fine artist. Whoever had arranged the exhibition had managed to find rhythms of colour and line between her portrait of Inna Markova – a farmer's wife with deep-set eyes and a flowered headscarf – and an exuberant tapestry of medieval village life, sewn over with neon bursts of colour. They had found a marriage too between her image of a crowd, scattering under mortar fire, one boy caught in the centre of the frame, not knowing which direction to run in, and an abstract canvas, painted in blocks of muted grey and yellows, with a single patch of red, like the recording light on a camera, blinking in its top corner. She realised with a slight shock that the red light was repeated on a small globe-like camera mounted just over the huge picture window. A fisheye lens which would capture the whole room.

She heard footsteps below, and turned in time to see a man in his thirties in a sage-coloured T-shirt and cream trousers climbing the stairs behind her. He had thick, curly hair, and his skin had a healthy tan, which could mean any sort of mixed ancestry, or a recent long holiday somewhere sunnier than Northumberland.

'Hiya,' he said. English, upper middle class, Tash thought immediately.

'Hi.'

'You're Natasha Bell, aren't you?' He came forward, holding out his hand, with an open smile and good eye contact. 'I'm Rupert. One of the flock hoping Jemima can sort out all my problems in a single week.'

She shook the hand offered to her.

'Call me Tash. How many problems have you got?' she asked.

He frowned, touching his finger to his chin. 'I don't think I love myself enough yet.'

'That sounds serious.'

'Yeah,' he said and shoved his hands in his pockets. 'It's been an awful struggle. Actually, a friend of mine came on one of these a while back. She was wiped out after seeing her company through its first funding round, and said this really helped her. I've got a start-up going to market later this year. Tech journalism.'

Rupert had walked over to one of her early shots of Kyiv. Blurred café culture in the foreground, tank traps in sharp focus at the rear.

His expression was intent. The light from the window fell across his face, creating pools of shadow at the top of his breastbone. Tash lifted her camera. He noticed, but didn't protest.

'Do you mind?' she asked.

'I'm honoured.'

He continued to look, and managed to avoid stiffening. Tash took the photo, revelled in the physicality of the pull and click as she wound on the film.

'I saw a documentary on war photographers,' he said, once the photograph was taken. 'Do you have PTSD?'

'Why? Are you worried I'll have a flashback in class?'

'No, just curious.' His attention returned to the photograph of the scattering crowd. A moment of suddenly intruding violence, caught, mounted and hung on the wall like a taxidermied stag. 'No offence, but isn't it just luck though, getting these shots? I mean, like this one of the boy. Right place, right time?'

He didn't seem to be taking the piss. Tash sat down on a bench under the picture window – make him squint if he wanted to study her – and took her time replying.

'Luck is a huge part of it. But so is training. You need to recognise the moment and get the shot.'

'You look too young to have been trained in anything.'

'So do you.' Tash was itching for a cigarette. She pulled the pouch from her pocket and started to roll one. 'I left school at eighteen. I was going to take a year out, ended up taking photographs instead. So I've been doing this for almost a decade.'

He stepped away from the photograph and nodded. 'You worked with Monty Young, didn't you?'

She concentrated on smoothing the paper of her cigarette, giving herself a second. 'Yes. I was with him when he was killed. Did you know him?'

'Shit. Sorry.' He ran his hand through his hair again. 'A bit. Did he talk to you about what he was working on?'

'We were all covering the same thing,' she said, keeping her voice even. 'The war.'

'Yes, I mean, obviously he was covering the war, but we met from time to time and he sort of half-pitched me on something before he went out. About tech and warfare. He was pretty cagey about it though. You know they say Ukraine has become a sort of lab for AI warfare?'

'You mean drones and stuff?'

'Yes – but he hinted that he had something more than that. Then he clammed up, said something about going to ProPublica. You know, that indie investigative journalism set-up. I've wondered about what that story was a lot since he died.'

'Yeah, I know who ProPublica are, but sorry,' Tash said, mechanically. 'I don't know what the story was.'

'OK.' He sighed. 'Shouldn't you be in France? Photographing these riots?'

'Riots?'

'Yeah, half the banking system seems to have imploded. ATMs aren't working, banking apps are just showing error messages. Now people have started throwing bricks through the windows of the Banque Populaire. Or the Banque not very Populaire any more, I should say. The guys at my office are scrambling to keep up with the story.'

'Shouldn't you be back in the office, helping them out?' Tash asked.

'Can't be in two places at once, and there will always be another crisis.'

She raised an eyebrow.

'Ha! OK. I see. Same is true for you.' He nodded to himself. 'I think you might be the tutor for me. Anyway, see you later.'

He jogged back down the stairs and the moment he was out of sight, Tash leaned forward, elbows on her knees, and breathed deeply. Her mouth was dry. The mention of Monty, out of nowhere, had made her chest tight. She heard a wail of sirens that she knew was only in her mind. She needed air. Needed to be alone. She touched her wrist, the woven leather bracelet, and noticed the staircase in the far corner of the tower again. Before she knew she'd made the decision, she had crossed the room, lifted the velvet rope and slipped under it.

6

Tash jogged up the stone staircase. It wasn't a spiral staircase exactly, but it curved, as if leaning on the inner wall. The air was dry, dusty and the only light came through arrow slits. She felt the walls shudder and a shower of plaster dust smattering on to her hair, gritty rain.

No. That was then. This is now.

It didn't matter. The urgent need to escape made her increase her pace up the worn steps. She had been indignant when she'd been medevacked out of Ukraine after surgery on her ruptured spleen, and started to search for flights back while still in her hospital gown. Her grandparents had protested, and their distress had guilted her into agreeing to wait a month, to make sure there was no sign of infection, before returning. Then came the night after the memorial service for Monty in London, and something – the way his mother held on to her hand, the unfocussed incomprehension in her eyes, his brother awkward in a suit so like Monty and so not – had broken her. She'd gone home, eaten noodles in front of Netflix, exchanging messages and making vague plans with contacts in Kyiv, then woken from a nightmare of the shooting in such a state of terror and collapse she had been unable to walk as far as the corner shop for a week.

The turn of the stairs continued and the light changed again, filtering through wood. She must be reaching the top of the display area now. She looked up and saw she was emerging into a sort of cabin at the top of the stairs, modern and more loosely put together than anything she had seen so far at Belford. It was as if someone had dropped a B&Q shed over the top of the staircase. The door was a latch, no lock, and it stuck and rattled as she shoved it open and burst into the fresh air. She bent forward. Hands on her thighs. Inhaled. Exhaled. Then looked up.

All Northumberland was laid out before her. After a minute, breathing deeply, waiting for the panic to pass, she lit her cigarette with shaking fingers, and inhaled deeply, before releasing the smoke into the breeze. In the distance sky and sea met in a blur beyond Alnwick and Alnmouth, and to the north the ground rose towards hills and a sky that was Scottish. To her right stood the main house, with the walled gardens behind it and the horseshoe of teaching studios round the fountain, small as a needle from this height. Behind her the ruins of the Abbey itself, walls without roofs, empty windows, foundations without walls, arches and doorways and stairs which led nowhere and to nothing; at the rear, sharing some of its walls, the neat Edwardian villa for the special guests. Its tall sash windows gave the house the look of a face, lazily observing her through half-closed eyes. It had its own stone terrace at the front, scattered with heavy-looking wooden garden furniture, tables with neatly furled umbrellas. Even from this distance, Tash could see the brass glint of the door knocker. She turned away, back towards the distant hint of the sea at the edge of the horizon.

It will get better. It has to get better. Then you can go back to work.

It took her ages to notice the bundle of white roses just under the low parapet. No card or wrapping, just a purple and gold ribbon holding the long woody stems together, and placed in a small earthenware vase. She glanced over the parapet at the long drop back to the turf, broken with ancient masonry. It looked kinder, more gentle than the track in Ukraine, but somehow she still caught the tang of blood, oil and frozen earth. She stubbed out the cigarette and put her hand in her pocket, feeling between her fingers the shape of a dark-blue thumb drive. She had carried it with her for eight months now. Then she touched her bracelet. It helped a little.

The door latch rattled behind her and she turned, wondering if Rupert had another question about her teaching methods, but it was a different man and he didn't look like one of Jemima's clients.

He was in his fifties, his white hair cut short, wearing jeans with a white buttoned shirt and a suit jacket.

'You're Tasha Bell?'

American. A nasty note of challenge in his voice.

'What gave me away?' she asked, lifting the camera slightly.

'I saw you from the house, and I want to ask you a question.' No polite smile. No offer of a handshake. She sat down on the parapet in case her legs were still shaking.

'Are you on the course?'

'No, I'm not. Why now?' he said. 'Why, after hardly speaking to your mother for years, are you here now?'

Tash did not think her fractured, long-distance relationship with her mother was any of this man's business. She studied him. There was something too tight about the skin at the corner of his eyes. A square jaw, a tan so deep it looked red in places. He'd missed a spot shaving though, just under his chin. Strange, given the brilliance of that white shirt, the flattering cut of his jacket and shininess of his brogues.

'Are you worried about something?' she said. 'Maybe you should watch one of Jemima's mindfulness videos.'

'What?'

He rocked back and curled his lip slightly. Tash lifted her finger to her own chin and he ran his thumb under his jawline till he found the unshaven spot. His frown became deeper.

'I asked you a question,' he said.

'I'm aware,' Tash replied. 'But it was kind of rude, and I have no idea who the fuck you are, so I decided not to answer it.'

She lifted the camera to her eye and took his picture. He flinched, like she had thrown something at him.

'I going to have to insist,' he said.

Tash lowered the camera. A jackdaw called in the distance, a chuckle of alarm or warning.

'How?' she said, her voice frost-cracked. 'How *exactly* are you going to insist?'

A vein on his forehead was beginning to throb. Bring it on. *Lose your temper, give me a chance to lose mine.* He was standing on the glass blocks of the skylight. They looked like a patch of ice melting under him in the sun of the summer's afternoon.

'My name is Frank Matthews, though people call me the Colonel. I'm the CEO of Charter Security and I handle the safety of some very important people who visit Belford.'

'Awesome,' Tash replied. 'I'm here because I'm not fit to go on assignment. Jemima offered me the job, so I took it. Satisfied? Now leave me alone. I didn't come up here for company.'

He studied her in silence for a second.

'I have my eye on you, Bell.'

'Really? Gosh, I feel safer already.'

A beat. Then he turned and walked back down the stairs. Tash rolled another cigarette, still sitting on the low parapet. By the time she had managed to finish and light it he was walking through the ruins towards Abbey Villa. He scanned his card on the reader by the front door and went inside. Her heart still leaped and plunged in her chest.

This was going to be harder than she had thought.

7

'Do you want a proper drink?' Jemima asked the moment Tash walked into her private sitting room. 'I'm ready for a gin myself. But I never know with your generation. Haven't you all given up drinking?'

Jemima and Bethan were sitting close together, staring at a laptop set up on a dark wood dining table in the middle of the room. The decor here was a contrast to the rest of the Abbey. Floor-to-ceiling bookshelves covered two walls, where doors allowed, while a third, dominated by a marble fireplace, was covered in pictures. An eclectic mix of photographs, bold prints and canvases. Tash spotted a couple of her own prints on the walls. Numbered editions with her signature in pencil under the image. Jemima must have bought them from the gallery in London.

'I haven't. Yeah, gin is good.'

'I'll get them.' Bethan sprang up and went to a sideboard cluttered with bottles against the fourth wall. 'You sit down, Tasha.'

Tash sat on an overstuffed armchair on one side of the fireplace, perching on the edge with her knees together as if she was facing the Mother Superior again, while Jemima took off her reading glasses and dropped them on the table, then stretched her arms over her head, arching her back.

'Ok, Beth, gift baskets and dinner vouchers for the River Café. I'll do the letters after supper, and charge it all to Notebook. Then we'll go with your captions.' She grinned at Tasha. 'Bethan has to check our Instagram posts don't give her the ick.'

Bethan returned from the sideboard, a gin and tonic in each hand. Ice and lemon had appeared from somewhere. She set one by Jemima, and the other she handed to Tash.

'Thanks.' Tash raised her glass in a silent toast, then drank. Good gin. Good tonic. She felt the chill of it going down her throat, felt it helping. 'Do you guys know you have an angry American patrolling the grounds? Frank Matthews. He followed me up to the top of the pele tower to ask me why I took the job here.'

'What were you doing up the top of the pele tower?' Jemima said, turning away from the computer, her drink in her hand. 'There's a sign. No unauthorised access.'

'I authorised myself,' Tash said. 'I'm in a shoot-first-ask-permission-later industry.'

Bethan snorted with laughter as she gathered up papers from the table.

'But the American?' Tash persisted.

'I didn't even know he was here,' Jemima replied, looking slightly accusingly at Bethan.

'He makes you twitchy, Jem,' Bethan said without any trace of apology, the papers held to her chest. 'He wanted to do an initial sweep of Abbey Villa now we have the new dates. He's heading back to London tomorrow – oh, and he'd like to see you after dinner tonight.'

Jemima rolled her eyes. 'OK. Officious little . . . Tell him I'm busy with the letters tonight. I'll come over to the villa first thing tomorrow and see him before he leaves.'

'Are you sure, Jem?' Bethan asked. 'I don't know why but he seems more on edge than usual.'

Jemima looked at her daughter. 'What did you tell him, Tash? About taking the job here?'

'That I'm fucked up and here for the money. I think. I was a bit abrupt.'

'I suppose I should play nice then,' Jemima said wrinkling her nose. 'Fine. Colonel tonight and letters and captions in the morning.'

'Probably for the best,' Bethan said. She picked up the laptop. 'I'll get those letters set up in the office.'

And she was gone, a cat in Louboutins.

Jemima settled in the armchair opposite Tash on the other side of the cold fireplace.

'The Colonel,' Tash said. 'He'd missed a spot, shaving.'

Jemima's glance was quick, assessing. 'That's not like him. I wonder what the hell is going on. It must be serious if it's making the Colonel nervous. He's the sort of man who prides himself on his nerves of steel.'

'Who is he doing advance for?' Tash asked. 'Is it something to do with the mysterious "more conference than a course week" at the end of July? Bethan told me you'd explain.'

Jemima crossed her legs, and drank before she replied. 'Yes. One of my private coaching clients is holding a getaway. A few of his advisors – including me – working through some of the ethical implications of his latest project.' She bit her lip. 'It's not the sort of thing which would normally give the Colonel the yips. Anyway, we cancel the usual course any week he's here. That's who the gift baskets are going to, visitors whose stays have been cancelled, but his advisors and their staff often want to take classes, or do workshops or use the spa, so we keep most of the staff on.'

'Coaching?'

'It's my bread and butter these days. Providing one-on-one support and guidance to business leaders so they can "maximise their potential"' – she scratched scare quotes in the air, with a crooked grin – 'and the value of their companies, of course.'

'How does that work?'

'It varies.' The other wall of the room was punctured with French windows which gave out directly on to a narrow terrace. In the distance the hills folded upwards to a pink and purple sky, scattered with stands of trees. 'I deal with CEOs of tech start-ups mostly and provide a mixture of business coaching and therapy. Some of these men, and women, they started off as engineers, then found themselves in charge of a company worth tens of millions, when they haven't had a chance to develop any of the necessary skills. I do in-person sessions when I'm in California. This time of year, either they come here for a day or two, or I have video sessions with them.'

'So you know all of their secrets?'

'Some of them,' Jemima said lightly. 'There is a lot of trust involved.'

'And who is this guy coming in July?'

Jemima finished her drink and put her hand out for Tash's glass. 'Want another? Bethan always makes the first one weak because she knows I drink them fast.'

Tash nodded and watched as her mother made them and returned.

'He's a bit of a special case. We started working together a few years ago, and then he took his company private just as the pandemic was receding. I don't coach him any more as such, but I'm an informal advisor, with a few others.' Jemima sat down again. 'Have you heard of Eliot Drake?'

8

Kharkiv, May 2024

Monty wiped pizza sauce off his hands with a paper serviette.

'Have you heard of Eliot Drake?'

Tash frowned. 'Yes, one of the quiet billionaires.'

Monty looked pleased. 'He's not a household name. Most people just look blank when I mention him.'

'I've read about him. He's an effective altruist, isn't he? One of those ones who believe the best way to help the poor is to earn a shit ton of money, then give it away.'

They were sitting at a small Formica table at the back of the pizza place next to the hotel. In front of them was a mess of crusts, oil and rocket leaves on a wooden board.

It had been a good meal. Monty knew how to listen, as well as how to talk, and he talked about being a reporter without any macho posturing. She'd noticed he had a half-smile, half-grimace, when he was afraid he was being too serious or self-righteous, she found attractive.

'And what do you think of "effective altruism", Tash?'

'A way for billionaires to stay billionaires and sleep at night.'

Monty laughed, winced, then put his hands behind his head and stretched. 'Sorry, four hours crammed into the back seat of a Fiat with two other correspondents. I'm still working out the kinks. Yup, that's him. Thirty-eight, and he's been a billionaire for four or five years. I don't think Drake would say he was part of the effective altruist club any more though. Too tainted by scandal and general fuckery. Though he still claims he wants to use his wealth for the greater good. He has many, many foundations . . .'

'Bless him. How did he make his money? I've forgotten. I just have a vague memory of a tall guy in loafers and thin brown sweaters.'

'Ah – the tech smart-casual look – it says, look, I'm like you. Just a bit better.'

He had a very expressive face, playful. Tash felt like a cat confronted by a puppy.

'He is an engineer,' Monty went on. 'Moderately successful start-up and it turned out he had a talent for, well, talent spotting. He became a partner at a venture capital fund, Notebook. Ending up buying out his partners. Then he started a data mining and informational intelligence company, Panopticon, which seems to be generating a lot of cash. You want anything else to eat?'

Tash shook her head and he lifted his hand for the bill.

'Wasn't the Panopticon a sort of prison?' Tash asked and Monty nodded. 'Why do these tech guys give their companies such creepy names?'

Monty laughed, thanked the waitress in Ukrainian and received a broad grin. While he counted out the euros for the meal, Tash searched for Panopticon on her phone. Yeah, a sort of prison designed so one guard could see directly into all the cells. Then she looked for Eliot Drake. The screen showed him to be as she remembered, a blandly handsome man in his late thirties, pictured in a button-down shirt, jacket and chinos. The shot she had found showed him cross-legged, sitting on stage at some event, finger on his chin, listening attentively to someone who had been cropped out of the picture.

'You use an incognito browser?' Monty said, as the waitress took the money back to the counter. She still looked pleased. Monty must have left a good tip.

'Yeah,' Tash said, still reading the article. 'Agency always tell us to use one when we're on assignment.'

'Seems like a quiet night. Fancy a walk?'

She slid the phone back into the pocket of her trousers. 'OK. So why did you ask about Eliot Drake?'

He held the door open for her and they emerged out on to the street. The air was cooler now, but Tash could feel the approach of the long hot summer in the May air. She thought of outdoor parties and passing vodka bottles around the bonfire and the smell of hay and dry soil, and wondered how long Monty would be staying.

'I was wondering if your mother ever talked about Drake. Apparently she acts as an advisor to him or something.'

He had agreed not to ask about Jemima, and technically he hadn't, but this still seemed like a sneaky way to *almost* ask about her.

'I don't speak to Jemima much.'

He didn't say anything, but she felt she had to explain somehow.

'I mean, you said you'd read the biography. You must get why.'

'She gave you up as a baby.'

Tash paused and tensed. A dull explosion in the distance. Too small to be a missile – a drone then. In the early days explosions like those had sent everyone running for the shelters. People hardly bothered to turn round now unless the sirens started wailing.

Outside one of the clubs, under trees covered in fresh foliage and fairy lights, groups of teens, in athleisure wear, were practising breakdance moves. Seventeen-, eighteen-year-olds maybe. Still too young to face conscription for now. The same age Jemima was when Tash was born.

'Yes. She wanted to do her A levels, go to university, but her parents said they'd cut her off if she kept me. My dad and his parents were super Catholic – I guess they talked her out of an abortion. So in the end, I went home with Dad. He died in a car crash two years later.'

Monty didn't pretend to be shocked or surprised. He'd have read those facts in Jemima's biography. He didn't tell her how sad it was either, or touch her arm and say he was sure it must have been an awful decision for Jemima. It was odd how many people did that, as if the thought would never have occurred to Tash over the last twenty-seven years. He was quiet, attentive, leaving her room to say more. She suddenly realised he was probably very good at his job.

'Her parents cut her off anyway. For having me rather than getting an abortion, I mean. So she did her A levels, got her degree and went off for her PhD in America without any help at all.' She turned round to admire the wide boulevard. Posters advertising a concert in the metro station. The local orchestra had taken to performing underground to avoid the endless night-time shelling. 'I'd get cards and letters growing up and we'd text occasionally, but then just as I was leaving school she started getting famous.'

'And you were far too proud to go running after her?'

'She tried to see me when she could when I was little, and she's made it clear she wants to know me, but she doesn't push.'

Tash hadn't realised how grateful she was for that until she said it.

'And now the future of humanity is in her hands,' Monty said.

'You what now?'

'Sorry. That sounded shit. But people like Eliot Drake – they can move mountains. I just hope she's giving him good advice.'

'Breathe deeply and spray lavender on his pillows, probably. Are you writing about Drake? Isn't that a tech reporter's job? In case you hadn't noticed' – she gestured at one of the shattered buildings further down the road, neatly taped off with warning signs – 'there's some shit going on here.'

'Yeah, there is,' he said, lightly, but not too lightly. 'Have you ever noticed technology and war have always gone hand in hand? Leonardo Da Vinci's designs for forts. Code breaking and computing in World War II. Now nations are using computers to attack infrastructure. There's this war – bombs and boots on the ground – but there's also a continual, hot cyberwar going on across the world and as long as we manage to keep things ticking along, no one notices. But the barbarians are at the gates. All this tech has made things very comfortable for us in the West, but it's left us vulnerable too.'

'This sounds more like a think-piece in *Slate* than reporting.'

'Ouch. Just you wait. Anyway, I'm curious about Drake's insights and plans.' He glanced at her and looked away again.

'The money you spent on my pizza was wasted then. I know nothing. Barely even heard of the guy and I had no idea he was working with Jemima.'

He smiled down at her and winked. 'Oh, I wouldn't say it was wasted.'

9

Belford Abbey, 29 June 2025

'I've heard of him,' Tash said. 'Someone told me in Ukraine you advised him.'

Jemima smiled, but it didn't reach her eyes. She was sitting with her back to the French windows, and the high back of the chair shrouded her face with soft shadows.

'I try.'

'Do you specialise in billionaires?'

Jemima studied her, as if trying to work out how much edge there was to her voice. 'Not many. Half a dozen perhaps, a lot more in the tens of millions range. That sort of wealth has a gravitational force to it.' She shrugged suddenly. 'All sorts of people come out of the woodwork, and there's a danger, when people get that rich, they find themselves surrounded with "yes" people, telling them how fantastic they are, and gaining perspective, retaining any humility, gets much harder.'

'Is that what you do? Humble them?'

'You make me sound like a dominatrix.' Tash grinned into her gin. 'No, I try to make them question their assumptions. Anyway. That's who is coming. Eliot Drake and friends, plus security and entourage.'

'Including the Colonel?'

'Yes, I'm afraid so. I really think he is devoted to Eliot, but he's made himself Eliot's guard dog. And his bite can be as bad as his bark.'

Tash thought of his coiled hostility up on the roof.

'One of the staff sold a picture of Eliot here to the newspapers,' Jemima went on. 'Nothing embarrassing, just us playing tennis, and I was inclined to let it slide. The Colonel insisted on us sacking her though. Anyway. It's a circus, basically. We'll keep it quiet as long as we can, but Eliot's jet is tracked and people talk, so we'll probably have protestors at the gate the minute he arrives.'

'Protestors?'

'Yes. They call themselves New Luddites. Maybe that's why the Colonel is getting het-up. I know they've been gaining momentum lately. Fears about AI, now this Paris thing will give them more coverage I suppose . . .'

'The Luddites are anti-technology protestors?'

'Yes, that's them. I'm sorry they are targeting Eliot though – I really do think he wants to help people.'

'Maybe he should try paying his taxes then.'

'Tasha . . .' She sounded tired, like Tash was being a child.

Tash let it drop.

'Why are there flowers on the top of the pele tower?'

'Flowers?'

Tash described them while Jemima frowned at her. Then she tapped her ring against the side of her glass. It was a huge gaudy thing, a piece, a piss-take of the gold bands and variable diamonds most women wore. She shook herself.

'It's not a secret. And you should know before they turn up. There was an accident, last year. One of Eliot's people, a man called Brandon Wallace, went up there in the middle of the night and fell. Dennis, one of the ground staff, found him the next morning when he came on shift. He'd broken his neck. No other clients around at the time, of course, thank Christ.'

'Jesus. Someone died? Is that why the sign's there?'

Jemima shook her head.

'No, the sign was there before Brandon decided to go and commune with the night. He authorised himself too.' Jemima rubbed her finger round the edge of her glass. 'There was a police investigation, of course, but not much in the papers. And this happened just after we had heard that you'd turned up injured and your colleague had been killed.' She sighed. 'It was hard to think straight. It got easier once we knew you were home and out of danger, of course. Your grandparents were very good about keeping me updated, you know.'

Tash didn't know what to say. She hadn't wanted Jemima to visit her in hospital. Hadn't really thought about her at all. She'd just replied to a couple of text messages. She felt an unfamiliar curl of guilt in her chest, like smoke from a candle.

'This will be Eliot's first visit to Belford since then,' Jemima finished.

She was staring at the ground again, making little circles with her slim ankle. The dark silk of her high heels caught the early evening glow from time to time. Tash didn't say anything, just watched.

'I've no idea who could be leaving flowers though. They were fresh?'

'Couple of days old.'

'Maybe Brandon made an impression on one of the staff. I didn't like him much. He introduced Eliot to the Colonel for a start.'

'You didn't throw him off the tower, did you, Jemima?'

She laughed out loud at that, a deep throaty laugh which made her eyes brighten. 'No, I did not. I think he spent half the time just getting Eliot psychedelics, or whatever. They were very close for a while.' She peered at Tash over the rim of her glass. 'You did sign that NDA, didn't you?'

'I did. Though I don't think "third hand report of tech billionaire taking drugs" would get me much from the *Sun* tip line.'

Jemima grinned, then stared down at her drink and her voice was quiet. 'I've been so looking forward to you coming here, Tasha, but it's frightening too. You're my daughter, I want to get to know you, but I'm not sure how to do that.'

The conversational tack took Tash by surprise. Somehow, what Jemima might feel about her turning up at Belford, war damaged and angry, had not occurred to her.

'I don't know. Slowly?'

'OK.' Jemima's voice was a little breathy and her eyes were damp. 'Thanks.'

'I do like teaching, you know,' Tasha said. 'And I intend to do a good job here.'

Jemima reached forward. 'I never doubted that for a second, Tasha.'

A ripple of bells sounded from the corridor and Tash looked at the clock on the mantlepiece. Six-thirty. Dinner time. Tash lifted her head. Somehow, in the midst of the conversation, the panic she had felt in the pele tower had receded, as if she'd moved from shade to sun.

Jemima sprang up, chin up, skirts swinging. 'I hope you're hungry.'

10

Dinner at the Abbey was farm to table food. Most of it made locally, they were told, and though she didn't recognise the names of most of the stuff put in front of her, it tasted good and there was plenty of it. Everyone sat at long communal tables in the old kitchens, though an end of one of them was set aside for Jemima and a group of students. Everyone, it seemed, was promised dinner with her during their stay. Quality time.

The room itself was high-ceilinged and stone-flagged, lined with antique dressers filled with the same mixture of earthenware and blue and white dishes the food was served on, plus copper pans, silver chaffing-dishes and the sort of junk shop curios Tash was always tempted to pick up before she remembered she didn't own a shelf to put them on. Vintage butter dishes, a rough pottery model of Bamburgh Castle, a ceramic seal, its whiskered nose high in the air. More cottagecore than sad beige. The staff passed up and down the gaps between the tables in their black polo shirts and brown aprons, telling the diners what the dishes were, answering questions. Efficient and friendly without being obsequious, flashing smiles, most with the local accent, Geordie with a dash of Scottish. Most of Jemima's clients were in their thirties. A scattering of people in their fifties perhaps, but no one older than that. Expensive haircuts, clothes which hung well on fit, well-fed and exercised bodies. No obvious logos. The women wore very little make-up, or they wore make-up that was good enough to be almost invisible, and the men moisturised.

Having money and comfortable lives didn't make these bad people, any more than having their home blown away in a missile strike made a Ukrainian a saint, Tash told herself. Still that obvious ease which came with their money grated on her. The solipsism of wealth, she thought. They believed the world revolved around them. But maybe they were right, because on some fundamental level, it did. She put a careful smile on her face and listened to the to and fro, trying to catch and remember the names of the diners around her. 'Oh, my God! Have you seen the pool?' 'The rooms are darling.' 'I feel a thousand times better already.' They would all be having appointments with nutritionists and personal trainers during the week, as well as group classes with Jemima, one-on-one sessions, and their creativity workshops. They could cook with Belford's chef, or even be sent home with bottles of micronutrients in convenient capsule form, prepared on the premises. One or other of them might say 'we've been so lucky', or 'we're very blessed', but they didn't mean it. They couldn't mean it, or the contrast between their lives and the shit most people went through trying to get to another payday would drive them mad. They had to think they were special, or perhaps they believed everyone else was being poor on purpose just to harsh their vibe.

Give it a rest, Tash, she told herself. *You are here to get better. Wellness Barbie wasn't wrong when she said this was a place to heal just because she was wearing five hundred quid high heels when she said it. Stop overthinking it. You can't walk on a broken leg, and you can't go and shoot conflict when you are jumpy as hell and seeing ghosts. So shut up, take the win and enjoy the fancy food and the soft towels for God's sake. It's just a temporary retreat. What's that French phrase? Step back, so you can leap further forward.*

Someone mentioned AI and the talk ranged across the reliability or not of Large Language Models, fake news, AI slop, which was apparently the term used for the uncanny pictures of kittens in storms, or Jesus with his arm around Donald Trump, which appeared on her social media feeds from time to time. Tash half-listened, till she realised someone had asked her a question.

'Sorry?'

'I asked what you think about the future,' a man with a touch of grey in his glossy dark hair asked. James. 'As a creative, aren't you worried?'

'I don't know. There is plenty to worry about here and now, so I just try and deal with what's in front of me on any given day.'

A round-faced girl, Zoë, laughed. 'You sound like Jemima! I don't know. I sometimes think these Luddites have it right. Perhaps we should smash up all the technology. Redistribute the wealth. Start again.'

James leaned towards her, touching shoulders, and Tash realised they were a couple. A couple having a good day. 'Careful,' he said. 'What if they come for your coffee machine?' He wrinkled his nose at his dining companions. 'It works via an app. She can operate it from bed. Espresso there and waiting by the time she reaches the kitchen. Can't imagine she'd want them to redistribute that!'

Zoë covered her mouth in mock horror. 'They are revolutionaries, not barbarians!'

Barbarians at the gates.

The group laughed along with them. The sort of comfortable laugh which suggested they all believed they were roughly on the same page, that their underlying principles were both shared and praiseworthy.

'What's the news from Paris?' another man asked in the clipped, precise vowels of Nigerian English. Jay. 'Anyone seen anything further this evening?'

One of the older women, with soft white curls and a scarf in jagged abstracts of pink and red, replied.

'Nothing good. They are using water cannons against the protestors on the Champs-Élysées, and a lot of the luxury stores in the Marais are getting looted. Or smashed up at any rate. I'm sure all the Birkin bags were moved to a safe place the moment the cash machines started playing up.' A moment of quiet while they all absorbed the news. Jay offered an appropriately wry smile to the comment about the bags. 'Do you think it is a cyberattack?'

'I'm sure it is,' Jay replied, then glanced at Tash. 'That is my field, Tash. Cybersecurity. People do not realise what an effort it is to fend off these attacks all day every day. I know of major banks who are now creating paper records of their holdings every hour in case an attacker gets through.'

Tash smiled at him, and found herself hoping he would sign up for photography.

'Perhaps it's just incompetence,' Zoë said. 'What's happening in Paris, I mean.'

'No,' Jay replied. 'It is an attack and a clever one.'

'Whatever the cause, people will die if this goes on,' the woman with the scarf said, running her fingers over the fine silk at her throat.

'Do you really think so?' James asked, a tiny furrow in his smooth brow.

'Yes,' she replied simply. 'People are angry already, this is just the sort of thing to push them over the edge. Most of my Parisian friends are going to their country houses for now.'

Tash flinched, thinking of Ukraine. The wealthy so often forgot most people did not have anywhere else to go.

A waiter arrived carrying more plates of food.

'Grilled Hispi cabbage with hazelnut dukkah,' he said, setting down a plate piled high with charred leaves. 'And this is saddle of rabbit with purple sprouting broccoli.'

The food was welcomed with a flurry of thanks and he winked and passed on.

'Who do you work for?' Zoë asked Jay.

'No one!' he said cheerfully, and served himself rabbit. 'I just sold my company to Notebook. I am here to start thinking about what to do next.'

'Have you met Eliot Drake?' James asked. 'That's the Notebook man, isn't he? The best sort of billionaire,' he added to the table at large. 'Lots of charitable foundations and no social media network.'

More comfortable laughter. The idea of the angry Parisian mob seemed to have been forgotten. Well, they were a long way away.

Jay pursed his lips and shook his head. 'No! My company was too small for a meeting with the man himself. Less than twenty million. I met with one of his subordinate's subordinates.' He put his hand over his heart. 'Though Mr Drake did send me a gift basket and a polite email. The honour.' Zoë sniggered. 'The gift basket included an invitation here, for which I am most grateful. I wonder how many of the people here are owners of businesses he has bought. He must acquire a dozen companies like mine a week. Cybersecurity, facial recognition, machine learning . . .'

'He funds all sorts of journalism start-ups too. That man, Rupert, who's here. He got his seed money from Notebook,' salt-and-pepper added.

'Well, I paid,' said silk scarf. 'Since my husband died there has been so much pressure over the inheritance. I'm looking for a little clarity and escaping my son's start-up ideas. He worships Eliot Drake. He says Drake makes Elon Musk look like an idiot.'

'I think Elon does that all by himself,' a long-haired girl replied.

Suddenly, Monty's ghost was leaning against one of the dressers. He caught Tash's eye and waved. Someone said something about Hearst and *Citizen Kane*.

Tash needed to ignore Monty. Loosen up. Let the chinks in her armour open up and let all this warmth in rather than resent it. *Contribute, Tash.*

Friends in London had bought or sent her books to read while she was convalescing. A new thing apparently, book gifting. One, a history of the great American titans of the gilded age, had painted a picture of a society grinding through its gears till the metal smoked, letting off a crunching screech of distress and dislocation in the wake of too many new inventions and innovations, trains, the telegraph, electric light. A portrait of progress falling over its own feet. But that was in America, and Tash was safe here, surely, behind these old British walls. Britain was, Tash thought, less than America. Less rich, less powerful, less extreme, less, she hoped, insane. Britain was perhaps sauntering downhill into an uncertain future with an umbrella over its shoulder, rather than careening off a cliff in a fully automated self-driving cybertruck.

She mentioned the book and the conversation swirled around what the past can or cannot teach us, till the party broke up in a mood of polite well-fed satisfaction.

II

Back in her pale, beautifully appointed room, she tried not to hate Jemima's clients, their smooth security. She thought of Bethan's *You will be kind to our clients, won't you?* and gritted her teeth; she had meant what she'd said to her mother about doing a good job. Though what her job would be when Eliot Drake turned up, still seemed unclear. She sat down on the window seat and faced the room. Monty's ghost sat in the armchair.

She froze and waited, staring him down.

Reality shifted and he was gone. She knew that Monty sitting there, in her tastefully upholstered armchair, was just her brain still processing the trauma of that day in the woods. Part of her wondered if she'd ever be free of these sudden appearances. They could be frightening, destabilising, but she was afraid she'd miss them a lot if they did stop. A print of the Abbey ruins hung over the fireplace. It reminded Tash of an outdoor version of Hamlet she'd seen as a kid.

She twisted in the seat and looked out at the view. The sky was finally darkening, though touches of purple and pink still softened the sky to the west, held aloft by oak and sycamore trees on the brow of the hill. She pushed open the window, pulled her tobacco from the pocket of her jacket and rolled a cigarette, trying not to think too much until it was lit and she could exhale, slowly, into the still summer air.

Eliot Drake. His friend falling from the tower. *Wealth on that scale has a certain gravity.*

A door shut, downstairs, outside, with a rattle and clack. The shot that killed Monty suddenly deafened her and her palms stung. The terrible now of it. Her heart plunged.

'Just a door. Just a door. I'm here. I'm in England.' She said it out loud. The night was silent again, the present struggled to assert itself and the past reluctantly withdrew.

She picked up the smouldering cigarette from the carpet – *fuck* – then stubbed it out on the outside of the windowsill. She wrapped the butt in toilet roll with shaking fingers and threw it in the bin in the bathroom. She washed her hands with soap that smelled of bergamot and lemons. A week here, and she wouldn't recognise the smell of her own skin. This place. The kingdom of Jemima Carter. Fairyland. The folk tales her grandfather read to her as a child had stern warnings about fairyland, and its many dangers. She breathed in through her nose, out through her mouth, waiting for the panic to subside fully.

Back in her room, she unpacked, then pulled the thumb drive from her pocket and plugged it into her laptop. Monty's thumb drive. A familiar untitled folder appeared on the screen. She double-clicked it for the millionth time. It asked for a password. She tried a fresh handful of random words.

Hamlet
Belford
Alnwick

The image shuddered, like it was shaking its head each time. Rupert had said Monty had pitched him a story about tech in the battlefield, hadn't he?

Techwarfare
AIwar
Robosoldier

Nothing.

She unplugged it and returned it to her pocket then touched the braided leather bracelet round her wrist. She hadn't taken it off since the day it was given to her. Karin told her she'd fought the nurses when they tried to remove it at the hospital. In the end they'd given up, wrapped a sterile bandage round it and got on with the operation.

She looked at the chair. She wanted him to come back. When he didn't, she spoke to the void where he should have been.

'Monty, when did you stop thinking of me as a source, and start trying to protect me? Christ, I never even noticed.'

Tears came into her eyes. At first she swiped them away. Then she didn't, and, trying not to make any noise the embroiderer or the artist might hear, she let herself weep.

12

Kyiv, June 2024

Monty and Tash were giving themselves a day off, after a week reporting on the Russian advances in the Donetsk region. The action was grinding and miserable. Tash had got the shots, and Monty had done the words, but the weariness and gloominess of it had got into their bones. An air strike in Kharkiv killed four people, and Tash found herself thinking, *That's not enough to get the front page*, and hated herself and everyone else.

She'd have got over it, pushed through, but then they drove through the devastation of the Holy Mountains. The area had been famous for its forests and hiking trails along the river valleys before the war. Now huge swathes of it were burned to bare bones and scattered with minefields. The news on the radio was filled with speculation about the American elections, the upcoming presidential debate, with a side order of the UK election news. She'd told Monty what she felt, and he told her they should get back to Kyiv for a couple of days. So after twelve hours of driving, their documents being photographed at every checkpoint, a shower and change of clothes, they joined the promenaders and day drinkers and tried to get the smell of smoke out of their system.

He talked about his childhood. His younger brother, who he admired, but didn't understand, the distance his ambition and love of books built up between him and his parents. How his mother's baffled admiration of him made him feel small. He left gaps for her to contribute as she wanted, but didn't press. It made talking easy.

'Jemima visited a few times when I was a baby,' Tash told him, 'but the first time I remember meeting her I was five, six, maybe? I couldn't work out why Gran kept cleaning the front room, or why I was wearing my good dress, but we weren't going to church.'

They had bought ice cream and sat out on the pavement in the warmth.

'The bell rang, and Gran called me, and I came to the top of the stairs and there was this woman there. I didn't recognise her, but I knew she was important somehow. She had bags from the toy shop in town in her hands, and red hair, then she looked up and smiled, and I thought she looked like a Disney princess.'

'When did you find out she was your mother?' Monty asked, licking chocolate from his wrist.

Tash wrinkled her nose. 'I must have been told, or I worked it out. I felt horribly shy. Anyway, Jemima bought art stuff, and we painted a picture together. I was finishing it off, colouring in the sun, when I heard Jemima and Gran fighting in the kitchen. I can close my eyes and see that particular shade of yellow now, feel the pencil, you know.'

'Ah,' said Monty. 'One of those memories.'

'Yup. She would have been, what, twenty-two then? I didn't see her for another three years.'

He hesitated for a moment before he spoke. 'You know, Tash, if you do talk to your mother, you should tell her to try and get away from Eliot Drake.'

'Oh, for Christ's sake. I rarely speak to her. It's hardly going to come up.'

'But if it does . . .'

Tash finished her ice cream, and started wiping her fingers. 'Are you going to tell me why?'

He dropped the end of his ice cream into the bin. His face becoming serious. 'I can't. Not yet.'

Maybe it was the drive through the savaged woods. Maybe it was the last story, but Tash's temper suddenly snapped. 'So what, you think I should drop her an email? Hi Jemima, it's your estranged daughter here – I know I've had sod all to do with you for a decade, but my friend Monty says you should ditch your billionaire client. Big kisses.'

He recoiled. 'No, for fuck's sake don't send an email, and don't mention my name.'

The reaction, so fierce and from the gut, shocked her. He saw her surprise and ran his hand through his hair. 'I'm sorry, I know you are taking the piss, Tash, and I'm sorry I made you angry, but never mention me or him in an email, OK?'

Behind him the people came and went, all smiles, choosing to forget, for a moment, what the future might hold.

'You mean it,' Tash said softly.

'Yeah. I do. But let's forget for now. I'm sorry I pushed it.' He tilted his head up, savouring the warmth of the sun. 'What do you fancy for dinner?'

13

Belford Abbey, 30 June 2025

The taster sessions on Monday went well. Yes, she assured the curious guests, what they learned here would also mean they'd take better pictures with their iPhones in the future. That seemed enough. When they were done, Tash bagged up the exposed film and waited at the side entrance to the house to hand the package to the courier from the printers. He arrived on a motorbike and listened to her comments and instructions about the developing, making the occasional note on an actual paper pad, but never taking off his helmet. Then she went for a drink with Jemima who, with gentle tact, asked her about Ukraine. What was it like when she first arrived? Mad, a sort of terrified elation as the initial invasion faltered and Kyiv remained under Ukrainian control. Where did she stay when she was in Kharkiv? A hotel? No, she rented a tiny second bedroom in the flat of a young widow with two small sons. It was cheaper, and anyway the Russians had started targeting hotels, especially if they knew journalists were staying there. Tash asked when Jemima had bought Belford.

'I don't own it, Tasha!' Tash blushed, suddenly feeling small and stupid as Jemima continued. 'The company owns it. It pays all the staff too. I'm the founder and CEO, but I have investors I have to answer to. Eliot Drake's the main one actually. Or rather his company, Notebook.'

'Doesn't that complicate the therapeutic relationship?'

Jemima made a face. 'A bit.'

* * *

Life in the house was frictionless. Food appeared on the table. Tash's laundry was taken from the basket and returned clean to her drawers. Waste bins emptied and the water jug in her room refilled. The drink with Jemima at the end of the day became a habit, and Tash found they could talk easily about nothing in particular, swapping light, interesting stories, feeling out the edges of each other. Most mornings Tash ran along the gently rising and falling tracks which wound up and down the hilly landscape of the park. She had started running the first time she came back from Ukraine, and it had become necessary to her now. This sort of running very different to the parks and embankments in London though. The sound of water was everywhere, streams cutting their way through the soil, sudden waterfalls, slower stretches softened by reeds, bright green ferns catching the sunlight under beech and oak. White-faced sheep, and the broad sweep of the Aln with abrupt banks and pebbled shores, crossed by half a dozen bridges, each one a different design.

In the morning, while the students had their yoga and meditation sessions, listened to experts preach the benefits of micronutrients or took one of the treatments available from the half-dozen beauticians on staff, Tash went through the results of the previous day's sessions, writing brief comments on sticky notes and affixing them to the back of the prints.

On Thursday, one, from Gloria, the woman in the silk scarf whose French friends had deserted Paris, stopped her in her tracks. It was a picture of dog roses, just past their prime, but the shot was miraculous. A shallow depth of field, so the blooms to the rear were slightly soft, while a single bloom to the left and just above the central point of the frame was pin sharp. The light seemed to cup and separate each petal, while the dark background and the slight blouseyness of the midfield blooms gave the image a sense of danger and change, a still moment of transience, a protest against the inevitable dying of the light. And though the shot was in black and white, it seemed to glow with colour.

Tash looked up. Monty's body was lying on the central table in the classroom. There and not there. She inhaled slowly through her nose and looked back at the print. Strong emotion unlocked him, as if it took down her defences and he pounced into her vision. She waited, knowing he wasn't there, hoping very much he'd be gone soon.

On the Friday evening there was a party where the guests showed off the fruits of their creative labours, and Tash was quietly proud of what her students had done. She signed copies of her book with honest dedications of encouragement and good wishes. Checking her email in her room that night, her headphones on, she saw a reminder from her publisher about going to sign books in Alnwick, and with a sting of surprise and guilt, realised she had not left the Abbey grounds all week. She sent a message apologising, and promising to go on Saturday morning.

14

Saturday, 5 July 2025

'Natasha! Thank you so much for coming in to do this – so appreciated!'

The owner of the bookshop, a nervous-looking man in his fifties with a neatly trimmed beard, an extravagantly flowered shirt and round glasses, took both Tash's hands in his own when he introduced himself, and Tash suppressed the instinct to pull away. She'd had a horror of being touched since she came back. The Belford spa facilities, the beauticians and masseurs, were wasted on her. He released her.

'Thanks for asking me,' she said automatically, remembering to smile. 'Lovely shop.'

It *was* a lovely shop, an eclectic mix of fiction and non-fiction with separate sections for poetry, art, and local history. 'Thank you! All new titles. There's a huge second-hand place down the other end of town, so we don't try and compete with them. They do a nice Welsh rarebit too if you fancy it. I've set you up in the office.'

He led her through a curtain into a functional back office of desk, computers and blue carpet tiles. The wall art showed soothing landscapes. The sort of thing one might like to look up at while wading through accounts in search of perspective. The stack of books waiting for Tash on the desk was larger than she had expected. A dozen, perhaps.

'Bethan at the Abbey said you have a great art and photography section.'

He blushed. 'Yes. It's a hobby of mine and I use my pictures to do Christmas cards and calendars. Not as exciting as what you do, of course. The local wildlife can be a bit elusive or uncooperative at times, but they don't shoot back.'

'That's an advantage.' She pointed at the landscapes. 'Are those yours?' He nodded. 'Lovely.'

'Thank you.'

She took her seat by the books, and he handed her a Sharpie. Then he hesitated. 'I'm sorry. I didn't mean to say anything, but you look so young! When I saw you on *The One Show* talking about the book . . . It broke my heart. I know I'm supposed to feel for your subjects, not you, but you're so little!'

Tash shook her head. 'I'm five six, and stronger than I look. And maybe it's good to be slight. Makes me harder to hit. And don't be taken in by my girlish looks. I'm twenty-eight.'

He blinked. 'Oh, sweetie, do you realise that thinking twenty-eight is grown up is a *sure* sign you're still just a baby?' He sighed. 'At least you're safe at the Abbey now. I'll leave you to it, and would you like a coffee? We've got a proper machine.'

Tash gritted her teeth and smiled. 'Sure. Flat white would be great.'

He mock saluted then bustled back into the body of the shop as Tash shrugged off her jacket and drew the first book towards her, smoothing her hand over the large-format glossy pages. She'd written the captions herself, brief words giving names and locations. The refugee charity which was receiving whatever profits the book generated had commissioned texts to go along with each photo too. Some were passages from Ukrainian literature, others were narratives from Ukrainians, both fighters and civilians.

Without meaning to, or wanting to, she turned to the last page and the photograph of Monty's body on the trail. A slight blur at the top left edge of the frame, the ghost of a dead branch from the tree she had hidden behind, then his hair, collar. The puffer jacket with press patch velcroed to the back. The shard of metal beaded with her blood. Her scar itched.

'I brought you your coffee,' a voice said.

Tash turned back to the title page and looked up to see a stranger coming into the office, a white porcelain mug in each hand. He was younger than the manager, in his thirties. Handsome, with a yellow-blonde beard, and hair short at the sides, longer on top. Scandinavian blonde, not English. Some red in it. He looked like he was taking a break from splitting logs in a Charles Tyrwhitt advert. Maybe that was because of the lumberjack shirt, worn open over a plain white T-shirt. The office seemed suddenly much smaller.

He set the coffee beside her and sat down on the other side of the desk, a polite, friendly smile on his face. His eyes were a startling icy blue. The sort that looked like frost on a sunny winter's day.

'Thank you. Do you work here?'

'No. I'm Harry, a friend of the owner. Well, I'm renting his holiday cottage next door for a couple of months so I suppose he's my landlord really,' he replied. 'But I think he likes me.' He pointed at the books. 'One of those is for me.'

Tash took the lid off the Sharpie.

'Shall I dedicate it to you?'

'Present for a friend of mine, actually,' he said, watching her pen hover over the title page. 'Could you sign it to Karin Chernkova?'

Tash paused, then signed only her own name. 'No need. I sent Karin a copy myself.'

She saw a flash of blue, Karin's shiny jacket, and smelled the mix of rotted pine needles and gasoline. Her scar stung, not itching now, but aching with the cold shock of the first cut. She breathed steadily through her nose without looking up, trying to tell her body she was not in danger, that she was in a bookshop in a small and peaceful northern town. Her heart still thundered. *Speak*, she told herself. *Make the body recognise where it is now.*

'Do you really know Karin, or are you just trying to make an impression?'

'Can't it be both?' he said.

In the silence which followed, she looked up again. Her perception shifting from threat then, in the woods, to some new threat, here and now. He sat back on his chair, giving her space, crossing his feet at the ankles.

'We spoke recently. I wanted to talk to someone who had worked with you. But yes, I am trying to make an impression. Karin said you were conscientious, brave but not foolhardy. Reporters, Monty included, thought highly of your work.'

Tash tried to imagine the conversation, under what circumstances it had taken place and, what else Karin had said.

'Are you a journalist?'

'No.'

Tash closed the book and passed it to him. 'So who are you then?'

He balanced the book on his knee, flipping through the pages with one hand, his coffee in the other. 'Normally, I'd . . . I don't know, be a friend of a friend who bumps into you in town and invites you for a drink. Maybe an aid worker you crossed paths with in Ukraine, but we haven't got much time and we decided, well, the psych evaluation team decided, that the direct approach might be best in the circumstances.'

He glanced up. Still had that polite smile on his handsome face, one that made the corners of his eyes crease.

'You're with the intelligence services? That's what you are implying, isn't it? All that, "normally I'd be a friend of a friend" bullshit.' She wanted to take her coffee, drink, but was afraid her hand would shake. 'Have you been hanging around all week, waiting for me to come in and sign? Was this . . .' She nodded at the pile of books. '. . . your idea?'

He half-shrugged. 'I suggested it.'

'Well, congratulations. You got me out of Belford Abbey. And now every conference room in MI6 can have a copy. If you are MI6.'

'We have more conference rooms than that,' he said.

Trying to go for the roguish charm, was he? Well, good luck with it. She could taste metal in her mouth. All senses on high alert. She had enjoyed whole days this week without this clenching, paralysing fear turning up at all, and now here was 'Harry' looking like he'd dropped out of a Hallmark Christmas movie and her hands were sweating.

'How are you getting on with Jemima?' he asked.

'Just fine.' She signed the remaining books, her signature reasonably steady, and put the lid back on the Sharpie. 'And I'll be heading back to the Abbey now. Hope you've had a lovely week in Alnwick.'

She reached behind her for her jacket.

'Please don't,' he said lightly. 'Your country needs you and all that.'

'Oh, fuck off.'

'We really do.'

She hesitated. MI6 recruited correspondents sometimes, didn't they? And photographers – particularly conflict photographers like her – were known for being observers, moving quietly round the edge of things. Near the action, but professionally invisible and uninvolved. They weren't spies, as such, or sources, but might talk through their impressions of people and places with friendly contacts like 'Harry'. Share information that wouldn't necessarily get into print, but the powers that be might want to know.

But until she could get a grip on these attacks of panic, and banish Monty's ghost, she wasn't going anywhere MI6 would be interested in.

'Look, I'm grateful, and thanks for buying the books, but I'm sure my country will manage. I can't go back to Ukraine. Not at the moment. I'm teaching here all summer, so whatever war zone you want me to snoop about in, you're out of luck.'

The metal taste was still in her mouth and she could hear air-raid sirens, their slow keen.

For a moment she was gone. Her fingers shook and looking down at them she saw her hands as she had in the basement of a house in Kharkiv. Smeared with concrete dust, under flickering lights, as she tried not to listen to the whimpering of children around her, their sharp intakes of breath as bombs came closer; the murmured reassurances of their parents, whose own voices shook. The terrible impotence of those moments. While powerful men lay awake in sugar-coloured palaces and told themselves they were serving a greater good.

Got to move.

She stood up, shrugging on her jacket as she did. He stayed where he was.

'Belford is the war zone I'm interested in.'

She stopped.

'Belford? It's not a war zone. More like heaven designed by middle-aged, middle-class people. And it's helping me.' The words jumped out of her mouth before she even knew they were true.

'Sit down, and let me explain.'

'Why should I?'

'Concern for your mother? Or if that doesn't fly, what about curiosity?' he said. 'What could His Majesty's Government want to know about what goes on within the walls of Belford Abbey?'

'Perhaps you all need help with your emotional growth.'

'We probably do. But come on, Tash, you know what this is about really. Don't you?'

15

'Is this about Eliot Drake?' Tash asked.

'Bingo! Yes. It's about Eliot Drake.' Harry made his fingers into a gun shape and fired them at her. She flinched. 'The new billionaire on the block. You'd be surprised how much time we spend monitoring billionaires these days.'

Tash only realised she had sat back down again when she saw him smile.

'So are you MI5 or MI6?'

'I'm Secret Intelligence Service, MI6, but it's a joint operation.'

That sort of wealth has a gravitational force to it. All sorts of people come out of the woodwork.

'How do I know you are with *any* British service?'

He put his book on the table and pulled his chair forward, its legs scraping over the carpet tile, and leaned his elbows on the desk. 'I have a warrant card, but those are not hard to fake. I'll tell you three things. Maybe that will convince you.'

Monty's ghost was standing over his shoulder, looking vaguely guilty. *What, was this 'I'll tell you three things' an established technique?*

'OK.'

He ticked them off on his fingers. 'One. You have a juvenile record for shoplifting that was expunged when you were eighteen. Two. You have been warned by your photo agency that you will not be sent to active conflict zones until you complete the mandatory counselling. Three. You described Monty's death in your first session, but missed your next appointment, then told your manager you would complete the course later in the year after spending the summer teaching here. Your manager thought that sounded like an excellent plan, and encouraged you to take all the time you need. He seems a good guy.'

She took hold of her coffee cup again. The impulse to throw the remains in his face was almost overwhelming.

'It's not hot,' he said. 'You'll ruin my shirt, but not my pretty face.'

'I've always thought mind reading was a pretty slimy party trick,' she said sharply. 'And drop the cute act, will you? You're not as fucking charming as you think you are.'

He looked surprised; his eyes flickered over her, reassessing. 'OK. But those are my bona fides. Don't you want to hear more?'

He had the sense to stay quiet while Tash adjusted.

'OK.'

'Look, I can give you the usual spiel about how it's useful for someone like you to have friends in the service. We can be very helpful. Just think of having MI6 as your own private concierge. We can be obstructive too, but I think threats will make you dig your heels in.' He sighed. 'And this is in your own best interests. Eliot Drake is a very important person in your mother's life. You'll be helping her, as well as yourself, by helping me.'

Perhaps they would open up Monty's thumb drive for her. That would be helpful. Then she could find out what the story was that had taken them into the woods that day, though maybe Monty wouldn't want her to hand his secrets over to the security services with a smile.

Should have thought of that before you got shot, shouldn't you?

A ripple of pain and anger shuddered out from her stomach to the tips of her fingers. She breathed through her nose, in and out, until it passed out into the air around her, and focussed on him again. He was watching her, head on one side, a slight smile on his handsome face.

'But what do you want me to do exactly?'

He rocked back in his chair. 'Eliot Drake is coming to Belford, with an entourage and at short notice. That suggests to me there is something big on his mind. His Majesty's Government wants to know what it is. You are a trained observer, good at paying attention while staying in the background, and part of the household.' He paused. 'I also think Eliot might be interested in you – Jemima is important to him, so there's that. And also he has that fascination with war a lot of men have.'

'OK, so . . .'

'So I want you to be my eyes and ears in that house. How about it?'

Tash was silent for a minute. When she was ready to go on assignment again, a friend like Harry would be useful.

'Maybe. If I agree to help you, I want to be able to ask questions. Like you said, he's an important person in Jemima's life. What's he doing that the government is so interested in? He's like into data mining and AI, isn't he?'

He stood up suddenly. 'Fancy a walk? There's a nice spot where we can sit and watch the world go by in the market square. I'll share what I can, Tash. The more informed you are the better.'

'You say you're a spy and now you just want to sit together in the square?'

'Avoiding being seen together in a small town like Alnwick is hard, so let's not try. I'm just a fan of your work who got chatting to you in the bookshop. We will become friends, meet up from time to time. I'll be working here over the summer – I've taken the cottage to write my novel. I'll be going on long walks for inspiration, hanging around in the pubs, that sort of thing.'

Tash remained in her chair. 'Why aren't you talking to Jemima? She has access I can't possibly have.'

'He owns her house and they've known each other a long time.'

'That it?' Tash said. He studied her for a long moment before replying.

'She's also very tightly surveilled – by Eliot, by his company and by his own security team. We can't risk an approach. But you, you might find a way to slip under their radar.'

They left the back office. The manager was at the cash desk, bent over the card reader.

'All right, Peter? Tash has finished signing.'

He looked up and blushed. 'The card reader is playing up again! My last customer said it's happening all over town.'

'Have you tried switching it off and switching it on again?'

'Yes, Harry, I most certainly have . . . oh! There we are! Back in business.'

'Good, because Tash has some purchases to make.'

Harry plucked one of the OS maps from the stack by the till. 'Hang on.' He crossed the shop floor at an easy saunter, then returned with a biography of Eliot Drake. 'There you go. If you're going to meet him you should know something about him.'

'Oh, is Mr Drake coming back to Belford?' Peter said. 'That's nice.'

'Yeah, don't think I was supposed to mention it though,' Tash said.

Peter mimed zipping his lips together. Tash smiled.

She presented her card and got the little confirmatory beep as money moved through the ether. 'Are they still having problems with these things in France?'

Peter wrinkled his nose and lifted up an iPad mini from behind the desk. It was playing BBC news with the sound off. 'I know it's a little unprofessional to have it running in the shop, but I can't take my eyes off it. Have you been to Paris?'

'A couple of times.'

'I love it there. God bless Eurostar! But honestly, look at it now.'

She looked at the screen while he talked. A montage of professionally shot videos mixed with scraps of mobile phone footage. Some lines at government foodbanks. People, well-dressed, prosperous-looking people, queuing for food. Restaurants with 'cash only' signs. Market stalls with people bartering for milk and cheese, handing over batteries, packets of salt or pasta.

'A website has gone up to help work out a bartering system,' Peter said. 'So resourceful and better than letting the fresh stuff rot, I suppose.'

A reporter spoke into a microphone outside a grocer's shop which was taking IOUs from regular customers. Then the image changed to a package of riot material. A line of police facing a massive crowd. A plume of tear gas. Someone in a yellow jacket putting a bin through the front of a McDonald's. Shuttered banks.

'What on earth will happen if they can't sort it out soon?' he said. 'It's been a week already. I thought technology was going to make our lives easier, but sometimes I think we'd all be better off with paper and pen.'

'I'll walk you back to your bike, Tash,' Harry said.

Peter tore his eyes away from the screen again. 'Thank you for coming, Natasha. And do pop in again. I so hope you'll be here for the Wild Hunt.'

'What's that?'

Peter smiled, Paris forgotten, and his hands fluttered madly into the air once more. 'Oh, what if you photographed the burning of the wolf, and the dancing! It's not a real wolf, of course, just a huge wolf's head made out of straw – the Rotary Club organise that, and it's a wonderful show.' He stopped himself. 'It's our version of the Lughnasa festival. Celebrating the beginning of harvest and we have it on the last weekend in July. But we've themed it round the Wild Hunt – a sort of ghost story about gods charging around the sky hunting down the souls of the evil men who've died during the year. Bit of pagan fun for all the family. There's a parade down Market Street, with masks – everyone dresses up – there's music, hot food, drinks, craft gifts. And after sunset there's a bonfire in the marketplace. That's when the wolf is burned.' He glanced back down at the screen showing the rioting, the queues, and his voice became slower and more doubtful. 'It's supposed to guarantee the harvest will be good, and we won't grow hungry over winter.'

'Yeah,' Tash said. 'I'll be here. Thanks for the coffee.'

Peter smiled at her, but his attention was already caught by the footage unspooling in front of him.

Harry opened the door to the street, and the bell jingled.

16

Kharkiv Region, June 2024

'What's winter like here?' Monty asked. He was sitting at a table in the garden of a shell-damaged village house, eating slices of the first of the season's apples drizzled with honey and yogurt.

He, Tash and Karin, his new fixer – a tiny woman in her thirties who had proved remarkably fierce when she wanted to get them past a checkpoint – were guests of the owners, a couple in their sixties, both round as berries and brown and wrinkled as walnuts, who had stayed when the rest of the village had been driven out by shelling. They were a three-hour drive out of the city and the countryside had looked lush and rich as they rode through the early morning mist. Sunflowers growing wild among the grasses, the stands of trees along the wide slow rivers, low distant hills. Most of the fields, growing wild this year, were mined.

Tash was enjoying taking pictures of the couple. The dappled light coming through the leaves, the neatly ironed tablecloth and the pinks and blues of the wife's headscarf. Karin translated the question and the couple laughed. Their reply was too quick for Tash to catch.

'Inna likes to knit, because she doesn't need much light, and Klym makes rugs with scraps,' Karin said. The couple were still speaking. 'They have electricity now. Last winter they had only a solar lamp a volunteer brought them, but they say winter will come soon enough. So we should enjoy the summer while we can.'

Monty smiled and nodded. The couple began to speak about the first winter, how one of their neighbours was killed by a sniper, how people began to flee leaving animals behind them to starve.

How Inna went from home to home keeping cows and goats fed and watered as best she could. How sometimes an invisible soldier would fire at her feet while Klym stayed behind the walls of their smallholding, repairing damaged walls, foraging for firewood when he dared.

'But we have the garden now. For food and the chickens. The fields are mined, but when they repaired the power lines they cleared a strip. Enough to plant potatoes.'

'Did you ever see any strangers come through here? Not Russians or Ukrainians?' Monty asked.

Klym shook his head, then Inna patted him on the arm.

'Twice,' Karin translated as she spoke. 'People came through with better trucks. In the spring this year. They flew tiny helicopters – that's drones, I think – over the village for a day or two each time. Then went away. They didn't do any damage. April, because the apple trees were in blossom.'

Klym nodded, remembering now. He picked up the earthenware jug from the table and filled their glasses. Last year's cider.

'Probably drone pilots, training, don't you think?' Karin said.

'Probably,' Monty replied.

Klym said something else.

'He hopes you have what you need.' Karin smiled and then broke off. 'I think they are lonely, Monty. They want to hear our stories.'

Monty put away his notebook. 'Come on, Tash. You too. Let's sing for our supper. What would they like to know about us?'

Karin laughed. 'Inna wants to know how long you and Tash have been married.'

Tash almost blushed.

Monty smiled at the old lady. 'I haven't persuaded her yet, but I shall work on it. Would she like to hear how I made an idiot of myself in front of President Zelensky?'

Klym chuckled at the story. 'He's a comedian. He'll understand. Do either of you know Bath? Inna likes Jane Austen.'

17

Alnwick, 5 July 2025

Tash emerged into the summer sun outside the Alnwick bookshop.

'We're heading that way,' Harry said, nodding towards a flagged alleyway a little further up the road. The streets of the market town were busy even though the school holidays hadn't started yet. Locals greeting each other, half of them with spaniels at their heels, mixed with small groups of teenagers wearing matching backpacks. Tash and Harry turned into the alley, which broadened into a yard with a restaurant and delicatessen. It led to the top corner of the cobbled market square, one side dominated by a three storey building with a colonnade, and high windows on the first floor. Several other, more irregular buildings around the square were mostly constructed of large blocks of sandstone; in the sunshine it looked as if the whole town had been fattened with honey.

Tash stepped to the side of the pavement, and looked around her. The movement of people, the generations weaving around each other. The smell of bread and bacon coming from the café, the way the sunlight hit the stones.

'Is it AI? The stuff that Eliot Drake is doing?'

'Machine learning,' Harry replied.

'I don't really get the AI thing,' she confessed, thinking back to the to and fro of the conversation her students had had at the beginning of the week. 'Humans aren't just brains in a body. What makes us useful in the world is as much about what goes on in our stomachs and spines as in our heads.'

'And that concludes your TED talk?'

She looked up at him, but he seemed interested.

'For now. Like and follow for further updates.'

He smiled. There was a stone cross in one corner, and benches with ornate wrought-iron backs facing into the square. A scattering of stalls – food, crafts, one selling fruit and veg – were set up on the cobbles. 'You may have a point, but you're thinking about the Large Language Models like ChatGPT – the stuff which sounds human and will summarise your PDFs for you. What Drake's done, as far as we can tell, is a lot simpler, but a lot smarter than that.'

'Go on.'

'Give me a minute, you've reminded me I am a being with a stomach. Bacon roll?'

She nodded, then waited on the pavement as he ducked into a bakery behind them. As he disappeared into the relative darkness of the shop, it occurred to her she could leave. Just unlock her bike, head back to the Abbey and tell Jemima about the approach. The Colonel, Drake, Jemima, they would all want to know, surely? Easy Brownie points from Mummy and friends. Then she could settle back into the cocoon of the Abbey. Snug. Monty wouldn't do that though. Not to mention the fact that, if Harry was with the service, she owed him.

And Harry said he would tell her things. She leaned against the edge of a metal bench. The back and sides, high and huge for street furniture, formed a wrought-iron frame twisted through with poppies and doves. She couldn't see him, but she could feel Monty at her shoulder.

'I'm at Belford for me, not you,' she muttered to him.

'Here you are.' Harry held out the roll in its brown paper bag towards her. She took it and they sat together on the bench to eat.

'So what's special about what Drake's invented?' Tash asked after the first minutes of eating were done.

Harry swallowed, and wiped the grease from his lips with the back of his hand. 'So you've heard of his company? Panopticon?'

She remembered that pizza place. Monty paying the bill. 'Data mining,' Tash replied.

'Yup. Kind of. Like I said, this is cleverer than Large Language Models, and simpler. So LLMs, they can write emails for you, condense documents, give you research summaries in a way that is convincingly human, right?'

Tash nodded.

'But they get things wrong, because they are trained across the whole internet and don't always pick and choose when it comes to their sources. That's why they occasionally suggest making a nice risotto with poison mushrooms, or adding glue to your pizza. Drake has gone another route. He's created a single system, Panopticon, that brings together a lot of advanced machine learning techniques and makes them work together. But Panopticon is selective about its sources and is more interested in getting things right than understanding natural speech, or reproducing it.'

'So what sources does it use?'

'Well, take all the geolocation and metadata from messaging as read. Emails, phone calls. Energy usage. Your search history, what vitamins you buy. Bookings, vouchers, documents stored in the cloud. Then from facial recognition to cryptography to video analysis. CCTV, GoPros, Apple Watches. Panopticon gathers everything' – he nodded towards a neatly coiffed woman in her sixties, striding over the cobbles – 'from her Waitrose points, to . . .' He sought out someone else. This time a girl a few years younger than Tash, holding up a camera for a selfie. '. . . to her Instagram account.'

An older man watching selfie girl.

'And his Only Fans account?'

'I'd lay money on it,' he said. He had a good voice, rich without sounding affected.

'There's no Waitrose between Newcastle and Edinburgh. But I get your point.'

He grinned crookedly. 'Fair enough. Make fun of the southerner. The point is, it's not bothering to ingest novels or the contents of Reddit. It's strategic in where it concentrates its compute. It doesn't pretend to be your girlfriend, but it is very, very accurate and can find key slivers of information, connections in the midst of vast amounts of data. It joins dots, and makes excellent assessments of the importance of the connections it finds.'

Tash chewed on her roll, frowning.

'Think of it like a very clever spider,' Harry went on, 'with an infinite memory. You can prompt it to answer a question, like "give me a list of the ten people in south-east London likely to be the biggest drug dealers in the area", or ask it about drug dealing in that part of London in general and it will write you a book. Or ask it about "anything of interest to law enforcement agencies in the following postcode" and it will give you a list organised by the different units of the Met.'

'And that's enough to make Eliot a billionaire? Helping the police round up drug dealers?'

'That's an example. The intelligence it can deliver isn't just limited to dodgy deals though. Perhaps a certain group of executives are getting together to organise a merger. Maybe one of the tech firms has a big announcement coming.'

'Ah. So people can make money off it?'

He laughed. 'They can make a lot of money. Or disrupt markets, bring down governments. And Drake owns it.'

'You said.'

Harry twisted round so he was facing her. 'No, I mean he *owns* it, Tash. He didn't just buy the right company and shout at the engineers. He made it.' He sighed and turned away again, his gaze ranging over the crowd in front of them. 'Well, with the help of a few friends and some strategic acquisitions. But he stitched it together, made it *think* about what it found. Most intelligence we use isn't actually secret you know, not any more. The difficulty intelligences services face now is sifting through the vast amount of information available and working out what matters. It's impossible to find the signal, the thing we should pay attention to, among all the noise.'

'And this thing, which Drake has made, it's better at finding the "signal"?'

'I said infinite memory, just now, didn't I? I suppose what I mean is infinite awareness. Panopticon has become, as far as we can tell, much better than any human at analysing the available data. It is constantly updating its knowledge, finding new sources and adding them to itself automatically, then it comes up with actionable intelligence again and again. Using it is like becoming omniscient.'

Tash finished her roll in silence, thinking, observing her own animal nature. The taste of salt and fat, the feeling of being sated. Perhaps those physical sensations didn't matter any more. 'You've seen it work then?'

'I was part of a team that had a remote demonstration. It was terrifying. Beautiful.'

He wiped his fingers and balled up the paper bag in his fist and Tash thought of her grandmother, her hands held together in prayer.

'Infinite awareness. Sounds like God,' she said.

The paper bag was thrown with casual accuracy into the over-sized black bin, with the Alnwick town arms picked out in gold. 'Yeah. And, like I said, Drake owns it, so you can understand why the security services might be interested in his thinking.'

'Can't you . . . buy it off him, or something?'

The question seemed foolish as soon as she'd asked it. Drake could buy this whole town and everyone in it – Duke and castle included – and probably not even notice it.

'No. We are allowed to rent it occasionally. Two years ago, when he started touting Panopticon to governments, large corporations, he'd come to us promising the moon. We'd award the company contracts for background reports for certain operations or projects, and what he came back with was good. Not stellar, but good. Then Panopticon started getting better at a much faster rate. Before we knew it, we were going to him, begging him to take our money. Now he's selective about what contracts his company takes on and which ones he doesn't. Pay enough, and you'll be able to get a ring-fenced portal to work with the system remotely. Of course we'd love to buy it outright, have exclusive access, but he's not offering that.'

'Do you know who else he's selling services to, other than you?'

'We know he's picky. Consults with his advisors about who to share his sweeties with. Their security is very tight, but every time I see a foreign agency get a good win, I assume they've gone through him.'

'And you seriously can't go to Jemima direct?'

He glanced at her sideways. 'No. One of our people made an approach through her business partner, Bethan.'

Tash frowned. She'd assumed Bethan was more assistant than partner.

'She was turned down flat and Eliot's people got our operative's picture, and that was a short step to her real name. She can no longer work the field. If you are going to help us, you really can't say anything to Jemima. Nothing at all.'

'Aren't you afraid of being exposed too?'

'Yes, but this is worth the risk. And I have the best cover in the world, you know: the truth. My name *is* Harry and I *am* writing a book. It's crap, but I'm trying. Pan can find my life online. A couple of courses with Curtis Brown Creative, a short story competition or two and otherwise a boring, OK-but-not-stellar career in civil service. Now on a sabbatical. We just met. We might run into each other again. We'll exchange numbers.'

'Can't they just switch on our phones and make them record our conversations?'

'Phones still get really hot if you try that. Anyway, one of the most frightening things about Panopticon is it doesn't need to listen to us; it knows what we're thinking without even bothering to do something as clumsy as switch on a microphone.'

'That does sound a bit like God.'

It was still only mid-morning, but the sunshine had tempted people out on to the streets for their morning coffees. Teenaged waitresses, their skin pale and faultless, in black tights and flat shoes, flipped open tables and chairs and set them on the pavements, and greeted the elderly couples who settled at them with broad grins.

She heard the lilt of the local accent, the practical warmth of it.

Then she thought of the Colonel, snarling on top of the pele tower, of the roses under the parapet.

'Would I be in danger, Harry? Talking to you?'

He lifted his hand to rest on hers for a moment. A casual touch, a reassurance. She flinched.

'Not today. If you help us, and are discovered, you might get expelled from Eden. But I don't think you'll be in any more danger than that. Not on British soil.'

He said it with airy confidence, but he was not looking at her as he spoke.

They walked to her bike. As Tash settled her tote from the bookshop into the large wicker basket between the handlebars, she noticed a florist on the other side of the road, its windows trimmed with purple and gold. So many pretty ways to separate a person from their cash.

'Jemima told me one of Eliot's entourage was killed in an accident the last time they were at Belford.'

Harry nodded. 'Yes. Brandon Wallace. He was a bright boy at school, made some money selling his first start-up then got into trouble over his taxes and went to work with Eliot. A very smart, confused man.'

'Was it really an accident? Brandon's death?'

'We believe so. The local police ran the investigation, and they are competent. There is security footage of him going up there alone.'

She studied her hands, flexing round the handlebars. He was convincing, but parts of his story didn't fit into hers, and the points where they differed felt sharp and dangerous. 'How do I know who you are? You sound right, but you could be anyone.'

'I knew about your record.' He sounded hurt.

'If you're MI6 why don't you just—?' She stopped herself and thought for a second. 'What about other countries, other spies? They must be interested in what Drake wants to do with his program too and they could get that information you have about me. What if you turn out to be a Russian? I need someone to vouch for you.'

He studied her carefully. 'I don't think we're ready for you to meet my mum and dad yet.'

She refused to smile, and saw a spark of irritation in his eyes.

'Christ, really? Doesn't your gut tell you to trust me?'

Trust no one.

'Maybe I don't trust my gut.'

He tapped his fingers against his jeans. 'OK. Pick a time. A time you can be outside tomorrow.'

'Three-fifteen.'

He nodded. 'A Chinook helicopter will fly over Belford Abbey at three-fifteen. Will that do?'

She laughed. 'Yes, that would do it. Wait – what? You're serious?'

'You want someone to vouch for me. I think the Royal Airforce should do it.'

'OK. Then what?'

'Like I said – I want you to be my eyes and ears. For a start, find out who will be joining Eliot at the Abbey. Use your initiative.'

'OK.'

'Good. Now give me your number.'

'You don't have it already?'

'Yes, but I want it to go into this phone today, now, while I'm standing next to you.'

She recited it. He thumbed it into the phone and then sent her a pair of emojis. A book and a pair of bacon rashers.

'Any text messages are between Harry the charming would-be novelist, and Tash the slightly bored photographer, OK? No spy shit.'

'Should I write that down? No spy shit on text messages.'

'Don't take the piss.' He inhaled slowly. 'Tash, I know you don't have any particular reason to trust me. And vague talk about the power of Panopticon might sound a bit . . . abstract. But this is real. It is happening. Eliot Drake and people like him are *happening* and they have the potential to make a real difference in the world, for good or bad. The power they've amassed makes them something utterly unique to our age and we don't know how to handle them yet. You really will be helping everyone – yourself, your mother, your country – by helping me.'

'An appeal to my sense of right and wrong? Is that what the psych eval team told you to try?'

He nodded. 'Maybe, and please remember, whatever their faults, at least someone *voted* for the people I work for. I don't think you're someone who's going to side with the oligarchs.'

She studied him. 'OK. I'll see what I can find out.'

'Thank you. And, run the route I've given you. Try it out if you think my bona fides are good. I'll meet you there later in the week.'

'What route?'

'It's on the map you just bought.' Then he put out his hand and Tash shook it, automatically. 'Make sure you set off at the same time every day. Been lovely to meet you.'

Then he disappeared into the growing throng of tourists.

18

Supper that evening was cold cuts in Jemima's rooms as there were no students in residence. Tash told them about her visit to the bookshop.

'I met a fan too. Guy called Harry. He's writing a novel.'

'Tell him to try Jemima's meditations for creatives,' Bethan said, serving salad from a large wooden bowl.

'Not sure he's the meditating type,' Tash said, and Jemima suppressed a grin. 'Oh, and those flowers at the top of the pele tower came from the florist in town. Their company colours were on the ribbon round the stems.'

'The flowers? I bought them and put them there,' Bethan said.

'I didn't think you liked Brandon,' Jemima said, the knife in her hand frozen over a quiche.

'I didn't much. A friend of Brandon's asks me to put them up there from time to time. It was Brandon's birthday last week.'

'Yule?' Jemima asked, then glanced at Tash. 'Yule is one of Eliot's inner circle. Probably be joining us at the end of the month.'

Tash had a name.

Bethan shook her head. 'No, just a girl who said she knew him and emailed through the website. Goes by the name of Star. She sends me the money via PayPal. She wanted them laid at the foot of the tower, but I didn't think you'd like that, so I put them on the top.'

Jemima had pouted over her salad. 'No, I wouldn't want a shrine there – it might freak out the guests, but what's the point of putting them there where no one sees them?'

'I guess it gives this girl "Star" a sense of comfort to think about them there. Doesn't do any harm, does it?' Bethan said, with the ghost of a smile. 'You're very observant, Tasha.'

'That's my job,' Tash replied. 'Oh, and I wanted to ask. I'd like to spend some of my free time taking portraits of the staff. Make it a project while I am here – the labour behind the luxury.'

Jemima brightened immediately. 'I think that's an excellent idea. As long as you don't make me look like I'm exploiting them.'

'You aren't, are you?' Tash asked.

'No, I'm not!'

'We should be fine then.'

Jemima looked at her narrowly. 'You're teasing me, aren't you?'

'A bit.'

Jemima twirled her fork between her fingers, then jabbed it into her salad with relish. 'Go for it. Bethan, can you send a message round saying I'm fine with that? Though if they don't want to be photographed, they don't have to be.'

'Sure.'

'Can I photograph you, Bethan?' Tash asked.

Bethan glanced sideways at Jemima. 'Of course. It's not very dynamic though; I spend half my day answering emails or on Zoom calls.'

'That's fine.'

The following afternoon Tash made her way to the pele tower at three and climbed the restricted stairway, her camera in hand. She reached the top, and scanned the horizon. Nothing but sky, and the early summer greenery.

She'd almost convinced herself 'Harry' was a fantasist and a fraud when she heard the heavy thrum of blades in the air. A Chinook helicopter, looking absurdly heavy, was moving across the sky towards her. Coincidence? The helicopter slowed and hovered at the edge of the park, then it dipped its nose towards the Abbey before continuing north.

'Well, fuck me,' Tash said out loud, watching it shrink into the distance.

So that was real. Harry was real. Her phone beeped and she pulled it out of her pocket.

Great to meet you yesterday. Hope to see you again. Another bacon roll maybe? Next Saturday?

OK, you're on.

A movement at the edge of the park caught Tash's eye. The Belford Abbey minibus, unmarked and an elegant navy blue, was approaching down the drive, appearing and disappearing between the tall pines. It crossed the stone bridge which spanned one of the deeper, wider tributaries of the Aln, then turned up the slope again to the house and the ruins. Another twenty-five or so well-moneyed men and women coming here in search of answers or peace. Below her she saw Jemima coming out of the house to greet them. She was in white today, or ivory maybe, a tight bodice and stiff skirts. Even from this distance, she noticed Jemima inhaling, straightening her shoulders, before the minibus crunched to a halt on the gravel outside the classical portico and Jemima stepped forward to greet her guests. Tash lifted her camera caught her with her hand outstretched towards them.

Showtime.

19

Shooting in Belford was different to street photography or conflict, where the impetus was to get close, catch the dynamism of a moment, report and witness. This sort of portraiture was about sinking into the background until your subject almost forgot you were there, witnessing their worlds. Tash had time to think of the framing, the light, and wait.

On Monday morning, as dawn was breaking, she shot the chef at Belford, Nisha Wells. She was a wiry woman, her black hair streaked with white and secured firmly in a bun. She wore square glasses and mauve lipstick from the moment her day started at five, baking bread for breakfast, to the end of dinner service. Tash liked the kitchen, a vast, high-ceilinged room with doors leading straight into the gardens on one side, and the old kitchens where the students ate on the other. The picture Tash got, the one she chose, showed Nisha in the midst of kneading dough, casting flour on to the board. With the light coming in from behind her, the flying flour made her look like a goddess casting snow over her frost kingdom. Tash knew she'd caught that; she hoped she'd caught Nisha's expression too – absorbed, satisfied. Someone taking pleasure in an act of creation. She only wished she'd been able to catch her Glaswegian accent, still thick despite years of working in London before she came here.

Satisfied with the shot, Tash finished the roll with still lifes of the pots and pans, the jugs, the notes of menus pinned up to the corkboard criss-crossed with the shadows of the mullioned windows.

'Do you cook for Eliot Drake when he comes here?' Tash asked, focussing on the neat, legible handwriting. 'Or does he have a cook in his entourage?'

'He's got half a dozen, but I cook for him here. I prep here and take it over to the villa to finish. I have a nice wee trolley.'

'Is he demanding?'

'No. I read a couple of interviews after he started coming here, and he's all "just the cheeseburger for me" in them. Didn't want to get caught eating truffles, I'm sure.'

Tash lowered her camera. 'What, is he a vintage-champagne-and-wagyu-steak man really?'

Nisha was still working the dough, slapping it down on to the table, kneading it with enough force to make the muscles of her upper arms tense. 'No, we've converted him to liking the stuff I make here. Local honey, raw milk cheeses. Mutton and traditional dry cures. Sourdough. Funny. Old stuff, stuff of the land, for a gadge who's all computer codes and private jets.'

She turned the dough, dropping it with a slap which sent up another shower of white dust.

'Some of his friends that are coming have special requirements. Yule is vegan, and if she could just get her food in pill form so she didn't have to look up from her screen, she would. Torrent hardly touches what we serve. Mind you, she's paid to think dark thoughts for a living and she knows I forage on the grounds sometimes. Probably thinks she's a fork away from death. Fran the cleaner says there is always muesli bar wrappings in her bin. John Allingham will eat anything, but he's often off carbs and has a fixation with liver of all things. And I can't bear to serve the Colonel beef because he insists on it being well-done.'

'I've met the Colonel. We didn't get on. He's going to keep an eye on me apparently.'

Nisha stopped kneading the dough for a second. 'Be careful of him, lassie.'

'Why?'

She paused. 'Because he keeps a very close eye on us. Not just when Eliot is here. He asked me how my sister was the week after I'd visited her; how did he know that I'd been to see her, or that she was ill? It gave me the creeps. I know that sounds like nothing, but it felt like a threat. I don't scare easily, but I kept out of his way more after that. Ach, maybe he just fancied me and was trying to make conversation, but he freaked me out. So if he's told you he's keeping an eye on you, well, watch your back.'

'What was Brandon like?'

'That'd be the one who fell?'

Tash nodded and Nisha eyed her cautiously, her brown eyes sharp behind those square glasses.

'Food-wise, neither foodie nor philistine.'

'And other than that?'

She formed the dough up on to a tray where the uncooked loaf sat with a dozen others and her mouth became a thin line. 'I only spoke to him once or twice.'

Tash thought of Monty, that way he had of saying nothing but looking politely attentive and letting the other person fill in the silence. It worked.

'But I saw him in the herb garden the afternoon of the day he died,' Nisha went on. 'He was hiding, I think. We don't ban guests from that part of the garden, but they aren't encouraged either. He was sitting between the sorrel and the rosemary, on a bench Fran uses when she fancies a smoke. He had his head in his hands, and he was crying.'

'Shit.'

'Yeah. I can't help wondering . . . What if I'd said something? He looked embarrassed when he saw me, so I just smiled and pretended I hadn't noticed.' The loaves sat in the morning sun, swelling, ready for the oven. Nisha looked at her watch. It was pinned to the top of her apron, an old-fashioned analogue one, like nurses used to wear in black-and-white films. 'You want tea? I know you're a fags-and-espresso-for-breakfast girl, but this will set you up, I swear.'

Tash nodded. Nisha washed her hands at the huge butler's sink under the window and dried her hands, then went to the Aga and poured something sweet and herbal into moss-coloured mugs. She didn't speak again until they were both sitting down at right angles to each other at one end of the long oak table.

'Has Jemima told you how I ended up here, Natasha?'

'She said she poached you from Soho House.'

Nisha smiled crookedly. 'That's kinda true, I suppose. But when I first met Jemima I was a coke-head, and declared bankrupt. A friend dragged me to one of Jemima's classes and, I'm not saying it was a moment of revelation that cured everything, but it made life feel . . . possible. I needed to get out of London though, I knew that, and I knew Jemima was buying this place and would need staff. I might not have been everyone's first choice as head chef at a place like Belford. But she took me on and she saved my life. Talked me through the withdrawal. Gave me the tools to stay sober.'

Tash put the lens cover back on to the camera and picked up her tea. 'But she does pay you, right?'

Nisha laughed, a bark of amusement that bounced off the stone walls. 'Aye, she does pay me! Very nicely. No, I'm saying, Tash, I wish I'd spoken to Brandon that day because I might have been able to get what he was going through, because I'd been there.'

'He was an addict?'

'He used. They said at the inquest that he had taken hallucinogens, and had been on uppers and downers for months. But I know how it can make you feel. Not the drugs, he and I liked different things, but the shitty, self-hating hell of needing them? That I know.' Nisha turned her cup between her fingers, tracing the artistically artisan curves of it. 'I remember times feeling so trapped, so fucking desperate to get away from myself . . . Let's just say it was lucky I didn't have a pele tower handy on those days.'

Tash sipped her tea. It tasted of hay and camomile, like thin sunshine on a winter's day.

'When I saw him in the garden and he looked up, that was how he looked,' Nisha went on. 'Trapped. Ach, I should've recognised that look and said something. God, and with real help – Jemima, I mean – just yards away! But he never went to any sessions with her. It's fucking tragic.'

The morning light was getting stronger, glancing off the polished copper pans hanging over the Aga. Nisha's kitchen staff would be arriving soon, ready to prepare and serve breakfast to the guests.

'So do you think he killed himself?'

'I don't know, love. When a person's in that sort of state the line between accident and suicide gets very blurry. It was a lovely night. Crisp cold days and clear skies. It would have been full of stars. Late November. But there is frost and the old stone gets slippery.' She drank her tea and sighed. 'But accident or suicide, if I'd said something, maybe he wouldn't have got in that state and decided it was a good idea to go up there at all. That's all I mean.'

'But he wasn't your responsibility. Surely one of his friends—'

'I don't know what they saw or what they didn't,' Nisha said fiercely. 'All I know is that I saw he looked afraid, and I got on with picking rosemary for dinner rather than helping him.'

Tash didn't protest further.

'A friend of his gets Bethan to put flowers up there from time to time,' she said instead.

'Really?' Nisha's expression softened. 'I'm glad to hear that. It's good that he is marked in some way.'

Tash cradled her own cup. Nisha was obviously ready to get on with her day, but Tash felt she was still edging towards something.

'Were the protestors about when Brandon died?'

Nisha retied her apron round her waist. 'What? Do you think they might have got into his head? They always are when Eliot is here. I suppose it's possible. Yule said Brandon left his money to the Luddites. I mean, that's the group of people who think everything he and Eliot do is evil and want to tear it down. Yule said it was like a suicide note in itself, giving his estate to them. A repudiation of his life's work.' She shook her head. 'Though talking about "his life's work" at thirty-five . . . That's when your life's work should be just beginning.'

Behind her, Monty's ghost, always and forever thirty-two, smiled sadly.

'Morning, Nisha! You all right there, Tash?'

Emily, one of the daily staff from the town, breezed in, her bicycle helmet dangling from her hand, her cheeks bright pink. 'It's going to be a beautiful day. Have you seen what's happened in Paris?'

'No?' Nisha said. 'Go on, out with it!'

Emily's eyes were wide. 'They got the banking apps working for like, half an hour this morning, and the French president was walking up to the podium to announce the end of it all, then everything fell apart again. Like, right when he was walking up. The video's all over Facebook. A fella runs up to him, and the expression on his face . . . I blame the banks. Just pawns in their bloody games, we are.'

Torrent. John Allingham. More names. And Brandon looked trapped the day he died. Tash wished them both good morning and headed off, pulling out her phone to check the news as she did.

20

Tash's students found it harder to focus this week. Towards the end of the lecture hour on Tuesday, when Tash asked for comments about the use of depth of focus on one of the slides, she was greeted by silence, and turned to see they were all looking at their phones.

'What is it?' she asked.

'Paris!' one of the younger women said.

'Have things got worse?'

'No,' she said. 'That is . . .' She tapped something on the screen and turned it towards Tash.

A tiny newsreader and a tinny voice. '. . . disturbing news that the failures in the banking system might have been, in part, caused by the sudden death of an engineer tasked with maintaining key defensive parts of the digital infrastructure of the banking system. The French president told reporters at a news conference this morning that while the death was natural, it left the system briefly vulnerable to attack. The name of the deceased man will not be released to the public. He again appealed for calm. Emergency food distribution was interrupted today in the Marais . . .'

The woman clicked it off. 'Bit of a coincidence, isn't it?'

'Coincidences do happen,' one of the men replied, with the air of someone delivering a rare and vital truth.

'It's bloody scary.'

Tash gave them details of the practical exercise. Portraits, using each other as subjects. When they came back next day most of the pictures showed students bent over their phones, their eyes focussed and their expressions tense.

The air felt thin and charged. Everyone's feeds filled up with hot takes about the possibility of contagion spreading to international financial markets. Calls for the French president to resign were growing, farmers were bringing rotting food into the city streets and dumping it. Retailers shuttered their shops entirely, afraid of an increase in looting. After dinner on Wednesday, Jemima made a speech about finding peace in uncertain times. She cracked jokes. Got them to laugh. Reminded them of the importance of community. It seemed to make them feel better.

Then the news came of three Parisian youths, shot by police. They had been at the front of a mob trying to break in the doors of the Banque de France. Two of the Belford students left that night, afraid of being out of reach of their families. They were ferried to Alnmouth by Craig, the local taxi driver. He told them on the phone he'd like to be paid in cash. One of the personal trainers almost went, only staying on Jemima's promise if anything happened in the UK, she'd get a week's wages in cash and the loan of one of the Abbey's vehicles. She didn't want her mother to be alone if things went sideways.

The mist clung to the fields around the Abbey as Tash stepped out of the walled garden and shut the gate behind her. The sky was already bright, the last pinks and purples fading into blue, but the air was chilly. She zipped up her running jacket and rested her foot on the metal railings which lined the path down to the edge of the Belford estate and the river to stretch. She clasped her hands behind her back and raised her arms, stretching her shoulder blades, then set off at a gentle jog down the track. It curved to the west, running along the river passed the Lady Well, then she turned off it as it crossed the river, running down along a narrower track to a gate in the high wall which ran for miles around the park. The gate was heavy, wrought iron and was operated by a switch set an arm's length away. And there was a discreet grey camera on the wall above her, facing in. She glanced at it, then pressed the release button and the lock buzzed. She went through and it clanged firmly behind her.

On the other side of the road was a sign for a public footpath, and Tash climbed over the stile, and followed it across the field to where it rejoined the edge of the river, shadowed by oak and ash. It dipped under a stone bridge, over which the traffic was moving in a steady stream, then brought her to the edge of a wide green pasture overlooked by the sprawling castle. So many windows, so many towers. After half a mile she reached another patch of woodland and a footbridge. She paused, breathing in deeply through her nose, out through her mouth. Harry was leaning against the wooden guard rail.

He nodded to her, then glanced at his watch.

'Good morning. Right on time.'

'My grandmother always taught me to be punctual.'

'Good for her.' He put out his hand. 'Give me your phone. Do you have an Apple Watch? Fitbit tracker? Anything like that?'

She shook her head and pulled out her phone from the zipped pocket of her running top and gave it to him. As she did, a woman, her dark hair pulled back in a ponytail, approached along the trail at a steady jog from the east. She paused and Harry handed her the phone. She slipped it into her pocket, nodded to him, and set off along the track.

'She better bring that back,' Tash said.

'She will. That's Janice. Up here for a week's holiday. If anyone asks you decided to run together after finding you were both doing a similar route. Three more miles through the woods, nice gentle ten-minute miles.'

'And Janice is?'

'One of ours. We have a support team from now until Eliot Drake leaves the country.'

He was wearing a North Face jacket, a mix of red and black, and walking trousers, the boots on his feet slightly grimy from the path.

'Can she order up a Chinook too?'

'No. We'll have teams of three at a time. All with solid cover as ordinary people up here on holiday. They'll be running interference in case Panopticon gets curious, and bringing me intel when I need it. Alnwick is small, but I can be spotted in the same area as them from time to time and it'll just look like noise. I hope.'

'Get you,' she said.

'Come with me.'

He stepped off the path and put his hand out to help her down the uneven bank, on to a sweep of gravel which extended under the bridge and a little further upstream. A daypack rested against a long flat rock. They were out of sight of the path and bridge here, a mossy corner where one of the Aln's tributaries joined it on the curve. The tributary had dug a deep channel through the soil, emerging with a gurgling fall next to the low flat stones.

He opened the daypack and pulled out a fleece, which he handed to her. She hadn't realised till he did so she was beginning to get cold now her body was at rest. As she pulled it on over her running top, he produced a flask and unstoppered it.

'You think of everything.'

'I doubt it. But I try. You said the Colonel's already been here once. I'm sure he'll do a priority look at all the Abbey staff and teachers. Panopticon would certainly notice if you stopped for half an hour in the woods and flag it. But thanks to Janice, it won't. She's running a route with no cameras so, unless we're really unlucky, we can meet like this whenever you run.' He poured coffee from the Thermos and handed her the cup. 'If I'm not here for any reason, don't pause, don't wait, don't even slow down. Just run the extra three miles.'

'And your phone?'

'My phone is back in the cottage, where I'm enjoying a long lie-in, of course.'

The coffee was welcome.

'OK, so what do I need to know?'

He reached into the daypack and handed her a folder. When she opened it she saw the pages weren't printed, but typed on an old-fashioned machine.

He noticed her noticing. 'We want to be invisible to Drake's systems. That means pen, paper, ink. All communications have to be in person, or in code. End-to-end encryption is useless, so physical dead drops if necessary, not virtual ones. A postcard is safer than a phone call.' The water gurgled over the rocks. 'I've spent the last couple of months getting trained in old-school tradecraft by men and women who were in the service in the seventies and eighties.' He poured his own coffee. 'Mean old coots some of them. They lost agents, sources, getting pictures anyone can find today on the open web, but I learned a lot.'

'What do your colleagues think of this?' She tapped the typewritten file.

'They call us Luddites, but most of them are shit scared of systems like Panopticon, so they also wish us luck and work on their escape plans. You'd be surprised how many senior intelligence officials have bought themselves small pieces of land off grid, buried food stashes and bought generators.' He noticed her expression. 'Well, you asked.'

Tash nodded. Then examined the file.

'I want to make sure you have some decent background on all of Drake's entourage, these great minds who are going to advise him what to do with Panopticon.'

'The Council of Heaven,' Tash murmured, opening the file and beginning to read.

'What?'

'It's in the Bible. Genesis and Job,' she told him as she turned a page. 'God has a council of divine beings who advise him. I was thinking about it after talking to Jemima about this gathering of advisors. Did you know they helped him come up with this set of protocols about the use of Panopticon? The Cap d'Antibes protocols?'

'I've read them.'

So had Tash, after Jemima mentioned them over their gins on Tuesday evening. Eliot Drake's little group had come up with a guide to best practice for wielding the power of Panopticon and systems like it. A dense and heavily footnoted document, it had chapters on bias, even-handedness, public consultation, transparency and legislation, democratic accountability and human rights. They seemed, as far as Tash could tell, to boil down to Google's old tag line 'don't be evil'.

'Yeah, well. If Eliot Drake is God, or owns God, his friends are the Council of Heaven. I have names for you. John Allingham, Torrent, and Yule.'

'Very much the inner circle then. Good. I'll get briefings put together for you. Our subject today though is Frank Matthews, known to Eliot Drake and friends as the Colonel,' he said, tapping the photograph paper-clipped to the first page of the report. Frank was shaking hands with a perma-tanned politician in front of a phalanx of American flags.

Tash studied it. 'So who is he? Other than a jerk.'

'Bit of a mystery,' Harry said, cradling his mug in his hands. The collar of his jacket was up, framing his face, and the light was highlighting the red amid the gold of his hair.

'I thought you guys knew everything.'

'No, that's Google,' he said. 'Or it was before it drowned in AI slop. But we know a fair amount. There's a blank area in our records – or in the records we can access anyway, but we know he served with a private paramilitary group in Afghanistan for three years. Silver Hawk.'

'What, like Blackwater?' Tash asked.

'Yes. A private company that takes on defence contracts. Often the Americans use them for security for top officials. After Silver Hawk he worked as a consultant for a couple of years, then reappears on our radar when he became best buds with Eliot Drake. Eliot invested in his private security firm, Charter, and hired him to run all of his own security. That was about three years ago.'

'Brandon, the guy who died, introduced him to Drake,' Tash said. 'Jemima told me that.'

'We're aware.'

She read slowly, then went through the photographs. Some bleary shots with a dusty background which looked like they'd be cropped. A black-tie dinner in a white and gold ballroom. The women in the frame looked bored – some seemed suspiciously young, others had pillowed lips and white-blonde hair. Then the Colonel's mugshot. The lighting did him no favours in that one: there was bruising on his face, and one of his eyes was beginning to swell.

Tash held it up. 'Nice.'

'We had to send an FBI friend of ours into the station to take photos of the hard copy of that. And the report. Pictures of the Colonel, particularly during his military days, are hard to find. That's not unusual with special forces members though.'

'Can't you just refuse to let him in the country if he's got a criminal record?'

Harry shook his head. 'He hasn't got a record. Read the arrest report.'

She did. The Colonel and Brandon Wallace had been at a strip club, when one of the other patrons had got out of line. Frank had taken it on himself to wait outside the venue, then beaten shit out of the offending guy in the parking lot. The man had declined to press charges, claiming the CCTV footage showed him falling over, and Frank helping him up. Repeatedly.

'The Colonel paid off the guy he beat up?'

'Brandon Wallace did actually.'

Tash stared into the water as it churned over the rocks. 'I wonder if the beating was because of his chivalrous nature, or to impress Brandon then. Did Brandon introduce him to Eliot after this?'

'Yeah. Quite soon after.'

'So the Colonel knows how to manipulate people then.'

Harry looked impressed. 'Looks like it.'

Tash squinted at the page. 'So he was in management with Silver Hawk for a while. And then running basically a one-man security consultancy . . . I don't get it. Why would a billionaire like Eliot Drake go into business with this guy – even if Brandon did put in a good word?'

Harry turned over a pebble with the toe of his boot. In the distance Tash could hear the whispers of traffic on the A1, the closer shush of water over the weir.

'What do you think?'

Tash thought about the soldiers she'd met in Ukraine: civilians and conscripts. Dark humour, a certain fatalism, a grim determination to make it through another day. Then about the men she knew back home. Her grandad, whose bookshelves groaned with thick volumes about WWII. 'That weird thing men have for war?'

'That's my theory. A lot of these tech bros, like Drake, worry they made their money at a keyboard rather than shooting elephants or building barns. Lots of them have an army man as part of their entourage. Sometimes they run their security detail, sometimes they are paid-for drinking buddies. The glow of masculine power they give off acts on the tech guys like animal musk.'

His voice dripped with contempt.

'You were in the army, weren't you, before you became a spook?' Tasha asked.

'Yes. How did you guess?'

She nodded towards the backpack. The coffee and the fleece. 'You're not just prepared, you're really prepared. Only people I saw like that in Ukraine were the ex-military security advisors some of the news services sent out with their people.'

'Ever the observer, Tash.'

'That's my job. So is the Colonel's company doing well?'

'Yes. Very well.'

Tash closed the file and handed it back to him. 'But hang on. Why would the person who owns Panopticon need a security firm? Or corporate intelligence?'

'Panopticon can't stand behind the velvet rope,' Harry said, drinking his coffee. 'It can't keep off autograph hunters, or tackle a stalker. So people like the Colonel are doing just fine. He's got a villa in the south of France and a bank account with just under two million in it. Not bad for three years' work.'

Harry didn't look like he had two million in the bank. He looked like a good education and a sense of civic duty had left him in a flatshare at thirty-five.

'Have you got anything else for me, Tash?'

'Someone called Star sends Bethan money for flowers for Brandon. And there's something else. The cook, Nisha, said Brandon Wallace left all his money to the Luddites and was crying in the herb garden the day he fell. She said he looked trapped. She put it down to drugs, but . . .'

'He was an unstable guy, but I'll look into it. Get ready, time to go.'

Tash looked up. Janice was approaching her, back straight and eyes front, keeping the same even pace.

'OK.' Tash stood and shook out the stiffness in her arms and ankles, as he took the fleece off her shoulders. 'But Harry, I need to ask you . . .'

'No time now. See you in a few days.'

Janice held out the phone and Tash took it like the baton in a relay race. Even Panopticon, with all its godlike power, wouldn't have felt the change.

By that afternoon the price of gold had gone through the roof and cash machines in London were emptying as the population started hoarding banknotes. The British prime minister, asked about the situation, made a bland statement of support for the French authorities and echoed the appeals for calm. Then he was caught on a hot mic telling his assistant if the French didn't get their shit together soon, the whole system would be fucked.

21

Most of the Abbey staff Tash could photograph in the day, but the night security guard, Wilf, only arrived after dinner. That evening, Tash went to find him. He seemed genuinely pleased to see her, welcoming her into his room, an old panelled office off the servants corridor close to the main entrance. He had a fold-up chair ready for her.

'This must be lonely work, isn't it?' she asked. He was too conscious of her at the moment, but there was a good chance with time and conversation he'd relax, and she'd be able to perform her magic trick of being there and not there.

'It's canny boring, a lot of the time,' he confessed. 'But I've got my radio and my puzzles. Also these items.' He tapped the monitor screens showing the feeds from a dozen cameras around the edge of the park, a dozen more showing images of the area outside the Abbey and among the ruins. A third showing the common areas inside the main house and stables where the guests had their rooms. 'They've been upgraded so if the image changes in a way that's suspicious, they sound an alarm. Hang on. It'll happen in a mo.' The tall window next to him looked out over the lawns at the front of the house. Above the hill a slice of dark sky was visible. He had a bookcase just inside the door and his own kettle and mini-fridge.

'There!'

The computer pinged softly – the electronic equivalent of a waiter discreetly clearing his throat – then one of the small images grew slightly on the screen, while the others shrank a little.

'Fox!' Wilf said with deep satisfaction and Tash watched as the creature approached the gate, its eyes suddenly white in the screen as it looked around, then slipped through the railings. 'Now there you go, it's usually a fox. I like them. My sister keeps chickens though. She hates foxes. Guess it's all a matter of your point of view. Anyhoo, sometimes it's like being paid to sit and stare at *Springwatch* and I don't have to worry about missing anything now because of all this cleverness.' He smiled up at her, his round face, covered in short white stubble, full of delighted mischief. 'I like to wonder what it sounds like when I go through the ruins. Ping ping ping, ping ping ping, and the windows all rippling away.'

Tash moved sideways so her shot showed him washed by the light of the screens, the white edge of the window behind him, the radio at his side.

'How often do you get humans on there?'

'Oh, once or twice a week some lad gets pissed and decides to hop over the wall with a mate. I just call the police in, and nine times out of ten they nab them before they're halfway up.'

She had the shot she wanted.

'Were you here the night Brandon Wallace died, Wilf?'

He folded his arms across his broad chest and rolled his eyes. 'Well now, bad business that. No. I was not. I get sent home, see – what is it the Americans say? – benched – whenever Mr Drake and his people visit Belford. The Colonel brings in his own team.'

'What do you think of him?'

'The Colonel?' He rubbed the side of his nose. 'Ach, I don't know. I'm ex-services myself and he's what my mum would call all fur coat and no knickers.'

The image was striking. Tash laughed and he grinned ruefully at her.

'Mind you, a lot of the Americans used to strike us squaddies like that. Nice kit, the Colonel's lot have. Bit of an attitude though. Always walking like they think they are being filmed in slow-motion.' He waved his arms back and forth without standing up, making his chair squeak. Tash laughed again. 'Maybe they'd have seen that poor lad if they ever took their dark glasses off.'

'So one of the Colonel's men was monitoring the screens that night?'

He nodded. 'Aye. Cannae say if they have someone on all night – probably do – but I know someone comes in, sits in my chair. They mess with my settings. When the Colonel's been, I come in an hour early to set up the screens again as I like them. Still, it's nice to have a week off. We've got a caravan on a mate's farm, Argill House. No phones, no computers. It's lovely. Fancy a brew?'

Tash did and he got up with a sigh and flicked on his mini-kettle, still looking over his shoulder at the screens from time to time.

'I'm not casting aspersions, mind. Poor fella tasked with watching probably felt awful when that young lad turned up dead.' He pronounced it deed. 'And there's no camera on top of the tower, or covering the ground where he fell. I mean, he should've seen the lad go up the stairs, there's a camera in the exhibition space, but maybe he was doing his rounds, or having a piss. And even if he did see him. Well, he might think of it a bit later and reckon he'd missed him coming down.' Wilf squeezed the tea bags against the side of the mugs and dumped them carefully in a little flip bin. He was one of those men who seemed to notice and take great pleasure in every movement, each small convenience of life. 'And as for when you walk around with the torch – it's more to make people feel secure in their beds, not examine every inch of the place. There's plenty of nights I wouldn't have thought to pass a torch beam over where that Brandon fell. I do now though.' He handed her the mug and sipped from his own, moving back to where he could watch the screen while staying standing. 'I do now.'

He made it strong.

'Not that it would have done any good, finding him sooner in the night. Coroner said his neck was broke. Dead the moment he hit the ground.'

Tash was confronted by the memory of Monty, falling sideways, suddenly a heavy object rather than a person, muscleless. She thanked Wilf for the tea.

'And,' he went on. 'I mean, if their brief is the same as mine, we're supposed to be watching for people trying to get *into* the park, or scanning for people who shouldn't be here, not spying on the folks who live here, or the visitors. End of the week there are always a few guests around where they shouldn't be. Jemima trusts me to turn a blind eye. It's one of her things that: we all need to turn a blind eye to things occasionally. In friendship, marriage, business. I'd say she's right.'

Tash moved to where she could see the screens again, and took another two, three frames with Wilf variously silhouetted against their shifting grey and black patterns. So many cameras.

'And all this is recorded?'

'Aye. When I first started doing security, ten years ago now for the Duke, we used VHS tapes still, and recorded over them after a week. Now it seems like there's infinite room to keep it all. Up in the clouds, they tell me. Gets sent up automatically and I don't think it ever gets deleted.' He leaned over the desk and put on his reading glasses, moved the mouse. The feeds made themselves small, bunching up together on two of the screens while he used the third to search.

'Aye, there it is.'

Tash leaned forward. The video was monochrome and showed the deeply shadowed space of the exhibition floor in the pele tower. Small whited-out patches showed the position of subtle uplighters around the edge of the room. A figure, bulky, in hoodie and jeans, emerged up the stairs and staggered sideways. Looked at one of the pictures, shuffled unsteadily, then headed towards the staircase to the roof. Tash could see him unhooking the rope, the 'no unauthorised access' sign to his right. He seemed to note it the same moment Tash did. He looked to his left for a moment, as if checking to see if he was observed, then lurched forward through the arch.

'There he is, poor lad, on his way up. Then Mr Drake went looking for him.'

'What?'

'Yup.' Wilf used the mouse to skip through a couple of hours of the footage. 'After they'd buggered off back to America, I had a scan through and saw it. Told my Charlie, he's a copper in town, and he passed on t'message but it wasn't mentioned at the inquest.

Though I marked it up for them.' Tash noted both Brandon's ascent and this next section had been flagged with a pink dot on the timeline. 'Here he is. Though of course, Brandon was already dead by then.' A tall figure, slim and unmistakably male, though Tash had no idea how she knew that, came up the stairs, rested his hand on the newel post at the top of the stairs, then headed towards the arch. Five minutes later, according to the time stamp, he returned and paused for a second in the exhibition room. The light glinted off his wrist – a watch perhaps? Tash touched her bracelet. The figure descended out of the frame and into darkness.

Wilf clicked at the screen and the windows rearranged themselves again. 'Right. Fancy a walk? It's time for me to do a run.' He grinned. 'Have you been into the Abbey Villa?'

'No, I haven't.'

'We'll have a deck then.' He unhooked his jacket from the back of the door, and picked up a torch.

They approached through the ruins, skirting the bottom of the pele tower first. Wilf shone his torch up its ragged sides. In its light the pale stone at the top looked as if it had been built from a full moon. Then the beam travelled over the turf at the bottom. A fierce burst of red made Tash flinch before she registered they were poppies, sheltering under the wall among clumps of borage and forget-me-nots. They re-entered the ruins proper via a clanking iron gate, then headed towards the villa.

'Isn't the villa the same as the rest of the Abbey though?'

Wilf ran his pass over the reader by the door, and it clicked open. Tash followed him in and it closed softly behind them. The front door opened directly into large lobby which ran across the full frontage of the house. To Tash's left was a huge fireplace, older than the house itself, she reckoned. Rugs were laid over huge stone flags and a trio of leather sofas surrounded the empty grate. The far wall was lined with bookshelves. To her right was a grand piano, another smaller fireplace and another arrangement of chairs and tables. Co-working space meets English country house.

Ahead of her a wooden staircase swept up to the first floor.

Wilf slipped his key card back into his pocket, and just past the foot of the staircase, where the lobby narrowed, opened a door.

'Dining room. When he has his people here, this is where they work mostly. So I'm told.' Tash followed him in, and he touched a light switch. A low glow diffused through the room. 'Night levels, in case someone was to come and sit here in the middle of the night, I suppose, without lighting the whole place up like a Christmas tree. This tech is magic. It knows what time of day or night it is and sets the levels to match. I wanted one in my house, but the wife told us not to be daft.' He spoke with soft pride.

A polished mahogany dining table dominated the room. Chairs for twenty people to sit round it, maybe more, and sideboards dotted with modern ceramics behind the head of the table and along one wall. Over the fireplace a huge painting thick with energetic streaks of paint, a vortex of drips and splatters.

'Bloody hell,' Tash said quietly.

'Thought you might get a kick out of seeing this, being an artist yersel',' Wilf said happily. 'Though I never really got along with Pollock. I'm more of a Hockney man. There's a good show on at the Baltic in Gateshead by the way. Twin girls doing lovely work. You should get yersel' down there.'

'I will. So is Eliot Drake an art fan?' Tash asked, studying the picture. It had a vigour and energy to it which got under your skin.

'Maybes. Emily says he sits in that chair' – he pointed to one of the ordinary dining chairs opposite the painting – 'and he studies it. Like he can see something there no one else does.'

'I thought he'd sit at the head of the table.'

'Em says he's always sitting in the middle, never the head. Mind you, no one else ever sits at the head of the table either. Not even Jemima.'

Tash could hardly take her eyes off the painting.

'It's not the real thing, you know.'

She turned to him, questioningly.

'I know. First time I saw the art in the villa, after he'd decorated, I had a heart attack. I was all' – he wagged his finger at an imaginary interlocutor – '"I know how much that bloody thing's worth!

We'll need to have security screens on all the windows now, and every crim from Newcastle to Edinburgh is going to try their luck getting in here and cutting it out with a Stanley knife." So the Colonel told us, patronising wee shite, that although Eliot Drake does own the original, that's actually in storage in France somewhere. In a tax haven or something. This' – Wilf nodded at the painting – 'is an exact copy produced by a studio in China.' He shook his head, sorrowing over the habits of the super-rich. 'It was gospel too. I looked it up when I got home. There are studios what specialise in doing copies for people like Mr Drake. Copies of works they own but are too expensive to have on a wall. Funny old world. I felt like a right Charlie.' He stepped out of the room, holding the door for Tash to follow him. As he touched the light switch, the side lamps dimmed to darkness. 'Still, my Fiona liked the little Monet I got her for Christmas that year.'

On Friday morning there was no sign of Harry by the bridge. Tash photographed Bethan at her desk, going through her emails, taking a call with a major Parisian stockist of Jemima's care products. Bethan was calm and kind – but even half-heard through Bethan's head phone, the Frenchwoman sounded panicked and teary.

It took some time, but after Bethan stepped out to talk to one of the personal trainers, Tash got what she wanted from the office. Her favourite picture in the end, though, was of Bethan stalking through the main entrance hall in her bandage skirt and high heels while the statues seemed to watch her with a mix of shock and admiration.

On Friday evening, as the students were celebrating their week, the lights of the French banking system switched back on. Jemima's guests assured each other they hadn't been that worried, not really. Perhaps the French had overreacted.

As Tash looked at the work the other creative groups had produced, and listened to Jemima's closing speech – affectionate, open and optimistic – she got a message from Harry.

Sorry can't do tomorrow.
Maybe next week?

22

On Saturday evening, as Tash made her way to the chapel wing and supper with Jemima and Bethan, she thought of the picture of the flowers Gloria had taken, the swell of emotion she had felt looking at it. She hadn't been able to say what that feeling was as it hit in its first wave. There had been too much of it to name it, to make it clear. But she knew it now. Her joy, looking at that photograph was run over with a fierce, rainbow-coloured jealousy. The image had captured something – a beauty which made room for the viewer and invited them in – which made Tash feel strangely vulnerable.

She was almost at the door to Jemima's sitting room, when she registered the door was open, and raised voices were coming from within. Well, one raised voice; that of Colonel Frank Matthews. Tash hesitated on the threshold. Bethan, standing by the sideboard where the drink and food was laid out, saw her, and beckoned her in.

'What the fuck do you want?' the Colonel said, spotting her. 'I'm trying to have a private conversation with you, Jemima! And the prodigal daughter can just wander in if she feels like it?'

The expression on his face was dark with frustration, fierce enough for Tash's muscles to tense for flight.

'Tasha is here because I invited her, Frank.' Jemima spoke calmly. 'You just turned up and started haranguing me.'

'What I'm telling you is important. You have to teach Eliot to control his temper before he gets us all killed.'

Jemima lifted her hands, palms open. 'Fine. I hear you! But why are you shouting at me about this now? What has happened?'

The Colonel seemed to stop himself. He glanced between the three women. 'Nothing. Teach him to control his temper. That's all.'

Jemima put her hands on her hips. 'Frank, that's not how this works! If Eliot wants more coaching, it's up to him to tell me, and to define his goals. You don't get to storm in and set terms. I work for him, not you.'

'Strictly speaking, Jemima, you work for the Notebook board of directors.'

'Still not you,' Bethan murmured.

Frank span round long enough to shoot her a dirty look, then turned back at Jemima.

'This is for all of us, Jemima. You must realise that things have changed now Eliot has taught Pan to think.'

Bethan pulled the ring pull on a can of tonic, which made the Colonel jump and scowl again. Bethan ignored the look, calmly mixing a gin and tonic and handing it to Tash.

'Frank, Pan doesn't think,' Jemima said. 'You're anthropomorphising it. From what Yule said this new upgrade sounds like a sort of brainstorming function.'

The Colonel swallowed, then spoke slowly. 'It's not a brainstorming function. It's an enhancement of Pan's strategic planning and real-time execution abilities. It's a game-changer. And as a result the pressures on Eliot are going to be huge.'

'I saw word has got out Eliot's coming here soon.' Bethan set her glass down on the sideboard. 'Are you worried about the Luddites turning up in force? The last couple of weeks in France have swelled their ranks.'

'Eliot has got a lot more to worry about than them.'

'Frank, you are paranoid.' Jemima said.

'That's my job.'

'And what's worse, you are making him paranoid,' Jemima continued. 'What are you worried about? You're in a bloody spa. A bloody fortified spa. In Northumberland. Try and relax.'

He pointed a meaty finger at her, a living bubble of frustration, about to burst. 'You have no idea how important that head is you are messing with, Jemima. You think you know him? You haven't got a clue. You see what he chooses to show you. You think he's an inch away from enlightenment, I think he's an inch away from greatness. But can we both agree that he needs to control some of his impulses if he's going to get there?'

Jemima stared him down. 'We might be able to agree on that, Frank. But I'm still not taking direction from you on any coaching I do with him. And this weekend is just about giving advice as part of the round table. We have no coaching sessions planned.'

He threw up his hands. 'Fine. I've done my best. Enjoy your little supper, ladies.'

Then he turned and stalked out of the room.

Bethan glanced at the salads and cold cuts laid out on the table. 'Do you think he'd respect us more if we were having raw steaks?'

Jemima smiled briefly, but she was distracted through supper, leaving Tash and Bethan to talk over France's return to stability.

When Tash got back to her room, she sent Harry a message.

How are the words going?

Good. Got a last minute place on a cool course. Will text when I'm back.

Tash went to bed feeling strangely bereft.

New guests arrived the following day to be inspired and rejuvenated. On Monday, when she went for her run, Janice was waiting for her by the bridge and another woman took her phone for its extra miles. Tash told her what the Colonel had said and was thanked. No chat, no attempt to build a rapport. Janice was all business.

On her way back to the house, one phrase from the Colonel kept going through her head: ... *before he gets us all killed.*

That evening, when Tash joined Jemima for a drink, she and Bethan were huddled round the laptop again.

'How was your day?' Bethan asked, turning around.

'Good,' Tash answered. She became aware of the air of tight concentration in the room. 'What's happening?'

Jemima was reading something on the screen, her slightly witchy reading glasses perched on the end of her nose.

'It's Eliot. Fuck, maybe I should have listened to the Colonel after all.'

Tash smiled. 'That bad?'

Jemima remained serious. 'He put up a blog post on the Panopticon site.'

Tash tried to read over her mother's shoulder, but the post was a single block of text in the minimum size font.

'What does it say?'

Bethan put a gin and tonic in her hand and set another by the computer. Tash noticed she had one herself this evening.

'Thought I might join you,' she said almost shyly.

'Cool,' Tash said.

'OK . . .' Jemima was scrolling down the screen. 'Increased security measures. Power of Panopticon must be carefully controlled. Now he's quoting a bit from the protocols we came up with last year in Cap d'Antibes.' Her frown deepened. '"In a world where people such as myself can become targets of misdirected anger . . . a guarantee that my own safety is tied to Panopticon's success and vice versa . . ." What the hell is he up to? Then there's some more general pablum.' She scrolled again, her perfectly manicured fingers stroking the touchpad. Bethan was reading over her other shoulder now. '"So, to that end, I am making it known that I have . . ."'

'He's done it, hasn't he?' Bethan said. 'He's put in the kill code.'

Jemima froze, leaned in towards the screen. 'Mother fucker!' Jemima exploded, slamming the laptop shut and pushing it across the table. 'He said it was a joke, and that he wouldn't do anything like that without talking to the rest of us first. Then he just does it!'

Tash sat down on a dining chair next to her.

Jemima's cheeks were flushed. 'Shit, sorry, Tasha. I shouldn't shout like that.'

'It's fine. I'm OK. What's a kill code?'

'A kill code,' Bethan said, sitting down on Jemima's right, 'is basically a long stream of numbers and letters that Eliot has to input every other day, or something like that. If he doesn't, Panopticon will start to degrade. And only he knows it.'

'It's nuts,' Jemima said fiercely. 'What if he gets hit by a bus? He'll destroy a company that's worth over seventy billion dollars.'

'Can't someone force the code?' Tash asked.

'No,' Bethan said. 'This is much too long. At least until quantum computing gets going.'

She crossed her legs and sat back, sipping her drink, scowling at the laptop.

'Why has it pissed you off so much, Jemima?' Tash asked.

'Sorry. Look, Panopticon is very powerful, and it gets more impressive every day from what I'm told. Once when they were here – oh Lord, before we went to France – Torrent, she's one of the inner circle, made the point that a lot of people and governments might want to get their hands on it, and what would be the safeguards if they managed to copy or steal the tech stack? You know, it's all fine when Eliot is in charge and vetting use applications according to the protocols we set out, but suppose North Korea, or China or Russia got hold of Panopticon?

'Anyway, Brandon made a crack about the *Mission Impossible* films – you know, "this message will self-destruct in ten seconds". They started talking about it. Yule and I pushed back, and Brandon basically told us not to get our knickers in a twist.' She took off her reading glasses and started chewing the armature. 'This kill code – it's irresponsible, childish and also . . .'

'Also?' Tash prompted.

'I don't *like* Eliot identifying with Panopticon. Tying their fates together. It's as if he and Panopticon are one and the same. God, I hate to admit it, but Frank might be right. This new ability to strategise, it could make whoever controls Pan . . . too powerful, and at the same time too divorced from the consequences of using that power.'

'Strategise? This is what the Colonel was talking about the other night.'

'Yes, Pan makes suggestions for steps forward towards a certain goal. Yule says it's very effective. I think it's the improvements that have been made there which have wound up the Colonel. He thinks everyone is coming after Pan now.'

'Maybe they are,' Tash said.

Jemima looked at her, and she blushed slightly and dropped her gaze.

'I just don't like it. The sudden decision to come here, the Colonel getting jumpy and now this.'

Tash thought about what the Colonel had said. '*Has* Eliot got a temper?'

'He can do,' Jemima said sadly. 'He is only human after all.'

Tash stayed awake into the early hours, reading, thinking and occasionally trying more possible passwords for Monty's thumb drive.

Cyberattack
Paris
Drake
Panopticon.

Nothing worked. She glanced over at Monty's ghost, who was watching her from one of the cream upholstered armchairs.

'So I have to find out for myself, do I?'

Monty's ghost smiled at her, a little apologetically.

For the rest of the week, Tash taught, got up early to catch the cleaning staff at work, and photographed them mopping the floors of the old kitchen, the morning light dazzling the stones. She photographed the beauticians, so they looked like nuns in their clean white coats, gentle smiles on their faces as they tended to Jemima's guests with infinite grace. Twice on her runs she met Janice who handed her a fleece and a briefing file on another of the members of the Council of Heaven, and each time Tash ran on feeling better informed and more in the dark than ever.

23

Saturday, 19 July 2025

On Saturday Tash stopped by the bookshop to tell Peter she would take photographs of the wolf burning, and to ask him to get permission for her to shoot from the external staircase outside the town hall. He was happy to help with that, and when she asked for another favour too.

Harry was waiting for her on the ornate park bench outside the bakery. The town clock above them clanged the hour as she sat down next to him and he handed her a paper bag, still warm.

'God, I'm starving,' Tash said taking it. 'I mean, hello, Harry. How have you been?'

He laughed, a warm and pleasant sound which caused one or two heads to turn. One woman let her gaze linger.

'That's yours too.' He nodded to a takeout coffee sitting in its cardboard tray between them. 'My week was interesting. Did you miss me?'

'It's been hell without you,' she said. 'Actually, I have a bit. Janice isn't exactly chatty. Where have you been? I mean, I presume you weren't really on a cool writing course.'

'I kind of was. I was in Paris.'

Her unwrapping of the bacon roll slowed down.

'Why?'

'Spy shit,' he said lightly. For the first time Tash noticed that this bench, although it was in the square, was so ornate, it would be hard for anyone to get close to them without being obvious. 'Though my cover was a four-day writing course at the Paris Institute, and some research for my novel, so I've come back primed with some wisdom on the unreliable narrator in contemporary fiction, if you'd like to hear it, and some bad photographs of various picturesque alleys where my characters can drink espresso and talk about their feelings.'

Still going for the rakish charm then, but his heart didn't seem to be in it today. Tash snapped the lid off her coffee and blew over the silky surface.

'Do you really think Panopticon might take that sort of interest in you, Harry? Monitoring your every move?'

He crossed his legs, his face twitching as he caught the slight snark in her voice. 'You're still missing the point, Tash. I'm not that interesting to Panopticon, no more than anyone else. No team of Eliot's minions is tracking me from one of those hangers full of screens like you see in the spy movies. The point is, they don't have to. Panopticon is doing it automatically. It's doing it to everyone. You, me. The guy who's just bought a pork pie from that stall though he really shouldn't. Every shopkeeper, teacher, tourist, butter seller and candlestick maker. Panopticon watches us all. Clue's in the fucking name.'

'In Alnwick?'

'Everywhere.' He looked at her, and Tash felt her bafflement was written on her face as clear as if she'd drawn a question mark on her own forehead.

'You've forgotten. Panopticon is God.' His voice was tight. 'Infinite awareness, remember? Look, my cover is fine, adequate. I took all the measures I could to meet with the people I needed to see in secret, but I don't know if I avoided the eye of the Lord. Perhaps there's a CCTV camera outside one of the businesses on Rue Pigalle which we didn't spot. Maybe it caught me going into a bar, then my contact following ten minutes later. Maybe there's a tourist's picture of me on a quiet street, and that's enough to isolate the burner phone I was carrying and track my movements around the city even when I left my registered phone in my room, or tucked behind a copy of the *Da Vinci Code* at the institute. It's all there. And Panopticon is always putting it all together in the background, seeing if the pieces form an interesting pattern. All the time. If it sees enough it will note me as a likely agent, and point me out to its human users even if they never think to ask it about me themselves.'

'Aren't people supposed to delete CCTV stuff after a while?'

'Depends. Railway and tube stations are, in Europe anyway. But doesn't matter if they do or not. Panopticon has already seen it, understood it and stored it away.'

'So why did you risk the Paris trip?'

'I told you. Spy shit.'

He looked like he hadn't slept properly for a while. She returned to her bacon roll and chewed for a while in silence. MI6 had kept him hanging around here for a week, waiting for her to turn up and sign books, then paid for a Chinook to fly over Belford Abbey. That would be a few grand. She'd looked it up. That suggested this – her, Belford Abbey, Eliot Drake – was important. Then, just as Tash had agreed to share information, he was off to Paris. From Northumberland. For days. They must have plenty of spies in London who could have popped over the Channel. Hell, they must have tons of spies in Paris too. Why pull Harry off her case to send him there? Unless of course, these two things were in fact one thing.

She looked up. A woman in a short white coat was watching them from the other side of the square. She didn't seem to be with anyone.

'For one thing, stop looking so miserable,' she said. 'Happy to see your favourite photographer, remember?'

He shook his head, but the wry smile was back, and he shifted in the seat to angle himself towards her.

'CCTV isn't that good. It can identify us and see we're together. It can't tell if I'm in a shit mood. Why? Are we being watched?'

'Just a woman on the other side of the square gave me the creeps. You're making me paranoid.'

'I'm trying to make you paranoid about electronic, unmonitored surveillance. It's fucking perverse of you to immediately spot a possible human watcher.'

She smiled back at him, happy Tash, talking to a handsome new friend.

'Let's finish these rolls at my place,' he said. 'There's a yard.'

He stood up, taking the chance to glance in the direction of the woman as he did.

'Like that is it?' he muttered, before smiling at Tash again and leading her back in the direction of the bookshop. She followed, and he stopped at a heavy black door a couple of yards past it.

'The code is 1234?' Tash said as he keyed it in.

'Peter's choice, not mine.'

The door opened into a flagged alleyway with tiny cottages named after wildflowers on one side, and a high wall of massive blocks of sandstone on the other. At the end it opened out into a yard, lined with planters and with a garden table and chairs in the middle. He set down his coffee and the bag with his roll on the table, and Tash settled too. The castle showed above the gate in the yard's back wall, its turrets framing the pale blue sky.

'Did you see the woman?'

'Yeah. So what news from the Abbey?'

'But I want to hear about Paris first.'

He shook his head and started eating like a man who hadn't seen food for days. 'No. I said I'd tell you some things. Not anything you ask.'

She tucked her hair behind her ear. 'Well, I'm not telling you shit till you answer at least one question. Was your trip to do with Eliot Drake?'

He stopped. 'Yes. Now tell me something.'

She drank her coffee. 'Give me a chance. Eliot isn't even fucking here yet. I take it Janice filled you in on the Colonel's visit?'

'Yes. Fair enough, that was of interest.'

'Bark first, then you get a treat. So the trip was about Eliot. Has he got some connection to what's been happening in France?'

Harry looked uncomfortable. 'That's what I was trying to find out.'

Tash thought, remembering how he talked about the demo he had seen. How every time he saw an agency get a big win, he assumed now Panopticon was involved. 'Have the French used Panopticon?'

A flash of irritation. Then he conceded. 'Every Western democracy has.'

She waited.

'OK. Six months ago the French arrested the bosses of a large-scale people-trafficking operation working between the Algerian coast and Marseilles. Incredible work. I've been in Paris to confirm that it was done with Panopticon's help.'

'But did they use it for information, or for strategy?'

His mouth was a thin line. 'This strategising option you told Janice about hasn't been offered to any agency or organisation I know of. It was intel only, but it was faultless.'

'What did that faultless information cost them?'

'For enough to bring down the whole operation and warn the next level players not to step up to fill the void? Two hundred and seventy million euros.'

Tash almost choked on her roll. 'Cheap at the price, I guess.' She paused. 'I suppose, if you are a security service and you get a chance to see what Panopticon can do, you might want to keep using it. And not pay that much each time.' She thought of the gathering at Belford, the people coming to advise Eliot Drake on 'ethical implications of his latest work'. She wondered what he'd been up to since the group published their 'protocols'. 'Or maybe, as an intelligence agency, you want to get on with your "spy shit" without running everything past Eliot Drake, the Colonel, my mother and whoever else he invites in for a chat.'

His face was blank. 'I barked. Give me my treat.'

She finished the roll and wiped her fingers.

'Jemima's really worried about this kill code — that's what his blog post was about.' She outlined the conversation and he looked interested, which made Tash feel suddenly like crap. Carrying general gossip back from Belford was one thing, but repeating what Jemima had said in her room felt worse.

'OK, my turn. My trip wasn't just about finding out if they'd used Panopticon to bust up the people-smuggling ring. I also wanted to know if the French had tried to brute force their way into Panopticon so they could keep using it as they saw fit.'

'And?'

He stared sulkily at the table top. 'My contact wouldn't confirm or deny it.'

'But your gut says the French government did try to use Panopticon again or steal it?' Tasha asked.

He nodded and her mouth went dry.

'So, do you think, are you saying that what happened in France – the cyberattack on the banks – that might have been *punishment*?'

'Yes. Though I don't know how . . .' The clouds of tear gas, drifting across the Seine. The keen of alarms. Harry rubbed his hand across his eyes. 'It's possible Panopticon suspended the French government's access to their alerts system. They, like us, having a rolling contract with Panopticon to watch for possible weaknesses in our digital infrastructure. Banking, power, communications. Panopticon issues a regular stream of patches and fixes and notices of vulnerabilities that need action. If the French were caught trying to get more out of the system than they paid for, he might have cut them off, but most of those things – they might cause small data breaches, slow service or local outages. Not a sudden and complete collapse.'

She cradled her coffee, suddenly glad to be away from the CCTV cameras in the square, and fighting the impulse to whisper. 'What about that man who died? The engineer who was key to the security of the systems? Suppose Panopticon knew that man was dead, and what it meant, and told Eliot so he knew when to suspend their access to the alerts . . .'

'At the moment it would cause maximum damage? Maybe.'

She bit her lip. 'Times we don't know we're lucky. Perhaps there have been a dozen times this year, a bunch of accidents or deaths, or just engineers with hangovers, have left us or the French open to attack, it's just we didn't know. But Panopticon does, and can send Eliot a little alert of his own.'

'All I know for sure is that the French president called Eliot Drake personally on Friday lunchtime. Within an hour he had fired the head of Directorate General and two senior officers. Then all of a sudden the financial system started working again.' Harry leaned forward on the metal table, his head low. He may not have had time to sleep, but he had still showered before they met. She could smell the coconut shampoo on his hair, and found it oddly touching.

'So the call was to apologise and beg forgiveness for trying to force their way into Panopticon?' Tash asked.

'That's my best guess at the moment.'

He lifted his head, trying to focus. 'I have a full briefing being prepared for you on Yule, but here's a sneak preview. Our team has been talking to our diplomats across sub-Saharan Africa about her charity projects. The consensus is she's extremely effective. She's set up cooperative workshops and training programmes in Nairobi and Freetown. Built roads in the DRC, but here's the strange thing; over the last year she hasn't run into any of the problems most NGOs do. Her kit doesn't get stolen. Her permits come through. Head of mission in Sierra Leone said she seems to have an uncanny ability to make allies with the most useful people in an area, and pay off exactly the right selection of the worst.'

'And we're thinking that might be thanks to Panopticon and its strategising?' Tash asked, watching the movement of the clouds over the high castle walls.

'Given what Jemima said to you, that's beginning to sound like a probably.'

Tash folded up the paper bag her roll had come in and put it in her empty coffee cup. Taking her time.

He looked away. 'I'm sorry. I really am tired. The French are freaked out and angry.' His mouth was a narrow line. 'But we need to talk protocols. I'll give you the briefing on Yule on your run on Monday, but today I want to go through some codes we can use on text too if it's harder to meet up when Eliot is here.'

Tash reached into her pocket and pulled out her wallet. From between the credit cards and ancient business cards she extracted a small semi-transparent envelope, which held four negatives.

'What's this?'

'They show the security screens at Belford. In case you need to sneak in at some point. Lots of the wall isn't covered.'

'That's excellent.'

'Do you know who the woman in the square was?'

'Another reason for the mood. I might have brought a shadow back from Paris with me. An angry shadow. But that's my problem.'

'OK. Harry, can I ask you something else?'

'Sure, but you got anything left to trade?'

'This question is about me.'

'Go ahead.'

Tash breathed in. 'When we met, why didn't you just say "Natasha Bell, you owe us. Time to pay up."?'

He said nothing.

'It was why I asked you to step it up with the bona fides. I thought if you were MI6, you'd have just reminded me you dragged me out of a fire fight.'

He paused for a fraction of a second longer. 'Different people are motivated by different things, Tash. We thought curiosity would work better than gratitude with you.' She was about to say something more. 'Come on, I need to go through some things with you.'

24

Pokrovsk, June 2024

Monty and Tash had spent the day among the ruins of a street where a double-tap missile strike had injured four children, then many of the first responders who had gone in to save them. They were going for the human interest story. Rather than just reporting the facts, Monty wanted to talk to one of the surviving ambulance drivers. How did they decide when to run towards the injured children? Did they understand a double tap was likely? Tash had tried to find a way of taking a picture which wasn't just the record of a hole in the ground, a broken toy. She hoped the photo the paper would use was one she took of the mother of one of the injured children, her face hidden, head lowered, a curtain of chestnut hair shrouding her face. One hand held the hand of her other son who was standing next to the sofa. He was older than the boy who was hurt and stared into the camera defiantly. Defending his mother? Defending his own right to live perhaps.

From a journalistic point of view, it had gone well. The story and the interview left all three of them shattered though. Karin just wanted to sleep and talk to her family back in Kharkiv, so went back to the room she'd rented for them. Tash did not want to close her eyes, in case her dreams were vivid or surreal versions of what she had seen that day. Monty looked sick and jittery too. They found a bar which served beer and bowls of stew and Tash queued at the counter while he found a space for them in the back corner, as, after two years, her Ukrainian could at least get them food. When she carried the tray over, the bottles chinking together as she moved, Monty was working with his phone and notebook. His screen showed the story of Vladlen Tatarsky, a pro-Russian blogger killed by a bomb in St Petersburg in 2023.

'What are you looking at that for?' she asked, setting down the tray.

'It's the feature story I'm working on. Someone just sent me the link.'

She handed him his stew and beer and settled into the corner to eat as he bundled away his notebook and phone. Silence. Monty tried to crack a joke. She ignored him, then felt bad. She could see by how fast his drink was disappearing he wasn't feeling any better than she was.

'It was the swing,' she said eventually.

'What?'

'The swing the girl was playing on just before the strike. The chain and those rubber seats, and the colour of the frame. It was just like the one in the playground at the end of Shields Lane in Morpeth where I grew up. Every time I picked up the camera it was like I was back there, and I wondered what my street would look like if Putin was chucking missiles at it.'

He nodded. 'Yeah. Today was a shit one.'

'Do you think what we do matters, Monty?'

The question just came up; she hadn't even known she was going to say it.

'Yes,' he said immediately. 'Yes I do. We have to force people to care, sometimes. What's the alternative? That we let the powers that be just play chess with us? We might just be pawns to them, but I'm going to make sure they know at least some of the names.'

Like her question, his answer had come too fast. She'd spoken without thinking, he was continuing an argument he'd already been having in his head.

'You think you are a pawn in this game?'

He drank his beer in great gulps and signalled for another. 'You and me, Tash, are the pawns of a pawn of a pawn in the great game going on around us. The politicians are pawns too, little mechanical dolls bought by billionaires. And all of us in service to the great god of shareholder value and the myth of infinite growth.'

She was surprised. He didn't normally sound so cynical. 'How did you ever work for *The Times* with an attitude like that? You sound like a revolutionary.'

'You'd be surprised how many left wing journalists work for the *Daily Mail*. We all have to eat. Nah, I admit I get some of this off my brother Simon. He's the radical in the family. Been protesting stuff since he was a teenager.'

'And now? City job, a kid and a mortgage?'

Monty shook his head. 'No. He's younger than me. He's a stonemason working at York Minster. Didn't go to college, just reads and thinks and shapes stone.'

'Why a stonemason?'

'He said even if machines can learn to carve, they won't be able to climb a ladder to fit a rainspout on a 16th-century church for a while.'

Tash smiled. The stew was good, but her appetite was weak.

'What was your childhood like?' Monty asked, scraping out his own bowl. 'Apart from the swing.'

She pushed her bowl towards him, and he started in on the rest of her stew, then she leaned against the wall, glad of the sense of security being pressed in the corner gave her. 'Lots of churches involved as it happens. My gran is super-religious. Mass-every-day-and-twice-on-Sundays religious. She's probably moved in to the church since I came here.'

The old living room had a corner in it where Tash would take a comic book and a torch and hide under a blanket. Hiding from the eye of God.

'So?' His spoon hovered halfway to his mouth. Behind him locals were collecting food from the counter, settling at the long tables. No one said much beyond grunts of greeting. Some had dust on their clothes, the tell-tale scrapes on their faces which meant they'd been caught by debris.

'So it was easy to get stuff wrong in the house. Apparently Jesus hates mess, and fuss, and children who make a lot of noise.'

He lowered his voice. 'I did not know that about Jesus.'

Tash squirmed. The owner of the place set down fresh bottles beside them. He looked like Hagrid, moon face and heavy beard, an apron over the great bulk of him. The bottles sweated in the heat, pearls of condensation running down the green, waisted sides.

'Don't be sorry for me,' Tash said. 'I had Grandad. And my photography with the shopkeeper down the road. And I love Gran. She raised me. But she'd lost her kid and I think she believed, a bit, that God had killed him for a having a child out of wedlock. No, she didn't believe that. No. Maybe she did.' She picked at the narrow label round the base of the bottle. 'Anyway. Living with her taught me to have an eye out for possible explosions at any time, at least. That's been helpful.'

He smiled at her.

'So you grew up with God watching you all the time.'

'. . . all the time,' she repeated in a whisper.

'What else did that teach you?'

'Move quietly. Keep your voice down. And how to keep secrets, of course.' She shrugged. 'What about you, did you go into journalism straight away?'

He shook his head. 'No, when I left uni I wanted to be a spy. I joined MI6, then I realised pretty quickly I preferred exposing secrets to keeping them.'

'And what secrets are you exposing now?'

She said it flirtatiously, but he looked uncertain. 'I've got a contact on the big story I've been chasing, but I have to confirm what he's telling me and that's tough.' He studied his beer for a second, and the quiet seriousness of his expression made her want to reach out, put her hand to his face. 'It's a huge story, I think. The world is being remade around us, and we aren't paying attention.'

'What do you know so far?'

He sighed. 'Move quietly. Keep your voice down. And trust no one. And nothing. Not even the evidence of your own eyes.'

25

Belford Abbey, Saturday 19 July 2025

Tash headed back to the Abbey two hours later with her head full of spy shit. After passing under the huge stone arch at the entrance to the park, and following the road on its first downward sweep, she got off her bike where one of the rills leading to the river went under the road. She paused then pulled the bike into the bracken, in case one of the Abbey vehicles needed to get by, and scrambled up the slope, close to the stream to try and catch the way the afternoon light was shining through the bracken and hitting the water. Soon her portfolio would be full of nature shots like the ones Peter the bookseller specialised in.

She had read the book on Eliot Drake now, watched a couple more videos, and scrolled through long streams of comments on Reddit boards. He didn't seem to divide opinion the way Elon Musk did. Perhaps it was because he was less showy, and more considered when he spoke or wrote. Articles on the politics of billionaires mentioned him in passing, just to say he hadn't contributed to either party at the last election, nor had, the reporters wrote almost glumly, any company or entity he was involved in. Libertarians tried to claim him as their own; the effective altruists pointed to his charitable foundations. Those seemed mostly involved with building infrastructure in underfunded countries, roads and internet capacity.

She lay on the turf, shooting up through the leaves, catching the falling play of the water slightly out of focus behind it. Then stopped, and just watched and listened to the splash and gurgle of the rill dancing over the rocks, watching the patterns in the pools where it shifted and spilled. Monty's ghost didn't appear to keep her company, leaving her to the white noise of her thoughts, weaving in and out of the sound of the water.

The day she came round in the hospital in Kharkiv, a woman who called herself Kelly had come to visit her. Long brown hair and red lipstick. She had held Tash's hand. Told her that she was so sorry E Squadron hadn't got there sooner. That an SIS training mission had picked up chatter that a Tash and Monty were in trouble nearby, and they'd been given clearance to intervene, but had not been quick enough. Told her that the Russian who shot Monty was known for his brutality. That Kelly was, on behalf of His Majesty's Government, gutted they hadn't got there in time. Tash could feel the pressure of her elegant fingers even as she lay here, on the turf, smell the disinfectant they used to mop the floors of the hospital with its shattered windows and exhausted doctors. Kelly had impressed on her that it was vital to keep the secret. They couldn't let Russia know the British had boots on the ground in Ukraine. Please stick to the story the soldier had outlined on the truck.

And Tash had.

But she could have sworn that when she spoke to Harry just now he had no fucking idea about any of it.

She groaned.

'Bloody Hell!' someone exclaimed, then gasped, a half-laugh. Tash turned round. Bethan was ten feet away, hand on her chest. 'You scared the life out of me! I had no idea anyone was there . . .'

She wasn't in a wrap dress right now. Light loose trousers, a thin fleece and walking shoes.

'Hey.' Tash scrambled down the slope to join her, brushing leaf mould and moss off her hands. 'I've been contemplating nature,' she said. 'You too by the looks of it.'

Bethan glanced down at her outfit. 'Yes, just thinking through a few things, and I sometimes find that easier when I walk, so I head off over lunch sometimes. Has Jemima messaged you about tonight yet?'

'Don't think so.'

'There's music on at the Tanners Arms. Emily is playing the Northumbrian pipes so we're going along to support. Do you want to come?'

She hesitated. 'Yeah. Is Emily good?'

'She is, and I've become a convert to the pipes since we started living here most of the year. Emily's playing at the wolf burning, so you'll hear her then if not before.'

Tash pulled her bike out of the bracken and rolled it back on to the road.

'Eliot Drake will be there that weekend, won't he? At the Wild Hunt? With the Council of Heaven?'

'With the what?'

Tash explained, and Bethan laughed, digging her hands into the pockets of her fleece. 'I think Eliot will want to come to the party, so the others will too. He likes a bit of local colour. The Colonel will hate that of course, but . . .' She shrugged. 'Lots of people dress up, wear masks and get their full pagan on, so Eliot should be able to pass unnoticed if he wants to.'

They started walking down the track, Tash pushing her bike. 'You said you came out to think,' she said. 'Tell me if you want to be alone.'

Bethan shook her head. 'I've done thinking. It would be good to have the company. Have you been in town?'

'Yup.' Easier to say nothing about Harry. 'Though I'm beginning to get what you mean about never leaving Belford. Everything is so easy here.' She thought Bethan frowned. 'I know it takes a lot of work to give that impression. I mean it's easy for me.'

'We're doing our work right then.'

The path curved upwards through a stand of tall pines. Another stream, lined with oak and beech, marked the border between wood and grazing land. In a moment the shingled path on which they were walking would turn again and the Abbey and the ruins would appear in front of them as if by magic.

'How's the teaching going, Tasha?'

'Good. I think. You tell me. The students have been filling in assessment forms, haven't they? I thought Jemima would be "feeding back" to me by now.'

'You don't need to say feeding back in a sarky way, Tasha. It's useful.'

'Tash. I prefer Tash.'

Bethan glanced at her, but nodded.

'OK. So what did they say?'

'"Ms Bell is a superb teacher and a remarkable artist. I'm inspired." "She was very patient and I am delighted with what I managed to accomplish in such a short time." "I would like a printout comparing the advantages and disadvantages of the best widely available film cameras up to the value of ten thousand pounds." "It's a shame she doesn't smile more as she is such a pretty girl."' Bethan rattled all of this off with hardly a pause for breath, her hands in her pockets and her eyes on the horizon.

'You're having me on,' Tash said. 'You remembered all that?'

Bethan laughed out loud, startling a grouse into a chuckling complaint which made her laugh even more. 'Your accent gets a lot more northern when you're surprised. Yes, I just remember things.'

'A human Panopticon.'

'Hardly. Though I don't know much about Panopticon. Jemima is in the meetings, but it all goes over my head. I just have to make sure they are looked after.'

'Are they hard work?'

'It's OK. You'd think the millionaires would be the problem, but really it's the assistants trying to anticipate the needs of the millionaires who are a pain in the butt. Added to which they treat me like a moron, which is annoying.'

'Nowt so queer, pet.'

Bethan laughed. 'You were brought up in Morpeth, weren't you?'

'Yeah, reet down t'road,' Tash said, playing it up, before lapsing into her usual voice. 'Gran hated the accent though. She got sent to elocution lessons when she was kid, and Grandad was in insurance before he retired, so he was told to speak "nicely" too. They insisted on me pronouncing my "t"s and using long "a"s at home.

It was a bit different at school, mind, and now my accent depends on where I am and who I'm with.' She paused. 'Did someone really say I should smile more?'

'Yup. He had all sorts of helpful suggestions for Jemima too.'

'That makes me feel better.'

Bethan walked on a few paces in silence, then sighed. 'Look, I can't tell with you, Tash. I don't know if you want to please Jemima, or you despise everything and everyone at the Abbey, her and me included.'

'It's harder to despise you when you aren't dressed as a Barbie doll.'

Bethan gasped, shocked and amused at the same time.

'As for Jemima. Ach, you know. Even if she didn't bring me up, she's still my mother, so I feel fourteen whenever I'm around her. So yes, I despise Belford, and think it's amazing. I think there's something obscene about the whole enterprise, but I want to please her and be praised for my work too.'

Bethan stopped dead, forcing Tash to stop too. 'You *are* like her!' It sounded like an accusation. 'I never have a clue what you are going to say next.'

'I didn't mean to—'

Bethan held her hand up, her eyes dancing. 'If you are about to say you didn't mean to offend, I shall forget that I'm a nicely brought up Barbie doll, and thump you one.'

Tash bit her lip, and Bethan grinned at her.

'Good to know where we stand, anyway,' Bethan continued. 'I'd be grateful if you didn't tell the guests you despise them though.'

'I've liked all the individual guests so far, as people. Well, mostly. It's the idea of them I can't stand. It's wrong for anyone to have this much money. Mum, them. Me too.'

'Even if you never spend it.'

'Haven't given it back, or to charity either, have I?'

'No.'

'I used to be a nicer person, I think. Before Ukraine.'

They had started walking again, and Bethan pointed to the side of Tash's head, without looking at her. 'You're only twenty-eight.

Your brain is still basically mushy. I didn't have any idea who I was until I was thirty-five.'

Tash said nothing. Monty was walking beside them now, resting his hand on the handlebar of Tash's bike.

'Why do you think Ukraine made you less nice? Doesn't seeing suffering make you more caring?'

'No. The opposite,' Tash said. 'You have to stop thinking of the dead as human sometimes. Then something sneaks under your defences and goes off in you like a hand grenade. And I find it harder to control my temper now. I don't know. I'm brittle . . . like I can snap at any moment. There were times in Ukraine when I had to move, to act without thinking. I got in the habit. Now I speak or act without thinking here sometimes. I don't mean to . . .' She hadn't managed to say even that much to the counsellor she'd been sent to. Maybe Wellness Barbie had secret powers.

Bethan sighed. 'You hide it well, Tash, but Jemima knew there was something up when you took the job in the first place. And she's seen you fighting it at times. Doing the breathing.'

The path turned and they were looking across the valley at the Abbey. Tash paused automatically to take in the view.

'You went right at the start of the war, didn't you?'

'Almost. I was in Paris on a romantic break with a guy I was sort of seeing. We walked through a demonstration in Place Saint-Michel, all these people with Ukrainian flags, weeping and singing. And I wasn't sad or afraid. I was excited at the idea of going there. Couldn't wait to get back to London and sort out my credentials and a route.'

'How did the boyfriend take it?'

'Not well. He was an ex before I got on the plane at Heathrow.'

'Have you told your grandparents how you're doing here? They'd be welcome to visit, you know.'

'Yeah. I sent a postcard. Grandad would come and visit. He might sneak up if we can arrange it. Gran will accept a house from Jemima, but not her hospitality. She's still a brazen hussy in Gran's book.'

'If she only knew the half of it,' Bethan said dryly.

A strange new idea occurred to Tash and when she looked sideways at Bethan, Bethan blushed. They climbed the track, switching back and forth up the slope to the house and ruins in silence. The pele tower reared above them.

'Do you think Eliot Drake will let me take pictures of the meetings?'

Bethan shrugged. 'Maybe. He's got a vain streak and I know he likes your work. Jem sent him a copy of your book. I'll email.'

'Thanks.'

As they got within range of the Abbey Wi-Fi, Bethan's phone buzzed. She pulled it out of her pocket. 'Only gone an hour and I have five missed calls and ten emails.' She scanned the phone. 'Oh, you have got to be fucking kidding me!'

'What?'

'That paranoid, self-important bullying shit!' She put her hand to her head. 'Sorry, Tash. It's the Colonel. He's issued a decree. We're only to use live-in staff while Eliot is here, for security reasons. Having our usual people coming and going will overtax their resources. Jesus! We'll have to try and bribe a couple of the maids to live in, and Cassie won't stay if she can't go visit her mum midweek. I better get started.'

She raised a hand in farewell and picked up her pace heading along the drive, then up the steps into the house.

26

Jemima drove the minibus into Alnwick herself and parked in the quiet market square. The market had packed up and gone, but there was still a steady movement of people and cars. It was only when she got out Tash realised her mother wasn't wearing her usual film-star gear. Jeans and a loose silk top, her hair tied back. Tash walked next to her on the way to the pub. It occupied a corner plot, just beyond one of the ancient gates which arched over the road. And as they approached they could already hear laughter and conversation pouring out of the open windows.

The centre of the main bar had a tree in it, apparently growing out of the floorboards and disappearing into the ceiling. It was hung with twists of fake flowers and leaves and festooned with winking white fairy lights. Jemima lifted her hand in greeting to the barman, who lifted a finger from the beer pump he was pulling in acknowledgement and nodded towards the far corner. There was a reserved sign on one of the small tables, almost next to the stools and stands and mini mixing desk set up for the absent performers.

Jemima took a seat facing the room and asked of a pint of whatever. Tash sat opposite her. The bar was beginning to fill up. Men in checked shirts with comfortable bellies; wives in heavy make-up and sparkly tops. A few people closer to Tash's age and a few who looked hardly out of their teens. The girls all had long, straight hair and the boys short at the back and sides, long on top. On the doors someone had stuck up a poster advertising the Wild Hunt. A cartoon wolf's head surrounded by orange and red flames thickly outlined in black.

'What are you thinking about?' Jemima asked.

'How long this place has been here,' Tash replied. 'And if people looked much different a hundred or two hundred years ago.'

Jemima took her coat off. 'Eliot says that he can see Viking blood in the locals. So maybe.'

'Do you like him, Mum?' Tash said as Bethan approached the table, three pints held between her outstretched fingers and a bag of crisps between her teeth. Tash took one of the drinks from her, and, unburdened, she sat on the other side of the table next to Jemima. Jemima's eyes flicked up, and Tash realised she'd called her 'Mum' and her cheeks flushed. Jemima looked away again.

'I'm not sure I should like or dislike people I work with. That implies a value judgement, and it's hard to help if you are busy judging people.'

'But would you like him, if you weren't working with him?'

She considered the question while pulling open the crisps and helping herself before proffering them to Tash.

'I can't think where we would ever meet. Or how we'd become friends. Or what we would talk about if we did. The tech people I work with look at me as a management tool, or self-optimisation tool. It can be quite calculated. They aren't trying to develop empathy, or emotional intelligence to be better people. They are doing it to become better negotiators, to get more out of the people who work with them. There's something very cold about it.' She took another crisp and waved it in the air to make her point before eating it. 'I try to get them to understand it's a good idea in itself to become a more rounded, empathetic human being, but it's like I'm speaking alien. Eliot is a strange man, but given his wealth he can't really be anything else. Sometimes he needs validation, and I'm flattered he comes to me for that. Sometimes I can tell he is only half-listening to me. Then again, when you work with someone a long time, you become sort of fond of them. Maybe. It's like that saying, you don't care for the things you love, you love the things you care for.' Her face froze. 'Shit, sorry. Tash . . . You know I love you, don't you? I always have. Even if I haven't looked after you.'

Tash felt her face burn. 'I know. Stop second guessing every single thing you say, Jemima. I'm not going to pull it all apart to find some reason to be angry with you.'

'I will though,' Jemima said. 'I can't help it.'

Bethan seemed to have gone tactfully deaf during this exchange, slightly turned away from them and surveying the crowd, pint in hand, her phone upside down on the table. It dinged and she picked it up, then sighed.

'Trouble?' Tash asked, eager to get away from the moment.

'No. Just the Colonel wants to let us know he and his "advance" team will be here at eight tomorrow morning. He has some new guys on the detail and wants to give them an onsite briefing.'

'If anyone tells me I'm overpaid, I look at those guys,' Jemima said, lifting her pint. It looked comically large in her small hands. 'Wilf could do just as good a job as his stupid "detail".'

'I'll put out a message on the company Slack,' Bethan replied, thumbing the screen. The door to the street seemed to be in constant motion now. 'Did Tash tell you what her name for Eliot's gathering is?'

Jemima shook her head.

'Council of Heaven,' Tash said trying not to blush. 'You know, God's advisors.'

Jemima laughed. 'About right. Though with bloody John Allingham there . . . He acts like he can't hear me.' She peered round the crowd, and waved to someone at the other side of the bar. 'I hope we have room for a dance later. Emily plays music you can't help moving to.'

'He knows you studied philosophy at Cambridge,' Bethan said not looking up from her screen. 'He's afraid you are going to point out his bullshit and show him up.'

'Better not tell him I was pissed and shagging about most of time, and barely scraped a two-one,' Jemima said.

In spite of what she had just said, that hurt Tash. She had always imagined her mother giving her up in order to take her studies seriously. She felt a touch on her hand. Jemima. 'I was messed up, Tash. Shit, sorry, I'm doing it again.'

The crowd parted, and Emily came through, followed by a handsome, dark-skinned man clutching a fiddle in one hand, a pint in the other, and a third, older man who made his way to the piano. The crowd cheered and the music began.

Jemima began clapping along with the music, unselfconscious, though people were looking at her from time to time.

'Jemima, do you know who that woman is?'

Tash jerked her head towards a woman at the bar.

'Oh shit. Yes, she's a journalist. Got a bit of a fixation with Eliot. Says he destroyed her career last year, but I think it was plagiarising half her stuff that did it.'

As they watched, a middle-aged woman in tight jeans slid off her stool and walked towards them. 'Good evening, Jemima.'

'Evening. We're here to watch the music, Marsha. That OK with you?'

The woman leaned forward, putting her hands on the table. 'I know he's coming to Belford next week. Do you have enough fancy soap in the place to wash the blood off his hands? Off *your* hands?'

Jemima held out the packet in her hand. 'Fancy a crisp?'

The woman curled her lip and retreated back to the bar. Tash hadn't meant her. She'd meant the older woman sitting next to her in the short white coat. The one who had been watching Tash and Harry in the town square the day he got back from Paris.

'What the hell was that?' Jemima said after she was out of earshot. 'Blood on his hands?'

'The corpse of her career, I guess,' Bethan said, then turned back towards the performers.

Jemima turned to the players, her face a mask.

Tash studied the woman and her companion. Thought about Harry, and Chinooks, and about motorcycles, and the first time she saw film being developed. About postcards and secrets and avoiding the eye of God.

'Jem,' Tash said, leaning sideways. 'I think I might go to Newcastle tomorrow. Wilf said there's a good exhibition on at the Baltic.'

'Excellent idea,' Jemima said briskly. 'Have lunch with your grandparents. They probably think I've got you under lock and key here.'

'I'll see if Gran can fit me in between masses.'

Jemima snorted with laughter, then reached out and squeezed Tash's hand briefly.

'It will be OK, you know. Eliot being here. And it's only a week. Then we can get back into the rhythm of things.'

'Are you reassuring me, or yourself?'

'Both of us. I think you've been healing since you got here, and . . . Eliot changes the atmosphere wherever he is. He makes the weather. And the kill code thing makes me think the weather will be stormy.' She folded her empty crisp packet into a neat triangle. 'And we'll have the protestors out front and the Colonel's goons all over the place. The protestors sometimes have sessions of banging pots and pans. They say it's "rough music" to shame Eliot.'

'You're afraid I'll be triggered.'

Jemima nodded. 'And you've been doing so well.'

Tash hadn't realised how much she had been seen in the last couple of weeks.

'I'll manage, Mum. And I promise I'll come to you if I can't.'

'Thank you.'

Jemima blinked a few times, then returned her attention to the stage, gracing the performers with her full beam smile.

They spilled out of the Tanners Arms at closing time, proud of Emily and high on the energy of the pub. The next day Tash left early for Gateshead, and walked through the exhibition, then spent a while in the café, writing. One letter she wrote was on thick creamy stationery with the Belford Abbey letterhead. When her grandparents joined her for a late lunch and told her forty times how well she seemed, Tash realised how sick she must have looked last time she saw them. She posted her letters on the way back to the station, thinking about where and how we learn to trust.

* * *

Tash's phone went on its extra run on Monday while Harry briefed her on Yule. He looked, if anything, worse than he had at the weekend. He quizzed her again on what the Colonel had said, trying to dig out any further nuggets of information on what 'strategising' might mean, but refused to say anything more about Paris or the angry shadow he'd brought back with him. Then he wished her luck.

Tash glanced back over her shoulder after Janice returned her phone and saw him leaning against the bridge, watching her.

Eliot's imminent arrival seemed to hum in the air, making everyone restless and Tash found herself unable to sit still. She walked through the house, through the ruins, going in circles as if she was patrolling or haunting them. She couldn't say which.

In the early evening Tash spotted the Colonel through the huge picture window in the exhibition space. He was carrying a stepladder up to a gate in the outer wall of the ruins. It looked slightly bizarre – him in his always semi-formal attire with the paint-splattered ladder. Tash peered out, getting as close to the picture window as she could. He was checking the camera above the gate. As Tash focussed, he turned suddenly, looking out towards the stand of oaks a little further down the slope. He clambered down, and set off towards them, and it was only then Tash noticed another man standing in the shadow of the trees and waiting. He made for a good figure in the landscape, giving a sense of scale, and alone. His hair was slightly long, and pale as straw. Tash took the photograph, and watched the Colonel approach.

'Oh, Tash, pet! That's splendid!' Tash smiled as Wilf examined his photograph. 'The wife will love it.'

Tash had come to Wilf's office to deliver her portrait of him, his face lit by the screens, his radio on the desk beside him, before he retreated to his caravan.

'Have a good week off. I hope the Colonel's men don't make too much of a mess of your settings.'

'Oh that!' Wilf leaned forward over the desk. 'Here. Have a look what I found when I came on this evening.' He searched with the mouse for a couple of seconds, then the screen was filled by an image of the Colonel in extreme close-up, his face distorted by the lens. 'He's fiddling with the actual cameras now!'

The clip played as Wilf giggled. The Colonel retreated and stood by the tree with his hands on his hips. Tash frowned. She lifted her camera and took a picture of the screen. 'Isn't that by the ruin wall?'

'Aye, that's right. That camera watches one of the gates to the villa.'

'And that time and date is right?'

'Yes, it gave me a shock. I mean just I come in, this evening, hang my coat up and turn round, and there's that bloke a-leering at me!'

Tash stared, then smiled. 'Hell of a start to your evening.'

The Colonel was still in frame, admiring the landscape. The blonde man Tash had seen, had photographed from the exhibition space in the pele tower, should have been clearly visible. But he wasn't.

'Never thought of the Colonel as a man to stand around admiring the view,' Wilf said. 'Perhaps I've misjudged the man.'

'I doubt it.'

He patted the photograph. 'Thanks again for this, Tash. I appreciate it. I really do. And I shall see you in a week.'

Tash smiled and wished him a happy holiday.

After supper Tash was working in her room, when some instinct drew her to the window. A fleet of black SUVs was approaching the Abbey, four of them, glimmering like coal in the evening sun. Tash felt her throat tighten and she rested her fingers on the glass as she watched them turn towards the Abbey Villa and disappear out of sight beyond the ruins.

PART II

The Council of Heaven

27

Kharkiv, July 2024

Tash's housemate and landlady, a war widow with two children, invited Tash to a friend's party on the edge of town and Tash asked if she could bring Monty. It was a good party, a mix of Ukrainians and the ragtag brigades of foreign civilians war brings in its wake. Diplomats, aid workers, researchers, journalists and a posse of EU workers who seemed to be arranging cultural exchanges and theatre workshops. Bringing over musicians to join in the concerts underground while the city shuddered above them. Poets and street artists.

The music at the party was loud, the room decorated with tinsel, and the alcohol plentiful. Tash flirted with a trauma surgeon, took photographs of the dancing in the narrow hallway, a girl, her face glistening with sweat and her face turned up towards a tinsel-shrouded light above her. Her eyes half-closed, glitter smeared across her cheek so it looked as if she was sweating gold.

Tash knew and liked several of the people there, but from the moment Monty arrived, kissed her on the cheek and added a couple of bottles of vodka to the kitchen worktop serving as a bar, she found she was always aware of exactly where he was in the room. It had come on slowly, this sense of him. Her disappointment in days when he was reporting elsewhere. The thrill of catching sight of him in whatever bar the press pack had chosen for the week. She realised she was narrating her days for him inside her head as she worked, telling him how she felt about this assignment or that. Inviting him here was a sort of test, of him and her. Her idea was to surround him with the hottest, horniest people in the city, and see where he decided to spend his time.

After about twenty minutes he sought her out, pushing through the crowd once he had exchanged a few hellos, and then didn't leave her side for the rest of the night. Not when one of the junior diplomats, a good contact for a reporter like him, tried to chat. Not when a girl with huge eyes and an almost see-through top tried to persuade him to dance. Not when one of the aid workers shouted something in his ear about a story, or one of the poets offered to cut up lines of coke.

She wasn't sure if there was any discussion about leaving together, she simply found they had done so and they were out on the street in the relative quiet, ears ringing and eyes sore from the cigarette smoke. Then he took her hand.

Tash had not had many first kisses, not ones like this anyway, which really did feel like the beginning of something – that lived up to the ideal. They were walking past a restaurant on Bohdana Khmel'nyts'koho, where the owners had strung ropes of lights from the summer terrace to the trees, and he stopped, and pulled her towards him. Cars passed, conversation drifted across from the restaurant, and the world paused as he bent towards her. When they pulled apart, everyone and everything around them was beautiful. He beamed at her, his expression a mix of joy, relief and hunger.

Tash bought overpriced vodka, tobacco and chocolate from one of the kiosks and they went back to her rented room, the uncomfortable sofa bed scattered with Tash's half-unpacked clothes, almost too eager to get the first time out of the way so they could sink into the next. Tash felt the delight shaking her head to toe and thought of the girl who looked as if she were sweating gold.

28

Newcastle Airport, Executive Centre, Tuesday, 22 July 2025

The jet landed on schedule. As it taxied to a halt, the convoy of black SUVs from Belford Abbey, driven by the Colonel's goons, pulled on to the tarmac to meet it.

Jemima flicked down the mirror above the passenger seat and checked her lipstick, pressing her lips together, then smiling to check her teeth.

'Here we go,' she said, then opened the door and hopped down on to the tarmac. Tash and Bethan got out of the back seat, though Bethan stayed by the car while Tash followed her mother. Tash turned back, surprised Bethan wasn't coming too. She had her arms folded and her pink, polite, professional smile already in place. The Colonel had ridden in one of the other vehicles.

The Executive Centre staff in hi-vis jackets positioned the airstairs next to the plane, and the door opened with a smooth hiss of hydraulics. A uniformed man trotted straight up the steps and into the cabin.

'They do customs and immigration on the plane,' Jemima said to Tash.

At the rear of the plane luggage was being unloaded. Shiny cases slid down the chute and were loaded into a waiting van, the sort of anonymous black transit used by mortuaries to ferry the dead between hospices and funeral homes.

'Do you feel nervous?' Tash asked. 'Before you meet him?'

She considered, then shook her head. Her red hair was in a ponytail today; it whipped back and forth behind her.

'Not usually. But today is different. I haven't seen him in person for a while. He's keen to meet you though. I'm glad you came to welcome him.'

Tash suspected Jemima hoped she'd make a good impression on the billionaire. She'd do her best. She owed her mother that much, at least. As they waited, a couple emerged from the private terminal and walked towards the cars. The woman, shorter than her companion and very slight, had blue streaks in her dark hair. Jemima waved at her, and the woman lifted her hand in response.

'That's Yule. She flew up from Porto this morning. And her assistant. The assistants are normally OK. Overworked and a bit panic stricken, but OK.'

'That's not what Bethan says.'

Jemima tapped her foot. 'Yes. Well, they have their moments. They don't realise how important she is. Sophie usually manages to get a few of them off the energy drinks while they are here. Not this week though.'

The Abbey had seemed strangely deserted yesterday night as most of the staff left, given a week off, like Wilf, rather than being forced to live in. The treatment rooms were shut, the apps where you could book your personal training or nutrition appointment greyed out. Tash and the other workshop leads had been invited to stay though, in case the Council of Heaven wanted a moment of creative calm. She focussed on the door as the man in uniform trotted down the stairs again and set off back towards the terminal. Strutting. Head up. His important business for the state concluded.

Eliot Drake exited the plane.

He paused at the top of the stairs, face lifted to the sun. He was wearing black jeans and a white T-shirt under a light blue unbuttoned shirt, his thick hair longer on top and parted to the side, a leather bag crossways across his body. Aviator shades. He tilted his head to one side then the other, straightening out the kinks, then he caught sight of Jemima, and sketched a wave before walking down the steps and wandering across the tarmac towards them.

Behind him came a small crowd of his fellow travellers. Torrent, a forty-something Asian woman in a dark business suit. A man, also in his forties perhaps, shouldering past her as she hesitated at the top of the ramp, in a crisp dark-blue collarless shirt and sports coat, Allingham. Then the assistants. The Council of Heaven had assembled. Tash lifted the camera, caught the billionaire as he approached.

The Colonel stepped forward, but Eliot raised his hand in greeting and kept moving towards Jemima rather than Frank. He was taller than Tash had expected, six-foot, but slender. He walked with a slight bounce to his step. Jemima stepped forward to greet him, her hands outstretched.

'Eliot! Hi! How was your flight?'

For some reason, Tash had thought he would be pale, but his skin was tanned and he was freshly shaved. A good jawline. He put his hands out and took Jemima's, squeezing them briefly, a half-smile on his face. On one wrist he wore a bracelet of wooden beads with silver accents, on the other a watch which Tash guessed cost as much as the SUV they had just arrived in. He was more handsome in person than in the photographs she had seen.

'Yeah, OK. Got some work done.' He took off his shades, hanging them off the collar of his T-shirt, then he turned towards Tash. His eyes were a very dark brown, so dark you couldn't quite tell where the iris ended and the pupil began. 'Hiya. You're Natasha, aren't you?' He put out his hand. 'I'm Eliot.'

Tash took it. The handshake was firm and his hands were dry. 'Yeah – Tash. Good to meet you.'

'I like your work.'

'Thanks – and thanks for letting me take pictures.'

'Sure. My lawyers went through all the releases, didn't they? They said you'd be like an official White House photographer. We get approval of anything you publish.'

He spoke quietly, a transatlantic accent. She nodded. 'That's it.'

'Yeah, I'm going to limit shooting to breaks and things. Though maybe we can fake a heated discussion for you at the end. Give you a vibe.'

Tash would never put her name to something staged, but no point getting into that now. 'Sounds good. I thought you might ban me after I told your head of security to fuck off.'

He half-laughed. 'No, you wouldn't be the first to tell him that. Jemima doesn't like him either.'

'I never said that, Eliot.' Jemima sighed. 'I said he satisfied a need.'

'Yeah, he's got a lot of operational, frontline experience.'

'That's not what I—'

He cut her off. 'You're sweet coming to meet us. No need though. And I'm half-dead so no point trying to coach me in the car. Did Tara update you? I want a rest day tomorrow, just suck in some of that Belford Abbey vibe, then we'll run scenarios for three days.'

She put her arm through his – she looked tiny next to him – and led him back towards Bethan and the SUV. 'Yes, she did. And I'm just welcoming you as a friend and a guest, Eliot. You can sleep in the car. What are the scenarios?'

'Torrent's people came up with them, but they are based on Pan's newer capabilities with some real-world feedback folded in.'

'Eliot,' Jemima asked, 'have you closed Belford Abbey to play games?'

He smiled. 'Kinda. War games. The Great Game. *Game of Thrones*.' Then he glanced at Tash. 'You won't take pictures of me drooling all over myself in the back seat, will you?'

Tash mock saluted. 'Scout's honour.'

'Hey, Bethan.'

'Hi, Eliot.'

Bethan opened the nearest back door for him and he climbed in, while Jemima went round the other side. Tash got in at the front, next to the driver. Bethan waved at them, then headed towards the Colonel. Tash twisted in her seat. They were directing the rest of the party into the other cars.

The lead vehicle pulled away, and they followed.

Even in the luxurious quiet of the SUV, Tash couldn't hear what Eliot and Jemima said to each other in the back seat. A few murmured remarks – nothing in the tone suggesting they were saying something of significance. She watched them intermittently in the rear-view mirror. Their heads were close together. Eliot looking weary but relaxed, Jemima all quiet attention.

When she next looked, he had gone to sleep, his head resting on Jemima's shoulder. The richest man in the world. Jemima caught her eye in the mirror and smiled – a tight, brief smile – before turning and looking out of the window.

The convoy skirted Alnwick and Tash noticed the signs advertising the Wild Hunt – 'Local Crafts! Hot Food!' – as the car turned towards the park gates.

'They were quick,' Jemima murmured as they approached the gate.

On the verge outside the entrance to the park a dozen men and women were setting up a banner, a sheet held between bamboo poles with 'New Luddites' spray-painted on to it and their logo, a grey triangle on its point. On the other side of the stone arch another sheet had been unrolled. The artwork was a lot more sophisticated. It showed a huge cartoon of a thin man dressed in black at a table, with Eliot's almost quiff and high cheekbones, knife and fork in hand, stuffing his face with huge slices from a globe sat on a platter in front of him. At his feet stick figures crouched, holding up their hands in supplication, or scrabbled around his shoes for fallen crumbs. They shared a single speech bubble. 'Hey, Eliot! Leave something for the rest of us!'

Tash recognised the image as a rip-off of an early 19th-century Gillray cartoon. In the original, though, the plum pudding globe was being shared between England and France. Here, Eliot had it all to himself. As the convoy approached, the protestors scrambled to pick up metal saucepans and began bashing at them with spoons. Discordant, clanging.

Tash gritted her teeth. *Bang bang bang.* Monty at the front suddenly, with pan and spoon, thwacking away gleefully. Eliot stirred, rubbed his eyes, and looked out of the window, his expression blank.

The gates swung open as the SUV in front of them approached slowly, in the midst of all the noise. Tash looked up, caught her mother's glance in the rear-view mirror. Jemima kept eye contact and breathed in deeply enough for her chest to rise. Tash echoed the movement.

'Take their picture, Tash,' Jemima said as she exhaled and Tash exhaled with her.

The protestors craned forward, lifting their pans, rattling them with the spoons, trying to see in through the tinted windows. They were all masked. Witches and ex-presidents in fleeces and T-shirts. A woman in a short white coat stood slightly apart, still as a sentinel. Tash was sure it was the same woman who had been watching her and Harry in the square. The shadow Harry said had followed him back from Paris. Her mask was of a hawk. Close to the gate, one man wore the skull and antlers of a stag. His fist raised. As the first car slowed on its approach, he pulled the mask off to look in through the glass and Tash was struck. He had a close-cropped blonde beard, and a strong, defined jawline. She lifted her camera, focussed, and took the shot as the driver slowed for the turn. One human face briefly exposed among the demons and goblins.

The picture, the breath had helped. Tash swallowed. Speak. Remind the body where it is.

'What's with the masks?' Tash asked as their car took its turn crawling through the crowd and under the stone arch. The demons pressed against the glass.

'I've no idea,' Jemima replied. 'Eliot, do you know?'

'They think it makes them anonymous, they are covering their faces to avoid facial recognition,' Eliot said. 'But gait is a better way to identify individuals anyway. Masking is pointless now.'

He was staring at them out of the tinted windows, his face still blank. The beginning of H. G. Wells's *War of the Worlds* drifted up into Tash's mind as she watched him. *Something about intellects vast and cool and unsympathetic, watching people like bugs under a microscope.*

'Maybe you should talk to them while you are here, Eliot,' Jemima said as they left them behind and the car hummed smoothly along the private road towards the Abbey.

He snorted. 'What – get thrown a bunch of gotcha questions with everyone's iPhone in my face?'

'I could invite a couple in. The Colonel can frisk them for phones. Show you are willing to have a conversation. You know they've gained followers since what happened in France.'

He shrugged. 'People will forget about that by the end of the summer, and about them. But maybe. Yeah. OK. *Vox populi, vox Dei* and all that.'

'Not that you believe that for a second.'

'Neither do you.' He sighed. 'Look what democracy has delivered in the last ten years. One disaster after another.'

They crested the hill and there was Belford, glowing in the sunlight on the other side of the Aln valley. Eliot leaned forward to peer through the windscreen at the view.

'Home sweet home.'

29

Tash was invited to the welcome dinner in the villa that night. As she showered and dressed, she rehearsed what she had been told about the members of the Council of Heaven.

Yule Collins. Born and raised in Berlin, then did her PhD in political science at Oxford. Taught herself to code as a teenager and set up anonymous servers and encrypted messaging systems for anarchists and social justice movements across Europe. Then she became an effective altruist while studying under Simon Pemberton, a philosopher who had enjoyed a solid if unspectacular career at the university until his ideas about the morals of wealth took off among the tech utopians of Silicon Valley. He was now enjoying a late and surprising second career as the best-selling author of almost impenetrable books.

John Allingham, a former journalist whose work popularised the philosophy of the ancient Greeks in an easy to digest form, peppered with anecdotes about tech founders and captains of industry. Harry's erratically typed briefing notes had been scathing about his scholarship, but gave him grudging respect for turning his light learning into a media career which included a top rated podcast as well as the books and a constant round of speaking appointments.

Torrent. Academically brilliant, majoring in computer sciences. Designer of a sprawling multiplayer online game in which, famously, people married and bought 'land' where they raised virtual flocks and crops from their studio bedrooms and basements. Some had even bought virtual burial plots in which to bury their digital selves. She now specialised in running red teams for tech disruptors, suggesting worst case scenarios about how their inventions could be abused or corrupted. The notes had said she was probably the most gifted of the Council of Heaven, and the richest after Eliot himself. Her consultancy work, it seemed, she did purely because it interested her.

Tash dressed as usual – the group didn't look as if they were the cocktail dresses and dinner suit types – then made her way downstairs and through the gardens. The entrance to the ruins was guarded now by two bulky, soft-bellied men in black suits. Their hands clasped lightly under their bellies. They wore earpieces – surely earpieces didn't need to be that obvious any more? That was probably the point though – you were meant to notice them, take them as proof these men were plugged into a higher authority. They nodded to her as she passed between them, but didn't challenge her. She remembered a story one of her colleagues, a cameraman, had told her about filming in 10 Downing Street once. He'd been loading kit in through the famous front door, and thought he should introduce himself to the policemen on duty. 'I'm Graham King,' he'd said. 'Oh, we know who you are, Mr King,' they'd replied.

As she walked between the ancient remnants of the destroyed monastery, her footsteps light on the neatly cropped turf, she noticed the guests and their attendants had gathered on the terrace. They stood or sat in small groups, but even if he hadn't been the tallest man there, she'd have been able to sense where Eliot Drake was at once. The attention of the group leaned towards him. He was chatting to Charles and Ingrid. Among the guests, Belford Abbey staff in black polo shirts carried drinks and plates of canapés, offering without interrupting conversations, quietly alert to the needs of Drake and his guests. Emily, Fran and Yasmin were serving. Bethan and Jemima had selected their oldest hands for the job. Jemima was sitting with the Colonel, her face a careful blank, complete with polite smile, while he leaned towards her, his hands chopping the air. All that money, Tash thought, all that success and she still has to just sit and listen to him. Jemima looked up and winked at her, but didn't make any move to interrupt the Colonel.

John Allingham sauntered towards Tash as she reached the terrace. 'Natasha Bell! War photographer!' he announced, beaming, and a couple of heads turned in their direction. She wasn't sure if he was announcing her, like a footman at a Georgian ballroom, or simply saying hello. 'Can I get you a drink?'

Emily was already at her elbow as she stepped up on to the terrace, proffering her some sort of champagne cocktail. The bottom of the glass was thick with fruit puree. Tash took it and thanked her.

'I'm John,' he said, offering his hand. The handshake was a little too firm and he patted her arm with his free hand, before picking his own drink off the table. Sparkling mineral water, Tash noticed. What a spartan. He looked like an older, faded version of Eliot. Not as fit and his blue eyes looked watery and a little red, as if he had something in his contact lens. 'Now, is it true that you called our little group the Council of Heaven? Jemima was just telling us, what a scream. How did you come up with that?'

He managed to smile without looking amused.

Eliot had come across to greet her too. 'Because I'm God, and you are my advisors. Council of Heaven is from the Book of Job, isn't it?' John looked startled to find Eliot suddenly so close. 'I must read it again. I think you were being ironic though, weren't you, Tash?'

Eliot was drinking one of the fruity champagne drinks too.

'Perhaps,' she said, lifting her glass to him. 'And yes, Book of Job, though something like it is mentioned in other places.'

He rubbed the side of his nose. 'Was the Devil on the Council of Heaven too?'

'It's hard to tell. But I think so.'

'Nice to have a scholar in the place.' If he noticed John flinch, he didn't show it. He looked around. 'Wonder who it is? I mean, Torrent's job is to play devil's advocate, but an actual devil would be interesting.'

'Are you religious?' John asked Tash.

'No. But I've been stuck in a few hotel rooms without internet access or anything else to read,' Tash replied.

One hotel room. With Monty. He had presented her the Gideon's Bible from the bedside table, shocked at how little she knew of the New and Old Testaments even after having been dragged to church every Sunday through her childhood. 'That's why I never read it,' she'd complained, but he'd persisted. 'It's the foundation of Western culture, for better or worse. Read it. I mean, skip all the x begat y stuff. But read it.' And she had. Then again while she was in hospital and she had felt him, sitting in the back of the room as she turned the pages. What he would say to her, ask her? Check your sources. Compare accounts. Look for the story behind the story. Plenty of meat on these ancient bones.

His ghost walked across the back of the terrace like it had somewhere to go and John cleared his throat, drawing her attention back to him. 'I'm writing a book about literature and war at the moment,' he said. 'From Homer to *The Hurt Locker*.'

'That should keep you busy.'

She knew that the rules of conversation meant she should ask some flattering question at this point. How fascinating! Do tell me more. She didn't, but he didn't seem to notice.

'We should have you on the podcast sometime,' he said. 'I'd love to chat with you about your experiences.'

His podcast had millions of downloads a week, but Tash suddenly, violently, didn't care. She smiled tightly and offered to put him in touch with her publicist.

'Eliot, can I ask you something?' she said.

'You can ask,' he said, vaguely interested. 'There's a lot of stuff I'm not allowed to tell people though. About my work and things. Even here.' He smiled. Politely attentive.

'A man I was working with in Ukraine. The one who was killed. He used to be a tech reporter and I wondered if you ever met him. Monty Young.'

Tash waited, watching him for any flicker of recognition, wondering about Monty's opaque hints about this man, his distrust of email, his bloody thumb drive.

Eliot rubbed the side of his nose. He was still wearing the bracelet of beads. It clashed with the Rolex, Tash thought. 'Don't think so. I met a lot of reporters when I was building Panopticon though.

Those were the days I was desperate to talk to them. Now it's the other way round.'

Jemima joined them from the other side of the terrace, in green again, but a more muted shade than the jewel bright hue she had worn on the day Tash arrived. This dress also flowed off the curve of her hips and rippled as she walked. It was the green of holly, late in the winter, and made her skin look very white. The diamond drop of her necklace and earrings were like frozen dew. She touched Eliot on the arm and he bent down so she could whisper in his ear, then she stood aside.

He nodded and put out his hand. 'Can I borrow your glass, Tash?'

She surrendered it, and he tapped it against his own to attract the attention of his guests.

'Hey, everyone!' They turned towards him, the silence immediate. 'Thanks, Tash,' he added, returning her glass. 'So, dinner is ready, but before we go in, I wanted to welcome you to Belford. I'm looking forward to our discussions over the next few days.'

Tash watched the other people on the terrace watching him. Charles and Ingrid standing close together, staring. The assistants and servers. Money might have gravity, but fame had its own gravity too. Fame made small moments, a greeting, an exchange, of no special significance to one person, bloom in the experience of the other into something to be hoarded with life's great moments. I met the King, we talked about fruitcake. I met Eliot Drake and we drank champagne and fruit cocktails on a terrace overlooking medieval ruins on a summer's evening . . .

'Now, the Colonel needs to share a couple of things with us.'

He stepped back, bowing his head slightly and the Colonel cleared his throat.

'Thank you, Eliot. Now I'm sure you all noticed the protestors at the gates. Usual ragtag bunch, but we're keeping a close eye on them. There is one person of interest in town. Looks like Marsha Connelly is here.' Yule and Torrent groaned. 'Yup. I know. We're keeping watch, but just wanted to make you aware in case she tries to approach any of you.' The Colonel smiled his thinnest smile.

'We've had to put new security protocols in place this week, and I apologise for the inconvenience if any of you were looking to have a massage or stock up on your micronutrients.' He didn't bother to try and hide the sneer in his voice. 'Most of you, I hope, won't notice any difference on the grounds.'

He looked back at Eliot, who nodded and pressed his hands together. 'Let's eat.'

30

There was a seating plan and by the time Tash followed Eliot through the French windows, the general arrangement was pretty clear. Eliot in the middle, the Council of Heaven surrounding him, then favoured guests, including Tash. At the outer edges were the assistants with smooth hair and good clothes, the only sign of their roles as helpers and facilitators to the great and good being the high attenuated buzz of their attention, focussed on their bosses. As the party settled, Tash amused herself working out who belonged to whom. Torrent appeared to have at least two. One woman, her hair scraped back in a bun, was ostentatiously working on an iPad and only greeting the others with wordless nods. Tash decided she was probably one of Eliot's.

The person sitting next to Tash, a shiny-eyed man of her own age, introduced himself as Perry and explained he worked for Yule. He had long, thin hands and an accent with a trace of Bristol to it. As the staff laid out sourdough on the tables, and pats of banana butter scattered with salt, he reached into his pocket and produced a small tin box with a sentimental image of Victorian children on it, and leaning across the table, handed it past Tash and along to his boss.

'Sorry,' he said, grabbing the bread. 'Micronutrients. Supposed to be taken with food. If I don't give them to her the moment she has to take them though, she'll get talking to someone and forget.'

Tash glanced sideways. Yule had obediently flicked open the box. She emptied the contents into her palm, then transferred them to her mouth in one go, washing them down with her first glass of white wine.

'Sophie the nutritionist here is recommending I take some of those,' Tash told him. 'Offered to whip me some up pills in her clinic.'

Perry nodded. 'Yes, Nature-first micronutrients. Sophie is one of the best, and of course all of her stuff is bespoke.'

'You must be sorry she's not here this week.'

'Oh, she left like six months' worth of Yule's usual capsules in my room in the stables. And reishi mushrooms for mental acuity.'

Tash sipped her own wine. Sophie had gently suggested ashwagandha to combat severe anxiety.

'The supplements are excellent at supporting the immune system, but I wish she'd exercise more,' Perry said, watching Yule. 'I'm at the gym, six-thirty every morning. I'd go mad without it. It's the personal training staff here I'm going to miss.'

'How long have you been working for Yule?'

'Two years. She's paying for my PhD,' he said, and started buttering his bread. 'I'm studying consciousness, mix of philosophy and hard science. I mean, everyone's talking about creating an artificial consciousness, but no one's been able to define what the one we have at the moment is yet.'

'I've been wondering about that,' Tash admitted.

He nodded. 'I mean, is it just "I think, therefore I am"? We know some of the decisions "we" make are down to our gut microbiome. Some say thoughts are just after-effects, like hallucinations, the mental trash left over from processes over which we have no control. So when you get to computers you have to ask, can something that doesn't eat, or move, be conscious in the same way we are?'

'So what do you think?'

He grinned. 'I've no fucking idea – that's why I'm studying. But maybe that's one of the things about artificial intelligence: it's forcing us to think about our terms a bit more carefully. Tough for some people, that.' His eyes drifted to John Allingham.

'Is that what these guys are going to discuss? Artificial consciousness?'

He shook his head. 'No. Luckily for us as a species, I think that's still miles off yet. Yule says they are talking through scenarios about the use of Pan in real-world situations. But she wants to talk about the Cap d'Antibes principles they came up with last spring and safeguarding. She thinks any use of Panopticon, any use at all, should be controlled by a two-key system. So no single person can use it or provide access,' he added when Tash looked blank. He leaned in closer to her. 'Apparently Eliot has access to Pan via his *phone* at the moment and it's driving Yule crazy. Torrent too.' He bit into his bread, staring at the polished surface of the dining table.

'Does it matter, in the end though, what Eliot does? Isn't the story of technology that someone always emulates it, or copies it?'

He paused, his eyes fixed in the middle distance as more staff brought out plates of starters to be shared along the table.

'In time, perhaps. But Eliot is a long way ahead of the game. He's a genius.' He caught a flash of scepticism on Tash's face. 'Yeah, I know that's often bullshit – plenty of billionaires have not-exceptional minds, but exceptional luck. Sometimes though there is an Eliot – someone who really has achieved a breakthrough no one else has got close to yet.'

'Jemima said something about Panopticon being able to strategise? Like brainstorming with LLMs?'

He buttered his bread thoughtfully, as if astonished to be holding something so simple and so ancient. 'That's like comparing the Matterhorn to the hill Belford is built on. I've seen that strategising in action this year, working with Yule. At the moment Panopticon is, well . . . imagine you had all the smartest people who have ever lived in one room. Shakespeare, Einstein, Tesla, Plato. Now imagine them working together, really happy, creative atmosphere, swapping ideas, building on each other's work.'

'OK.'

'So that's what Eliot has done: built the space for them to work together, with all the information that Pan has access to to inform their thinking. Though, it's not like they need to look something up. All that information is part of them. Part of the air. If you take away Panopticon, it'll be like all those great minds spread out across time and space again. Not talking to each other. Not sharing ideas.'

'You make Panopticon sound rather beautiful,' Jemima said. Tash hadn't realised she was listening to them. Neither had Perry. He sat up straighter in his chair.

'It is. It can be. It depends what you use it for.'

'But those people, the ones you chose to name,' Jemima said, 'they're all white men for one thing, so a very traditional Western idea of genius, and they are all people we like to think were morally good as well as brilliant, aren't they? So we sort of assume, without even thinking about it, that the work they would do together would be good. Great even. But what if it's not? Would your metaphor be any less accurate if you said Panopticon can be like having Vlad the Impaler, Stalin, J. Edgar Hoover and Machiavelli in a room, working together in harmony?'

He swallowed. 'No, Jemima. It wouldn't be. Interesting point.'

She smiled at him.

'Slippery fucking things metaphors. Make sure you're not secretly tricking yourself into a biased opinion, Perry.'

'But, Jemima, you're pro-Panopticon,' he protested.

'I'm pro it being used with the protocols we set out.'

Jemima turned away and Perry concentrated on his food for a while.

The plates were piled with smoked potatoes and pickles, cheese with butter mushroom and truffle sources, tiny salads of pale leaves and herbs. Tash had seen the greenhouses, photographed them, the delicacy of the gardeners tending and harvesting. She wondered if Inna and Klym were still on their smallholding, gathering summer fruits for lunch among the drone of insects.

'Did you know Brandon, Perry? The man who died here last year?'

He hesitated, and the truffled sauce he'd scooped up on his bread ran down his fingers. He set the crust down on his plate, wiped hands on the fine white linen of his napkin.

'A little. He was kind of an arse to the assistants. The work he did on AI image generation was impressive, Adobe would have killed for it, but I never really saw how it fitted in with Eliot's vision.'

* * *

As the plates were cleared away, Eliot nodded to the assistant with the iPad. She produced a folder from his backpack and began handing printed sheets out round the table. John Allingham flicked open his reading glasses and looked at his.

'Another Non-Disclosure Agreement? Eliot, I have enough of these to paper my room already. Is it really necessary?'

'It is,' Eliot said, unsmiling.

Allingham huffed, but signed anyway. The others did so without even bothering to read. Tash did the same. Given her relationship with Harry, this was all a lie anyway. Jemima read through hers, then borrowed Allingham's pen to sign.

'Thank you,' Eliot said once the signed papers had all been gathered in, and stood up. 'I have an announcement to make. As you know we are going to game out some scenarios over the next few days, looking at how Panopticon's advances in strategic planning might affect the services we offer to governmental and private clients, and how to manage oversight and accountability. I also want to give you some news for a bit of added context. Panopticon has, since yesterday, entered into partnership with one of its sister Notebook companies, Frank's Charter Security. I've been interested in ways in which Panopticon can lean forward, more actively assisting clients both in the digital realm and in the real with minimal intervention. Trials we've been running have produced excellent results. We'll brief further tomorrow evening; for now, take tomorrow to read through the scenarios and do feel free to discuss them informally, request any extra research, touch grass . . .' A few people smiled. 'I look forward to your thoughts, but I'm very excited . . .'

'You can have mine now,' Yule interrupted fiercely. 'No. That's a terrible idea. Panopticon is already a threat to civil liberties, but we put in safeguards. The biggest ones were no agentification, and no real-world action automation. Pan must not be allowed to take independent decisions and act on them. *Every* active step needs to be examined by humans, and cleared by humans with yes/no authority. That's the only way to make sure accountability is built in.'

'Eliot hasn't finished yet, Yule,' the Colonel said.

'He might not have finished, but he's stopped making sense. And you can call me Dr Collins, "Colonel".'

'Yule,' Eliot said, 'look, we'll run the scenarios with the human intervention and agentified versions of Pan, but you know how slow and cumbersome some of these guard rails make things. We're giving away half of the advantage Pan offers us with this endless box ticking and double verifications.'

'Our advantage, Eliot? Who's "we" here?' Jemima asked, her voice light.

'Merely shorthand for the advantage we offer our carefully and *ethically* selected clientele, Jemima,' he said.

'Christ, you can't even say ethically without sneering,' Yule said. 'How long have you been running these trials? What trials? Bloody hell, you had us all working our arses off coming up with a code of ethics, then you just fucking ignored it!'

'Calm down, Yule. Just take tomorrow to think,' Eliot said. 'Then we can convene to talk on Thursday. The trials mostly consist of automatically monitoring the digital space for enemy action taken to counter any Panopticon strategy. Then the agentification or ordering downstream actions in real time.'

Tash felt lost, but Jemima's face was tight.

'Eliot, this partnership with Charter,' she said. 'Might this agentification of Panopticon involve, say, Pan ordering Charter personnel to take specific actions? So Pan issuing instructions to human employees, downstream of the main goal?'

He nodded. 'Exactly, Jemima. Once parameters are set on an operation-by-operation basis. For example, say one of Yule's foundations needs a human agent on the ground. Maybe to give a bribe, or even check an area for mines. Yule, you can't go on every trip to action those deployments of money or personnel on a case-by-case, moment-by-moment basis. But under Pan's protection and guidance, Charter personnel could. Just take the day to think about it.'

'I don't need a day,' Yule said quickly. 'This is a terrible idea. Pan cannot operate without continual oversight. It is a machine, with no soul, no social contract, no sense of accountability. It can't be shamed, or put on trial or made to realise the moral consequences of its action, and that means you can't just ditch the guard rails for convenience. Those choices can be difficult. A human should be taking responsibility for them. Torrent, you must agree with me?'

The other woman hesitated, then shook her head. 'I'm going to take the day, Yule. Think it through.'

'Bullshit. No. It's just wrong.'

'I for one . . .' Allingham began.

'Oh, fuck off, Johnny,' Yule said. 'I'm not going to listen to one of your arse-kissing speeches about philosopher kings. Did you know about this, Jemima?'

Tash's fingers tightened around each other in her lap. Her mother looked calm, a polite but not entirely convincing smile on her face.

'No, Yule. This is the first I've heard of it. Eliot, what are your proposed checks and balances for this new phase? What is the nature of these trials? Do you have an org chart or any other material we can look at tomorrow about the relationship between Panopticon and Charter?'

Yule opened her mouth, but Jemima held up her hand, and to Tash's surprise, Yule stayed quiet. Eliot wrinkled his nose.

'Let's not get bogged down in the details now,' he said. 'We can talk about all that on Thursday, Jemima,' he said. 'Though, FYI, in my first company the org chart was me, then everybody else.'

'But this isn't a piece of business software. This is Panopticon, and if you're talking about integrating it with Charter, you are talking about weaponising it,' Jemima said.

The temperature in the room seemed to drop by several degrees.

He shook his head. 'No. You're being overdramatic. But the world is a dangerous place, and Pan can do so much to protect our way of life. We shouldn't have to work with one hand tied behind our back.' He looked at the Colonel. 'I recognise there have to be some safeguards in place, but . . .'

'Whose way of life are we protecting?' Yule said. 'Yours? Mine? Do you mean you want society to stay as it is now, forever, or are you harking back to some happy day when I couldn't get a credit card in my own name because I'm a woman? Why do *you* get to say who is protected and who isn't?'

'Because I built Pan,' Eliot snapped. 'That's why.'

Yule's eyes widened. The Colonel leaned back in his chair and blinked, his face neutral.

Jemima smiled. 'OK, Eliot. We're behind you, you know that, but coming up with a new way of managing Panopticon over a couple of days is a big ask. Even with me and John here.'

John and some of the assistants laughed politely and the tension in the room lessened a little.

'This week is just the beginning, Jemima. A chance to talk through hypotheticals so we can feel out the edges of the issues.'

'Work that should have been done months before you started any "trials"!' Yule exclaimed.

Eliot clenched his hands so he was leaning his knuckles on the table. 'I don't know if you noticed, Yule. But this is all pretty secret stuff.'

'And you have kept the secret well,' Jemima said smoothly. 'So you'll have to forgive us if we're all surprised, Eliot, won't you?'

Eliot controlled himself. He nodded. 'Good point. Yes. Yule, I'm sorry you're not hearing me, but I'm happy to talk about all the issues. I mean, that's why I invited you all here.'

Yule folded her arms across her chest. Her face mutinous. 'You're blindsiding us. Are you really asking anyone for advice or feedback any more, Eliot, or is this just a loyalty test?'

His face was flushed under his tan. 'That's enough now. Thank you to Jemima, Bethan and their team for this wonderful evening. I for one am going to get an early night, and I'd suggest the rest of you do the same. All the facilities are available to us tomorrow, even if we've had to reduce staffing levels a bit. Have a swim, work out. Take a class. Fill the well, people. Then we'll get into it.'

'Fill the well? You've got to be fucking kidding me,' Yule said. She got up from the table, her chair scraping loudly against the floorboards, and slammed out of the room while Eliot was still standing, watching her go.

Up in her room, Tash plugged in Monty's thumb drive and tried another half-dozen possible passwords.

Protocols
Guardrails
Notebook
Charter

While she did, she tried to understand what she had heard, the mix of jargon and hypotheticals made it all hard to get a grip on. She thought of the example Eliot had given of Charter personnel helping Yule's foundation. Monty sat in the window seat, staring at her.

'I know you'd understand all this. I'm sorry. I'm just pictures.'

He continued to sit there. Tash examined him, the solidity of him, his weight creasing the fabric of the cushion. She was watching her own mind at work, interesting when it wasn't frightening. She'd tried to touch him once, and her hand, not in on the illusion, somehow had travelled through thin air.

'Was it these trials, Monty, that you'd heard about? Monty, *why* were we in the woods that day?'

He didn't answer.

Her phone buzzed. A message from Harry.

Did you meet him?

Yeah. Interesting guy.

31

When Tash went to open her studio the following day, Eliot Drake was waiting for her, sitting on one of the benches near the fountain, his head tilted back so the sun fell on his face. He looked absurdly young. When he heard her footsteps on the gravel, he opened his eyes and smiled at her.

'You're early,' Tash told him, scanning her card on the reader by the door and pushing it open. He stood up and followed her, hovering in the doorway while she put down her bag and wedged the door open. 'Sleep well?'

'Like a baby,' he said. 'I always do here. And I've been meditating. Had a swim. I feel wonderful.'

'Good. None of the rest of the council bothering you with questions?'

He nodded sideways. One of the Colonel's goons was standing by the entrance to the ruins. 'He's been given strict instructions to keep people away until I've finished my morning routine. It's one of my favourite perks. Did you sleep well?'

'Fine. You done any photography before?'

'I used to. Before . . .' He shrugged.

'Before what?'

'Whenever I see a good view, one of my PRs snaps me looking thoughtful in front of it.'

She smiled in spite of herself. 'Do you want a coffee or anything? We can order from the kitchen or there's a kettle at the back there.'

'Tea!' He smiled suddenly. 'I like drinking tea when I'm here. What do you want?'

'If you can work a Nespresso machine I'll have one of those.'

He glanced at it dubiously. 'I can work it out. I'm a generation-defining genius, you know.'

Tash laughed, picked up one of the student cameras and checked the lens was clean and there was no film loaded, trying not to think about the fact a billionaire was making her a coffee.

'I had my people check the records,' he said.

'I'm sorry?'

'To see if we had any record of Monty Young contacting us or interviewing me in the old days.' He frowned at the coffee pods. 'He asked for an interview after we put out the Cap d'Antibes protocols, but we couldn't fit it in. Came to the conference about it though. His coverage was pretty positive apparently.'

'He was interested in technology and warfare.'

Eliot looked up, his expression friendly and bland. 'None of the companies I own or have holdings in manufacture drones, or anything like that.'

'Where have you been running your trials, Eliot?'

'Sorry, Tash. The world is at war. Can't say anything about that.'

'Hi, am I early?'

They both turned round to see Yule at the door. She smiled at Tash, then rocked back a little spotting Eliot at the coffee machine. He glanced at her. Then hit one of the buttons on the coffee machine and grunted with satisfaction as it began to whirr and hiss.

'Come on in, Yule,' Eliot said. 'Ceasefire during class about the business, though, yeah? Out of respect to Tash. Coffee?'

'OK.' She came in cautiously and set her bag on the table. 'I looked through your book last night, Tash,' she said, while Eliot set to work on another espresso. The kettle for his tea clicked off, and he jumped slightly. Then smiled at it, as if delighted by its helpfulness. 'It's amazing.'

'Thanks,' Tash replied, fetching and checking another camera.

Eliot brought over their coffees and retrieved his tea before sitting at the bench along from Yule. One of the assistants appeared at the door and Tash beckoned him in. Eliot didn't offer to get him a coffee. She put cameras in front of them and broke open a pack of ISO 400 films. Good for daylight. The canisters rattled in the cardboard boxes as she handed them out. Yule looked uncertain, the assistant intimidated, and Eliot was all bright, conspicuous attention.

Tash didn't go behind the desk at the front, seemed daft with just four of them in the room. 'Great. So we'll just go through the basics, the exposure triangle and some ideas about composition, then we can shoot in the gardens and ruins.'

She turned to the laptop to bring up the simple triangle of aperture, shutter speed and ISO. When she turned back Eliot had his hand up.

She grinned. 'You don't need to put your hand up, Eliot. What is it?'

'Just before we get started, I wanted to ask you something. That OK?'

Tash leaned back against the desk, folded her arms and nodded.

'If you could end war, would you?'

She hesitated. Next to Eliot, Yule stiffened. 'I reject the premise of your question,' Tash said eventually. 'You can't end war. Humans are violent animals.'

'What if you control them then?'

'Then they wouldn't be really human any more.'

He seemed to ponder this for a second. 'Maybe that would be best. Isn't that what being an altruist really is? Taking action for the greater good?'

Tash hesitated. He was looking at her expectantly.

'I'm a photographer. There are plenty of philosophers knocking around the place if you need one.'

He grinned and shook his head. 'Lived experience can provide a useful perspective.'

'For fuck's sake, Eliot. You are not God,' Yule hissed. 'You can't end war. And what happened to respecting Tash and not talking about work?'

'Just exploring hypotheticals, Yule. Some of the big questions.'

'There is no God,' Tash said, 'and sometimes I think free will is a bit of a stretch.'

Eliot studied her. She was beginning to recognise this particular look: open, friendly, but a certain stillness behind the eyes that was unsettling.

'Yes,' he said. 'I think free will can be overrated. Though, as long as people think they are free, maybe it doesn't matter if they aren't.'

'I said I thought it was a stretch, not that it was overrated.' He smiled, conceding the point with a lift of his eyebrows. 'If you want fresh perspectives, maybe you should invite in some of the protestors, like Jemima suggested.'

'It could make for a good photo, don't you think? "Eliot Drake meeting the people who want him dead".'

'It would,' Tash replied.

'Eliot, when did you start referring to yourself in the third person?' Yule tutted. 'And the point wouldn't be a photo op, it would be to listen to them, because they have just as much to contribute to the conversation as you do.'

'They really don't though. I mean, all human life is valuable, but let's not pretend. Some lives really are more valuable than others. Especially now I've put the kill code in. Mine's worth about seventy billion.'

'The kill code is a ridiculous, immature . . .'

He ignored her. 'By the way, Tash, I didn't even ask, have you fully recovered from your injuries?'

'Yes, thanks. I had excellent care.'

He pulled a notebook from his pocket and set it down on the table. 'Sorry. Back to the triangle thingy.'

32

The lesson went well, as far as Tash could tell. All three of her students were engaged and, she hoped, briefly lifted out of their own concerns, concentrating on light and focus. The day was sunny, but with frequent clouds passing high above, making fleeting shadows in the gardens, then in the ruins where she watched them experimenting with framing, using the empty windows, or scraps of ivy in the foreground. The assistant, one of Allingham's, only dared ask her anything when Eliot was out of earshot, and he seemed so hyperaware of the billionaire's presence, she wondered if he'd remembered to focus any of his shots. He handed her his roll of exposed film, and thanked her, then scuttled off. Yule shot two reels, asking Tash to act as a model for much of the second, then left without saying anything to Eliot.

He was working more slowly, and as he'd handed over his second reel she pointed out the knees of his chinos were stained from the grass.

'Good sign,' she said as she labelled the roll of film with his initials and put it in her messenger bag with the rest. 'No good photographer has clean knees.'

'Come back to the villa with me for a minute?' Eliot asked. 'We could have a beer?'

'OK.'

He got them out of the fridge himself and flicked off the caps then handed her one.

The kitchen in the villa looked domestic, if luxury. More of a snack station, Tash realised, seeing plates of cold cuts in the fridge with the beers, a basket of bread products and preserves next to the toaster. A large oak table stood on the slate floor and Eliot drew out a chair to sit down, inviting Tash to do the same. One of the Colonel's goons stood by the door, a human draught excluder.

'I bet you get asked what it's like to get shot at a lot,' he said. 'Does that mean you've got a good answer, or are you bored of the question?'

She smiled, turning the beer in her hand. 'I don't mind people asking, but it's hard to say. It's scary. Your heart beats faster, time does seem to slow down a bit. But it might only seem that way because the memories stay so vivid. But being shot at is different for everyone I think.'

'How come?'

Behind him the Colonel came into the kitchen. He didn't seem surprised to see them. He filled a glass of water at the sink and came to sit down with them, exchanging nods.

'I'm grilling Tash about war,' Eliot said. 'Go on, Tash.'

'You learn pretty quickly if you can take it or not,' she said. 'Everyone is afraid, especially at first. Some people freeze, other people keep moving, and you can't tell which one you are until you hear a live round zip over your head. Turns out I keep moving. I made a lot of mistakes when I first went out. But I was lucky, and the mistakes didn't kill me. Now I'm a bit smarter.'

'What sort of mistakes?'

'A white T-shirt is not a good idea in an area with sniper activity,' she said, and he beamed at her.

'And do bullets really make that zipping noise when they fly overhead?'

'Yeah. They really do.'

'Oh yes, rifle bullets anyway,' the Colonel interjected. 'The soundscape is different under mortar fire.'

'Any close calls, Tash?' Eliot asked, ignoring him.

Harry's team had got a lot right about these people. Tash supposed that should give her confidence. 'More than I'd like. I probably had a lot I never even knew about.' She paused. 'You know how often you're not in the room when big decisions about your life get made?'

'Like if your company fires you, or something?'

'Yes. I mean that I might have been inches from death a dozen times and never had a clue. Perhaps we got the good soldier at a checkpoint, not the psycho who was coming on an hour later. Or a mortar team decided to fire on the market instead of the café we were in.'

'Invisible terrors. Invisible saves.' Eliot drank his beer, looking past the goon through the window at the hazy, rolling countryside. 'The CIA, the British Secret Services – protecting us from those invisible terrors used to be their job. I don't think they can do it any more. The world has got too complex, but it is exactly those dangers I want to use Panopticon to protect us against. All the invisible terrors, the minefields we walk through without even knowing it. And normally they are impossible to see. But to Panopticon they are obvious! She tells us about them, then we can go out, clear up the minefield . . . Or go even further back. Stop it being laid in the first place! Who wouldn't want that?'

The Colonel cleared his throat, and Eliot looked slightly irritated, but stopped talking.

'That sounds like *Minority Report*,' Tash said, swigging her beer.

'It's a good film.' He sounded snappy. So someone just clearing their throat was enough to irritate him.

'And there was this of course.' She touched her finger to the scar on her cheek, and Eliot nodded, examined it. 'But there was one in my first month. A sniper opened fire on the car I was in. Probably Ukrainian friendly fire, the car had "TV" on the side instead of "Press". Russian vehicles often had "V"s on the side, so mistakes were made. One bullet smashed the lens off the camera I was carrying and buried itself in the back seat. Here.' She reached round the back of her neck and undid the catch on her necklace before pulling it off and giving it to him.

He cradled it in his hand, and she noticed for the first time how long and thin his fingers were. Like a pianist. A detail from the biography drifted to the surface of her mind. He'd played in his youth. She wondered what the world would look like if he'd become a musician instead of an engineer.

The necklace had two pendants. A bullet and a St Christopher medallion.

'That's the one,' she said, as he rolled it round his palm. 'I keep it for luck.'

'Shit.' He sounded awestruck. 'You know, I've never even fired a gun?'

'I keep offering to take him to the range,' the Colonel said.

Eliot ignored him.

'But you don't believe in God, Tash. Why the St Christopher?'

'For my Gran. She asked me to wear it, so I do.'

'So you believe in luck, but not God?'

'Everyone who's been in a war zone believes in luck. You see people who act like idiots and survive. Some people do everything right and still end up . . .' She trailed off, expecting to see Monty's ghost peering in through the window. She was ready to tell him she didn't mean him. He hadn't done everything right. He'd gone chasing after his contact, his big story, when they knew things were risky. Too risky. She breathed in through her nose, out through her mouth and realised that she'd seen Eliot do the same thing when controlling his temper in the workshop.

'Personally, I believe in training. Did you do any training, Tash, before you went skipping off into a war zone?' the Colonel said, and sat back from the table, arms folded.

'No, I just stuck a daisy behind my ear and put on my favourite unicorn sandals,' she snapped. 'Of course I did the training. I can flank a position and dodge into doorways like a Navy Seal. First aid. But you still need luck.'

The Colonel tutted and leaned back in his chair so the front legs came off the ground.

'Maybe.' Eliot handed her back the necklace. 'Or just complete situational awareness.'

'Well, I . . .' the Colonel began.

'I'll see you later, Colonel,' Eliot said.

The older man had the sense not to protest, just stood up and left the way he had come.

'Want another beer?' Eliot said, heading to the fridge.

'I'm good, thanks.'

He fetched one for himself, then went and picked up Tash's book from the coffee table at the other end of the room. Opened it as he sat down and cracked open his beer.

'Jemima's really proud of you, isn't she?'

'Yes, I think she is.'

'I hope she'll be proud of me too. In the end. But it would be criminal not to use Pan to her full capacity.' He looked up. 'Does it freak you out, my relationship with her? I mean, Jemima wasn't much of a mother figure to you, but she sort of has been for me.'

'It's complicated,' Tash said. 'But I'm proud of her. Or at least, I'm becoming proud of her.'

His gaze returned to the book. 'You're very honest, Tash, aren't you? It comes across in your work. And you are one of the few people I've met in the last few years who doesn't look at me like a nodding dog.' He bounced his head up and down, eyes fixed on hers, but with a slightly panicky, tight edge to his expression. She laughed.

'That's because I don't want anything from you, Eliot.'

He seemed to ignore the comment. 'Yule says what she thinks too, obviously. But I'm finding her energy a bit of a drag. Your mother told me once to take stock: when you come out of a meeting with someone, do you feel more energised, or less? If it's less, consistently, then the relationship isn't working.'

'Sounds a bit cold-blooded.'

'Are you calling me cold-blooded?' He pushed the book towards her, so sharp and sudden she flinched. 'You're the one who took a picture of your dead friend two minutes after he'd been shot, then published it in a book.'

'I didn't say *you* were cold-blooded,' she snapped. 'I said that way of assessing friendships was cold-blooded. I thought you were supposed to be a genius. Can't you understand a simple English sentence?'

Eliot's eyes narrowed and that flush of colour appeared again under the tan. Tash could feel her own cheeks, hot with anger, felt him study her. Then he laughed.

'You've got a temper! Me too. It's an issue I'm told I have to work on. Well, if we share a mother figure, I guess that makes us brother and sister. That felt like a sibling spat, didn't it?'

Tash picked up her stuff. She didn't want to be placated. There was something clear and comforting about being angry.

'I wouldn't know. I'm an only child.'

'Me too. You know that old question, if you had to choose a superpower between invisibility or being able to fly? What would yours be?'

She stood up. 'Invisibility, of course.'

'Mine too. I think Yule and Jemima would rather fly.'

'See you later.'

'OK. And Tash?' He waited until she was looking at him again before he went on. 'It's not always that they want something from me, that nodding-dog act, not always. Often it's because they are afraid of me.'

He returned his attention to the book, and she left. The body guard murmured something into his cuff as she closed the door behind her.

33

Ukraine, 2024

After the first night in Tash's rented room, she and Monty worked together whenever they could and shared their cars, rooms, and whatever beds they could find. Tash had never even known this kind of eager happiness existed. She'd woken on the second or third day, knowing they had to go to work soon, lying across his chest, worried that it could kill her career. Not the relationship, no one gave a toss about who slept with whom in the field, and both of them were single anyway. She was afraid she'd worry about him, and that would screw with her work. Luckily the next time they came under fire, she felt exactly the same mix of excitement, terror and focus she had always felt. And he knew how to handle himself.

Monty was secretive at times. There'd be hours when he'd work at the other end of the bar, head bent over articles in the WSJ, 404 Media, Wired and wouldn't say why he was interested in them. Times when he'd slide out of bed, and she'd wake and find him gone, only to see him pacing the balcony in the pre-dawn darkness, the phone clamped to his ear, or making notes by the blue neon wash of the sign over the club opposite.

The Big Story became a sort of running joke between them. She wasn't offended he wouldn't tell her what it was; it seemed, in the heat and pleasure of their days, to be a charming eccentricity. She knew it had started at a conference he was at a year or so previously. That his attention sharpened, differently, whenever a Russian target was killed on Russian soil. That was all.

She woke up one morning to find him hunched over the desk, phone in hand.

'It would be very boring if you were sending dick pics to other girls.'

He jumped, almost dropping the phone. 'I only have eyes for you, dear. Soz, didn't mean to wake you. I'm taking pictures of my notebook in case I lose it.'

'What, the cover?'

'The individual pages.'

She yawned. 'For your world-changing story?'

'You look like a cat when you yawn. I sense mockery. Yes, for my world-changing story.' He got up from the table and walked towards the bed. 'Let me show you how serious I am.'

He fell forward, full length on top of the mattress, which made her laugh then suddenly he did look serious. He tucked her hair behind her ear.

'Will it change the world, this story?'

He ran his hand over her bare shoulder. 'I'm not sure any story can change the world. I know I'm a bit romantic about being a journalist.' She made her eyes wide with mock disbelief, and his mouth twisted into a half-smile. She liked that half-smile. She liked his hands on her. 'I know, but I think we can push, question. At the very least set the cat among the pigeons.'

'Is that a known technique?'

'One of the best, actually. It puts people, organisations, ideas under pressure. And people show you who they are when they are under pressure.'

He slipped his arm under her, drawing her closer, then with his free hand, whipped the sheet into the air, so it fell over both of them.

'I'll remember that.'

'I've seen you under fire, Tash. And you've seen me. You know who I am,' he said, and then he kissed her.

34

Belford Abbey, 23 July 2025

Eliot played tennis after their beer. She saw him on court – a doubles match with him and Jemima versus Torrent and John – when she went out to hand over their films to the courier. The courier didn't turn up. She had her phone out, wondering who to call when Bethan came and found her.

'They've stopped him at the gate,' she said. 'Come on, I'll run you up there.'

They walked to her car in the parking area behind the court, discreetly screened by conifers.

'It was Jemima that got Eliot into tennis, you know,' Bethan said as they climbed into her Mini. 'She's helped him a lot.'

'Did you understand what they were talking about at dinner, Bethan? All this agentification?'

'Not really, I thought that was letting ChatGPT book a holiday for you. This seems a lot more serious.' She changed gear as the car climbed the slope towards the gates. 'I know Jemima's pissed about the kill code, but I'm not surprised he's a bit paranoid. The security services are interested in him.'

'Really?'

'Yeah, someone approached *me* a year ago. I was meeting suppliers for some of Jemima's product lines in Newcastle and this woman "got chatting" with me and made a pitch. Eliot was here at the time, and the Colonel was waiting in my office when I got back. Said he knew I'd been contacted by a "known agent". Freaked the shit out of me.'

'Did you tell Jemima? About the approach?'

'No. Didn't want to worry her. She has enough on her plate dealing with Eliot and the egos.'

Bethan drew up ten yards from the gate and they got out of the car. When the Colonel's goon saw them approach, he stood in the middle of the road. Hands clasped in front of him, legs wide, face impassive.

Behind him Tash could see a courier, surrounded by protestors. He raised his gloved hand in salute as he caught sight of her. The protestors, bored probably, began rattling their pots and pans.

'All right,' Tash said. 'Stand down superman, I'm just dropping off the films for the courier.' She handed him the jiffy bag.

He opened it, and pulled a clear plastic bag from his pocket. Each roll of film was removed from its little plastic canister, the canister shaken, and the film examined before it was returned and the canister went into the clear bag.

'For God's sake,' Bethan said. 'You're taking the piss now. This another of the Colonel's security measures?'

The goon remained impassive. 'Yes. We'll give them to the courier, Ms Bell. Have a pleasant evening.'

They returned to the Abbey. Bethan's mouth was a straight line as they drove.

'I hope none of the staff we still have see any of that – the going through stuff at the gate. It'll piss them off no end and I'm not sure we can manage if anyone else leaves. Emily will be off before Eliot leaves anyway, to play at the festival.'

'Push comes to shove, my gran taught me how to make a bed properly.'

Bethan grinned. 'I'll keep that in mind.'

As they left the car, they could hear the sound of the tennis ball being struck, hitting the ground, behind the conifer hedge.

35

Nisha served a buffet in the old kitchen for the assistants and staff, and another in the villa for the select few staying there. Eliot had only been there a day, and the tensions in the house made it feel as if the air was sliced with steel wires. You could cut yourself to shreds walking through a room and never know it.

Perry appeared, looking for Yule, her box of micronutrient pills clutched in his hand. She hadn't had supper at the villa apparently. Then he got a message, made a sandwich from the old kitchen buffet and headed off with it, his pill box and a sense of purpose. Tash wondered where Yule had hidden herself. When she'd finished eating, she followed the corridor past the silent treatment rooms and opened the door into the greenhouse.

An unusual sort of greenhouse. It was lined with palms and ferns, scattered over the heavy flags in huge pots, but at its heart was a vast swimming pool. It snaked through the greenhouse in a gradually widening and deepening river till it became a pool which extended through the open end of the structure into the garden itself. Beyond the edge of the greenhouse were loungers and low sofas, a natural water shower. More sheltered tables and chairs were also scattered among the palms and ferns. A discreet QR code on each one meant you could order drinks direct to the table.

Golden hour was approaching, and the uplighters in and out of the water were beginning to glow. Tash paused on the threshold of the room. All of Belford could feel like a fairy tale, but this place in particular seemed heavy with the potential for other-worldly encounters. The hour, between day and night. The water and solid ground, the way the pool and the far open end of the building meant she was both inside and outside the Abbey. A liminal space for trolls, demons and the fae folk.

And Yule had something of the fae about her, with her slight body and blue hair. She was sitting at one of the tables, the remains of her sandwich and a silver ashtray in front of her, a roll-up in one hand and a glass of whiskey in the other, her eyes fixed on the horizon and nothing at all. She glanced round as Tash came into the greenhouse and nodded.

'Hey.'

It could have been an invitation. Tash sat on one of the high-backed wrought-iron chairs at her table and got out her tobacco.

'Do you mind if I join you?'

'You English are so polite. It's a free country. And I'm hiding from John, not you. You don't witter.'

'Does he witter?' Tash asked.

'Sort of. I heard one of the maids say it and it's my favourite new English word. Like "wheesht". Your mum said that to John once and I could have kissed her.'

'Wheesht only works up north. Londoners wouldn't understand you.'

Yule shrugged, the movement hardly detectable under her oversized hoodie. Her fingers were painfully thin, pink around the knuckles and the cuticles red and bleeding. She shifted position and Tash wondered if she'd been caught staring.

'John's one of those men who think if they just repeat themselves again and again people will give up and agree with them,' she said.

Tash half-smiled, lit her cigarette and for a while they smoked in silence. Yule fiddled with her phone.

'Yeah, you're definitely not a witterer. How was beer with Eliot this afternoon?'

'Fine.'

'Did he ask you what being in a war was like?'

'It is what most people ask me,' Tash replied. Yule nodded, still looking towards the horizon.

'Most people ask me what it's like to be rich.'

'And what do you say?'

'Something facetious, or faux humble, you know. Amazing to have the opportunity to help people or some bullshit.' She turned towards Tash, observing her over the rim of her glass. 'I'll tell you the real answer if you tell me yours.'

Before Tash could reply the door to the main building of the Abbey opened again, and Fran appeared. She had two glasses on a tray. Yule tossed off what was left in her glass and placed it on the tray, taking off the two fresh glasses and handing one to Tash. Fran left with her thanks and the dirty plate. Tash raised an eyebrow and Yule waggled her phone at her.

'Joys of technology.'

'Thanks. Eliot asked me what it was like to get shot at actually. But you want to know about being at war in general?' Yule nodded, and Tash considered for a second. 'OK, the real answer is a cliché, but it's true. I was shit scared sometimes, bored a lot. Overwhelmed at others. But I felt very alive out there. Nothing mattered other than surviving, getting the pictures, getting them back to the agency. Whenever I came back to the UK, it was hard to do anything normal for a while. Paying bills. Talking to people about their partners or jobs. All the usual day-to-day stuff seemed so small in comparison to dodging bullets.' She tasted the whiskey and smiled. It was the American sipping whiskey she preferred. Lucky guess from Yule, or all part of the Belford service? The latter she guessed. 'It's made me impatient, and' – she thought for another second – 'brittle, I guess.'

'Fair enough. My turn?' Yule said and Tash nodded. 'Being rich saves time. That's all money is for in the end. Since I sold my company I haven't been grocery shopping, or clothes shopping or cleaned my house. I have a cat, but I don't have to empty the litter tray. I have a car and the tank is always full. I haven't had to wait in a queue or fill in a form for three years.'

'And what do you do with all that time?'

'Try and work out the best way to spend any given billion dollars. So I read a lot. Talk to experts. Lie awake at night crippled by existential dread. Can't find anyone to do that bit for me.'

Tash laughed. Dusk was coming on fast now, the sun setting behind the hills throwing up a feast of purple-pinks and greys into the sky behind it.

'You've used Panopticon for your aid work? This strategising?'

'Yes. It's been fantastic. First of all, we know the right people to talk to anywhere in the world. Pan has found us local experts, community leaders. The strategising takes a goal – build this road, say – and breaks it down into steps. Who to talk to, how to get the contractors we needed. But I don't know. Sometimes I'm afraid of machine learning, AI, all this stuff. It hasn't made us smarter or more efficient, it's just made us lazy. Creatively lazy, intellectually lazy, and now I'm worried it might make us morally lazy too. That's the key danger of Pan. Especially now.'

'When you used it . . .?'

She shifted in her seat and sighed. 'It gave great strategic advice. Told me to invite this person to a reception, send this person a "gift", flatter someone else and it provided a handy digest of his tedious books so I could do that. But *I* still had to do those things. Make the decision and have the party, or send the watch or have the conversation. Eliot . . . I'm afraid by using Charter, he's making it so I wouldn't even have to do anything other than press a button while he sips a craft beer on one of his yachts. Just hit select all and enter, and either Pan or Charter employees would do the rest. Then there's this "safeguarding in the digital realm" aspect. I'm not sure what he means, but I have my suspicions . . . Is he talking about safeguarding those personnel? How? It's impossible to hide in a world blanketed in CCTV where everyone has a smart phone and cloud photo storage.'

'You sound pretty unhappy about all this.'

'Something's gone wrong, Tash,' Yule said quietly. 'I think something's gone very wrong with Panopticon.'

She continued staring at the table, a rough mosaic of blue and white tiles.

'Why do you say that?'

'I used to have access to the system,' she said quietly. 'Not just the interface, but the back room. The whole tech stack – that's the set of the different frameworks and languages which make it work. Remote, then from 2022 only from the office in Palo Alto, but still full access. Then I realised I was quietly being shut out from parts of it.'

'Quietly?'

'Yeah. It's like . . .' she frowned, searching for the right words. 'OK, suppose you lived in a house, you know all the rooms. But when you look at it from the outside it looks like it's grown, like the walls are a foot taller and further apart. But the rooms inside all feel like they are the same size they always were. And, maybe, I don't know, there are sounds in the walls. Or odd echoes that didn't seem to be there before. That's what it feels like when I access the system now.'

'Sounds subtle,' Tash commented, watching her.

'It is,' Yule conceded with a quick smile. 'But I'm good at what I do. It's why I'm rich.'

'You must have asked Eliot.'

'Yeah. He said he was building in some new systems but they were too buggy to fully join up at the moment.'

'Don't you believe him?' Tash noticed her flinch.

'I did at first, but now I'm not so sure. Safeguarding, agentification, the capacity to let it "plan", to put together trials. . . . I didn't know anything about that. I think that's what he's been hiding. And I think it's dangerous.'

'And why are you telling me?'

'You signed the same NDAs I did and I have to talk it through with someone.' She shook her head and fell quiet for a moment, watching the shifting water in the pool. 'I wonder if Brandon noticed it too and that's why he was so miserable last time we were here. I thought he was just pissed that Eliot was spending so much time with the Colonel. Now, I'm not so sure.' She sipped her whiskey, her fingers curled round the glass. 'Brandon was a really good coder. The work he did on video analysis and manipulation was amazing. Hollywood loved him.'

'What was he like?'

'An idiot. Clever, but an idiot.' She said it with affectionate exasperation. 'But he had a heart of gold. Kind too, but used to drive me mad, you know. He'd go to strip bars and become convinced some girl or other there needed rescuing. But he wanted the best for people. Romantic. Lots of ex-strippers with good degrees now, thanks to the unofficial Brandon Wallace Scholarships.'

John emerged from the changing room area in long swimming trunks, a towel over his shoulder and nodded to them before heading towards the deeper part of the pool. They fell silent for a while, watching him, with their cigarettes in hand, as he began to swim in and out of the greenhouse, doing a disciplined front crawl. He swam well, the water receiving him without complaint.

'Good. You scared him off,' Yule said. 'It was typical of Brandon to die while high and going to look at the stars. You know the kill code was his idea? I think he just said it as a joke. "Eliot, people would kill to get their hands on this . . ."'

'And it really can't be broken?'

'It would take years.'

'Eliot must have written it down somewhere.'

She shook her head. 'No way. He'll have used his memory palace thing – it was his party trick at school and we used it to go card counting in Vegas.' She smiled briefly. 'That was fun until we got banned. We'd fly up for the weekend from the Bay and stay awake forty-eight hours straight. I used the winnings to bank roll my first start-up.'

John had paused at the far end of the pool, staring out at the darkening sky, and the first stars scattering across the vault of heaven. Then he turned and swam back towards them.

'Can't you talk to your assistant about all this?' Tash asked. 'He seemed smart.'

Yule was watching John climb out of the pool. He was a lean man, better muscled than Tash would have imagined.

'No. Perry is too much of an Eliot fanboy. Anyway, he's so obsessed with the idea of artificial consciousness he can't seem to understand it's the least of our problems. Not in a world where Panopticon exists.'

John had picked up his towel. He wandered past them, running his eyes over the drink and the ashtray, but didn't comment on that, or any shred of the conversation he might have picked out.

'What about these trials Eliot's been running?' Tash asked when John had disappeared back into the changing rooms.

'Yeah. He has developed superpowers, so of course he wants to use them. I was an idiot to think he'd abide by the Cap d'Antibes protocols, or talk to me or Jemima first. The Colonel has been whispering into his ear about "taking action" for a couple of years now. So he'd be all for it.'

'The Colonel seems to be getting a bit nervous now.'

The darkness was thickening over their heads, deepening the shadows between the plants around the edges of the greenhouse.

'Really?' Yule said, blinking at her. 'Jesus, how far would Eliot have to go to make him nervous?' She crossed her legs, folded her arms across her chest. 'And John's been telling him he is somehow qualified to make "hard decisions", whatever the fuck that means. They're telling him he's a philosopher king – our great techno-feudalist leader– and I think he's believing them.'

'What does Jemima tell him?'

Yule snorted. 'How to run meetings. No. She made him a much better CEO, and she's tried to make him a better person. I like her, she has a decent moral compass, and I know Eliot has always really respected her, but I think her help has made him more . . .'

'More what?' Tash said quietly.

'I don't know. Better at pretending to be a good person, maybe. God knows what tomorrow is going to be like.'

A murder of crows passed by, cawing to each other and silhouetted by the last light in the sky. Yule watched them, and Tash thought her expression was of longing.

'Eliot told me he wanted to be invisible when he was a kid. That was his chosen superpower,' Tash said idly. 'Mine too.'

Yule's jaw tightened, and she started to roll another cigarette, her fingers acting automatically while she focussed on something else. Tash could almost see it happen. The cascade of thoughts, the connections being made.

'You OK?' Tash asked.

'Fine. I'm fine.'

The fingers holding her cigarette began to shake and she set it down, unlit.

'Yule?'

'No. I don't know. I'm freaking out and that should be Torrent's job.' She started picking at the skin around her nails, pushing one nail under the skin surrounding another. A fresh bead of blood appeared and she sucked it. 'You reminded me of something, something Eliot . . . He told you the best superpower would be invisibility, yes?'

'Yes, he did. So what did I remind you of?'

'Something else he could have been hiding from me in Panopticon.' She shifted in her chair, leaned forward, staring at Tash.

She's trying to see if I think she sounds mad, Tash thought.

'Look, Eliot and the Colonel were messing about when we were here last year, before Brandon died. I was smashing John at chess while they watched and the Colonel said something about my white knight. I don't know, there was something in the bro chuckle they had over it. I wondered if it meant something. Started looking for references to white knight in Panopticon, as a phrase or the number they start on on a chess board – B1 and G1. It was after that Eliot shut me out of the system.'

Tash couldn't see the connection. 'What's special about the white knights – in chess I mean?'

'Nothing. Well, nothing in particular. White normally has the advantage in a chess game because it plays first, but more than that? I mean, if you're playing against someone who is not that good, the way the knight moves can be very hard to predict, it seems to come out of nowhere.'

Yule went still. She wasn't just thin, she was gaunt. Like an anchorite locked in her cell, eating nothing and praying for all humanity. She stared up at the stars.

'So Panopticon makes everything visible,' she said. 'The whole world's an open book to it. But what if it could make people completely invisible too. What if Eliot is . . .?'

'I don't understand,' Tash said.

Yule got hurriedly to her feet. 'Sorry, I have to go.' She shoved the tobacco and papers into her pockets. 'I can't be right, but with John and the Colonel whispering in his ear . . . Why else would he mention that superpower thing?' She leaned forward, her hand on the back of Tash's chair like she needed the support. 'He used to listen to your mum, Tash. She could make him laugh at himself, you know? Maybe she can get through to him. I can't. And John just says what he thinks Eliot wants to hear.'

'Yule,' Tash said, reaching for her arm, feeling the tension in her arm muscles through the hoodie. 'What was he like before?'

The question stopped her in her tracks.

'Funny.' She smiled again. 'He used to be quite sweet in a dorky kind of way. Shit, I don't know. I was thinking about the difference between him and Brandon before you came in. Both of them had that macho saviour-complex thing. Brandon wanted to save humanity one stripper at a time. And he'd boast about how smart they were, how well they were doing.' She blinked rapidly and looked up. The sky above the greenhouse was full of stars now. Too many to name. Numbers too big for the human mind to wrap itself around. 'Eliot wants to save humanity too, I'm sure of that, but *he* wants to do it. You know, I can't work out what matters more to him: that humanity is saved, or that it's *him* who saves it. I don't know, whatever was off in him before, Pan has warped and twisted it somehow into something monstrous.'

She pulled away. 'Night, Tash.'

Tash climbed the stairs back to her room an hour later, settled in one of the armchairs by the empty fireplace, her laptop open. She switched off the Wi-Fi and Bluetooth before she clicked Monty's thumb drive into the port. On her Finder window the drive appeared with its single unnamed folder. She doubled clicked, her mouth a little dry and the slightly old school window appeared as usual telling her a password was required. 'Whiteknight', she typed, and the window shimmered sideways and the computer beeped, sullen and absolute. 'Whitenights'. Again, the beep and shudder.

Tash thought about passwords, how you were always told to use numbers as well as letters, how Monty, who was brilliant and mercurial and someone she had loved, was also lazy at times, impulsive – reaching, at least at first, for the first thought, the first idea. 'WhiteknightsB1G1' she typed. And the folder opened.

Nights were still short at the end of July, and the chill dawn began lightening the window as Tash read. Notes from interviews with American veterans, with CIA and SIS contacts. What looked like background conversations with professors at MIT, start-up founders. A list of what looked like made-up words. Notes from the same biography of Eliot Drake that Tash had read. Notes about the Colonel.

And all handwritten. Monty had photographed each page of his notebook and stored it here, the files numbered 1, 2, 3, up to 142. The words swam in front of her eyes. She read each page, then read them again, her frustration mounting. Nowhere had Monty written down what his story actually *was*. She went through again. A page of dates, phone numbers. Not all his shots were in focus. Only one image had any other sort of file name, it looked like the sort of code given to photographs taken with an iPhone. Something Harry once said drifted into her mind.

We had to send a friendly FBI officer to take pictures of the hard copy . . . She opened it. A shot of four men in military fatigues, and centre left was the Colonel.

36

The security guards at the Abbey Villa opened the door for her with a nod and Tash walked through the house into the kitchen where she'd had a beer with Eliot the day before. Yule and Eliot were both sitting at the main table, toast and coffee in front of them, little bowls of jam and marmalade, milk jugs and sugar bowls, repurposed hand-painted tin cans holding cutlery.

'Your prints,' she said, setting them down.

At the other end of the room, among the leather sofas, Torrent sprawled, reading from her laptop. Yule pulled her folder towards her and started flicking through it.

'It's like Christmas, isn't it?' she said. 'You have to wait and see if you got what you wanted.'

Yule grinned, suddenly and wide, joyful. 'Look!'

She pushed the opened file towards Tash and Eliot. It was a photo of Tash against the ruin, and the sky, spattered with clouds, giving the frame the feel of an epic western. Tash's eyes, and the neat scar on her cheek were in sharp focus. The broken stone of the ruins, the grass, even her hair, slightly soft. Tash was on the left of the frame, her shadow inked behind her on the stone and she looked . . . stunning. She looked young. She looked like someone thinking of something both painful and beautiful at the same time and she realised, looking at the print, that this was how Monty had seen her. And that was why he had loved her.

He had been dead now longer than they had known each other, and the terrible cruelty of that realisation made her lean forward and touch her fingers, tented, onto the table to support herself.

'That's a good picture,' Tash said.

'That is . . . ,' Yule replied with relish, 'a fucking amazing photo. Look, Eliot!'

He put down his phone and grinned. 'Nice.'

They had forgotten, in that second, they were enemies today. Then Yule remembered and she closed the file, tucked it under her arm.

'Thanks, Tash.'

She picked up the last bit of her toast. 'See you in the dining room.'

Tash sat down heavily at the table, exhausted. A long night, then the shock of that photo with the Colonel. Eliot had pulled his own file of prints towards him now.

'Do you prefer working with film?' he asked as he opened it.

Tash struggled to focus. 'Different tools for different jobs. But I do love working with film. It's like writing with a pen; a sort of enforced slowness is useful at times.' She thought of Monty's notes. Drake. Panopticon. Charter. Colonel. They were on every page. Tash was living in the middle of Monty's story, whatever it was.

Eliot grinned, lopsided, and pushed his hair back off his face. He looked rested, relaxed.

He studied the first print, then turned it towards her. To her surprise she saw another image of herself, this time crouched down next to the assistant. In the foreground the edge of the fountain and the waving grasses of the flower beds were out of focus, and she liked the way it was impossible to tell what she and the other student were looking at.

'Good.'

'But if you were going to criticise?' he asked.

'The composition is a bit flat, and I like the blurring in the foreground, but maybe it hides too much of the image. There's something slightly voyeuristic about it. Not that that's a bad thing. A lot of street photography has that vibe.'

'Appropriate for a photo taken by a man who owns Panopticon,' he said, dry, and unruffled by the criticism.

Another half-dozen shots of the garden followed. Then another, again with the voyeuristic vibe, of Torrent sitting in one of the gazebos, studying her iPad, her expression, mostly hidden by her hair, intense and concentrated while the garden seemed to bloom and thrive in a desperate attempt to get her attention.

'I like that,' Tash said.

'I should call it "the broader picture". Something Torrent obsesses over. Whenever anyone says money can't buy you happiness, I think of her.'

'I'm right here,' Torrent said from the sofa, without looking up.

'And are you rich?' Eliot called.

'Yes.'

'And are you happy?'

'Not particularly,' Torrent replied and Eliot smiled.

'Does money make you happy, Eliot?' Tash asked.

'Not in itself,' he said, turning to a shot of the ruins, 'but I like the things it gets me. They make me happy. Being tired at the end of a day makes me happy. Doing meaningful work. It's like your mother says . . .'

'Meaningful work?'

He blinked up at her. 'What I do, what I have done, is meaningful. What was it that philosopher John likes said? Archimedes – "Give me a lever long enough and a fulcrum on which to place it, and I can move the world." Well, I've invented a long fucking lever.'

Torrent called up from the sofa. 'He was a mathematician, not a philosopher.'

'All the better.'

'I'm not so sure,' Torrent said, shutting her laptop. 'Mathematicians describe what's possible, it's the philosophers who work out how best to respond to those possibilities.'

Eliot's upper lip twitched, but he didn't reply, just turned over another sheet, and then stopped. Tash glanced down to see what had caught his attention. It was a colour picture – it looked, in fact, as if it had been enlarged from a smaller print, the details were a little fuzzy. The copy of a copy. It didn't show anything from Belford though. It was the image of a group of men in US Army fatigues standing in front of a jeep. Four of them. All unshaven.

The man in the middle of the group was unmistakably the Colonel, though a good decade younger than now.

'What the fuck?' Eliot said.

Tash shook herself, looked. 'That's the Colonel, isn't it?'

'Yes. I know this picture.' He peered at it again. 'Or a version of it. Frank has it on his office desk. That guy on the right of him is an old friend of his. It was taken when they were serving together in the Special Operations Group.'

'The what?'

'Covert military operations for the CIA, recruited from Navy Seals mostly. Very hush-hush, but the things he's told me . . . The version on his desk is cropped though. Just him and the guy on the right. And what the hell is it doing here?'

He dropped it and thumbed out some message on his phone, rearing away from the picture slightly as if it were contagious.

Tash picked it up, and turned it over.

'The Newcastle lab didn't process this. Look, the paper stock is different.'

'So?'

'So someone must have come in and added it to your folder when it was in my classroom. The prints are left there first thing every morning. Is it, I don't know, a gift?'

'Why would I want it?'

'Jesus, Eliot, how should I know?' Tash said.

Her irritation gave him pause. 'So you didn't . . .?'

'I have no idea where it's come from. Why would I be interested in pictures of the Colonel? He's not my biggest fan. Maybe this is his way of telling you not to waste time farting around with cameras or something.'

Eliot took the picture back and stared at it. Torrent had got up from the sofa and come to join them, her hand on the back of Eliot's chair, leaning over his shoulder.

'He might do that,' she said. 'Weird way of sending that message though, isn't it? And subtle is not really his thing.'

'And why this version? With the extra guys?' Eliot added.

'Do you recognise them?' Tash asked.

'Never seen them before in my life.' He glanced over his shoulder at Torrent and she nodded. 'Do me a favour, Tash, and shut the door, will you?'

She did so, and glancing back she saw him take his phone out of his pocket, unlock it with his fingerprint, then tap the screen. By the time she returned, he was unlocking another app on his phone and hovering it over the photograph.

'What are you doing?'

'Perks of the job,' Torrent answered for him. 'He's seeing who the Colonel's friends are.'

He tapped again and after the lag of a few seconds, a calm woman's voice began to speak.

'Norman Peter Jakes was born in Points West, Michigan, in 1981, the second son of Norman and Cassie Jakes.'

'Skip to military service.'

'Certainly, Eliot. Norman was a member of the National Reserve from . . .'

'Was he a Navy Seal?'

'No, Eliot.'

Tash held her breath, afraid if Panopticon knew she was in the room, it might stop speaking.

'What about the other guy?' Torrent asked. 'On Frank's right.'

'Is Torrent an approved participant in this conversation, Eliot?' The phone asked.

'Yeah, yeah.'

'OK, Torrent. Robert Halls was a National Reserve guardsman from 2012 to 2020.'

'Is that Panopticon?' Tash asked.

'Is Natasha Bell, photographer, an approved participant in this conversation, Eliot?'

'What? Yes. Pan, where was this photograph taken?'

A moment or two of silence. Then it spoke again. 'It was taken two miles north of the US–Mexico border in southern Texas, while all four men pictured were serving in the National Reserve.'

Eliot plucked at the rings of wooden beads around his wrist. The silver accents sent a spatter of reflected light across the ceiling.

'Is this photograph available online, Pan?'

'No,' Pan replied and Eliot's face crumpled in rage.

'Who could have added it to the folder, Tash?'

She paused, thinking. 'Anyone. The classroom is unlocked in the mornings.'

He lifted his phone again. 'Pan, run checks again on everyone who has been in Belford today. Just the building itself. I don't want to know the sordid history of the protestors.'

'What am I looking for, Eliot?'

'Any connection to the Colonel.'

Another few seconds of quiet.

'Cleaning staff: Jane Marshall is the Colonel's third cousin twice removed. They have never met and appear unaware of the connection. Bethan Jones and the Colonel were in the Savoy Grill for the same half hour in 2014. 27 July. The Colonel owns two paintings by Charles Porter. He attempted to sell one on the private market in 2023 and was unsuccessful. The Colonel is closely associated with Panopticon and Notebook and has had frequent contact with you, Eliot, and your guests here at the Abbey. Would you like details of one-on-one communications between John Allingham, Yule Collins, Torrent and the Colonel?'

'Go ahead.'

'The Colonel and John have met for drinks in London seven times over the last three years. In September of 2024 the Colonel messaged Torrent "Stop freaking Eliot out with your paranoia." Torrent texted back "That is literally my job."' Eliot glanced up and he and Torrent grinned at each other. 'Yule emailed the Colonel in March of 2024. Quote: "Fuck off with your bro shit." The Colonel responded with a laughing emoji.'

'That'll do for now, Pan. Sleep.'

'Acknowledged.'

'That's fucking terrifying,' Tash said, looking at the phone.

Eliot nodded. 'So I'm told. It's just code though.'

'Eliot, have you ever run a Panopticon search on the Colonel?' Torrent asked.

He looked at her steadily. 'No point. I told you, the Special

Operations Group the Colonel led were covert. Pan still doesn't have access to the details, just weighted speculation. Anyway, Troy Huntley vouched for him.'

'Troy Huntley?' Tash asked.

'Former director of the CIA,' Torrent murmured. 'Now a non-executive director of the Colonel's company. Charter. I think he has stock options.'

'I trust him,' Eliot said.

Torrent folded her arms. 'Of course, so do I, but when you say he vouched for him, do you mean he wrote to you confirming details of the Colonel's service record? Or just at dinner you asked about him and he was like "Oh, yeah, Frank! Good guy!"'

Eliot looked grim. 'The latter.'

'Huntley could have known him through the private military contractors,' Torrent said. 'He did three, four years with Silver Hawk, didn't he? And they worked with the CIA.' Eliot nodded. 'You must have those records, Eliot.'

'Wake up, Pan,' Eliot said to the phone.

'Hello, Eliot.'

'Pan, did the Colonel meet Troy Huntley before or after he was employed by Silver Hawk?'

'Possibility for error occurs, but it appears the Colonel met Troy Huntley after he took up a management position with Silver Hawk.'

'Fuck.' He pulled at his bracelet. The loops of it slid easily over his hand and then he flung it on to the table top. Tash stared. Not a bracelet at all, but a set of prayer beads.

'Are you going to speak to him?' Torrent asked.

'Yes, of course I am,' Eliot said quickly, standing up and taking the file. 'Now.'

They watched him go, then Tash felt the other woman's gaze move to herself.

'Where did you get that photo from?' she asked.

'Nothing to do with me,' Tash said. 'You are the ones who've known him for years.'

Torrent nodded. 'That's true.'

'What's with the prayer beads?'

'The Colonel told Eliot they belonged to Abu Bakr al-Baghdadi. The Islamic State leader. The CIA took him out in a covert op in 2019. The Colonel said the soldiers who killed him took the beads from his body and gave them to the Colonel, as a thank you for his leadership on similar ops. Then the Colonel passed them on to Eliot.' She spoke very calmly, then took out her own phone and held it over the unspooled beads. 'Hmm. Some very similar ones are available on Etsy.'

'Did Panopticon just tell you that?'

'No. Only Eliot can access Pan through his phone. I used Google image search. Maybe al-Baghdadi had an eye for a handcrafted bargain.'

'They represent the ninety-nine names of God, you know, the beads,' Tash said, staring at them.

Torrent sighed. 'Yes, I know. Who wants to tell Eliot 'Drake' isn't one of them?'

37

Tash met Jemima coming from the main house on the edge of the ruins.

'You were at the villa?' Jemima said at once. No smile.

'Yes.'

'What the hell happened? I just saw the Colonel and Eliot in the garden. Eliot looked like he wanted to kill him.'

'Something about his service record, I think. Eliot's just found out the Colonel wasn't in the Special Operations Service after all.'

She told Jemima what had happened that morning. Her mother's face was tight with concentration as she spoke, then, when Tash had finished, Jemima surprised her by putting her hand on her arm, and leaning forward so her forehead touched Tash's shoulder.

'Do you know where that picture came from, Tash?'

She hesitated a fraction of a second. 'No.'

Jemima straightened and looked at her watch. 'Do me a favour. Distract me. I'm supposed to go in there and be a calming influence, but Eliot is scaring me. I need to shake myself out of this.'

'Scaring you how?'

'He's fixed on doing this deal with Charter, and Yule is right. The idea of marrying up Panopticon with a private military contractor is horrific.'

'I thought the Colonel just supplied security guards.'

Jemima shook her head. 'No, they do paramilitary operations. Like providing security for some of Yule's projects in areas where the governments are unstable or out of reach. Education in Afghanistan, road building in the DRC. But distract me!'

'How?'

'Anything.'

Tash cast round for a subject. 'OK. Why lilac? Why is that your signature flower?'

'I . . .' Jemima froze, then smiled. Her full beam smile. 'Because of you, Tash. The day you were born. It was 15 May and you were born just before dawn. I had a private room, and I was sitting with you in my arms by the window and there was a lilac tree outside. It was only for a couple of hours. Then your dad and your grandparents came and they took you.'

'Mum . . .'

Jemima turned away with a half-laugh. 'Well, that was certainly a distraction.'

'Mum, I'm sorry I ever thought you didn't care.'

Jemima put her hand on the half-ruined wall next to her. Her pale hand with its perfect manicure formed a strange contrast with the old stone, blooming with yellow grey lichen.

'That's OK, Tash,' she said. 'It really is. That's the reason, anyway. Go on. I can't go in there weeping either.'

'OK. What was Dad like?'

Jemima blinked and looked at her.

'Surely Nancy and your Grandad told you all about him?'

'Yes, but I mean, what was he like really? You know Gran. Dad and Jesus were always in a run-off for top position in our house. In her telling, he was a saint. I want to know what you thought of him.'

Jemima folded her arms across her chest, looked out across the gardens.

'He was funny. And he had his own car. That seemed pretty cool. My parents were very middle-class, very uptight about "what people would think" so I was raised to be constantly anxious about doing the right thing. Then I met your dad, and he didn't give a toss. He was loud and impulsive and enthusiastic. I loved the energy of him.'

'Gran made it sound like he spent his life helping the poor or in prayer.'

Jemima snorted. 'I mean. She's not wrong. He would always lend a hand. And if he saw someone homeless he'd not just drop a quid or buy them a sandwich. He'd sit down, have a conversation. My mother would have died rather than sit down on the pavement and split a tinny with some guy. But he wasn't pious about it.' She studied Tash's face. 'You have his nose. Definitely.' She breathed in steadily. 'Thanks, Tash, that helped.'

'Bethan told you to call me Tash, didn't she?'

'Yes, that's OK, isn't it?'

Jemima's attention drifted to the villa behind Tash. A door slammed. Tash turned in time to see Eliot striding off into the gardens. The Colonel came hurrying after him, calling his name. For once Tash did not taste something bitter, and her heart rate remained steady. She realised Jemima was watching her.

'I guess the session will be starting late,' she said.

'Can you' – Tash was surprised by her sudden need – 'can you tell me any more? About Dad?'

'He liked birds.' Then she laughed, seeing Tash's expression. 'No, actual feathered birds. He picked me up once for a day out and I thought we were going to Newcastle or whatever, but he had sandwiches and tea and took me to a nature reserve to look at birds. He had this really heavy pair of ancient binoculars he'd bought at the flea market. We hadn't really cottoned on to eBay back then.'

'Weren't you bored?'

'No. Back then I would have been happy spending the whole afternoon just looking at him. I was sixteen and very much in love. But he talked about them in a way that made it interesting too. And the sandwiches were good.'

'He got that from Grandad. He had a thing about the birds on his allotment. God it was like the fifties, growing up with them. Battenberg cake and allotments.'

'Yes. But you got out of there. Like I did.'

They went in through the side gate and both paused, looking towards the villa. The security men standing either side of the door.

'Yes,' Tash said. 'Into a war zone and a luxury prison.'

'Clever us,' Jemima said and leaned into her again so their shoulders touched. 'I better go. I'm glad you are here, Tash.'

'More grenades flying around than there were in Ukraine,' Tash said, and Jemima smiled. 'Good luck, Mum.'

'Thanks. By the way, your publisher forwarded some fan mail. It's in your studio. I'm afraid the Colonel's men opened the package.'

38

In the silent studio, Tash flicked through the bundle of envelopes the package from her publisher contained. The Colonel's men hadn't bothered opening the individual envelopes. She paused at one in a pink envelope addressed to her as Tash, rather than Natasha, in a girlish, looping script. She opened it.

Dear Tash,

I was surprised when I got your email or at least when I got the email from the bookshop man, but I suppose I never asked Bethan not to say anything. I guess it's nice you seeing the flowers and asking, because I never get to tell the story about how good Brandy Boy was to me, because, well, you'll see. Wow! It's weird writing an actual letter, like something out of an old film.

I didn't have much luck when I was young, it was all kind of messy with my family, you know. Long story, but I ended up stripping at Spearmint Rhino. That was OK, I guess. And well you've seen dead people and stuff, so I guess you won't be shocked, but I did a couple of pornos too when I was too young and stupid to think of what that meant. I was like eighteen, maybe? Anyway, I was twenty-five when I met B in SR and getting sick of it. The money was good, but I was bored and like, that can be dangerous, you know? Brandy was a nice bloke – I love an American accent – and we got chatting for real. I said I wanted to be a nurse. I was sick when I was like seven, and got more love in the hospital than I ever did at home, but I reckoned there was no chance. Especially not with those pornos out there. Total cringe. But he encouraged me. And we were friendly on and off for a bit, not just at the club. (That's not really allowed, but everyone does it.) Anyway, he was sweet and helped me apply for the course and paid all my fees and then some. I guess he was one of those men that like to keep girls grateful, but I was grateful! And he was never anything other than nice to me. No weird stuff, you know? Vanilla. Romantic. I was still worried about the pornos – there were clips all over Pornhub and stuff – but he said he was working on that, then one day he turns up at my flat and tells me they're gone. I look, and he's right! Not a sign of them. Funny, some of the scenes were still there, but the girl performing didn't look anything like me any more. Some of them looked a bit weird, like in a game. I was so happy I burst into tears! I'd like it if you didn't tell anyone about the pornos, but I wanted you to know Brandy deserves his flowers, and I'll keep sending them. I think he did the same for a couple of other girls too. I mean, I always knew he had lots of girlfriends. Millionaires do, don't they? Anyway, anytime I look now, if I see a girl who looks a bit weird, I think – I wonder if that used to be one of Brandy's other friends? I like to think the flowers are from all of us.

I'm in my second year now and it's going well.
With warmest regards,
Star

Interesting. She'd got Star's email from Bethan's computer during their morning of photography, and emailed from the bookshop before she met Harry in his post-Paris meltdown. She looked up to see Monty sitting where Eliot Drake had been the previous day.

'Proud of me?'

His ghost did not react.

Tash sat down behind her desk and read it again. Brandon. Image manipulation. Great for regretful porn stars, but how did that fit in with Panopticon? This couldn't be anything to do with the story Monty had been interested in. He had talked about tech and warfare, not Hollywood or visual effects. What had Brandon done, for Star? Then she realised. He'd made her invisible.

Tash texted Harry.

I'm bored. Fancy a coffee?

And got a smiley face and a thumbs up in return. Then she rehearsed what she planned to tell him as she biked up the road. Star. The Colonel's stolen valour. Monty's notes were on the thumb drive in her pocket, but she wasn't sure about handing those over yet.

Doesn't your gut tell you to trust me?

Maybe I don't trust my gut.

What did she trust these days? Old friends, and the instincts of old friends.

The last bit of the road to the gate was on a gentle slope. She'd found if she freewheeled down it, the tracker on her bike activated the gates, allowing her to glide through without dismounting. Today though, they didn't.

She put on her brakes, and one of the Colonel's goons stepped out of the gatehouse.

'Are you going into town, Ms Bell?' he said. Pleasant smile, and aviators like Eliot's.

'That's right.'

He nodded. 'I'll call up your escort from the main house. Should only be a couple of minutes.'

'I don't want an escort.' She said it loudly. The goon glanced over his shoulder to see if the protestors still camped outside were listening.

'I'm afraid we have to insist, ma'am. It's for your own safety and the safety of everyone here.'

'You can't keep me in here against my will.'

He took off his glasses now, his eyes were bright green and edged with crow feet, but he was not soft bellied like the men she had spotted at the entrance to the ruins.

'I have no intention of doing that, Ms Bell. If you do not wait for the escort from the house we will open the gates. As the bike is the property of Belford Abbey we can and will insist it stays here.'

'Then I guess I'll walk,' she said, adding an American twang.

'Then I'll come with you. There's no law against me following you, Ms Bell. It causes us some inconvenience if you won't wait. But you're not going alone. If you don't let me follow you, or if you shake me off, you will not be allowed back on to the grounds while Mr Drake is in residence.'

'What, because of those guys outside the gate?'

'I have my orders. I don't need to know the reasoning behind them. Now will you wait for the escort?'

'No.'

Tash got on her bike and headed back towards the Abbey.

'What is it, Tash?'

The Colonel had emerged from the villa on to the terrace. He had shaved properly today, but there was still strain around the eyes. 'I don't like leaving the meeting.'

'Surprised you are in it at all, given what happened this morning. You're a fake and Eliot knows it.'

'I asked what you want.'

It was warm today, the sky clear. 'I don't want anything from you. I want to go into town and your goon at the gate' – she jerked a thumb over her shoulder – 'he said I had to have someone following me.'

'Yes. If you must leave the park, we don't want you to go alone.'

'Why not?'

'Because, sweetie,' he said with an acid grin, 'it's a dangerous world full of naughty people. I have to look after Mr Drake and if that inconveniences you, then, well, I don't give a shit actually. You can leave on your own, but if you do you won't be allowed back into the park. I don't care whose daughter you are.'

'You think I'm going to catch "protestor" out there, like Covid or something?'

'These are the protocols. If you don't want an escort and need something from town it can be fetched.'

'I'd like someone to bring me a sense of personal liberty, please.'

He stepped off the veranda, pushing her back, and put his hand round her throat almost lifting her off her feet, keeping her off balance. She choked, head back, unable to breathe.

'I've had just about enough of you, you little bitch. I don't know how you got that photo, but I'd bet my balls it was you that put it in the file. We've looked after you, for Jemima's sake, but her usefulness and our patience is not never-fucking-ending.'

Her back slammed against the ancient curtain wall which fringed the ruin, then he released his grip and took half a step back. She bent forward, coughing and sucking in air. He watched, his face still purple.

'Am I understood?'

She pulled in another breath, retched.

'I said, am I understood?'

She held out her hand. 'Yes! OK. Understood.'

He waited until she had stood up straight again, then walked back to the villa. The two security guards by the door hadn't moved an inch. She glanced at the security camera which gave a view over the terrace and this end of the ruin. The assault, that sudden hand round the throat, the way her body was propelled across the turf and slammed against the wall would all have been hidden from view by the solid square body of the Colonel. He must have learned something about camera angles since he assaulted that creep at the strip club.

Tash steadied herself against the ancient stone. Then sat down heavily on the nearest chunk of masonry and pulled her tobacco out of her pocket. Her neck hurt. Brian Duffield had picked her up by her neck once at school when she was twelve and he was fifteen, just lifted her off her feet and set her aside. That hadn't left a mark, but she remembered the sense of utter powerlessness. She felt the skin under her jaw. This might bruise. And she would cover it, she realised. She would find a scarf, or a shirt with a high collar. Why? For Jemima. Because whatever she was dealing with, seeing those bruises would make everything harder.

The scars we hide in the name of . . . love. Yes, love probably.

She thought of lilac, then lit her cigarette and turned sideways, leaning against the sun-drenched stone so the two guards at the gate could see her. A small act of defiance. Let your boss assault me then. See if I care.

Monty's ghost was sitting on the terrace, beer in hand, watching her. But when she lifted her cigarette to her lips, she wasn't shaking any more.

Her phone buzzed. Harry, his message a single question mark.

She wrote back.

Sorry. Got held up. Maybe better next week.

Three dots.

No worries.

She went back to her studio and thought. About Harry, about Monty and his notes. About Star and Brandon and Wilf's cameras.

About what 'better next week' actually meant. She took out the thumb drive and plugged it into the computer in the studio and went through the pictures again. She switched her phone into incognito and looked up a couple of the dates. The assassination of a Russian pro-war writer. An ammunition dump exploding. She looked at the next image. And the next.

Monty had written a date at the top of one page. And underneath 'confirmation trials'. Then 'WK'. That must mean White Knights. An exclamation point, on its own and so large she hadn't noticed anything else on the page when she looked last night, but now she zoomed in, and examined the bottom of the page. 'Romantic', Monty had written. Then alongside it 'Story title? The Altruist'.

And Tash finally understood.

The knowledge, the sense of the pattern becoming a picture, came on her so suddenly and with such violence she thought she was going to be sick. She stumbled to the sink at the back of the room, ran the cold water, letting it chill the dumping blood at her wrists, then pictured Eliot's face and spat into the vortex of water disappearing down the plughole.

When she finally emerged, Eliot and John were sitting at one of the small tables in the walled garden, leaning against the blush brick stone as the light softened.

'Hey, Tash!' Eliot called out. 'Come over here, would you?'

She did, not rushing. John and Eliot both had one of Nisha's concoctions in front of them. Tall glasses, paper straws, a pale-lime-coloured drink decorated with mint leaves.

When she was ten yards away, she knelt and took their photograph. Eliot mid-sentence, his hand raised, palm up. John inclined towards him, eager, smiling wide enough for his perfect teeth to be exposed.

'Always working, aren't you, Tash?' Eliot asked. 'Hope you get your shot tonight.'

'What's happening tonight?'

'We're having a couple of Luddites to dinner. Jemima selected them. When she told them they wouldn't be allowed to bring in their mobile phones, some of them refused to come!' He laughed. 'Luddites! Who won't be separated from their mobile phones!'

Tash didn't join in the laugh, though John did, and Eliot looked annoyed.

'Well, I thought it was funny. One of them coming refuses to carry a mobile at all. I suppose he's pure of heart at any rate.'

'What happened with the Colonel?' Tash asked. 'You seemed pretty pissed at him this morning, but he was back in the meetings by lunch.'

Eliot sipped his drink through the striped straw. 'Oh, yes. Well, he did exaggerate his experience, but your mother always taught me to judge people by their actions.'

'He lied about his service record. That's an action.'

'I mean their actions towards me,' Eliot said pettishly.

'It's you he lied to.'

He set his drink down. 'Leave it, Tash.' Tash bit her lip and he continued more mildly. 'Look, perhaps he exaggerated, but I remember when I claimed all things about Pan which weren't true when I was first touting for business. And my lies contained a truth, even if they were not exactly true at the time. I'm very happy to be working with the Colonel, and I might not have hired him if he hadn't spiced up his story at first.'

'So the ends justify the means?'

'Often. Something we've been discussing at length today.' He stretched like a cat.

'You're wearing the beads again,' Tash said.

'I think they mean more now, rather than less,' John said, his voice dark honey.

'How so?'

'None of your business, Tash,' Eliot said, returning to his drink and stabbing at the ice with his straw. 'I just want to remind you, that anything you learned about the Colonel's service record is covered by the NDA you signed. Actually, both of the NDAs you've signed. Anyway, see you at dinner.'

'How are the talks going?'

'Fine,' Eliot said, though his tone suggested they were not. 'Though Yule and John keep repeating themselves at higher volume. I should go play tennis, just get the executive summary at the end.' John drew breath, but Eliot held up his hand. 'Yeah, yeah. The process is important. See you at dinner, Tash.'

Tash took the bike out again, up to the gate to hand over her films of the day to the courier. There were a lot of canisters to send off for processing. The goon, shaking the canisters and dropping them into the clear plastic bags, didn't comment. Tash and the waiting courier exchanged waves through the arch at the park entrance, then she headed back down for a shower before dinner.

39

The dinner with the party of Luddites was a success, from Eliot's point of view at least. A man and two women were ferried down from the gatehouse in one of the SUVs. The man, young and earnest, stuttered and stared when he found himself opposite Eliot. Eliot relaxed, and tried to draw him out, listening to him with every appearance of attention and grace. The women had tended to veer off into cul-de-sacs of conspiracy, which he greeted with polite bafflement. In the end it was Yule who got pissed off with them, leaning on the table, yelling at them that they were missing the point. Asking them what they thought of surveillance in society, then growling with disappointment when one of the women said she was getting shadow-banned on Instagram. They were all focussed on Eliot's wealth. He talked about the foundations. Declared he was happy to pay more tax.

Tash's pictures of the evening would be excellent. Eliot, seated, flanked by Yule, Torrent and John. The Luddites opposite. Neither Harry's angry shadow nor the pissed-off journalist had been invited. As the discussion became heated, the man pushed his mask to the top of his head; it was a carved face, caught in a pout and with more regular features than his own. The pictures would show Eliot as a sympathetic and beautifully lit still point at centre of the storm of argument around him. They would remind viewers of Renaissance paintings of Christ on trial, caught between his disciples and the Pharisees, in the midst of things yet somehow above it all, watching, with sorrow and sympathy, the passions of mortals playing out around him.

A shiver of rage and repulsion went through her, like a current.

* * *

Night. Only a sliver of moon in the sky, and that half-hidden by the trees. The darkness in front of her was perfect, a solidity. Tash took the path to the north-east, slowly at first, letting her eyes get used to it, then pushing faster as she climbed. When she turned, finally, near the top of the slope the house was already far behind her, tastefully washed by uplighters, the ruins and pele tower only visible by the jagged darkness they cut out of the field of stars.

There had once been a circle of stones here. Now only two remained, covered in green-grey lichen, five yards east of a stand of thick-trunked oak trees. One stone was tall, narrow. Its last remaining companion lay on its side. Tash took the long, thin case off her shoulder, then set up her tripod and camera, pointing them down to the house and the ruins, adjusting the frame so the sentinel stone appeared on the left of the frame. These stones were here when the Abbey was built – when the first monks arrived and put up wooden shacks, hired stonemasons and began to work. They were here when the monks were thrown out, and watched as the walls crumbled and the Palladian mansion appeared. They would be here, Tash hoped, when those walls came down too. She sat on the stone, holding the shutter release cable, studying the outlines of her mother's domain. Still as the grave. She pressed the release, hardly breathing while the shutter remained open, one long second after another, gathering in all the light it could. Seeing more in the dark than she did. She wanted to make Belford look as if it were drifting free among the stars.

She felt, more than heard, him arrive, a shift in the silence rather than a sound.

'Hey, Harry,' she said quietly. 'No sign of movement at the Abbey. I think we're alone.' He sat down carefully beside her. 'How did you get over the wall?'

'Four years in the army. And a grappling hook.' She shivered and he moved closer to her, instinctively sharing his body heat. 'It was easy to find a convenient blind spot with that picture you took of the security guard's screens. Thank you.' She didn't say anything. 'So you OK, Tash?'

'Not really. I underestimated the Colonel.'

'Tell me everything. Start at the beginning.'

She started with what else she'd learned about Panopticon's strategising. Then Eliot's decision to go into partnership with Charter. And the Colonel's stolen valour.

'I see.'

'That's it? I thought you'd be more shocked.'

'No. Plenty of people claim to have been in special ops, so that is not a huge concern. On the partnership with Charter? I'm not shocked, but I'm worried. It depends how good Charter's people are.'

Tash looked at him sideways. 'It's easy to think the Colonel's a joke, but I don't think he is. And he has deep pockets, doesn't he? I mean, with the private security detail half the point is to hire people who look the part. It's like Wilf said, it's about making people feel safe. He could hire serious professionals when he needs them, couldn't he?'

'Yes.' He looked out over the moon-shadowed landscape. 'Yes, he could.'

'There's more.' She told him what Eliot had said about protecting agents in the digital realm. 'I think Panopticon can wipe people from the record, from the internet, in real time.'

She heard his tiny intake of breath. 'That's impossible.'

'I don't think so, Harry.' She told him about Eliot's favourite superpower, about Yule's memory of white knights which came from nowhere, then what Star had said about disappearing from porn videos thanks to Brandon, and the Colonel apparently admiring the landscape alone on the video feed when she had seen him talking to a man under the trees. She reached into her backpack, pulled out one of the elegant Belford folders. 'There's a print of my photograph in there, of the Colonel and the man talking. And there's a picture of the still from Wilf's screen there too.'

'Bloody hell, Tash. This is good stuff. Can you get the matching footage too?'

'I don't know. But search for that man, and I bet you won't find him. The other picture is him at the gate. The Colonel has embedded him with the protestors, I think. It's easy to test my theory, just upload the photo to the cloud and see how long it lasts.'

'I thought you'd be observant, Tash, but this is exceptional work.'

'That's my job. And I'm not just doing it for you.'

She could feel the warmth, the solidity of him. The muscles and flesh under his clothes. Hear his breathing. There was comfort in it.

'For Jemima?'

'Her too in a way, but mostly for Monty.' Harry didn't move, as if he was scared he might startle her back into silence. 'Monty was investigating Eliot. I thought he was just interested in him in a general way, another billionaire he'd come across when he was a tech and national security reporter for *The Times*. But I was wrong. I think Monty's big story was that Charter has been training soldiers to work with Panopticon in Ukraine. And I think they've been going on active missions into Russia using Panopticon strategies, and under its protection. Those are Eliot's trials; that was Monty's story.'

He was silent for a moment. 'But how could Monty possibly know . . .?'

'He had a source, Harry. In the inner circle. The whole reason he went to Ukraine was to find proof. Someone on the ground was letting Eliot do whatever he wanted there in exchange for strategic help – probably targeted assassinations in Russia, attacks on ammunition dumps and airfields in Belarus. Of course they'd let Eliot and the Colonel play with their White Knights for that sort of assistance; they need all the help they can get.'

'Tash, it can't be possible,' he said. 'We'd know. We'd see them. We're not Panopticon, but we're not stupid either. Neither are the Russians. There would be chatter, photographs.' She could feel his breath on her cheek. 'I'm not saying we'd identify operatives before they struck, but we'd be able to trace the ripples back at least.'

'I just told you. They're invisible. His White Knights are being wiped from the record as soon as it is made. But we know they exist, don't we?'

'We do?'

'I met them. It was Eliot's White Knights who rescued me.' He flinched, but said nothing. 'The men that drove off the Russian patrol weren't MI6. You did your best to cover, Harry, but I could tell you didn't know what I was talking about when I asked why the British Secret Services didn't just call in the favour I owed them. You didn't have a clue about what actually happened in the woods that day.'

'You are good at noticing things.'

'Like I said, it's my job.'

'OK, Tash. You're making a compelling case.'

She bit her lip and gave herself a moment, looking up into the night sky before drawing breath to go on. 'But the thing is, the thing that means you have to take Eliot Drake down, Harry, is I don't think that patrol was part of the Russian military either.' She swallowed. 'I think they were White Knights too and they put on a little play for me and Karin. Panopticon probably suggested it. "Goal: to prevent publication of Monty Young's story, without arousing the suspicions of the British Secret Service, and protecting Natasha Bell. Step 1: Contact Monty Young. Pretend to be one of the White Knights who is having a crisis of conscience and is willing to talk. Step 2: Give Monty Young coordinates for a meet. Step 3: Execute Monty Young, then swoop in to save the ladies while firing blanks out of your AKAs." '

'Didn't they sound Russian? The patrol who killed Monty?'

'Yeah, they did. But Panopticon is international, isn't it? Not like they'd have any trouble recruiting a few Russians out there. More money. Work for Eliot Drake not Putin.'

'So you really think it was a set-up?' He sounded cautious.

'Yes. They found out that Monty was getting close, then Eliot and the Colonel murdered Monty. Karin and I were saved, because I'm Jemima's daughter, and Eliot is fond of her.'

What makes her so fucking special?

She saw those men again, crouching by Monty's body.

'They took Monty's notebook. Then a week later Brandon was killed – here – falling from the pele tower. Monty doesn't name

Brandon as a source in his notes, but something must have given him away. He wrote 'romantic' on one page. That's what everyone says about Brandon. So they worked it out and murdered Brandon too. Funny. Mum was distracted just before he died because she'd heard I'd been injured. Maybe, if she'd been able to help Eliot control his temper that week, he wouldn't have killed his friend.'

She thumbed a tear from the corner of her eye, then got up to adjust the angle of the camera. When she turned back, there was Harry by starlight, sad and beautiful as one of the marble watchers in the entrance hall of the Abbey. She sat back down beside him.

'Monty was a spy once,' she said.

Harry put his arm around her shoulders. It felt good and she let herself relax, just for a moment. She was desperate to rest.

'He must have trusted you to tell you that. Yes, he was. Promising too. But it wasn't for him.'

'How much of this did you already know, Harry?'

He hesitated. 'We suspected Ukraine had access to other help, beyond us and the Americans. Some sort of elite group of freelancers, and what you said about your rescue gave us a lead. Those targeted assassinations within Russia need very specialised resources as well as high quality intelligence. But we found nothing. No trace of them. You might call them White Knights, but we talk about ghost attacks. We hadn't . . . We hadn't got close to connecting them to Panopticon and Drake until you turned up and asked why we weren't telling you to act grateful.'

A shape, low and fast, moved across the grass below them. A fox, quick as thought. Almost invisible.

A light appeared outside the Abbey, a torch, moving back and forth over the grass. They froze, waiting, till it turned the corner. A routine inspection.

He sighed as the light disappeared. 'You know, there was an analyst at GCHQ who suggested the possibility of footage being automatically overwritten in real time. He thought he'd caught it, a couple of times, an erasure. From footage taken in Moscow last year. Just looks like a tiny glitch. We sent him on holiday. Finding those alterations will be like looking for a needle in a haystack. But the needle is invisible and the haystack is the billion hours of footage that is generated every day.'

She watched the passage of clouds across the sky and took another frame. Another minute of exposure. The camera would see more stars than she could.

'I want Eliot Drake on trial. Him and the Colonel. For plotting the murder of a British citizen.'

'That's what I want too, Tash.'

'Do you swear to me, Harry, you'll see justice done?'

'I swear.' He said it softly. 'I'll do everything I possibly can. Why?'

She handed him the thumb drive. 'Here are Monty's notes. I worked out most of the story about the training from there. The password is WhiteknightsB1G1.' He almost snatched it from her, tucking it into the inside of his jacket. 'And I think I can provide a much smaller haystack for GCHQ to look through for altered footage.'

'What?'

'The film from the night Brandon was killed. Someone went up the tower with him and pushed him off, so you will be just looking through a few seconds of material as he goes through the exhibition area. Maybe finding that will make it easier to see where other changes have been made elsewhere. And I think I can prove it was Eliot, so even if you can't reconstruct the original footage from the glitch, you should still be able to arrest him. I'll run tomorrow. Be there.'

'I will. Anything you need from me?'

'What happened to your French friend?'

'She disappeared a few days ago but we managed to speak before she left. She has some theories of her own about the collapse in France. Beyond alerts getting cut off . . . I thought they were insane, but after tonight, I'm not so sure.'

'Tell me?'

'I will when Eliot's gone, or under arrest. Till then, Tash, honestly, it's probably best you don't know. And you have to get back to the house.'

'What are the French going to do?'

'They have no evidence, and no idea what to do about it, but – three of their citizens killed during the riots, they've been humiliated on the international stage, suffered catastrophic financial loss. It's fair to say they are out for blood.'

She heard the click as the shutter closed.

'So am I.'

PART III

The Wild Hunt

40

Friday, 25 July 2025

Tash headed down the stairs to the first floor in her running gear. The night lights flickered on as she descended, laying a subtle carpet of light at her feet to guide her through the dark. She walked through the staterooms, through the drawing room where she had watched Jemima talking to her guests on the day she arrived, then down the main staircase into the entrance hall. It was one part of the house Jemima and Bethan hadn't modernised in anyway, leaving it as the first owners had intended. A chequered floor, fringed with statues of gods and virtues, elegantly draped, some turning away from passing visitors, marble fingers to their cheeks, others, clutching spears or clubs, staring out, defiant. One, Mercury judging by the wings on his sandals, reached out a hand to her. His expression was such that she felt sure he was bringing bad news. The one that reminded her of Harry.

She opened one of the concealed doors to the servants' corridor, near the entrance, and walked to the half-open door of Wilf's little office. One of the Colonel's men was sitting in Wilf's chair.

'Morning,' she said, scratching at the door. He span round.

'Morning, Ms Bell.' American, like his boss. Not one of the pair who had witnessed him throttling her yesterday and done nothing. 'You're up early. Can I help you with something?'

Tash wrinkled her nose. 'Yes, I just wanted to check, the park is closed today, isn't it? The Colonel didn't change his mind about letting people in . . . I wondered because of the festival in town tomorrow . . .'

'No, ma'am. The park is still closed. Have you seen someone here who shouldn't be?'

Tash hesitated.

'Always best to speak up, ma'am.'

'Yes, of course. I thought I saw a woman from my window. She was going round the far side of the pele tower. White coat. Scarf round her hair. Might just have been a trick of the light.'

'White coat, you say?' He was already picking up his jacket from the back of the chair. 'I'll go take a look.'

'Can't you just . . .?' Tash waved vaguely at the monitors.

'There are some gaps in the coverage there,' he said firmly. 'If you don't mind waiting here?'

Tash nodded helpfully and he left.

She had five minutes, she reckoned, to find the files she needed. She worked quickly, one eye on the other screen as the soft pings and rippling thumbnails showed the guard's progress across the front of the house. He disappeared out of range of the cameras.

She got the section showing Brandon climb the stairs, the sideways lurch which could have been a drunken stagger, but could have been him being shoulder-barged by someone. His sideways look, which could have been him looking out of the window, could have been him speaking to the invisible man.

Then the second section. Twice as important. She was still searching as the screens began to ripple and ping again with the goon's return.

Got it.

Eliot climbing up the tower, his left hand on the rail. Eliot going up the arch which led to the roof. Eliot returning. She imagined the path of the security guard back through the house. In through the east wing side door, past the old kitchen.

Come on, come on.

Done.

Now just the fragment that proved the erasure of certain people, the selective blindness of the system. The clip of the Colonel admiring the landscape which Wilf had shown her. Monday 21 July.

Footsteps echoing in the silence of the corridor.

The goon turned into the room. 'Ms Bell?'

Tash was leaning up against the bench by Wilf's mini-kettle.

'Find anyone?'

He shook his head.

'Sorry to waste your time.'

'Always better to speak up, Ms Bell.'

'That's reassuring,' she replied with a tight smile and walked out of the office. The tiny thumb drive Harry had given her fitted into her phone socket. She transferred the footage as she walked. Then headed for the garden, pulling down the sleeves of her running jacket, her fingers brushing the leather band.

41

Kyiv, 2024

A last weekend in Kyiv before the ground froze solid and they had to return to Donetsk for the grind of the winter offensive. Tash had spent the morning adding to her portfolio of shots of Kyiv, this time in the Monastery of the Caves, photographing the worshippers in the small chapels and the bodies of saints set into alcoves, to the sound of the Orthodox chant, which always hovered on the edge of discordant but remained somehow other-worldly.

Monty had been meeting contacts in the capital. Another angle on his big story. When they met for dinner in a restaurant by the golden gate he was puppyish with excitement.

'I have confirmation. Well, partial, and I can only say government source, but it lines up with what I've heard from my contacts back home. Big step forward.'

'Still not going to tell me what it is?' she asked. They were drinking wine tonight rather than beer, and the table had a cloth over it and a fake flickering candle. The waiter approached and they ordered. Steaks and dauphinoise. As if they were in Paris.

'No. But it's a morality tale for the technological age. What happens when we move fast and break things.'

'What happens?' She put her chin in her hand. Made her eyes wide.

He grinned at her. 'Things get broken.'

'Monty!'

'Sorry.' He laughed. 'I don't mean to be a dick. I suppose it's about power, and what people do with it. Road to hell paved with good intentions.'

It was a good restaurant. A bit cheesy perhaps. The waiter came and refilled their wine glasses, and a trio of young women came out on to the small stage at the far end of the room. They wore head-dresses of dried flowers, and full embroidered skirts.

'Bet you twenty quid they'll sing the "Carol of the Bells" first.'

'I'm not taking that bet.' The song had appeared in a million Christmas adverts over the years, a haunting chant which sounded like a peal of bells sounding in a snowy landscape. Tash had been in the country long enough to know it was originally called *Shchedryk*, Bountiful Evening, and was a carol of new year. The song of a swallow flying through a house, promising the inhabitants a bountiful spring once the winter was over. The women began, singing in Ukrainian, and she and Monty remained silent and listened.

'So is your article just going to be a collection of vague proverbs?' she said over the applause which followed.

'I think that should do it – no, it's going to be full of solid investigative reporting. Sort of thing I became a journalist to do. So far most of my career has been rewriting tech press releases, or chronicling the horrors here. This is going to be different, but I can't give you much more than a thematic overview till the thing is fully sourced and written up. But I have a lead now which might take me all the way there.'

'This is very frustrating.'

'I know. Soz. Let me distract you with presents. You're a girl, that'll work, right?' She stuck her tongue out at him, and he slid a packet wrapped in tissue paper across the table towards her.

'Are you proposing?'

'No.' He fluttered his eyelashes. 'I assume when I ask you to marry me, you'll want one of those staged proposals with doves and shit. And a videographer there ready to capture your surprise for Instagram.'

'Ha, bloody, ha.'

'I had the meeting, and I was on the way here and I passed a stall on the way back and . . . Look, just open it.' He was blushing.

Tash unfurled the tissue paper. A bracelet of thin braided leather straps with a simple silver clasp. Unshowy. Well made. Perfect.

'Did I do good?' he asked.

'Yes,' she replied, and put out her arm so he could fasten the clasp for her. 'You did very good indeed. I love it.'

She stood up a little so she could reach over the table and kiss him. He put his hand to her face. 'Tash . . .' Then he stopped. 'Food's here.'

42

Belford Abbey, 25 July 2025

Tash headed to the gate at the back of the walled garden and found the Colonel and one of his men waiting for her among the lavender and roses. The Colonel's man was in running gear.

'Morning, Natasha,' the Colonel said coldly. 'You're later than usual this morning.'

Tash stared him down. 'Yeah. Thought I saw someone from my window. Told your colleague. He didn't find anyone.' The Colonel would have had that report in the next three minutes anyway. 'But why are you waiting for me? I'm not going into town, just my usual river route.'

'Greg here will be running with you this morning,' the Colonel said. 'As your route takes you out of park grounds, and given the presence of the protestors—'

'You have got to be shitting me!' Tash exploded. 'They are on the other side of the park! And you met them. They are about as dangerous as a nasty cold. And I like to run alone. And how do you know what my route is?'

He smiled thinly. 'Nevertheless. We don't want anyone bothering you.'

He was looking at her neck, searching for the bruises he'd left there. The collar of her running top was zipped up to her chin.

'You won't know I'm there, ma'am,' Greg said.

'Don't fucking "ma'am" me, I'm not your boss. This is ridiculous.'

'It's happening,' the Colonel said.

'Fine! Come on then, Greg. And watch your feet. Hate to have you trip and fall flat on your face.'

Greg remained stony-faced. 'I'll manage, Ms Bell.'

Tash pulled open the gate and set off at an easy warm-up pace, leaving the Colonel with his thin smile to watch them go.

Harry would be waiting at the bridge, Janice, or whoever was covering the run, ready to take her phone.

Harry's a spy, she told herself. There's that long stretch in front of the castle – he'll see me coming. See I've got a goon with me. She began to plan, and her pace picked up. Greg stayed behind her, not crowding her and running with a light tread, matching her pace, but still close. Bodyguard close.

When they reached the broad swathe of green, the castle reaching up its turrets into the sky, she sped up, pushing herself. She had no hope of outrunning the guy. He remained at exactly the same distance behind her, and as her breathing started to strain, he was running without any apparent effort.

Shit.

They plunged into the copse on the far side of the castle at speed. The bridge was just ahead of her. No Harry. No Janice. Good.

She hissed and clutched her side, her hand inside the pocket of the thin running jacket, palming the tiny drive. She put her hand on the first post of the handrail and bent over, panting.

'You OK, Ms Bell?' Greg asked. Not even a ghost of breathlessness, the bastard.

'Stitch. Give me a sec.'

What did she have on her? Nothing. Her phone. Her key card for the gate.

That would have to do.

She straightened up, pulling it out of her pocket as she did, letting it fall at the bottom of the post.

'Your key card, Ms Bell.'

'Oh fuck, yeah.' She crouched down, hoping like hell Harry or Janice were watching from somewhere, picked up the key card and left the tiny memory stick in its place in the grass.

'Feeling better, Ms Bell?'

'Yes, thanks.'

They set off down the path again at a slow jog. Harry would go for the drive at once, surely. But even if he found it would he know what he was looking at? It was the second part which was key. Eliot going up the stairs, his hand on the newel post. Then coming back down.

Three miles through the woods, then the loop back, turning it over in her mind, trying not to look for Harry or Janice. Finally, on the rise leaning back to the gate to the gardens, she slipped, going down hard on her left wrist.

Monty's body lay in the grass beside her. She stared at it, tears pricking her eyes. She wanted to stay, just lie there next to him, even if he was dead, even if he was a dream – she still wanted to stay.

'Do you need a hand, ma'am?' Greg was standing over her.

'I'm fine. I'm fine.'

She struggled back on to her feet.

She got a text message from Harry an hour later.

How you doing? Fancy a coffee?
Words have gone well today.

Went for a run today, almost broke
my wrist. Still busy. Next week?
Might be at fair thing tomorrow.

Oh yeah, soz, you said. *Thumbs up.*

43

When the delivery arrived Tash was on the villa terrace, waiting for a chance to photograph the Council of Heaven on their break. First, she noticed the security goons on the terrace speaking into their wrists, touching their earpieces, until one went into the villa and then re-emerged with a sense of purpose in his stride and opened the wrought-iron gate set into the curtain wall. A couple of minutes later she heard the crunch of wheels on the west track, and a pair of delivery men walked through, carrying a large, flat wooden crate between them. They took it into the flagged entrance hall of the villa and Tash followed, watching as the purposeful goon signed the clipboard then saw them out again. The delivery guys left quickly, turning away from Tash's camera as they did. Strange. People tended to stop and stare when they came in here.

Eliot emerged from the dining room, his assistant at his shoulder and the rest of the council following him.

'I'm so sorry I missed it, Eliot!' Tara protested. 'I've never dealt with Henri before, so I thought it was spam.'

He turned on her. 'You thought an email from my art advisor, confirming I wanted the *original* Pollock sent here, for no fucking reason at all, was spam? Seriously? Get your shit together, Tara.'

'I will, I . . . I'll call Natural Le Coultre now. Perhaps the delivery crew can turn round. Surely, it's a mistake.'

'Has it been scanned?' the Colonel asked.

'Usual checks at the main gate,' one of the goons replied. 'Came up clean.' The Colonel was examining the edges of the crate, peering at the heads of the screws holding it together. 'We wanted to consult before opening it fully, Colonel, given we understand the item is of considerable value.'

'I think this has been opened and resealed,' the Colonel said. 'Natural Le Coultre normally put wax over the screw heads. Eliot, perhaps it would be best if we opened it in a controlled environment.' He looked over his shoulder. 'We have protection suits on site?'

'Yes, sir.'

Eliot glanced at Tash. 'I feel lucky. Forget that shit, just open it up.'

'But, Eliot . . .' the Colonel protested.

'Your man said it went through the usual checks at the gate. That means swabbed for explosives or anthrax doesn't it?' The Colonel nodded and Eliot looked around. 'Anyone hear anything ticking? No? Then let's look at it.'

Tara was scrolling through her phone with shaking fingertips. 'Natural Le Coultre say they received shipping instructions the day before yesterday. The serial numbers on the package and the email they just sent me match.'

Jemima was examining one of the other corners of the box. 'Eliot, is this really safe? There's a reason the Colonel has these procedures in place.'

'Fuck procedure. I said open it.'

'Typical,' Yule said bitterly. 'We come up with procedures to keep everyone safe and as soon as the mood takes you, you blow right through them.'

One of the goons glanced at the Colonel and when he nodded spoke into his cuff. Then they waited. The group seemed disinclined to talk. Torrent took her laptop to one of the sofas. Yule sat on the piano stool. Perry patted Tara on the arm and she cast him a look of teary gratitude.

Then Dennis arrived with his electric drill.

'You want this undoing then?' he asked, nodding towards the box.

Jemima put her hand out for the drill. 'Thanks, Dennis. You can pick this up before dinner.'

He shrugged, but handed it over with a curious smile before retreating. Jemima watched him go, then handed the drill to Eliot.

'You want to open it, go ahead.'

He took it. 'Oh, is this a teaching moment? Excellent.' He sniffed, then approached the box and put the drill to the first screw. It took him a second to work out how to use it. The drill buzzed and the first screw was withdrawn, hanging from the magnetic bit like a tear. Eliot plucked it off and dropped it to the floor. Turned his attention to the next. Two screws in each corner. Top right, bottom right. The high-pitched buzz was the only sound in the hall. No one helped or stepped forward to hold the crate. Only the Colonel hovered within arm's reach. Bottom left, top left.

Eliot plucked the last screw free, handed the drill to Jemima, then pulled off the front of the box. It fell to the floor with an ear-splitting bang.

A moment of silence. No puff of gas, no hiss of a pipe bomb. No visible coils of red and blue wires. Tash lifted the camera and caught Eliot, looking over his shoulder in triumph and realised that her heart rate was still steady, even after the crash of the crate.

The section Eliot had pulled away was lined with black protective foam, and the back of the canvas was visible now, snug in a thick layer of the same lining which kept its edges away from the edges of the box.

'Lift it out then,' Eliot said.

'Eliot,' Tara squeaked. 'It needs special handling. You paid over sixty million dollars for that.'

'Yes, I did. Lift it out and turn it around.'

'Eliot, there's white paint . . . on the foam.' John Allingham was pointing at splatters on the protective surroundings.

'I see. Get it out!'

The two goons came forward and, ignoring Tara's whimpers, lifted the canvas free of its lining and turned it to face the room.

'What the *fuck*?' Yule breathed.

Tash recognised the edges of the canvas from the reproduction in the dining room, but the centre of it had been daubed over with white paint, the ghost of the original just showing underneath, and over the white layer, smearing it in places, someone had painted in thick, red and uneven letters: 'Bertrand Caron, Fabian Pascal, Godard Martel.'

'Oh, Jesus!' Tara squeaked, lurching forward, her hand out.

'Don't touch it, Tara,' Jemima snapped. 'Call Eliot's art advisor and tell him the picture has been vandalised. Ask if there's anything we should be doing with it now to minimise the damage. Colonel, get it into your clean room in the stables and keep it there until an assessor arrives.'

'What are those names?' Yule said. 'Eliot, do you recognise them?'

'No,' he said simply.

'Can you ask Pan who did this?' Tash said, framing up, focussing on the daubed names, then stepping back to catch the expressions of shock and confusion on the faces of the watchers.

'I don't need to,' Eliot said. 'It was the French. A slap on the wrist for cutting their access to the alerts system.'

'I did warn you,' Torrent began.

'And I told *you*!' Eliot spat back. 'I fucking hate ingratitude. They tried to get into Pan.'

'And that decision cost them billions,' John said. He was stroking his chin, studying the ruin of the picture.

So they all knew that much now.

Eliot took out his phone and pointed it towards the ruined painting. 'Pan, what are the chances the French secret service did this?'

'High,' the voice said. 'The painting, *Number 47, 1948* by Jackson Pollock, was routed through France and delayed three hours in French customs allegedly due to Brexit paperwork. Agent Amile Breton had a coffee at a service station just outside Calais at 2 a.m. today. Amile Breton is a senior intelligence analyst who has referred to Panopticon in minuted meetings as a nightmarish abomination. She also referred to the French president as weak and craven in a WhatsApp message to her romantic partner, shortly before your phone call with the president, Eliot. It is possible she was in the room with the president at the time the call was made. She has visited Alnwick three times in the last month.'

'So this might be a rogue operation? Not sanctioned by the higher-ups?' Eliot asked, head on one side.

'That is likely.'

'But what do the names mean?' Yule persisted. 'Who are they?'

'Is Yule Collins an authorised part of this conversation, Eliot?'

'No, she is not. And put together a timeline of Amile Breton's presence here, Pan. I want to know exactly where she has been and who she has spoken to since she got here.'

He put the phone back in his pocket.

'Eliot,' Yule said quietly. 'You asked us to imagine, yesterday, what would happen if we removed some of the safety features in Pan.'

He took a step towards her. 'Shut up, Yule. Just stop thinking.'

He turned round and looked at everyone.

'Let's take a break for lunch, and we can continue our conversation after that. I'm going to eat in my room. Get something sent up, Tara. Think you can manage that?'

'Yes, Eliot.'

He set off up the stairs to the first floor, leaving them all staring after him. Then they scattered. Tash photographed the maimed painting being replaced in the case and carried out of the hall. Yule watched till it was gone, then snatched up her laptop and threw herself down on one of the sofas.

44

An hour later, Tash, watching from her studio, saw Yule, her head down and her hood up, striding across the walled garden, heading towards the main house. She checked her watch. The Council of Heaven should just be getting back from their lunch. Tash picked up her camera and followed her as she took the path round to the front of the house.

She caught Yule up on the driveway, standing next to one of the stone lions on the edge of the gravel in front of the main entrance. Yule was staring at the road leading up the hill and out of the park, clenching and unclenching her hands. She jumped when Tash said her name, and ran her hand through her tangled blue hair, knocking back her hood. The skin around her mouth was white.

'I'm waiting for a cab to drive me to the airport, then I'm getting out of here,' she said, adjusting the strap of her shoulder bag. The skin around her nails was raw and beaded with blood.

'Why?' Tash asked, walking across the gravel.

'Those names, the names on the Pollock picture. Do you know who they were?' She was still craning her neck, looking up the road.

Tash shook her head.

Yule span round, her face taught. 'I do! It took a while, but I found them. You know what makes it worse? So much worse? The Cap d'Antibes protocols we came up with are good. Really good. They provide a solid framework for the international community to deal with technological advances like Pan responsibly. I was building support for them. Talking to the leading AI companies about signing up, discussing legislation. But Eliot was wiping his arse with them the moment we got out of the meeting.'

'Yule?'

They turned. Jemima was walking quickly towards them from the villa.

'Yule? What on earth are you doing?'

'Oh, Christ,' Yule said. 'Don't bother, Jemima.'

Tash stepped back as Jemima approached, sinking into the scenery, deploying her superpower.

'Of course I'm going to bother!' Jemima said. 'We need you! Eliot needs you. You can't leave now. We have to find a way to prevent actions like these alerts about cyberthreats being switched off with no warning. We need to push for your two-key solution. Eliot has to agree to it.'

Jemima came forward, her hands in front of her, but Yule sprang back as if she were contagious.

'Jemima, Eliot has given himself complete control of Pan. He's never going to give that up. Did you read the email I just sent?'

'No, it came up saying "I'm going", then you undid send, so I came to find you.'

Yule bit her lip hard, and when she spoke again, her voice was shaking. 'I did not hit undo send. Pan did. Remember Eliot's vague scenarios about protecting agents in the digital realm? They're not "possible implementations", he's built and actioned them already. And as for "protecting agents" – you think Pan's not protecting itself? And Eliot?'

'So what did your email say?' Jemima asked quietly.

'Those names.'

'Eliot just told us. They were the people who died during the Paris attacks, the riots.'

Yule laughed, a horrible hysterical laugh. 'Bullshit! I mean Pan's probably already rewritten half the internet to make it look like that, but those three men died *before* the attack, Jemima! They weren't rioters. They were all French IT workers. The French president was wrong, it wasn't just the death of one man which left the system open to attack. It took three deaths. Three!' She held her fingers up. 'Three ordinary men maintaining very important pieces of software. And they all died in the week before the French finance attack. A car crash, a heart attack and an accidental drowning.' She counted them off on her fingers.

'I don't understand.'

'Eliot was angry, so he set Pan on the French! Pan didn't exploit a weakness it cleverly saw in the system, it created one – killing those men and then corrupting the system.'

Jemima stepped back. 'But Pan can't . . .'

'Fake a car crash? Drown someone? Poison someone else? Pan can't, but Charter Security personnel acting on Pan's orders bloody well can!'

Jemima shook her head. 'No. Yule, you can't believe Charter had anything to do with those deaths! It's just too outlandish. If Pan spotted something, a weakness because of those accidents, and that's bad enough, but . . .'

Yule stepped forward and suddenly grabbed Jemima's shoulders, making her flinch. 'Jem, listen to me. You have to listen. I know what they did. You don't know Pan like I do. This is not outlandish. This is the only explanation for what happened.'

'I can't . . .'

'You were there when we all agreed to give the French access for the people-smuggling operation. You know they tried to force the system afterwards.'

'And Eliot admitted he stopped the alerts! He admitted it was rash, he's on the verge of agreeing to the guard rails. The two-key system.'

'Stop saying that like it's some magic spell! Even if he agrees to it, he'll just strip it out whenever he's really pissed off. Seriously? You expect him to give up being a god and turn human again? There's no chance. I've watched you try every trick in the book with him and it's not working. It's not going to work. I don't care how good you are, Jemima, he's too far gone. You have to face that.'

Now Jemima was trying to pull away, but Yule held her close, staring into her face as Jemima tried to look away.

'You see he's different, don't you, Jem? Look how much worse he's got since last time. He used to be 90 per cent pretty cool, 10 per cent narcissist control freak. But that's reversed now.'

'Yule . . .'

'Jemima, get away from him. I swear, he's dangerous. Really dangerous.'

Jemima was pleading. 'He's a genius.'

'I know that,' Yule said. 'He is. That just makes it worse. And he will not listen to you.'

She released her grip on Jemima's shoulders, and now Jemima tried to grab her hands.

'Yule, I have to have an ally here, or there's no chance. We have to make him see he's accountable. Perhaps those deaths . . . Could they have been accidental? Perhaps he didn't mean to action the plan.'

'What? You're classifying assassinations as an industrial accident? Regrettable growing pains of Panopticon? They are built in.'

'He *can't* have known.'

'He did! I'm telling you, Jemima, it's all over. He's crossed the line. For God's sake be careful.' She noticed Tash again. 'Forget what I told you, Tash. Please. For your own sake. And everything that you saw this morning. And get out. Oh, shit.'

Eliot was strolling towards them, hands in his pockets. He was wearing a tan cord jacket over his white T-shirt today. The Colonel followed a few steps behind. Yule held up her hand.

'Eliot, I'm going. You can't stop me. The cab's on its way.'

'I cancelled the cab,' he said.

'You did what? I'm not staying here.'

'Yule!' He held up his hands. 'Jesus, I'm not trying to stop you. One of the Colonel's men will drive you wherever you want to go.'

He sounded reasonable, if a little disappointed, but Yule stepped back, almost tripping onto the turf. She steadied herself automatically, one hand on the flank of the old stone lion guarding the Abbey, the other clutching her bag across her chest like a shield. 'You've got to be joking. I'm not getting in the car with any of *his* men. No way. How many assassins have you got in town, Eliot? Bet you couldn't resist bringing them close. Having a little peek at them while you're in Europe?'

'What is she talking about, Eliot?' Jemima asked.

Tash knew. She thought of the disappearing man talking to the Colonel. The same man who removed his mask as the car passed through the gate. He hadn't been trying to see Eliot, he'd been letting Eliot see him. Give the boss a thrill.

Eliot looked innocent, a little offended. 'I promise, all of the security team here have Facebook pages. Their wives and girlfriends are on Insta. You can look them up.'

'Yes, but who might we meet on the drive, Eliot?'

'Oh, Yule.'

'I said no!' She was shouting now, her eyes bright. 'Where are the fucking bicycles? There was something in the handouts about a bicycle.'

Eliot smiled. 'Can you even ride a bicycle?'

'I'll learn!' Her voice, cracking with panic, echoed against the pale stone frontage of the house.

'You're being silly, Yule!' Eliot said, more sharply. 'I'm trying to help you.'

'Fuck.' She jabbed her ragged fingers at him. 'Off.'

'The car's coming round now, Eliot,' the Colonel said.

'Thank you, Colonel.'

'I am not getting into a car with your men, Frank.' Yule looked as if she might cry. 'I won't.'

The main door to the house opened and shut again with a rattle. Bethan was walking down the wide shallow steps. Flowing skirts today which rippled round her ankles, hair in soft curls. Handbag worn across her body, and she was twirling a set of car keys.

'Will you get in a car with me?' she asked Yule.

'Bethan! Yes, I will. Yes, please.' Yule turned towards her, desperate.

'How did you . . .?' the Colonel began.

Bethan pointed over her shoulder. 'My office is on the ground floor. Hard to avoid hearing. Come on, Yule. We'll take my car.'

'Yule's upset,' Eliot said. 'Been saying all sorts of mad things. You remember we have your NDA, Bethan, love?'

'I remember . . .'

'If you leave the premises, you will not be allowed back while Mr Drake is in residence,' the Colonel growled. 'Not unless one of my men has been with you at all times.'

Yule reached out and touched Bethan's sleeve. 'Please,' she said, very quietly.

Bethan glanced casually in Jemima's direction. Jemima's chin moved a fraction of an inch.

'I'm sure the staff will manage without me for a day or two,' Bethan said, her voice still light and relaxed. 'I'm only a WhatsApp away after all. Come on, Yule.'

Tash walked swiftly up to Yule and hugged her, hard. 'Ask Bethan about Wilf,' she whispered into the other woman's hair. 'Take care of yourself,' she added, stepping back and squeezing her hand.

Yule looked confused and surprised. 'You too.'

Bethan was walking towards the garages, her pace unhurried. Yule shoved her hands in her pockets and started jogging to keep up with her long strides, and looking back over her shoulder, the panic still in her eyes.

They watched until the two women disappeared round the edge of the house. They didn't speak until Bethan's dark-blue Mini climbed the hill towards the gate house.

'What are you going to say to her assistant?' Jemima asked. Her voice hollow.

'Perry? I thought I'd offer him a job,' Eliot replied lightly. 'Perhaps he can feed me Yule's special micronutrients, if she's left them behind. Put some extra pep in my step.'

'I'm sure he'd love to work for you,' Jemima said. She looked older today.

'Yes, like you always say, Jemima. Try and create a win–win.' He rubbed his hands together. 'Let's get back to it. Still plenty to talk about.'

'That wasn't true, was it, Eliot?' Jemima asked. 'What she just told me about France? The engineers?'

'Of course not,' he sounded sad. 'I mean, I did turn off the alerts. The rest – I think that French agent is running a psy-op.

Giving us those names then planting some shit on the internet for Yule to find.'

'OK,' Jemima said quietly. 'I guess that makes sense.'

'Eliot?' the Colonel said. 'We could still stop them at the gate.'

'Oh relax, Colonel.' He was already walking away, giving a half-wave over his shoulder. 'What's she going to do? Hide?'

45

Ingrid and Charles left the same afternoon, quietly, but not so quietly Tash didn't spot them in the car park with overnight bags.

'Jemima said things were a bit tense, might be best to give them space,' Charles told her comfortably, opening the passenger door for the tiny French embroiderer. 'We'll go up to Seahouses on the coast. Stay till Monday.'

Ingrid leaned out of the window.

'You can come, Tash, if you like. The cottage has an extra bedroom. Sea air? Leave them to hash it out.'

Charles leaned against the roof. He was dressed in white linen, complete with a Panama hat. 'You'd be welcome. I'm not as good as Nisha, but I'm a decent cook.'

'You'll miss the wolf.'

'Pfft,' Ingrid said. 'Overpriced drinks and bad sausages. I'll see more genuine ghosts and legends from our porch at the cottage anyway. All those drowned sailors to keep us company.'

'I'll stay. I promised Peter at the bookshop I'd take pictures.'

Ingrid shrugged, arranging her summer shawl over her thin shoulders. 'Good luck. You might even manage to make it look interesting.'

Charles seemed to find this charming. 'High praise indeed. Sure you won't come?'

'I'm sure,' Tash said. 'But can you give me a lift to the gate? I've got films for the courier.'

At the gate they went through the usual performance with the film canisters before they were handed over and, as they were transferred into the clear plastic bag and the rough music of the protestors started up, Tash realised that she was staying put while the French left. Again. She walked back to the Abbey as the sun began its slow decline.

Tash was halfway into her room before she noticed him. Eliot Drake was sitting in the chintz chair next to the fireplace. Her laptop was open on the desk behind him, playing the BBC news on silent. A city skyline in Ukraine, the blue sky marred by a column of smoke. He was watching, chin in hand, as she came in.

'Hey, Tash,' he said, turning. He waved at the screen. 'Just catching up on the news. Been a busy day.'

The door closed, and Tash realised the Colonel was standing behind her.

Eliot smiled. 'We'd like to have a chat.'

She sat down carefully on the end of the bed. 'You could have just messaged me. Not done the creepy waiting in my room bit.'

Eliot glanced at the Colonel. He stepped forward and grabbed Tash by the shoulder, and in the same move struck her, open handed across the face before she could move to defend herself. Her vision swam and her ears rang.

'What the fuck?'

'It's actually more private up here than in the villa,' Eliot said calmly. 'What with Charles and Ingrid away. Anyway' – he was still watching the screen – 'the Colonel has a question.'

He grabbed her again, lifting her up off the bed and screaming into her face. 'Who the fuck is Harry? Who is he?'

Jesus. A shudder of cold ran through her.

'What? Get your hands off me.'

'You stupid bitch, I'm going to beat you to death and piss on your corpse. I said who the fuck is Harry?'

He threw her down on to the neatly made-up bed, among the tasteful overstuffed cushions embroidered with wild flowers. Her back and side protested. He loomed over her, hands in fists.

'He's a writer!' she cried out. Lifting her arms to shield her head. 'Just a writer! I met him at the bookshop.'

He grabbed hold of her wrist, pulling her arm across her body, then struck again, open palmed, the other side of her head this time. The pain blossomed across her temples.

This couldn't happen here. The obscenity of it. The psychotic bulk of the man towering over her as she lay sprawled and dazed on the ivory bedcover, the highest possible thread-count sheets. He dropped her again and took half a step back. She coughed, wiped her face with her hand. Her nose was bleeding.

'He's not a fucking writer. Who is he?'

He feinted towards her and she put up her arms. She might be able to kick him from here, but it would have no force in it and he was between her and the door.

'He is! He's working on a novel. We've had coffee a couple of times. Now leave me alone!'

She didn't need to try and sound hysterical. It was there. The room was so small. Her laptop, the kettle, anything which she could have used as a weapon were all blocked from reach by Eliot. He was watching, his handsome face impassive.

The Colonel took a fistful of her hair. Dragged her up and close to his own face.

'No. He. Fucking. Isn't.'

She tried to brace herself for the pain to come, the next blow. Nothing.

Eliot was holding up his hand. The Colonel dropped her. She felt like a bird deposited at the feet of the master by an obedient game dog.

'Eliot?' she said, her voice cracking. 'Please. He's a writer. That's all.'

He ignored her, and woke his phone. 'Pan, can you give me a summary of our previous conversation about Natasha Bell. You don't need to bother with the biographicals.'

'OK, Eliot,' the calm female voice replied. 'Greg Martin reported this afternoon to the Colonel that, on consideration, Natasha Bell's behaviour on her run this morning aroused his suspicion. She claimed to have a stitch as they entered a small area of woodland on the river Aln, and fell on their way back up the south-west path from the edge of Belford Park to the walled gardens. He was not convinced that either event was spontaneous. The area of woodland is not covered by CCTV or visible from the road. He dismissed his suspicions at first, but given the arrival of the painting and the news a French agent had been recorded in the area, decided to report.' Tash breathed heavily, her hair falling over her face. Shit. 'Later examination of both areas found no evidence of a drop, though there was naturally a delay between the incidents and Mr Martin reporting his concerns. On hearing the report, you, Eliot, asked me to examine Natasha's movements since her arrival at Belford Abbey.'

'I go by Tash,' she said.

'Eliot, is Nat—'

'Yes, go on.'

'My apologies, Tash. I shall refer to you as "Tash" going forward. I reported that Tash has socialised in Alnwick on two occasions with a temporary resident of the town, Harry West. Harry West is an agent of the Secret Intelligence Service, colloquially known as MI6.'

'Bollocks,' Tash said. She couldn't do shocked, but maybe angry would be close enough. 'He's a writer! He's on leave from the civil service. He did courses.'

'He did do courses, Tash,' Pan said, smooth and helpful. 'But spies can try their hand at fiction writing too, you know! I have high confidence in my supposition that Harry is an agent. As well as a considerable amount of circumstantial evidence, he was also seen in conversation with the French agent Amile in the early part of last week in Alnwick. He visited Paris in the aftermath of the disturbances and was filmed entering the Musée des Arts on 15 July by a passing cyclist. Agent Claude Simon spent two hours at the same café on the same date. Shall I take you through my reasoning?'

'I don't give a shit about your reasoning. Maybe Amile was asking directions! He was on a *writing* course in Paris. If you've got any proof, show it. Otherwise fuck off.'

Pan didn't respond. Eliot shrugged. 'Coincidences do happen, Tash. But why was his phone at the Paris Institute when he entered that café?'

'Maybe he forgot it!'

'Yes, but you have to look at the *weight* of the evidence,' Eliot said with a slightly impatient sigh. 'The number of times travel or cash cards associated with him have popped up around MI6 headquarters, for example. The numbers of phones he uses, and Pan has found two false sets of documents with his picture on them. He is a spy. Certain as I'm sitting here. But we think you knew that.'

'I . . . I didn't . . .'

The Colonel hit her again. Twice this time. One blow to one side of her head, one to the other. She tasted blood.

'Look at our messages if you want . . .' It came out as a whimper.

Eliot sniffed. 'We have done. We're not morons, but then neither are you.'

'He did . . . He has asked about you,' Tash said, gasping, wrapping her hands around her head. 'You're one of the richest men in the world, of course he did. But I haven't been to town since you got here, so I just said what I knew then. My mother coaches you, one of your friends fell off the tower, you have a fake fucking Pollock on your wall.'

The click of heels on the stairs and someone scratched on the door, then pushed it open a crack.

'Tash? You OK? I want my gin . . .' Jemima's eyes flickered from the Colonel to Tash. 'What the hell are you doing to my daughter?' She stepped into the room and the Colonel shifted back. 'Tash?' she asked. Her eyes still on the older man. 'What's happening?'

Though she be but little, she is fierce.

'They think Harry is a spy,' Tash said, 'and that I knew it.'

'Hi Jemima. Harry is a spy,' Eliot said from the armchair.

'Harry? Your writer friend? He's not even French. Jesus, Tash, your nose is bleeding!'

'You think your government don't want to know everything they can about our business?' the Colonel asked. 'Tash's friend Harry is MI6.'

'Eliot.' Jemima walked towards the billionaire, a slight shake in her step. 'If that thug of yours has laid a hand on Natasha, while you watched . . .'

He stared at her, his eyes oddly cold. 'What? You'll be severely disappointed in me? And spare us the devoted mother bit.' He sat back in the chair, crossed his legs. 'Let's face it, Jemima, you hardly know Tash. And your guilt makes you blind. You have no idea what she's been up to since she got here. A snake in the garden of Eden, your daughter. So, Tash, did you really get a stitch today when you went out running?'

'What?' Jemima said.

Eliot held up his hand.

'I went too fast on the stretch in front of the castle,' Tash said. 'I needed to catch my breath and I didn't want to tell Greg that so I said I had a stitch. But I did fall over, and it fucking hurt.'

Eliot smiled, something almost kind in his expression as he turned to the phone. 'Pan, is Tash lying?'

A pause, a long pause.

Then the voice on the phone replied. 'Tash was running approximately 30 per cent faster than her usual pace before stopping suddenly for one minute twelve seconds by a footbridge over the Aln west of the weir. She ran more slowly afterwards. Her voice pattern also indicates that she is telling you the truth, though she appears to be in some distress.'

Tash put her head down, fighting a surge of triumph. Amateurs. If Eliot had asked if she'd made a drop, she'd have had to lie and that nasty little box of tricks might have outed her. If they'd made her answer when they asked if she knew Harry was a spy rather than hitting her, she'd have had to lie then too. But Eliot had allowed her to be truthful.

'I still have questions,' the Colonel growled.

'You're not asking them here,' Jemima said. 'Not like this.'

'I want to know . . .'

Jemima stamped her foot. Her stiletto heel thumping into the carpet.

'Enough. Let's see if Pan thinks I'm telling the truth now.' She took a breath. 'There are three cleaners, a handyman, two cooks and two kitchen assistants on site. If you touch Tash again, Colonel, they will throw you out of the Abbey. In a brawl your men would win, I'm sure, but I'd have rung the police and told them some of my guests had become violent and were refusing to leave by then.'

'Well, Pan?' Eliot was smirking a little.

'Jemima Carter does not seem to be lying, Eliot.'

'Really, Jemima?' the Colonel said, pointing at Tash. 'That girl is a stranger to you. She's fucked up. Staring into nothing, moody as shit. Not a word out of her for hours, then she throws a temper tantrum. She's damaged goods – easy pickings for any pretty-boy agent wanting to eavesdrop on you and Eliot. And you trust her?'

Eliot turned the phone between his fingers. 'Jemima? Thoughts?'

'I trust Tash to do the right thing. This Harry had a good cover, I take it? A good story?'

Eliot nodded.

'We all trust the wrong people sometimes, Eliot. Misread them. Why should Tash think some guy she met at the bookshop was a spy? They are trained to lie, and she's trained to trust the evidence of her own eyes.'

He blinked. Then slapped his hands onto his thighs and stood up.

'That's an excellent point. We'll leave it for tonight then. Come on, Colonel, let's see what Nisha has prepared for us this evening. Are you coming, Jemima?'

She kept her voice perfectly calm. 'I'll be late for dinner.'

'I know you looked at the footage of the night Brandon died this morning, Tash,' Eliot said. 'Why did you do that?'

'Everyone said he was high the night he died,' Tash replied, not looking at him. 'I wondered if it was true. And he did stumble. There was another bit marked. It showed you going up the tower a couple of hours later, then back down again. Wilf had marked the one of the Colonel up the ladder too. I wondered why. I guess he thought it was funny.'

'And did you really see someone from your bedroom window this morning?'

Yes. Monty. Every day.

'I wasn't sure what I saw.'

'Pan?'

'Tash appears to be telling the truth, Eliot.'

But not the whole truth. Yule was right, Pan was making Eliot lazy in all sorts of ways, thank fuck.

They left and the door shut behind them.

46

'Are you hurt?' Jemima asked as soon as the door closed, approaching Tash cautiously.

Tash lifted her head and Jemima gasped.

'No, I mean my ears are ringing a bit.'

'Your nose is still bleeding.' She was already on her way to the bathroom, on the way back, tissues in hand, she opened the mini-fridge and pulled out two little bottles of Lindisfarne Gin, kicking the fridge closed again with her scarlet heel.

'You're not going to pour alcohol on a bloody nose are you?'

'No.' She shoved the tissues into Tash's hand, snapped the lid off one of the bottles and drank it.

Tash smiled, which made her face sore, and dabbed at her nose. Jemima snapped the lid off the other bottle and gave it to her.

'I am so sorry, Tash. I never thought for a second you would come to any harm here.'

Tash drank. 'I know. Do you know what's going on, Mum?'

She sipped at the bottle. 'Eliot told us the French had tried to create a back door into Pan and he switched off their zero-day alerts in retaliation. Without those warnings and updates their systems were uniquely vulnerable, so the hackers had a free hand and caused chaos. But those accusations Yule made can't be true.' She lifted her gin to her mouth again, her hand shaking. 'I don't know what to do. We could go to the police. Get the Colonel banged up for hitting you. Go to the newspapers with the story about France . . .'

Tash closed her eyes. Her mother hadn't known – the relief running through her tasted like cold spring water on a hot day.

'Mum, what could we say? The Colonel might get a slap on the wrist. And there's no proof Panopticon has anything to do with what happened in France.'

Jemima was silent for a minute. 'Tash, do you think . . . Those people, those names . . . What Yule said? Is it true?' She sounded as if her heart was breaking.

'Yes, I do.'

Tash put her hand over her mother's. Jemima's fingers shook under hers.

'So what can we do?' Jemima asked.

'I saw Harry last night. Gave him some stuff. He's promised me Eliot will pay.'

Jemima sighed sharply, then downed the rest of her gin. 'Sounds like you can still think and move under pressure, Tash. So you knew Harry was a spy?'

'Yes. And I was a fool – I didn't think I was spying on Belford, just Eliot.'

'I suppose I should have expected you would sell us out, given you despise us.'

Tash wove her fingers through Jemima's. 'If Bethan told you that, she must have said I wanted to impress you too.' She sighed. 'I am sorry. Monty was working on a story about Eliot. I thought if I traded gossip with Harry he might explain it to me.'

Jemima sighed. 'I can forgive you.' She squeezed Tash's fingers. 'And if this is true, I'm only sorry I wasn't able to help you. God, I better go and have supper, or they'll come back. So what happens now, Tash? Can this Harry stop Eliot?'

'I'm expecting him to turn up and arrest them any second. But until he does, please be careful.'

'What do you mean?'

'Don't provoke Eliot. I think . . . Look, I think he and the Colonel have people in Alnwick.'

'People? Like the "people" Yule says killed those engineers?'

Tash nodded.

Jemima shuddered. 'It's frightening Tash, I thought I knew him. I mean, fucking hell.'

Tash leaned her head on her mother's shoulder. Jemima flinched with surprise, then leaned her head back. For a moment mother and daughter drank in silence together.

'Are you angry with me for leaving you with your grandparents?'

'You have to go to supper.'

'Please? I need to know.'

'I wasn't angry, Mum,' Tash said slowly. 'I mean, not really. I was confused, and I was sad. I can be sad, can't I? Without blaming you, or being angry?'

Jemima let out a long sigh. 'Yes, of course you can. Can I be proud of you, while acknowledging I've had bugger all to do with who you are today?'

Tash grinned. 'I will allow it. And there are genes. I'm sorry I didn't get your red hair, and I definitely got Dad's chin but there must be a lot of you in me.'

'You have my eyes,' Jemima said simply. She glanced at her watch again. 'I need to go.'

'Be careful.'

'Yes. I know. Slight confusion, sympathy for Eliot. Pretend I think Yule is crazy. I can keep that up until this Harry guy swoops in and arrests him.' She stood up. 'Are you OK, Tash? There are loads of blankets on my sofa. You can stay there if you don't feel safe here.'

'I'll be OK. I'll put a chair under the door handle.'

Jemima touched her cheek. 'You're very resourceful, Tash.'

Then she left for dinner.

Tash got out her phone and texted Harry.

You're a fucking spy. Eliot and the Colonel just told me. Delete my number.

47

Saturday, 26 July

Tash slept deeply and woke late, sore and headachy. She showered, letting the hot water treat her bruises and unwind her muscles. There had been no response from Harry. What was he doing now? She dressed and sat by the window of her room most of the morning, waiting to see the cavalry arrive. Sirens perhaps. Harry might not come himself, but he had the footage. He'd send the police and Eliot would be arrested.

No one came.

At noon hunger drove her downstairs and she found Nisha and Fran in the kitchen preparing lunch for the villa.

'You coming to the Wild Hunt tonight, Tash?' Fran asked as she came in. 'Eliot and his lot are going.'

Tash was making up a plate at the sideboard from the breads, meats and cheeses constantly laid out there. 'What? You're kidding? The Colonel's just letting Eliot out to wander in the crowd after this week?'

Nisha was stirring something on the stove. 'We got our orders first thing,' she said. 'They want a good lunch and then a light supper ready for when they get back from Alnwick, late this evening, so that sounds like they are going to me. Perry, the one who worked for Yule until yesterday, messaged me. Eliot's fired his girl. And one of the goons brought down fancy masks for them to wear at the burning.'

Tash's phone buzzed. She pulled it out, hoping it would be Harry telling her when he was sweeping in. Her message was from Perry too.

> Eliot asks you to join us for the festivals in Alnwick. Cars leave at 5 p.m. Or take your bike. You will be allowed to return to the Abbey after the burning. Until then he regrets all discussions are private.

The heat of the day had softened into a gentle warmth in the centre of Alnwick by the time the party from Belford arrived. Tash had already been there an hour, photographing the parade. The Colonel's SUVs followed the stragglers to a spot by a water fountain close to the square. The party got out and followed the crowd into the square itself. Cloth bunting, intricate patterns of vintage cotton prints, had been strung along the shop fronts, and round the edge of the square hot food trucks were doing a good business. The air smelled of toasted cheese and bread, the apple tang of cider. Some people wandered through the craft stalls with plastic glasses of Prosecco, others with pints of beer or mead.

A stage had been set up by the market cross with an arch of rippling lights around it, and a mixing desk under a shaky-looking gazebo nearby. Emily, her face pink and her blonde curls bouncing as she played the Northumbrian pipes, and a young man on the fiddle. The third player had a tabor today, a thin drum he played with a double ended stick held in one hand. He played thrumming, rippling beats with it, rising and falling with their own music. Emily saw Jemima across the crowd, and lifted her hand to wave. Jemima was in red, one of her film-star dresses, and wore a fox mask made of feathers which stopped just above her scarlet mouth. Eliot, standing next to her, in jeans and T-shirt, wore the face of a wolf, also fashioned in feathers.

In front of the stage a group of morris dancers performed on the cobbles, dressed in black with red handkerchiefs round their necks. Some of them wore headdresses crowned with antlers that reached high above their heads, wound with ivy.

Lots of the crowd wore masks. Badgers, green men, mice and eagles circled each other. Among the children Tash spotted unicorns and dragons.

In the middle of the square, surrounded by low metal barriers, was the straw wolf's head ready for burning. Six feet high, its jaws open and its ears pulled slightly back as if caught mid howl, it sat on a base of logs and kindling. A booth by the barrier invited visitors to write their wishes and prayers on scraps of paper, which would then be added to the fire.

Tash saw the stall was manned by Peter from the bookshop. He spotted her and grinned, before turning to deal with the crayoned prayer of a little girl, who was passing it to him with great solemnity. He mirrored her energy, offering a small bow. Tash lifted her camera and took the picture.

Allingham and the Colonel stood in the queue for the beer tent, reading handouts about the fair. Torrent had refused a mask. She stood on the edge of the square, leaning against the wall of the bakery in wide-legged trousers and huge sunglasses, watching the band and the dancing.

Tash climbed up the steps of an external stone staircase which led to the town hall and looked for Harry in the crowd. No sign of him. Jemima was on her own now, standing by the mead stall, a tiny sampling glass in her hand, looking right and left. Then Tash spotted Eliot in his wolf mask heading towards Northumberland Hall, which made up one side of the marketplace. He moved with purpose through the oblivious crowd, brushing past the other creatures of forest and fantasy, till he reached the east corner of the building, his way barred by high iron gates. As he approached them, they swung open and a man and a woman stepped out to welcome him. The man shook Eliot's hand and beckoned him inside.

Harry. Harry, the man Eliot knew was a spy. Harry, who knew Eliot was a murderer. Shaking hands. The woman, Amile, who thought Panopticon an abomination, who had vandalised Eliot's sixty-million-dollar-Pollock with the names of his victims, looking on.

Tash began walking down the stairs.

'You OK, Tash?'

Jemima was waiting for her at the bottom. She blinked behind her fox mask, then, seeing Tash's expression, pushed it back off her face.

'I don't know. I just saw Harry and a French agent with Eliot, but they were shaking hands. Mum, I think we've been screwed over.'

Her mother wore her best 'interested and relaxed' smile, but her voice was low, tense.

'There's a French agent here too? Look, Eliot has bought out the Colonel's share of Charter. He owns it all now, just likes he owns Panopticon.'

'And the Colonel?'

'He'll stay on as CEO. He's acting like he's happy with it, but I think Eliot forced him into it. I'm sure those "people" you mentioned are here. God, it's creepy. It's like I can feel them in the crowd, watching us.'

Tash struggled to concentrate. Harry and Eliot, shaking hands.

'Was there anything about France this morning? About what Yule said?'

'I asked. Eliot said something like that was theoretically within Pan's abilities. The Colonel looked like he was going to throw up and John gave us a speech about the art of war and the *theoretical* need to make an occasional show of strength. I nodded and frowned and chewed my lip.'

Allingham and the Colonel had got their beers now, and approached them. John was grinning broadly. 'I finally got Frank to buy a round,' he said in his smooth baritone. 'Think he can afford it now.' The Colonel looked grey. 'So, Jemima, what's with the wolf? I've been reading the handout but it's all adverts for mead.'

'Why are you acting like this is all OK?' Tash asked. 'Yule ran away.'

John crumpled his forehead. 'Yule made some rash and unfounded accusations. She's brilliant, done more good in the world than many of us can dream of, but the strain of working with corrupt governments has got to her. She had a breakdown.' He put out his hand. 'But she's fine! Perry, her old assistant had a message from her. Told Eliot about it. More crazy accusations, but she's taking a bit of time for herself.'

'Fuck me,' Tash said, staring at him. 'You actually believe that, don't you?'

'Tash,' Jemima said quietly.

She waited until Tash nodded to her, then walked away into the crowd. John shrugged and headed off in the other direction. The Colonel finished his beer in a single, wide-throated gulp, then turned back to queue for another.

Ten minutes passed.

Twenty.

Eliot emerged alone from the hall and Perry, the assistant, jogged up to him offering him a grilled cheese sandwich and Yule's pill box. Eliot swallowed the pills, then took the sandwich. He did not look like a man under arrest.

Eager little Perry, handing over Yule's message and now her pills and pick-me-ups. They should have given him a weasel mask.

48

As dusk fell, the mood began to change. The families drifted home, and the music became faster and more insistent. The morris men were leading the dancing, moving through the crowd, rattling and clacking the bones to encourage them to dance faster. Tash shot reel after reel. She was still waiting for the moment when the police would arrive and make an arrest. The handshake must have been some sort of strategy. Not real. Not real.

Eliot appeared and put a cup in Tash's hand. 'It's nearly time. You should toast the wolf.'

'You, or the one they are setting on fire?' she said, taking it.

'You can toast us both,' he said. 'You must have heard I've bought the Colonel's company. Poor Frank.'

'Hardly poor if you just bought his company.' She looked at the cup. 'What is it?'

'Hot mead. Woman on the stall said it makes your sweat taste of honey. But that seems unlikely. No, the Colonel is not financially poor, but he didn't want to sell. I'm sorry you and I haven't got along, Tash. Maybe we got off on the wrong foot though. I'd like a fresh start.'

'You had me beaten in front of you.'

'You spied on me.'

Tash drank rather than reply. The mead was sweet and warming. 'No time for a fresh start, Eliot, you'll be gone tomorrow.'

He placed a hand on her shoulder and her nerves screamed at the touch. 'I'll be with you in spirit. Always.'

'I saw you with Harry.'

'Yes, we met. And we came to an arrangement.' Eliot smiled. 'He says you had no idea who he was, but it's important that you know I don't believe him, Tash. Not for a minute.'

'What arrangement?'

The wolf smiled at her, squeezed her shoulder and let go. 'I got angry. I still need to work on my emotional regulation – you know what that's like. I need Jemima for that. So I have to make a sacrifice to show I'm sorry and will behave better in future. Well, it's a good evening for it. I'm going to watch the show with Torrent.'

He disappeared back into the crowd.

What arrangement?

The music from the stage reached up into a frenzy, then stopped suddenly. The dancers relaxed, a wave of chatter and laughter reaching into the corners of the square, like the ripples of water reaching the shore, then the bell above the town hall rang out the hour chime and everyone went still. Two morris dancers with ivy-strewn antlers were standing sentinel on either side of the arched tunnel under the clocktower. A shape approached along it as the chimes continued, and as they finished, echoing off into an eerie silence, a figure emerged. It was a man, his form made strange and outlandish by the long stiffened cloak he wore, and his mask looked like the bleached skull of a stag, the antlers reaching three feet above his head. He carried a flaming torch, held low, which cast his shadow against the walls behind him, the antlers seeming to tumble and chase each other across the stone as the flames flickered.

He walked towards the bonfire, the morris men forming an honour guard keeping back the crowd as he approached the wolf. The barrier was lifted away and as his foot touched the cobbles at the edge of the square, the violin and pipes started up a low drone. The whole crowd seemed to inhale. Tash glanced round. Other stags had appeared at the back of the crowd. They didn't carry torches, but wore the same bleached bone masks with high antlers and heavy black cloaks.

Some of the crowd noticed them, looking behind and between them, jumped and laughed in a mix of confusion and fear, covering their mouths, shifting closer to their family and friends. The torchbearer reached the wolf, and the drone of the pipes and violins grew louder, then began to scatter into running arpeggios, nothing of a tune, a cacophony, a building pressure. The bearer lifted the torch, then, as the tabor thrummed under the fiddle and pipes, he thrust it into the bonfire. The tabor boomed and snapped, the violin and fiddle cut off and in the next heartbeat broke into a dance tune, all joy and release as the flames caught and the wolf began to burn.

The crowd roared with approval, and the torchbearer pulled off his mask and grinned. It was Peter, looking flushed and happy in the firelight as his friends slapped him on the back, handed him a drink. Tash caught his smile in her frame, by the light of the fire. Beyond him Eliot was saying something to the Colonel. The older man crumpled slightly, his shoulders slumping, but Eliot turned away, joining Torrent and Jemima, and walked towards the SUVs parked on the far side of the hall. Tash jogged back up the stairs to watch. The Colonel was following them, but as he got close one of the drivers got out and held up his hand. Torrent opened the door of the second SUV. Jemima, still in her fox mask, looked at the Colonel and said something to Eliot. Eliot shook his head and ushered her in, then they drove away.

The Colonel was shouting at the other driver, but he remained impassive.

He had not wanted to sell. Eliot must have used the photograph, the accusation of stolen valour, to blackmail him into it. The Colonel turned away from the driver and for a minute Tash lost him in the crowd. Then he was coming up the stairs towards her. He grabbed her arm.

'Natasha, you've got to help me. Do you have a car?'

She shook him off – his face looked sweaty in the firelight.

'I came on my bike, and why should I help you?'

'I didn't hurt you, not really. And you're tough, aren't you? Tough, clever, Natasha.'

'Fuck off, you told my mum I was a basket case yesterday. If your ride has ditched you, you'd better walk.'

'No!' His voice became a high whine. 'Please, they are going to kill me.'

She blinked. 'Why would they do that?'

He took hold of her arm again, squeezing and releasing her as if he were massaging her. His eyes were bright with tears.

'The French! They call it justice, but no trial, no nothing. I'm being executed. It's immoral.'

'You're talking to me about morality?'

'It wasn't my idea,' he said desperately. 'Eliot asked Pan for the strategy. He gave me the names, that's all. He lied to me. Said they were targets the French authorities wanted taking out. Said it was part of a deal he'd made with them. A live trial in Europe. I didn't know what he was really doing!'

Monty was watching them from the bottom of the stairs.

'I swear, Natasha,' he whined, 'I only ever thought I was working for the greater good! For freedom! Security! I saved your life. It was a risk, but we saved you.'

She almost spat in his face. 'You mean when you murdered Monty, you let me live. That's not really the same thing, is it?'

'Please! I'm begging you. I'll do anything, anything you want.'

She pulled away from him again. Stepped back. Behind him in the crowd, one of the bone-masked figures seemed to pause and stare at them before moving on.

'We could do such wonderful things in the world, Natasha, with Panopticon and the White Knights. We can save people. We just needed time to put everything in place, and if Monty had written his story then it would have shut us down! One life! One life and then we could save thousands. Millions, even. Just think – cartel leaders, dictators, people traffickers, crime bosses – the world could finally be free of them. And all the decisions going through the Council of Heaven – that's almost your idea. You named them. The only person who fucked up was Eliot, pushing Brandon off the tower. I told Eliot not to confront him. To leave it to me. Now the French and British are holding it over him.'

'So it cost two lives. And you don't get to decide who lives and who dies.'

'But Eliot does? He's made a deal with the UK to avoid a murder charge. Eliot's freedom for access to Panopticon, and me out of the way.' His eyes darted around the crowd, and he groaned.

'If you're afraid,' Tash said, 'just go to the police. What can I do for you?' She nodded towards one of the uniformed officers – a man with the face of a pink bath bomb who was posing for a selfie with the flaming wolf behind him.

'No, the White Knights can get to me in custody. You don't realise how powerful they are.'

'Don't you control the White Knights?'

'Not any more. Now they are his! I had to sign over my control to Panopticon when Eliot discovered I had embellished my record a little.'

'Lied through your teeth you mean. Just walk away!'

'That was your fault. Him finding out. I know it was! My blood will be on your hands. Tell your mother. Make her persuade Eliot to change his mind. Tell him to rescind the order.'

'Talk to her yourself. She's gone back to the Abbey.'

'You don't understand. I'll never make it. Please, you're a good person.'

'Why the hell would you think that?'

'I know it.'

She studied him again. Fear had made him small, sucked all the hot air out of him. 'If I help you, will you tell the truth about what happened to Monty? Will you give evidence?'

He looked sick. 'Yes, I'll do anything. I just need tonight. I need to survive tonight. A place to hide. Then tell your mother she has to make Eliot cancel the order. I'll give the French the money I got from Charter. Call it a fine. Restitution for the families. That will work. I'll campaign for AI safety.' She looked at him. 'Yes, OK. I will testify against Eliot.'

Tash could feel the panic and hope coming off him, the stench of the battlefield, acrid and corrosive. 'There's a door. Next to the bookshop. It's on a key code 1234. It lets you into a lane between the shops. Be careful, my friend Harry is renting one of the cottages back there, but there's a yard at the end of the alleyway with a gate leading into the castle drive. Maybe you can hide there.'

He looked sick with relief. 'Thank you. Thank you, I'll find a way to pay you back. I promise.' He released her and plunged immediately back into the crowd, weaving among the dancers. One of the stags turned its head, following his movement. Tash climbed back up the stairs, searching for Frank in the throng. He'd headed into the thick of the crowd. She caught sight of him, trying to push past the shuffling revellers, his bullet head half-forward, shouting, heading past the butchers into the flagged yard which led to Narrowgate and the door. Another of the stags was standing by the dark windows of the deli. For a moment Tash thought it was watching Frank as he struggled past, then a man approached it, two full glasses held above his head to save them from spilling, and the stag mask was removed to reveal a young woman, fluffing up her flattened hair, laughing.

Tash took another step up, she could just see the entrance to the back lane beside the bookshop from here. Frank was still forcing his way through, a swirl of annoyance and irritation marking his place in the crowd. He was twenty feet from the gate now. A breeze pulled at her hair, and she turned slightly. Another man. Not part of a group of family or friends, he moved more smoothly through the throng, wearing the mask of a green man, leaves pouring from the carved corners of his mouth and the dark holes of his eyes. He wore a black fleece, the collar up, and he was following Frank.

Tash opened her mouth to shout, but the noise was impossible. She lifted her arm, waved. Frank didn't look in her direction. He stumbled, his head disappeared briefly and then he was being lifted up again, pushing back the jokers and long-nosed Mr Punches, the witches and fae folk who surrounded him. He elbowed his way forward, shoving them aside. Behind him, the green man followed, and the fairy-tale figures seemed to make way for him, dancing around him like eddies in a stream so, as Frank was blocked and sabotaged, the green man moved ever closer. They passed in front of a bar, hung with bunting.

Tash took the photograph. There couldn't be enough light, but it was all she could do. Perhaps she had something of them both in the wash coming through the plate glass windows of the pub. Frank was nearly at the door now. The man in black ten feet behind. Frank twisted round, looking over his shoulder. Did he see him? Would he recognise him? Tash felt her throat close up as she zoomed in on Frank's face, its distorted panic. The green man was just a few feet behind him now. Frank broke through the crowd, and stabbed at the mechanical keypad. The door opened. He plunged into the alley, pulling the door behind him. He'd made it. Tash felt a surge of relief. The green man reached the gate, his hands in his pockets. He pushed lightly on the door, then pulled out his phone. A moment of him standing there, his mask horrid in its blue light. Then he tapped the number into the lock, and pushed the door open too.

The spell broke. Tash ran back down the steps and over to the grinning policeman.

'Excuse me! There's a man. I think he was in trouble. Someone was chasing him.'

Perhaps he made it. Perhaps he had got through the back yard, found sanctuary in the castle grounds.

'OK, love,' the policeman said, looking politely curious. 'Where was this?'

'By the bookshop on Narrowgate. He went through the door into the lane, the other guy followed him.'

'Why do you think he was chasing him?' The policeman was looking her up and down.

What could she say that wouldn't sound insane?

'He's called Frank. The man who was being chased,' Tash said. 'I know him. He's a friend of Eliot Drake's and there have been all those protestors at Belford Abbey.'

The policeman nodded and brought his radio close to his mouth. 'Control, just going to check something. Possible assault off Narrowgate.'

The response came back in a burst of static. 'OK, lead on then. What's your name?'

'Tash. Tash Bell.'

'I'm Steve. Right, show me where you last saw them, Tash.'

His uniform had the same effect the green man had had, the crowd edging away to let him through. They reached the alleyway in a minute and Tash punched in the code. The yard light was out, and the second they stepped in to the narrow alley, the summer night seemed to enfold and deafen them. The policeman flicked on his torch.

'You sure it was down this alley, Tash?' he said. 'Doesn't sound like there's a fight going on.'

'I'm sure. There's a back gate, maybe they got out that way.'

'All right then, well you stay here and I'll take a look.'

He moved cautiously down the alley and Tash followed him, watching as his torch beam swept across the flagstones. The neat porches of the little holiday cottages on one side, the huge mossy stones of the neighbouring house on the other. Then he paused as the alley opened out into the yard, his torch light glancing off the green wooden gate at the back, the blocks of sandstone surrounding it. Tash's phone buzzed. She pulled it out and looked at the screen.

Back at Abbey with Eliot. You need a lift?

She thumbed back a reply.

No. Mum, be careful.

Three dots appeared, then disappeared under her message.

'Hello, sir? You all right there?'

Tash put the phone back in her pocket. The music had stopped again in the square, there was some sort of announcement, an indistinct, amplified voice, and then cheering. Festivities coming to an end.

She stepped forward. In the yard behind the table and chairs where she'd eaten bacon rolls with Harry, the policeman's torch beam had come to rest on a figure. It was slumped against the back wall and wearing the Colonel's sports jacket, but his face was masked. The green man. The policeman stepped forward again.

'Sir? Can't let you just sleep it off there, I'm afraid. You mind waking up for me?'

The figure didn't move. The policeman crouched down and shook his shoulder. 'Sir?'

He turned and saw Tash standing behind him. 'I told you to wait for me. This the man you saw being followed?'

'Yes, but he wasn't wearing that mask. The guy following him was.'

The policeman sighed and gently pulled up the mask to reveal the Colonel's face, white in the wash of the torch, eyes shut.

'Sir?'

This time when he shook his shoulder, the Colonel slipped sideways on to the ground and the torch caught the slick of blood pooled beneath him.

'Shit!' The policeman rocked back on his heels, touched his hand to the dry flagstone. Then steadied himself and put his fingers to the Colonel's neck. He began to talk into his radio at the same time. Tash leaned against the back wall of the bookshop, biting her lip, listening to him give the code for the gate, the place on Castle Drive where the back gate opened out. Moments, and a blue light washed up the castle walls. Steve's hands were bloody, it smeared across his hi-vis jacket. He opened the gate. Paramedics, more police. From the shadows, Tash reloaded her camera and took her photographs.

PART IV

Darkness Visible

49

The red light on the camera in the corner of the interview room blinked off, then the door opened and Harry walked in.

He held himself differently – his back straighter, his movements sharper – than when he was charming Harry, wannabe writer. He carried two takeaway coffee cups and her camera and put them awkwardly on the table, pushing one of the coffees towards her.

Tash picked up the camera instead. The film had been removed.

'I used Peter's machine in the bookshop,' Harry said, pointing at the coffees but he didn't smile.

'You did a deal with Eliot. And you murdered a man.'

He sat down opposite her and crossed his legs, flicking a scrap of lint from his knee. 'Not personally.'

'Not personally!' She spat it out. 'I bet that's what Eliot says. About the French engineers, about Monty. What, you think that just because you are giving orders to assassins rather than doing your own dirty work that makes you less of a murdering arsehole?'

He waited for a few moments before speaking again. 'Maybe not. I won't insult you by denying it, Tash. And we couldn't have done it without you. Panopticon will now be a key partner to the British government, and the French. At no cost to our taxpayers. Eliot will still be able to sell his services to other governments and individuals, though he's agreed to keep us informed.'

'Fancy suit,' she said, her voice dripping with bitterness.

'Thank you. Thanks to you, I've just introduced the head of the service to Eliot Drake. Virtually anyway. We had a very useful Zoom call from Northumberland Hall. I wanted to look nice for it.'

'Where is Eliot? Where's Mum?'

'Back at the Abbey. With Torrent and John Allingham. They know the Colonel is dead, by the way, and that you are safe.'

'Why didn't his security guards help him? I saw him getting turned away from the SUVs.'

'Because they've been trained, when necessary, to turn a blind eye. By Frank Matthews himself. And they had to choose between doing what Eliot told them, and what the Colonel said. They chose to obey the billionaire who had just become their boss.'

He looked at Tash's neck, where the bruising left by the Colonel's fingers was visible in the harsh light of the interview room. 'You don't owe him any sympathy, Tash.'

'You think I don't know that?'

'Well done for sticking to the cover story last night.'

She thought of her terror, sitting there under their eyes, protesting her innocence. Jemima's fierce intervention and now this casual, offhand praise. It twisted like a knife between the ribs.

'So what now?'

He smiled. 'In a couple of months I'll be taking on the Colonel's role as CEO of Charter. Advising and guiding Eliot. We'll try and find ways to discover the kill code he added to Panopticon, he'll try and stop us. Should keep us all busy.'

'What about your French shadow?'

'She'll be running his foundations in Africa. It's a new dawn of cooperation between the French and English security services. A long time coming too. You heard of the "five eyes" group?' Tash shook her head. 'Britain used to share its intelligence with the US, Canada, New Zealand and Australia. We're moving towards a more Eurocentric strategy. Panopticon will keep working with all those governments, of course, where we all agree it is appropriate. But the French government and our own will be a new axis of power in the world.'

'So that's the deal? You hold the evidence of Brandon's murder over Eliot's head to make sure he gives you what you want. He gets to stay alive and play Batman when it doesn't interfere with your agenda and keeps entering his code to preserve Pan?'

Harry nodded.

'Where is Yule? Are the White Knights after her?'

'We don't know where she is at the moment. She'll turn up. And there is no need to put a target order on her for now.'

Tash drank her coffee, remembering how he brought it to her in the office behind the bookshop a thousand years ago.

'Why did you give the French the Colonel? He said Eliot told him those French engineers were targets selected by the French government. He didn't know he was helping Eliot destroy their banking system.'

Harry tutted under his breath. 'Maybe he didn't at first. But I'm sure he worked it out long before Eliot got to Belford.' Tash remembered that unshaved patch on his chin the day the cash machines stopped working in Paris. 'His death was necessary to seal the deal with the French. They needed Eliot to sacrifice something for tearing a hole in their economy. We wanted to make sure Eliot knew his actions would have consequences.'

'Did you know about the painting?'

'No, that was all Amile. She wanted to set the cat among the pigeons, like you did with the photograph of the Colonel.' He paused. 'You just printed it out and added it to Eliot's folder, didn't you? How did you know it was important?'

Tash swallowed, the coffee tasted suddenly more bitter than usual. 'Monty thought it was important. He wouldn't have added it to the thumb drive otherwise. And you said pictures of the Colonel during his military service were hard to find. I wanted to know why it was important.'

'Well, you succeeded there, Tash.' He sighed. 'Amile's stunt with the painting could have backfired, of course, but now she's going back to France with the Colonel's scalp and Panopticon. They'll give her a medal and a corner office.'

Creating a win–win situation. Maybe Harry had taken one of Jemima's courses too.

'Though all that photograph did was give Eliot the leverage to take control of Charter.'

'There is that.'

Tash swallowed and tried to speak calmly. 'Harry, Eliot is mad. This can't work. You have to shut Panopticon down.'

He recoiled. 'No. We want to use it. Push back against the hackers, flood the dark web with light. Secure our infrastructure and get back on the front foot. And we'll be responsible. We want to reinstate privacy, ringfence data collections. Any kill orders will go through a rigorous review process. Really, Tash. This is an excellent outcome.'

'That was always the idea, wasn't it? To take control? You never intended to arrest Eliot. That night on the hill, you lied to me.'

He looked at her, a certain fondness in his eyes. 'Of course I did, Tash. Did you really think we would just destroy Panopticon? I told you how remarkable it was, and we didn't know half of what it was capable of then.'

'I really hoped I could trust you.'

'And I am sorry.'

'What about my mum?'

'She'll continue working with Eliot. Yule leaving, the Colonel's death. It's been a lot. He'll need her support.'

'What if she doesn't want to give it?'

'I don't suppose Eliot will give her any choice.'

'You're a cold-hearted bastard, Harry.'

A flick of irritation. 'Like you keep saying – that's my job.' He sighed and leaned forward on the desk, more like Harry the writer again. 'I'm not really though, I swear to you. I know you feel betrayed. I know you think we should arrest Eliot, let Panopticon fall apart . . .'

'Yes, of course I fucking do!'

'But the power it—'

'No. That's the point. Humans shouldn't have that much power. We're too stupid, too greedy. We can convince ourselves that any act is justifiable if it's for the greater good! You know this! You're building hell on earth, and calling it heaven because you get to control it.'

'Panopticon will save thousands of lives.'

'And destroy how many others? Are you going to use it to cover up political scandals? Get rid of any sort of speech you don't like? Destroy one company and pump the value of another? And anyone who gets run over in the process is just collateral damage? You let the Colonel be stabbed in an alleyway. You let that local copper try and staunch the blood. You remember what blood smells like, Harry?'

'Yes, I do.' He stared at his shiny black shoes for a second, his jaw tight. 'You know why Monty didn't make it as a spy? Too bloody self-righteous. Just like you. Sometimes the ends do justify the means.'

'That's just the shit murderous arseholes like you tell each other so you can sleep at night.'

For a moment it looked like he might say something more, then he changed his mind, stood up and walked out, letting the door to the interview room shut behind him with a gentle click.

Half an hour passed and the copper, Steve, who had found the Colonel, stuck his head in the door and asked if she wanted a lift back to the Abbey.

'We can stick your bike in the back.'

'Don't you need a statement from me?' Tash asked, already knowing the answer.

'They found him,' he said as she climbed into his patrol car. 'The guy who did it. One of those protestors you've had at the gates. The one who came in for a chat with Mr Drake.'

'Are they sure?'

'Oh, yes. He did a good job of cleaning himself off – the DI thinks he wore gloves then threw them in the bonfire after. But there's no doubting the CCTV from outside the bookshop. He's there, following the American into the alleyway; you can even see the glint of the knife in his hand.'

Tash looked at her own hands. Was there blood on them too? Of course Panopticon chose the man who had come into the house for dinner when looking for someone to frame. So much footage from the Belford cameras to work with. She could insist on giving a statement. Who would believe her over the CCTV footage? Perhaps the man's phone could prove . . . No, he'd said he refused to use one at all. He had done everything to make himself the most useful fall guy possible.

50

The patrol car crunched on the gravel in front of the house and Tash got out, thanking Steve, and then stood looking up at the elegant frontage of Belford Abbey as he pulled away. The door opened and Jemima ran down the stairs and hugged her. Tash couldn't relax into it.

'Tash, I . . . Eliot told me they've arrested one of the protestors, but I think he was smirking when he said it. And his lawyers emailed with a contract for counselling for next year. Double the money, and double the hours.'

'Congratulations.'

'Oh, sod off. Yule was right. He's stopped hearing me. He nods when I talk about oversight and control but . . . And your friend Harry is here. The spy.'

'He's not my friend.'

On cue Harry appeared at the top of the steps with Tash's laptop under his arm. He ignored Jemima. 'Hello again, Tash,' he said.

She looked at the computer. 'So that's why I was waiting half an hour? So you could go through my room?'

'Yes.' She thought of the night on the hillside, leaning up against him. 'And the only copy of the footage of the night Brandon died is securely stored with MI6. Wilf's machines are cleansed.'

Jemima put her arm round Tash's shoulders. 'You utter arsehole,' she said.

He offered her a tight smile.

'Doesn't this bother you at all, Harry?' Tash asked. 'Panopticon is dangerous and Eliot is a murderer. He murdered Monty.'

Jemima stiffened next to her.

He squeezed his eyes shut. 'Yes, it fucking bothers me. But Panopticon – God, the potential – no more drownings in the Channel. No more right wing terrorist attacks. No more Russian propaganda! We can't give it up. And without Eliot Drake there is no Panopticon, so yes, we are willing to protect one to save the other. And it's not me who decides that – it's the governments in Paris and London. The *democratically elected* governments. This is as near as we can get to putting Panopticon in the hands of the people. It's done, Tash.'

'I can still go public.'

'No,' he said it almost sadly. 'No, you can't. And I don't mean because of the NDAs and Official Secrets Act. I mean because you'll be scrubbed. We know it can be done. It's been done before. Whatever you publish will disappear. Any mention will be removed before it even appears on the screen. It's beautiful really. In the instant between you hitting publish and the words appearing on the web, Panopticon can reach down and pluck them out of the air. You could buy an old typewriter and bash something out. Send round photocopies I guess. See how far you get with that.'

'Eliot did it to the journalist, didn't he? The one who had a go at us in the pub. Wiped her out?'

'Yup. It's another very shiny toy he is offering us. One among many. Look, this is a huge victory, for the service, for the country. I wish you could see that, and take pride in it. Goodbye, Tash. Good luck.'

'I'm going to need it in this world you and Eliot Drake are building. It would be a fucking joke if it wasn't so frightening.'

He handed the laptop to the driver of the SUV, signed a clipboard, then climbed in. 'You have a beautiful home, Ms Carter,' he said.

'Fuck off, Harry,' Jemima replied, her voice clipped and businesslike.

He nodded to the driver and they pulled away. So that was it. Eliot had won. Or perhaps Panopticon had. Monty's story, the one he'd died for, would never be told.

'Mum,' Tash said. 'I think I'd like to sleep on your sofa tonight if that's OK.'

'Of course.' She drew breath to say something more.

'Can we talk tomorrow?' Tash felt heavy, weak with it all. 'I know there's more I need to tell you. I'm sorry . . .'

'Tomorrow then,' Jemima said. 'Come on.'

And she put her arm around her daughter's shoulder.

51

Tash stirred from an uneasy sleep. A hammering in her dreams, the thump and crunch of mortar shells, became a knock at the door.

The door to Jemima's bedroom opened, casting a golden light across the polished floorboards.

The knocking came again.

'I'm coming!' Jemima said.

Tash stayed where she was, hearing the rustle of fabric as her mother pulled on a dressing gown. A click of an old-fashioned key in the lock and a sigh of hinges as her mother opened the door to the corridor.

'Eliot! What are you doing here? It's the middle of the night.'

'I'm sure the contract says you're available to me twenty-four hours a day, Jem.' He sounded a little drunk. 'I've had a very busy day, and I need to reflect.'

'That doesn't mean you can just turn up, Eliot.'

Tash didn't move. If Jemima was going to say something about her lying there in the darkness, she would do it now. She didn't.

'I think I can. Maybe I should look into giving you a bonus. A hundred thousand to hear me going on after midnight.'

'Don't be silly. Fine, what do you want to talk about?'

'Loyalty. I want to talk about loyalty. And gratitude. Loyalty and gratitude. I need it, and I'll reward it when I can, but I can't always. And I'm sad about that.'

She heard her mother sigh and the scrape of a chair. 'Sit down, then. We'll talk about loyalty.'

'I want a glass of water. Can I have a glass of water?'

Another sigh, and footstep, then the sound of the mini-fridge opening and closing.

'Have you had your eggs frozen?' Eliot asked.

Tash heard the metallic snap of the water bottle being opened.

'What?'

'I hope so. You're, what, forty-four now? You might have some viable ones left. Bet you've done it already. You wouldn't need to carry it. Get a surrogate.'

'I already have a daughter.'

Tash could make out Eliot's reflection in the glass covering her print on the wall by the fireplace. It hovered, ghost-like above the scene in the Ukrainian café. A disembodied, haloed presence over the drinkers and the ruins. Jemima was only visible by the hole her body left in the light surrounding him.

Her silhouette handed him the water and he set the bottle down on the table.

'I know, but it was just dumb luck that Tash turned out OK. I mean, maybe she is a spy, but she's brave. Anyway, heir and a spare. That's what you need. I could father them, if you like. Think of it, my brains and your emotional intelligence. I think it's time for me to have a family.'

Jemima's voice was careful. 'We've discussed, Eliot, frequently, that emotional intelligence isn't something you are born with. It needs to be learned. Most people learn through relationships they value.'

He yawned. 'Just an idea. I could put a hundred million in a trust fund for each one. I mean, Tash's smart, don't get me wrong, but wouldn't you and Bethan like a few multimillionaire children running about?'

'You said you wanted to talk about loyalty.'

'Yes. Maybe sharing offspring is a way to build loyalty. Maybe I should have offered Yule a child. Yes, loyalty. Are you loyal, Jemima? Can you be trusted? When we consult about what kingdoms to raise, which to tear down. Who to make rich or poor. Or will you be sneaking off to warn any worthy souls who might get hurt in the process?'

'What do you think?'

'I think, I think perhaps you can be trusted, but not out of loyalty. You're a realist. That's your whole schtick, isn't it? How to be a realist, but a thoughtful one. Do what you have to do, then have a cry and light a scented candle.'

'That's not my schtick, Eliot.'

'And you're a good little capitalist. You like being successful. Like Yule. Did you know Yule has houses in London and the valley, as well as Porto, but hardly ever uses them? Travelling around the world spending the money from my foundations while her houses and staff are paid for by her dividends. Amazon and Uber stocks. All those workers, underpaid and underinsured, generating shareholder value, so she can run around the place spending money on rewilding the Scottish highlands or building roads in the DRC. And she never saw the irony in that.'

'I think you underestimate her, Eliot. I think you are in danger of underestimating a lot of people.'

Tash felt Monty's ghost settle on the floor next to the sofa. Put his hand on hers. She could swear she felt the warmth of his touch. Eliot didn't say anything for a long time.

'I thought Brandon was grateful. Little shit. He should have known I'd find out. Why did he come here? Once he started talking to that reporter, he should have stayed as far away from me as possible. Though the White Knights would have got him in the end. It was cruel of him, really, to make me do it myself, after everything I've done for him.'

'Eliot' – Jemima's voice was tight – 'are you telling me that you murdered Brandon?'

'Yes. I thought it might be important for our therapy. No reason you shouldn't know. The authorities are letting me off as a trade for them using Panopticon.'

'What happened, Eliot?'

'Oh, you know. Brandon and I went up the pele tower together. He fell. Then I went down alone. We got Pan to take me out of the footage afterwards. It wasn't till I got to the villa I realised I didn't have my beads. The ones the Colonel gave me.'

'Jesus, Eliot!'

'Tash noticed on the CCTV footage I wasn't wearing my beads when I went up again, to, you know, "look for Brandon" and was wearing them when I came down again. Keen little eyes, she's got. Maybe a White Knight should pluck them out. She'd have to stay with you forever then. Maybe you'd like that? Just say the word.'

'That's disgusting, Eliot.'

'While I have the kill code, they'll allow me some latitude, I'm sure, for personal projects. Still, your daughter has clipped my wings. I'm not pleased about that.'

Jemima's shadow leaned forward, her fingertips to her head. 'Why didn't you wipe yourself off that footage too? Of you coming back for the beads.'

He scratched behind his ear. 'Should have done. Didn't want to push it. The AI overwrite left some traces back then. The Colonel said me going and looking for Brandon fitted the timeline too, in my role as caring friend.'

'You murdered your friend.'

'Yes. You know, Tash is right, you never feel more alive than you do in a life and death situation. There was a moment there where I thought he might throw me over, but I was fitter than him. All that tennis you recommended.'

'Eliot . . .'

'I'm living with my difficult choices. We've talked about that too, haven't we?'

'Eliot, how can I help you if you threaten Tash?'

'Find a way. I know I'm not a bad person, Jem, because I am really sorry about what happened to the Colonel. He was loyal and grateful, but that wasn't enough in the end. Bloody French. That's sad. I see that's sad. But he'd understand, if he thought about it, that it was necessary.'

'The Colonel was murdered by an extremist. Wasn't he? One of the trio we invited here for dinner.'

'No. I had to do penance for France.' He sighed. 'The White Knights were your idea, you know. Well, you inspired it. You said sometimes turning a blind eye to bad behaviour was a necessary skill in management.'

'The White Knights?'

'Hasn't Tash told you about my band of happy warriors moving through the world yet? Untraceable. Invisible. But deadly.' He started speaking faster, leaning forward. 'I have my own band of 007s! It's so cool.'

'Are you high, Eliot?'

'Oh, relax. I've just had a couple of edibles. I know I'm a good person. I can do so much good in the world, and I want to, and I don't need to be worshipped. That's good, isn't it? And I like being a little bit invisible, like your clever daughter. Moving in mysterious ways.'

He sighed again, stretched out his legs in front of them and crossed his ankles. 'We can reforge the world, Jemima. You, me, Torrent and John. We could be like the Fates. Spinning in the background.'

'John's an idiot, Torrent's a sociopath, I'm a brand more than a person these days,' Jemima said, 'and I have no idea what you are.'

'Ideal representatives of the populace then. You know, Oppenheimer was a hack. "I have become the destroyer of worlds," he says. Big whoop. That's not power. Power is being able to move through the world like a shadow. Making moves. Making the road through history that other men walk down, never knowing it was you who decided the direction and the destination. That's power. That's what I can do. France was too much. I see that now. But I was angry. That's why I need you, to help me control my impulses.'

'That's too much power. Why should you remake the world? What gave you the right?'

He reached forward suddenly grabbing the collar of Jemima's dressing gown, yanking her towards him. She gasped. Tash tensed, watching in the reflection. His face was an inch from Jemima's, and the lines of his body taut.

'"Where were you when I laid the earth's foundation?"' he snarled. Jemima remained perfectly still. '"Have you ever given orders to the morning, or shown the dawn its place? Have you journeyed to the springs of the sea or walked in the recesses of the deep?"' His mouth an inch from hers. 'See, I've been reading Job too. Like Tash. I'm sorry if she's still upset about her boyfriend.'

Tash felt the tears on her cheek, but she made no sound. No movement. Monty's ghost squeezed her fingers.

'"I know that you can do all things",' Jemima said very carefully. '"No purpose of yours can be thwarted."'

He laughed and released her. 'So you've been reading it too? Quite the little study group, aren't we?'

'Eliot.' Jemima put out her hand, Tash watching in the reflection as she reached across the table and laid her fingers on his arm. 'Eliot, it's too much. Can't you destroy it? Panopticon? Don't input the code, just let it die. You're destroying yourself otherwise.'

He stared at her, then laughed. 'Oh, my God! Fuck, Jemima, you're sweet. Maybe not loyal, but sweet. I'd end up in prison! Even if I did destroy it, someone else would just reinvent Pan in a few years.'

'Maybe we need a few years to get ready for it. You said difficult decisions have to be made, sacrifices. If you did something which deserves prison . . .'

'Don't be stupid. I can't waste my time in prison.' He snaked his hand in the air. 'I'm building my road through history. The French had to be taught a lesson. OK, they got the Colonel and I'm sorry about that, but they aren't trying to force their way into Pan now, are they?'

'People have died.'

'People do that all the time! Can't make an omelette without breaking eggs . . .'

'Eliot, don't enter the code. Let Panopticon collapse. I'm begging you, for your own sake.'

'No, Pan is mine, and watch your tone. Shall I ask Pan to cook up a scheme that would destroy you completely? Your business, relationships, health even. Let's ask her now. Come on, it'll be interesting.'

'Eliot, if you won't listen to me, if you aren't honest with me, if you use threats, I can't work with you. I won't.'

He sighed. 'Yeah, you will. I'll get Pan to make the plan and send it to you. Then you'll get it. I think you should stop teaching other people though. All these fucking also-rans tramping through Belford. They congest it. Like phlegm. Let's keep Belford for us. Anyway we can talk about all that another time. And you should have a think about the egg thing. I'd like it. I'll get one of the lawyers to call you.' He stood up. 'Night, night, Jemima. Lovely to chat as always.'

'Eliot!'

He left, ignoring her, and after the door shut behind him, Tash heard his footsteps disappearing down the corridor, and her mother taking slow deep breaths. It was a full minute, maybe two, before Jemima spoke.

'You heard all that?'

'Yes,' Tash said. 'I heard.'

Monty's ghost squeezed her hand again. She ran her thumb over his knuckles, pulled herself up till she was sitting on the sofa, still holding the hand of a dead man.

'He has to be stopped.' Jemima came to sit on the sofa next to Tash.

'It's impossible, Mum. I've been thinking, but it can't work. The British don't want him stopped. I think they'd do anything to have access to Panopticon. The French too, now they've had their pound of flesh.'

'How long have you known about all this?'

'Not long, and not much. Monty was investigating him, so they set him up and murdered him.' She told Jemima what had happened that day, the patrol, the rescue. 'They weren't Russians, or special forces. They were Eliot's White Knights. Putting on a little show.'

Monty's head rested on her knee.

'There has to be a way. Just let me think.' Jemima pressed her fingers to her forehead.

Tash felt her shiver and lifted up one of the blankets and wrapped it round her shoulders.

'Thanks, love.'

Then they sat in silence watching the night begin to thin around them. Would people even know, Tash wondered, that they lived in Eliot Drake's world now?

'Harry told me lots of senior spies are buying land off the grid,' Tash said eventually. 'Getting generators and cabins and burying food stocks. Maybe I should buy a set-up like that with the money you gave me. You and Bethan can come and we can forage in the woods.'

She smiled. 'Yes, maybe we should. You better tell me everything, from the start, Tash. In case I've missed anything else.'

She did and Jemima listened without comment. 'I thought I could go public if Harry screwed me over, but he explained last night that with Panopticon operational, that's impossible. It will eradicate anything I publish.'

'So the secret services keep Eliot alive and out of prison, and in return he keeps Panopticon running. That means you can't publish. Do I have it straight?'

'Yes, Eliot and Panopticon are keeping each other alive, and they are both very well protected,' Tash replied.

Jemima was quiet for another couple of minutes. Then she shook herself. 'I have loved being here, you know.'

'Are you leaving?' Tash asked.

'I bloody well hope not. I want to spend the rest of my life here. But sometimes you have to be willing to risk everything.' She was looking through the French windows. Dawn was already smoothing the sky from dark blue to purple. 'Tash, what do you know about Yule's assistant? The one who Eliot has hired.'

'Perry? Likes to work out a lot. He's in the gym every morning, he says.'

'His room is in the stable with the other assistants,' Jemima said, half to herself.

'I don't know what you're thinking, Mum. But he's Eliot's man now,' Tash replied. 'Remember as soon as he got that message from Yule after she left, he went running to Eliot with it. He won't help us. You won't be able to recruit him.'

'I'm not going to. The fact that the little shit sold Yule out like that has just made things easier, that's all. Give me five minutes to get dressed, then we're going to go for a walk.'

Her movements were decisive now. She stood up, pulled her hair back into a ponytail, and tied it up.

'Where?'

'Down the hill, there's a stand of oak and beech on the slope, remains of an iron age hill fort. We should find what we need there.'

Monty's ghost squeezed Tash's hand once more, then disappeared.

52

Jemima told her the plan on the way and she was right, what they needed was there among the shadows, the ancient ripples in the earth, the last remains of some forgotten castle, in the grey light of dawn.

'I'm not going to ask you about him now,' Jemima said as they began walking back to the house. 'But sometime, if this works out, I'd like to hear about Monty.'

Tash's throat closed up, but she nodded. 'Yeah. I see him all the time, you know. Sometimes it feels like I'm making it up, daydreaming. Sometimes it's – what's the therapy word? Intrusive.'

'That's the therapy word. Let him come and go as he pleases, and when he starts to appear less – and he will – try not to hang on to him.'

'OK.'

Monty peered round Jemima at Tash, looking a little sad, but not resentful.

'Any word from Bethan?'

'I got a pawprint from an unknown number. So I guess Yule has told her enough about Panopticon for her to be using a burner.'

'A pawprint?'

'It's our "I'm safe, I love you" signal when we haven't time to call.' Jemima looked at her shyly.

'I like Bethan.'

'Good.' She glanced at her watch. 'When does Yule's assistant work out?'

'He said 6.30.'

'We better get a move on then.'

Tash stopped and put her hand on her mother's arm, looking down at the charming little wicker basket she was carrying, full of the result of their foraging trip.

'Are we really going to do this, Mum?'

'Can you think of another way, Tash?'

Tash shook her head.

'Then I don't think we have any other choice.'

They walked into the house past the marble watchers in the hall and towards the treatment rooms in the basement in silence.

Eliot Drake's party was due to leave the Abbey at ten. At a quarter to, the fleet of black SUVs rolled up to the front of the house, and Fran and Yasmin brought out the luggage and stowed it. The assistants, coming from the stables, carried their own suitcases. Most looked uncertain, and the girl who had managed the Colonel's diaries and messages had obviously been crying. Only Yule's former assistant, Perry, moved briskly, with his post-workout glow. He didn't look in their direction.

Greg, Tash's running partner, appeared to be in charge for now. Just before the hour, John and Torrent strolled out of the walled garden. Jemima ignored Allingham, but she stopped Torrent.

'Torrent, is this really what you want?'

Torrent looked at her steadily. 'Yes. I wish I could persuade you, Jemima, to get your thinking clear. Democracy as we've known it is too messy, too unpredictable for the challenges we are facing, but people value it. Panopticon means people can still vote, have their say, but there will be a stronger guiding hand in the background. A triumvirate. The French, British and Eliot, advised by us of course. In time we'll be able to pick those governments ourselves – I don't think the spies have worked that out yet – but in five years, say.'

'So Eliot is better than democracy?'

Torrent smiled. 'Managing one man is easier than managing a whole population. So yes, Eliot is better.'

'What if someone else builds another system like Panopticon?'

Torrent wrinkled her nose. 'I don't think we'd allow that.'

She didn't wait for a response, but climbed into the waiting SUV. Greg closed the door for her.

Eliot came last and, as he approached, the SUVs started their engines, emitting the soft, ethereal humming of electric cars. He was wearing shades, aviator style, and his white T-shirt and dark jeans look.

'Still taking pictures, Tash?'

'All the time, Eliot.' He just stared at her, his expression unreadable behind his shades. 'Our own invisible girl,' he said finally. 'You're going to find being that harder in the future, you know.'

Tash tightened the frame. The viewfinder filled with the black of his sunglasses, the pele tower reflected in them. He turned to Jemima.

'Another eventful stay,' he said. 'The next one should be calmer. My lawyers are writing to you about closing the place to guests.'

'I'll take a look,' Jemima said, then she took his hand. 'Eliot, will you not at least consider shutting down Panopticon? Can't we at least discuss it, when you've had a chance to process the Colonel's death?'

'That's been processed. No, Jemima. Pan lives. Pan will be your friend, your guardian.' He leaned towards her and kissed her on her forehead. '"No weapon that is fashioned against you shall succeed, and you shall refute every tongue that rises against you in judgement. This is the heritage of the servants of the Lord."'

'More Bible study, Eliot?'

'I've found a lot of wisdom there, Jemima. Rules to live by. Especially in the Old Testament. Remember those words, won't you?'

'I will.'

He got into the SUV. Greg closed the door on him, climbed into the front seat and the convoy pulled away.

'And now we wait,' Jemima said. She reached out and took Tash's hand. 'Can you do it? Put on a brave face and carry on as usual?'

'I can do it.'

'I'm so sorry, Tash. That Harry betrayed you.'

'I'm disappointed, but I had my doubts about Harry from the start though. I hoped he was planning on doing the right thing, but . . .'

'Why?' Jemima asked, watching Eliot's convoy climb up the hill. 'Because he didn't know about the rescue?'

'Not just that. He said he'd spoken to Monty's fixer, Karin, but he didn't know Monty and I were a couple.'

Jemima looked at her. 'I don't understand.'

'That means either he was lying about talking to her, or she didn't trust him. I don't trust my gut instincts, but I trust hers.'

'But you told Harry everything, Tash,' Jemima said, folding her arms. 'You gave him the only copy of Monty's notes.'

Film has a certain quality . . . My first teacher was a bit of a traditionalist . . . A postcard is safer than a phone call, 'It's like Christmas, isn't it? You have to wait and see if you got what you wanted.'

'I *might* still have a copy of the notes. Depends if Plan B has worked.'

'What was Plan B?'

'Old school,' Tash said. 'Plan B was old school.'

The first news came through on Tuesday afternoon, after Tash had taught her introductory workshop to her new batch of students, talking them through the familiar slides, encouraging them to experiment with focal length. The alert flashed up on her phone while they were working in the studio, photographing the arrangements of wild flowers Tash had scattered through the room: lavender and rosemary in tiny earthenware vases they used in the old kitchen.

> Stock price in Notebook holding firm after hospitalisation of founder, Eliot Drake.

One of the students had gathered poppies from the fringes of the walled garden, laid them out flat on the wooden shelf under the window. Now he was placing the camera as close to them as he could.

'Is this going to work?' he asked Tash over his shoulder. The poppies were blood red against the grain of the wood.

'I think so.'

53

West of Kharkiv, November 2024

'This is it, Tash, the story,' Monty said. She was still half-asleep, called out of a dream by him reaching for the phone.

'Still not going to tell me what it is?'

'Not till I've talked to this contact, then filed. He's been skittish as fuck. Then I'll buy you the best dinner we can find and tell you all. You know how impressed you are with my general brilliance?'

'It's a battle not to faint from admiration every five minutes.'

'Time to up your game because this will blow your mind.'

'Shame the best dinner you'll find to celebrate round here will be pizza.'

He slung his arm around her naked back.

'I like pizza, our first meal together was pizza.'

She leaned in close to him, half burying herself under his body. He was warm, and the mornings were cold. The battlefield had become monochrome, ice and frozen mud. He laughed, giddy with excitement. Then ran his hand down her spine. 'But actually, fuck changing the world, let's just stay here.'

His phone buzzed. He rolled away from her and picked it up.

'Yes! OK, my guy's sent coordinates. Skittish bastard.'

'Where?'

He gave her the numbers.

They pointed to the edge of a village where the frontlines were shifting in unpredictable ways. Dangerous, but nowhere was particularly safe this winter.

He kissed the back of her neck while she looked at her phone screen. 'I want photos, but they'll have to hide his identity. You can handle it, can't you, Tash? Reassure him?'

'Yeah. No worries. So how did you find this bloke?'

'A lot of cautious fishing but I eventually got a bite. I had to do lots of long trust-building conversations on Telegram while you were asleep.' He thumbed something on the phone, then rolled out of bed, grabbing his underwear from the floor, his T-shirt from the sofa where they'd finished their evening the night before. Tash pulled herself upright and began to dress more slowly. Monty was singing to himself as he pulled on his trousers, performed a neat little turn on his heel as he did up his belt. 'Fucking A. On the ground confirmation! You can take pictures of his kit too.'

He pounced on to the bed like a cat, almost knocking her off the bed.

'Monty!'

'I've been chasing this story for over a year.' He kissed her. 'And now the day has come. What will you wear at the Pulitzer ceremony? You can wear jeans if you like. Just as long as you are there.' The phone buzzed again. 'Karin will meet us downstairs in ten minutes.'

Karin had got coffees for them. Tash gulped hers down, feeling it shiver deliciously to the edge of her nervous system. As they walked to the car, faces pinking with cold as soon as they were outside the lobby, a Volvo sped close to them, then braked hard, spinning its wheels in the snow. The driver leaned on the horn, and the passengers leaned out of the windows. The correspondents of *Le Monde*, and France 2.

'Late night *encore une fois*, Tash!' their camerawoman called through the window. 'Oh, to be young and in love!'

'They came for war, but they found love. *Quelle histoire!*' the driver shouted.

Monty and Tash gave them the finger in unison. The camerawoman laughed, and the driver leaned on the horn again, then sped away. Heading west.

'Shit, if the French are going west, maybe we shouldn't be going east,' Tash said, watching them leave.

Monty showed Karin the coordinates on his phone. 'What do you reckon?'

'How important is it, Monty?' Karin asked, stamping her feet and tucking her chin into the collar of her sky-blue puffer jacket.

'Very.'

'OK. Let's go. This will take an hour, maybe two there and back. And it's too fucking cold to stand out here talking about it.'

Tash was bending over her laptop setting up the slides for the landscape class on Thursday when she heard a woman behind her swear.

'Shit, Eliot Drake is dead.'

Tash didn't turn round straight away. She breathed in, slow and deep, felt Monty's kiss on her neck, smelled the diesel of the beaten-up old Ford they drove into the forest.

The woman read from her phone. '"Despite making considerable progress on Wednesday afternoon, Mr Drake's condition took a sudden turn for the worse this morning, when he showed signs of multiple organ failure",' She sounded like she couldn't believe it. '"A hospital spokesman said that the billionaire's decline was dramatic, and despite the best efforts of his doctors, irreversible."'

The man next to her shook his head. 'Damn, he was one of the good ones too, wasn't he?'

The reader nodded. 'Yes, a real altruist. Bummer.'

'It's up there,' Monty said, pointing south-west.

'Where?' Tash asked. The road had turned into a logging track. Churned by military vehicles and frozen into impossible troughs.

'We can't go further in this car,' Karin said. They had stopped at the edge of the track.

'Fuck, this is a stupid place to meet,' Monty muttered. 'The guy is paranoid though. Did I mention that?'

Tash, checking her cameras in the back, leaned forward to squeeze his shoulder. He reached up to pat her hand absent-mindedly.

'Yeah, like twenty fucking million times,' Karin said. 'Come on. Nice winter walk in the forest.'

It took about twenty minutes. The woods were quiet, the only sound their footsteps cracking the frost. Signs were hammered into the trees on either side of them. A white skull and crossbones on red. 'Danger! Mines!'

Monty frowned.

'What is it?'

'Nothing.' He reached into his pocket and pulled out a dark-blue thumb drive. 'Just got a weird feeling. Can you hang on to that for me till we get back to the hotel?'

Tash put it into the inside pocket of her puffer jacket. 'Yeah, 'course.'

She was still looking down, doing up the zip, when the track curved, and they saw the Russian patrol. Four of them.

'*Kto vi?*' The bulldog in charge shouted. '*Ruki vverkh! Idite syuda!*'

Who are you? Hands up. Come here!

'Shit. Time to turn on the charm, babe,' Tash murmured.

'Leave it to me.'

They walked forward, very slowly, lifting their hands, showing their palms.

'Tash, you know I love you, don't you?' Monty said.

'I do. I love you too. It's going to be OK.'

'Yeah, yeah it'll be fine.'

The Russians came closer.

'*Na kolenyakh!*'

On your knees.

Tash threw the first slide up on the screen and turned round to face the group.

'Sorry,' the woman who had read out the news said with a smile, and tucked her phone into her pocket. 'We're listening.'

EPILOGUE – PLAN B

Sunday, 10 August

The three men were sitting on camp chairs by a small shed on the west side of the allotment on the bank of the river Wansbeck, the gatehouse of Morpeth Castle in the distance behind them.

Tash led the way towards them, with Jemima and Bethan following, both in their off-work clothes as Tash had come to think of them. The men stood up as they approached and Tash stepped forward to hug the oldest of the three first.

'Tash, pet!'

'Hi, Grandad, how was the asparagus this year?'

'Thought they'd be washed out, but they've been very nice.' He kept his arm round Tash's shoulder as he reached out a hand to Jemima.

'Afternoon, Jemima.'

'David. Hi.' She introduced him to Bethan.

'Mr Race, great to see you,' Tash said.

'I'll never get you to call me Arthur, will I, Natasha?' he said taking her outstretched hands in his own. He still looked, to Tash, exactly as he had when she was a child. The unruly eyebrows, the checked shirt with a thin knitted tie under his cardigan.

The two older men were both dressed for allotment work. Cord trousers, worn shiny at the knees and tucked into wellington boots. The other man, much younger, did not look like a gardener. On his lower half he wore biking leathers, but he'd taken off his jacket. He wore a T-shirt, with the logo of the New Luddites printed on it. He hung back, waiting for Tash to get the first round of introductions out of the way before catching her eye. She hugged him. He smelled of sun and sweat, and under that, something familiar which brought a wave of sadness out of the soil and closed her throat so at first neither of them spoke.

'And you are Monty's brother,' Jemima said. A statement, not a question. 'Simon, isn't it?'

'Yes. I'm Simon.' He flushed pink under her smile.

David and Mr Race unfolded more chairs and fussed with Thermoses and half-clean cups till everyone who could be persuaded into tea had a mug in their hands. Tash watched Bethan resisting the urge to help. Then Mr Race picked up a newspaper from the little camping table and handed it to them. They had read it online already, but it seemed only polite to look at it again, in black and white.

Death of Eliot Drake
sends Notebook shares plummeting

'Are you safe?' David asked. 'Because if there's any evidence you need burying, we have just the spot under the gooseberry bush.'

Tash grinned.

'Eliot's tragic death has been ruled an overdose,' Bethan said.

David looked at her, his blue eyes sharp. 'I know you might have heard I'm a God-botherer, ready to tell you that murder is a mortal sin, love. But that's the wife. And this wasn't murder, this was putting down a mad dog. If you did it, Jem, it'll be the best thing you've managed since you gave birth to Tash.' He sniffed. 'Now, tell us the truth. The whole truth. You owe it to this lad.' He patted Simon's thigh. 'And you know you can trust Arthur. He hardly ever talks about anything. Ask him what time it is and he'll want to know why you're so curious.'

Mr Race grinned, apparently very happy at this description.

'Tash?' Jemima asked.

Monty's ghost leaned against the chair over his brother's shoulder.

'I trust them, Mum.'

'So how was it done?' David asked.

'Biohacking,' Jemima said. 'Sort of. Yule, one of Eliot's advisors, was very into supplements. She took fistfuls of pills every day, some of which were made by the nutritionist at Belford. When she left, well, when Bethan helped her escape, Eliot hired her assistant and started taking her supplements himself. I think he thought it was funny.'

'Where did you escape her to, Bethan?' David asked.

'She's been staying in our security guard's caravan,' Bethan said. 'Tash told Yule to ask me about Wilf. She did, and I know about the caravan, so we put two and two together. It is the perfect place to hide out. No phone signal, no internet, no neighbours.'

'So these supplements . . .' Simon said.

'Death cap mushrooms grow on the Abbey estate,' Jemima said. 'I thought of them – and went and harvested them.'

'We went, Mum,' Tash interrupted her gently. 'I know you're trying to protect me, but I'm not ashamed.'

Jemima glanced at her. 'Fine. *We* went and collected the mushrooms from the fort. Then we used Sophie's, our nutritionist's, kit to freeze dry, grind them and make them into pills.'

'While the assistant was doing his workout,' Tash went on, 'I replaced the pills Sophie made for Yule with the death cap ones. Perry had them ready in the tin for Eliot, his day's worth, just like he did for Yule.'

'Won't Sophie get into trouble?' Mr Race asked.

'It was just the pills for that day I replaced,' Tash said. 'All the real Belford pills Perry had in his luggage are safe. I hope Sophie never finds out.'

Bethan sighed. 'Oh, Sophie knows exactly what you did. And she's not the only one.' Jemima and Tash looked at her, surprised. 'You left the equipment very clean, but she works there every day. Some things weren't put back in exactly the right place.'

'And she told you that?' Jemima asked. 'Tash, if it comes to it, I'll swear blind you were nowhere near any of it. And if you have any respect for me at all, you'll let me take the blame, OK? It was me who got involved with Eliot Drake in the first place; I helped him become successful, so it should be me—'

'Jem?' Bethan interrupted. 'Shut up, babe, and let me finish.'

Jemima shut up.

'Sophie came to see me. Apparently, after the news that Eliot was sick came out, she went and had a talk with Nisha. Then they had a talk with Wilf. You did well, but the corridor camera caught you both going into Sophie's clinic, and you on the stairwell in the stables where the assistants were staying, Tash.'

Jemima was still looking baffled and concerned.

Bethan smiled. 'OK. Best if I tell you in the same way she told me. Sophie stared over the top of my head and said she'd found a little disorder in her room when she came in on Sunday evening, but I shouldn't worry because she and Nisha had had a very thorough clean-up. And also, says she, did I know the Colonel's men must have been fussing with Wilf's settings again, because there were a couple of cameras that had footage missing all of a sudden. The one outside her clinic, and the stairs in the stables.' Mr Race and David grinned. 'Then Sophie looked me in the eye and said, "Now, Miss Bethan, there it is. And I'm telling you for all three of us if we see a penny more in our Christmas bonuses, more than what we're due, we'll be insulted." I told her I understood, and we've said no more about it.'

'Well said,' David grunted.

Jemima shook her head. 'I don't deserve them, any of them.'

'Did it hurt?' Simon asked. 'Would Drake have died in pain?'

Jemima took a moment before she replied, looking into her tea mug. It said 'I dig my allotment' on the side. 'Yes, probably. Though I'm sure he was given relief. He probably didn't fully understand what was happening to him.'

Abdominal pains, nausea, vomiting, and diarrhoea, followed by a period of apparent recovery, then organ failure, seizure, coma and death. Tash had gone to the library in Alnwick to look it up in an actual book.

Around them the birds chorused, someone on one of the other allotments laughed.

'What would you have done, Mum, if Eliot had said he was willing to reconsider, that morning before he left?' Tash asked.

'Found a way to stop him taking the pills. But I would have kept them handy.'

'We could have brought him down, brought him to justice,' Simon said. 'With everything Monty found out, and you, Tash.'

'No, we couldn't have done,' Jemima said firmly. 'He would have wiped it off the face of the earth. There was no choice.'

'You have to believe that though,' Simon said.

David patted Simon's knee. 'Maybe. Doesn't mean she's not right.'

'But Simon, now Panopticon is starting to decay, we can publish the story,' Tash said.

'I thought MI6 had all Monty's notes?' Bethan said.

Mr Race opened the newspaper and took out a thick folder of prints.

'I had a back-up,' Tash said, taking them from him and flipping through them. Perfect. 'Simon has been our motorcycle courier since Eliot arrived.'

'What?' Bethan and Jemima said together.

'I wrote to Simon the day I went to see the exhibition at the Baltic, the day after we went to see Emily play at the Tanners Arms. Monty had told me Simon was a stonemason at York Minster, so I wrote to him there. I explained who I was and what I was asking him to do. I also sent a letter to the printers on Belford stationery asking them to use our specialist courier when he turned up, rather than their own guy, and a letter to Mr Race telling him he might get some film delivered.'

'I was tasked with developing it, then hiding the prints in a drawer until asked for,' Mr Race said with considerable satisfaction.

Tash smiled. 'Thing was, I had no idea Simon had even got my letter until the films I'd marked for Mr Race didn't come back with my prints the day after my session with Eliot and Yule.'

Mr Race sipped his tea. 'Darkroom got quite the workout. Yes, Simon dropped off the films Tash marked for me, then took the rest on to your usual developers in Newcastle. I still have the flat over the shop, so if Drake or his minions ever tracked Simon's phone, it just looked like he was in the habit of buying a Coke and a Mars bar on his way.'

'I had a burner of course,' Simon said. 'And a false name. The printers bought the story I'd been hired by Belford Abbey and never asked for ID checks.'

'But what were you sending to Mr Race?' Jemima asked.

'The White Knight at the gate. Photographs of notes I made. Pictures of Star's letter. Then when I opened Monty's file, I photographed each of page of his notes from my screen,' Tash said. 'I printed out the picture of the Colonel and his friends, the uncropped version. Then photographed that too along with everything else.'

'Boring work. Fiddly too,' Mr Race said. 'Still Tash did a good job. Tricky to photograph screens. Got to be careful of the exposure.'

'You taught me well,' Tash said. 'Thank you.'

'It was, and always has been, my pleasure, dear,' Mr Race said. 'There's some lovely work at the start and end of the reels. Portraits and so on. Couple of lovely starscapes.'

In the distance a car backfired. Tash registered the noise, but her heart rate remained steady.

'Will anyone be prosecuted for the Colonel's death?' Bethan asked.

'Fuck that murdering shite,' Simon said. Then when David tapped him firmly on the leg, he added, 'Sorry, Mr Bell.'

'The guy they fitted up for it has already been released "for lack of evidence",' Tash said. 'So that's good. I don't know if they'll ever find the White Knight who actually killed him though.'

'As Panopticon degrades, he and his friends might find it more difficult to hide,' Jemima said.

A footstep crunched on the gravel behind them and they turned.

Harry.

He was walking down the path towards them, alone, hands in his pockets. He was wearing his writer Harry outfit. Jeans and fleece, the blonde quiff. Tash and Simon stood up.

He stopped, ten feet down the track.

'How did you know we were here, Harry?' Jemima asked.

'Panopticon is degrading, but it's not entirely useless yet. When I saw you were gathering, I thought it might be a good opportunity for a chat. I come in peace.'

'This is the fucking spy?' Simon said. 'Why should I give a rats arse what you come in, you wanker? Come in fucking clown trousers if you want.' He jabbed a finger at Harry. 'You were going to go into business with that monstrous turd.'

Harry stared him down. 'I have a deal to offer you. Do you want to hear it?'

'Grandad,' Tash said, 'perhaps you and Mr Race should—'

'No,' Harry interrupted her. 'This is a family affair. You dragged them into this.'

'We were happy to help, as it happens, sonny,' David said.

'What's the deal?' Jemima asked.

Mr Race fetched another garden chair for Harry, and he seemed momentarily baffled by this small courtesy.

'I know you're planning to publish with ProPublica, so somehow you managed to keep a copy of Monty's notes. And you intend to publish it under his name as well as yours.'

'So you've read my emails,' Tash said as Mr Race settled back on to his chair with a grunt. 'You can't expect me to be surprised about that. Like Mum said, what's the deal?'

'You do not mention me or the secret services in your reporting. At all. Report Monty's murder. You can even report the killings in France and the attack on the banking system as "suspicious" and say that intelligence sources have linked them to Panopticon. You can say that the Colonel was killed as a result of a power struggle at the highest levels of the company, and the evidence against the Luddite was fabricated.' The skin around his mouth was white. He did not, Tash thought, like having his shiny toys taken away. 'Fuck it, imply that the Colonel managed to poison Eliot's tea before he was killed himself, if you like. But not a breath of the security services getting involved, British or French, beyond our careful ongoing investigations. That's it.' He was hunched in the chair, toad-like. 'And we want a final copy of the article twenty-four hours before you publish.'

Tash pulled out her tobacco and rolled a cigarette. Made him wait. She lit it, inhaled, and let the smoke drift out between her lips. No one else spoke.

'OK, Harry. Those are your terms. And what do we get?'

His eyes flickered over them all.

'Away with it. You get away with it, Tash.'

In the silence the robin began singing again. Otherwise it was so quiet, you could hear the river whispering over the rocks.

'We have to be able to report on the White Knights in full,' Tash said at last. 'Everything that Monty got from Brandon on their training and early missions in Russia. Everything about how Panopticon can wipe people out of footage, or pluck reports off the internet before they are even published. With credit to a senior intelligence source, who is – what shall we say? – leading the investigations into possible abuses of machine learning?'

'Fine. I'll check the preferred accreditation when you give me the finished article. But yes, report out the White Knights.'

It was too easy. Tash blinked. 'Fuck, that's why you are letting us report it rather than slapping us with a super-injunction. You *want* us to report on it. The White Knights will need a home, won't they?' Tash said. 'You're going to recruit them. Use the article to get them to come in from the cold. Few messages on certain Telegram message boards? Little breadcrumbs to lead them to their nearest MI6 recruiting officer?'

Her voice twisted.

'We have to try and retrieve something from this clusterfuck beyond what we can suck out of the system before it collapses entirely. I know you think I betrayed you, Tash. But I was doing what was best for this country.'

'Working with Panopticon was never what was best for our country. You got the maths wrong somewhere, just like Eliot did,' Jemima said. She was staring at the turned earth, her hands still clasped round her cooling tea. 'Torrent said they were planning to choose the governments of Britain and France within five years. You never stood a chance.'

He stood up without replying. 'Are we agreed?'

Simon was still on his feet. 'Monty was a very good reporter, wasn't he?' he said. 'I always thought he was a bit of an arse, but he was just one bloke with a phone and a notepad and a nose for it, and he fucked you all right up. He was way ahead of you.'

Harry's expression tightened. 'Yes, he was. He was very good. I'm sorry for your loss.'

Tash blew smoke into the air. 'OK, Harry. You have a deal.'

He looked as if he was going to walk away, then changed his mind. 'What are you going to do next, Tash?'

Tash felt her mother look at her, then look away.

'I'll carry on teaching at Belford for the rest of the season.'

Jemima took hold of Bethan's hand, squeezed it, tried to hide her smile.

'After that, I don't know. But I think I might stay out of war zones for a while. I would hate to become callous about the loss of human life. It rots the soul.'

He tried to suppress a sneer, and didn't entirely succeed.

'You know Panopticon will be rebuilt, eventually,' Harry said. 'The New Luddites won't succeed any more than the old ones did.' He glanced at Simon's T-shirt again. 'It's coming. AI, machine learning, facial recognition, data mining – the whole lot. And someone will control it. Who is to say they won't be worse than Eliot? You've bought yourself a bit of time. Maybe a couple of years at most.' He looked round at them. 'So what are you going to do with it?'

They didn't reply. Harry shook his head, and headed back down the path the way he'd come. The others sat in silence, and a robin started singing. Tash looked up, expecting to see Monty's ghost, but he had disappeared into the morning and the liquid silver music of the bird's song.

AUTHOR'S NOTE

Though the capacities of 'Pan' are an exaggeration of the current state of affairs, they are not that much of an exaggeration. I only hope that we collectively come up with a better long-term solution to the issues arising than Jemima and Tash's. Eliot Drake and his company are of course, fictional players.

While all implausibilities and exaggerations are my own, I've spun off creatively from the work of some fantastic tech journalists and commentators. Hat tip to 404 Media, The Verge, Wired and The New Yorker. I learned a great deal through listening to thoughtful conversations on Tech Won't Save Us, Dystopia Now, Hard Fork, The Ezra Klein Show and The Bunker.

Bedford Abbey is my invention, though those with local knowledge might notice it occupies Hulne Park. My apologies to the Duke of Northumberland for the land grab. Alnwick, where my father's family is from, I have tried to portray faithfully, and I sincerely recommend The Accidental Bookshop on Narrowgate, the full English breakfast at Melvyn's Cafe in the Market Place, and a visit to the town museum as well as the castle. Peter and the Wild Hunt are fictional, as are the Luddites, at least as they appear in this book.

ACKNOWLEDGEMENTS

I owe a huge debt to my agent, Broo Doherty and the team at DHH for their support and advocacy, also to my editors at Hodder – Nick Sayer, who was a fantastic sounding board for my initial ideas for this book – and Audrey Linton who steered it masterfully to completion. My thanks to them and all the team at Carmelite House.

I think I owe half the writers of London a pint, and in all honesty I'm not sure how anyone manages to write fiction without the support of their peers. Whether it's raising a glass to successes, commiserating on failures, or supplying a steady supply of advice, stoicism, gossip and bad jokes, their company and friendship is invaluable. My sincere thanks and I promise I'll get the next round in.

Particular thanks too to my agent, Broo, Audrey, and all my friends, co-writers and collaborators for their many kindness during my father's last illness which took place during the writing of this book. I will forever be grateful for their support, sensitivity and help in difficult times.

And most of all to my husband Ned, for sharing in the many adventures and challenges of the last couple of years; not to mention providing a steady flow of cheese, coffee and negronis depending on the needs of the moment. All my love.

Want another pulse-pounding thriller from Marina Palmer? Then don't miss *The Russian Doll* . . .

When Ruth Miller is offered a job from super-rich Elena Shilkov, she is whisked from a dreary shared house to a world of unimagined luxury.

Then the sinister truth begins to reveal itself, that nothing is quite what it seems in Elena's dangerous, deceptive world.

Ruth should get away.

But it's already too late.